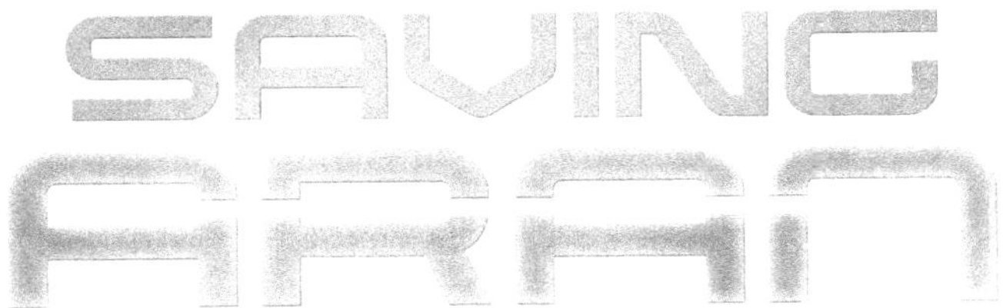

G. S. KENNEY

Saving Aran

Copyright © 2022 by G. S. Kenney

Cover art: Deranged Doctor, derangeddoctordesign.com

Praise for G. S. Kenney's award-winning Ascent of Eden series

A Warrior of Eden

"This is a well-written book with lush descriptions. The mystery and adventure keep the reader guessing... Once you have read this book, you will be clamoring to read all the others in the series."
— **N. N. Light's Book Heaven**

"Fast-paced, engrossing story about a strong, resilient heroine... The writing engages the reader with its finely-honed observations of character and intricate descriptions of the future world that is Eden. I highly recommend this book to all ages."
— **Amazon Reviewer**

Freeing Eden

"From the very first sentence, *Freeing Eden* charms with compassionate characters, and seduces with its intriguing premise. If you're looking for adventure alongside your romance, this warm and beautiful novel delivers!"
— **Elaine Isaak, author of *The Singer's Legacy* series**

"An intriguing story, well told, set in a rich, unique world. Send in the clones."
— **S. C. Mitchell, author of the *Xi Force* series**

"What an innovative sci-fi romance! I loved the premise of a clone learning their identity and the plot twists and turns kept me reading. I highly recommend this story."
— **Bookbub Reviewer**

"I read it in one sitting and then went back a week later and read it again, just to enjoy the detailed story and intense characters again."
— **Amazon Reviewer**

"...the planet Eden is a cleverly conceived, intentional throwback civilization...Against this backdrop, the well-developed main characters ground the story in an intimate discovery—of self and one another—that keeps the reader engaged throughout."
— **Amazon Reviewer**

The Last Lord of Eden

"A deeply thoughtful, swashbuckling sci-fi adventure. You'll get swept away and lose track of time, as you race to the end, hoping beyond hope that Kell can save his home planet without betraying the woman he loves."
— **Suzanne Tierney, award-winning author of *The Art of the Scandal* and *Blooms of War***

"Beautiful and thrilling, this book truly is the perfect Sci-Fi romance."
— **NetGalley member review**

"Skillful plotting and memorable characters abound in this well-conceived interplanetary adventure...So caught up in the fast-moving, intricate plot, I had difficulty leaving the book for meals or bedtime. Highly recommended."
— **Amazon Reviewer**

"Once I got into it I had trouble putting it down. (But you have to sleep sometime)"
— **Goodreads Reviewer**

To sign up for G. S. Kenney's newsletter and get a free copy of a future history of Eden's world, please visit *https://www.gskenney.com*.

Contents

Part I:
Saving Dilia

Chapter 1

Cort Earns His Knife

The cry of pain echoed in the alley and flowed out into the street like a liquid. Like blood. Cort drew in a sharp breath and touched the scar on his arm. "That's a child! He's in trouble!"

"None of our business," his friend Lor advised. His voice carried a warning.

Cort jogged a few steps to look into the alley, and his heart fell. It was Karl, the biggest bully in the school, with some of his gang. No friends of Cort, and a lot bigger than he was. Two of Karl's cronies were holding a struggling child while Karl was trying to cut the boy's arm. "No!" the child screamed. "No, stop!"

"Just cutting my initials." Karl said. There was a sneer in his voice. "Hold still."

Cort's friends had caught up with him at the mouth of the alley. "Four of them," Tark said. And three of us, he didn't have to say. "Leave it." Four fifteen-year-olds against three thirteen-year-olds were bad odds.

Cort touched the scar on his arm again, his breath coming more quickly. He'd been only eight when a gang of bigger bullies, teasing him about his father, had gotten nasty when he'd fought back. One of them had drawn a knife, and if a teacher hadn't intervened just then, he probably wouldn't have survived to help this child today. "Can't," he said.

He drew a deep breath, let it out in a whoosh, and stepped into the alley to rescue the child that Karl and his gang were tormenting. He waved his arms and trying to appear bigger than he was. "Hold off!" he shouted. "Soldiers coming!"

The gang members looked up, loosening their hold on the child, who ran off crying.

Of course, no soldiers came. It took Karl only a moment to grasp the situation. "You all alone, Street Scum," he said. "Now I cut you instead." He swept his knife in a broad, threatening gesture.

Cort drew back.

"Savage!" Karl's leering, singsong taunt cut the air like his knife.

"Not!" Cort retorted. His heart pounded so loud the sound seemed to fill the alley. He breathed shallowly and too fast, looking from right to left and back again. His friends were gone. No blame for that, but he sure wished that one or both of them had his back now. At least the poor kid had gotten away. Good.

But there was no escape for Cort. If he turned and ran, he was as good as dead. His back would provide too easy a target for four knife-wielding fifteen-year-olds.

Cort stood his ground.

"Where's your knife, Savage?" Karl passed his own knife from his right hand to his left, then back again. He made a mocking jab at Cort, who jumped back to avoid being cut.

Karl's three friends were moving around to block his escape.

"Yeah, where's your *bone* knife?" teased the boy at his left.

It had been a mistake last year when Cort had mentioned that knife—the only possession his father had left him. The school bullies never forgot. Cort clenched his fists, then forced them to unclench. If only he had a stunner or, even better, one of the starmen's lasers! He'd blast all of them, especially Karl.

By Earth, he just wanted to survive the next five minutes.

He didn't have much of a chance. The older boy was fast and mean, and, unlike Cort, he had a knife. But the odds were better against Karl alone than against Karl and his three friends. "So why does it take four of you to blast one person half your size?" he taunted back. "You afraid of me, Karl?" He tried to keep an eye on the three boys to his sides and rear. "You afraid I can beat you one-on-one?"

Karl snorted a contemptuous laugh. "I can take you, Savage," he sneered, his eyes narrowing. "I can blast you to Earth without a ship."

"Then get your friends off my tail."

Karl signaled with a jerk of his head, and the three other boys moved to the side of the dead-end alley where they had trapped Cort. Karl slashed at Cort, hard and vicious, not mocking this time.

Cort scraped against the wall as he ducked. "I'm going to cut you into little pieces and jettison them like garbage out the hatch. No one going to find the body." Again he jabbed forward.

Cort grabbed his arm and pulled. Off balance from the extended thrust, Karl fell to his knees. In an instant Cort was on the older boy's back, fighting for possession of the knife.

But Karl was bigger and stronger. He rolled over so that Cort was locked underneath him. Still, Cort refused to let go of his knife-wrist. Karl twisted so that he faced down toward Cort, now pinned to the street under the bigger boy's bulk. And he began driving the knife toward Cort's chest.

With every fiber of his strength, Cort fought to keep the knife away, but centimeter by centimeter Karl pushed the knife downward.

Cort's arms burned with the effort. When they started trembling, Karl's sneer turned to a grin.

Cort could hold Karl away no longer. Just before his arms gave way, he squirmed hard to his right. The knife meant for his heart plunged into his left arm. The cut seared like fire.

Cort forced himself to pull away, ripping muscle and skin.

Someone yelled, "Karl! Soldiers!"

In an instant, Karl jumped up, and he and his friends were gone.

Cort sat, pressing his right hand over the wound. Blood ran through his fingers and down his arm.

A squad of six soldiers ran down the deserted street toward him. Not aliens, of course. The starmen seldom visited the city, not even the few alien soldiers. Judging by the uniforms, these were in a private army, working for some rich kingpin who could afford to hire his own protection. Maybe even Sleb's, the kingpin who owned the block Cort lived in. It was a job requiring little education, and Cort and his schoolmates usually scorned it—but right now he was thrilled to see them. Behind the soldiers were two boys—Cort's friends.

Breathing a sigh of relief, Cort tried to stand. He felt faint and stumbled.

"Bad wound you got, boy," said the first soldier to reach him. The soldier supported Cort as he stood.

"Babies playing with knives!" another soldier said. "It makes me want to puke."

"Easy, Osk," said the first, "we all played with knives when we were little. You aim to fly a ship, you need a practice run or three."

"Osk was probably one of the worst," added a third soldier.

Lor said, "He was trying to save a little kid."

"Were you, now?" the third soldier asked Cort, studying him as intently as if his face might reveal how to save, not just a little boy, but all the khena trees of Aran.

Cort drew a breath and straightened up. If the soldier laughed at him, he would have no regrets. He'd do it again if he had to. By Earth, he'd save all the khena trees of Aran, too, if it came to that.

But the soldier just nodded, then fumbled at his pouch and withdrew something. To Cort, he said, "Hold still, boy. This is a starman bandage. It'll stop the bleeding and prevent infection, too." He started to wrap the bandage around Cort's bleeding arm.

"What're you doing, Garn?" Osk said. "Sleb'll blast you to Earth if he finds out you wasted one of his expensive bandages on this street rat."

"Weren't you ever a child once, Osk? The boy did a good deed, so we'll do one for him, too. Sleb isn't going to find out, now, is he?"

Osk was silent.

Garn finished wrapping the bandage, then patted Cort on the shoulder. "Get out of here, boy, before those thugs come back."

"Thanks," Cort breathed. "You saved my life. I won't forget."

The soldier laughed and said, "Save someone else's life sometime."

"Hey, think big," Osk muttered. "Save the whole buggin' planet." He turned to leave, and the other soldiers followed.

Cort made a vow to himself that he wouldn't forget. He wouldn't forget the kind soldier, and he'd save other lives, too, if he ever had the chance. More immediately, he wouldn't forget Karl, either. He intended to repay both.

The house was small, only one room, with one door, one window, one worktable, and one shelf for storing cooking utensils, but Dilia was grateful to have any kind of home at all. In the lawless nighttime people died out on the street, or went missing, which amounted to the same thing.

She was kneading dough for the bread that would be their dinner when she heard the door open. Preparing dinner was her responsibility, since Cort went to school, and his mother Mara had to work. Dilia turned to see Cort silhouetted against the glare of daylight. He was thirteen, the same age as her, but taller. Someday soon, if he kept growing, his head might almost reach the top of the doorway. She put a hand up to shield her eyes while he, uncharacteristically awkward, took off his pack and closed the door.

Dilia caught sight of a fresh white bandage on Cort's arm, and her heart leapt in fear. Had he been in a fight? How badly was he wounded? Might he… Dilia had trouble even thinking this…die? An injury could easily mean death in the city, where infections were not unusual, and the medications the aliens used were hard for the city people to come by, even on the black market.

She covered the dough with a damp cloth and came over to look at his arm more closely. The bandage was shiny and unusually white. "Is that an alien bandage?"

He nodded and looked at his arm, as if he too was still marveling over the exotic dressing. And maybe he was.

Dilia felt a wave of relief. With one of the aliens' bandages, whatever wound was underneath it would heal quickly, and it wouldn't get infected.

She turned his arm one way and another, examining the shining white bandage as if she might by sheer intensity see the cut underneath. "Is it bad? Does it hurt?" she asked in a shaky voice. Dilia loved Cort as something like a brother and a best friend, rolled into one. His death would be devastating, as bad as losing her father, as bad as then losing her mother. Cort was a bright flashing danger sign that said, "Don't dare love him too much. You could lose him, too."

Cort shrugged. "No, it's nothing. I'm fine—really." But he winced when she turned his arm a certain way, and Dilia now understood that he'd been awkward with the door because he was favoring that arm.

"What happened?" she asked. "Are you in a gang?"

"No," Cort said, looking away.

Maybe he wasn't, yet. But in another year or so, he and his school friends would all be in gangs, making trouble and getting hurt. There must be a hundred gangs ranging from school children to adults, city-born to newcomers newly arrived from the forest. Everyone was out to get what he could, however he could. Anyone not out making trouble was bound, sooner or later, to be a victim. Someday, Cort would be seriously hurt. And there was nothing she could do to prevent it.

Dilia had to stop thinking about this. She took Cort's school tablet out of his pack and sat against the wall with it, using her bedroll as a cushion. "We're really getting your money's worth out of your tuition—two for the price of one."

Cort flopped down to sit next to her, rearranging the bedroll so that it would pillow both of them. He smiled at her. "I learn more, too, when we go over it together."

Instead of attending school, Dilia worked in a shop near the gate to the base. Her meager earnings barely paid for her food; anything left over was added to Cort's mother's earnings and to whatever Cort managed to steal so that they could pay the tuition to keep sending Cort to school. But Dilia had no complaints. She was grateful to Mara for taking her in, and she loved being part of this family. Besides, she was learning so much just by sharing Cort's homework.

Turning to today's Mechanics lesson, she hunched over the tablet as if it contained all the riches they owned, her long auburn braid falling over her shoulder. But the lesson might have been written in a code for which she had no key. She couldn't concentrate. All she could think was that Cort was going to get himself killed.

"And then, when I get out of school, I'll be able to support you and Mama by myself," Cort said. "I'll make sure you have everything you ever wanted."

Dilia patted his hand affectionately and gave him a wan smile. "Not if you keep getting hurt in fights."

"I don't plan to," Cort said, a defensive tone edging into his voice. He turned back to the lesson on the tablet.

Maybe he was already in a gang. Dilia shivered. "Oh! And you think this will be under your control, do you? So tell me how you got that wound."

He looked away. "They were bigger boys. Bullies, picking on a little kid. Couldn't have been more than ten or eleven. I gave the kid time to get away, that's all."

Dilia stood up. She could just picture some gang of sixteen-year-olds turning on Cort when the child ran away. Their long knives would already be out, flashing in the sun. Adults' knives. Sharp. How many of them would there be? Four? Five? She walked the five steps to the far wall where the door was, then back, upset all over again. She tried to shake off the image, but she couldn't. She pictured Cort facing the bigger boys alone, without a knife. "Maybe it's time for you to start using your father's knife," she said.

Cort drew in a breath. He had coveted that bone knife ever since Dilia could remember. Maybe he would take it this time. It was the only thing besides his name—Cort-anaran, a savage name—that Cort's father had left him, his father who had come, already a grown man, out of the primeval forest into the city, fathered Cort, and then disappeared.

Cort stood and gave the tablet back to Dilia. He reached up and touched the high shelf where they kept the knife. Then he paused and lowered his hand. "I'd like to, but I'm not ready for it. I'm not going to take that knife until I know I can win with it."

"And how are you going to know that?" Dilia asked, suddenly angry. "By fighting some more? You'll get yourself killed!"

"I'm not that stupid!" Cort returned anger for anger. "I'm going to find a way to learn, that's all." Then he softened, smiling at her. "Don't worry. I wouldn't want anything to happen before I'm ready to take his knife, now, would I?" He touched her cheek, and she couldn't help but return the smile.

"You're lucky you have that knife," she said. "I wish I had something of my father's to remember him by."

"Come on, Dilia; don't be jealous. You actually remember your father. That's more than I do." Cort's mother said that his father had gone to Earth, but Dilia thought it was improbable that a barbarian from the forest would go to the starmen's home planet. Going to Earth was simply the slang phrase people used to say someone had died. Died, like Dilia's own parents.

"Yes," she said, "I remember my father, but so faintly and long ago, almost like a fairy tale, kind of shining in sunlight and unreal. I remember him smiling at me, and then putting his arm around my mother."

Dilia sighed, a feeling of sadness stealing over her. Her parents used to always hug each other, but all of Dilia's memories were of looking up at them touching while she remained on the ground below. It was like, in some deep way, she was defective. Unlovable. Not like them.

Regardless of whether anyone would ever love her, at least she had one true friend, Cort. And now he seemed to be heading toward an early death. She wanted to scream at him. *Take the damned knife! Protect yourself!* But it would do no good. She gave up on studying and turned back to the bread she'd been working on for dinner.

There was no hiding the shiny white bandage. Everyone at school saw it. Though Cort refused to talk about it, he heard enough of the gossip: the incident became known as a stand-off between him and Karl. And for thirteen-year-old Cort, a stand-off against fifteen-year-old Karl, one of the terrors of the school, was decidedly a victory. This was going to be a problem.

Cort took steps to improve his situation.

Karl was a bully, but he wasn't the best knife-fighter in the school. It was commonly agreed that that honor belonged to Stas, a classmate of Karl's. Fifteen, tall for his age, and wiry, Stas had skin and hair so light that from a distance he could be taken for a starman. There was a rumor that Stas was a halfbreed, and he encouraged it. Everyone knew that after he graduated Stas intended to serve in the aliens' army, up at the base, not down here in the city. Maybe even in one of the elite squads that guarded the power station. Most of the boys were eager to stay on his good side. The right connection with Stas could make a person wealthy one day. His gang had it made.

Cort didn't care much for Stas; he disliked his constant preening. But Stas had something that Cort wanted. Cort began hanging out on the fringes of the older boy's gang. He tried to be unobtrusive, while making himself useful when he could by running errands or passing messages. One of the gang members, though older, was in Cort's math and science classes, and Cort helped him with his homework.

Cort was almost accepted as a fringe member of the gang, but he had never asked Stas's permission to join. One day Stas decided that this situation had gone far enough. "Why you tailing my fleet, runt?" he asked. "You think you're such a big shot because you got away from Karl, now you can ship out with the older boys?"

"No," Cort answered honestly. "I was lucky with Karl. I might not be so lucky next time."

"You think we're going to shield you, you're wrong."

"I'm not looking for a shield! I got to stand on my own firepower with Karl."

"How you going to do that, runt?"

"I want you to teach me how to fight."

Stas's eyes widened; whatever answer he expected, it wasn't this. He rocked back on his heels, running his fingers through his blond hair, and studied the smaller boy. "Why should I? What's in it for me?"

"You should do it because you're good, and I'll work hard at it until I'm good, too. And everyone will say, 'Stas taught him. Stas is the man.' And I'll... Stas, I'll give you whatever I can, whatever I have if you'll just teach me." *But not my father's bone knife. That's mine.*

Stas breathed out a disdainful snort of laughter. "You ain't got nothing I want. Get out of here, runt."

"There must be something! I'll fence for you. I'll steal for you. I'll do whatever you want."

A glint lit in Stas's eyes. A new idea, and probably not a pleasant one. "You be my slave?"

Cort didn't see where he had any bargaining power. Hadn't he just offered whatever Stas wanted? He drew in a deep breath and lowered his eyes. "As long as you teach me."

Stas nodded slowly, and a disagreeable grin spread across his face. "You call me Master. I call you whatever I feel like calling you."

"Teach me for at least an hour every day."

"You call me Master, starting right now. You do whatever I tell you."

"Two hours on Seventh Day and holidays." Then Cort took a deep breath and forced himself to add, "Master."

Stas's grin widened, and some of the gang snickered. "I think I'm going to like this," Stas said.

Stas was using Cort to boost his ego, but Cort would be learning knife skills from a master. Cort thought Stas was unpleasant, but he wasn't malicious like Karl. He kept his side of the deal. And Cort kept his side, too.

The first two months were rough. One day, Stas ordered Cort to undress and run naked down the street, to the extreme amusement of his entire gang. Then he made his slave beg and kneel before him to get his clothes back. Another time, he made Cort crawl through a pile of garbage, and Cort had been ashamed to go home because he smelled so bad. Cort endured names like Rat-butt and Garbage-breath until what he was called no longer mattered to him. And through his calm perseverance, he found a kind of acceptance among the gang of older boys.

And he practiced. The knife he used was small, a child's implement, but he kept it sharp. Every moment that he wasn't at school or doing his homework with Dilia or fulfilling his obligations to Stas, Cort practiced.

He fell away from his friends and confided little even to Dilia or his mother, who always asked for news from school. He knew he was hurting them by pulling away, but he'd hurt them even more if he told them of the risks and the humiliation he was enduring. Some things were more important than pain.

Dilia remained Cort's one steady light during that period. The strength of her devotion to him sometimes was all that held him together when he felt on the verge of breaking under Stas's ridicule.

He had to get the best job he could, and that meant getting top grades, of course, but also being the kind of person who could be completely relied upon to keep his promises—whatever the humiliation, risk, or danger. Someday, he would find a way to do good in the world. Maybe even, like he'd promised that soldier, save someone's life sometime.

Cort's opportunity came when he was fifteen. Gangs in the city seldom fought one another. For the most part, the gangs knew their territories and stuck to them. But not always. Karl's gang began pushing into Stas's territory, a corner that bore a lot of traffic because of the nearby shops.

It was a rich location for petty thievery, the usual gang practice of the schoolchildren. And Stas wasn't about to let anyone take anything that was rightly his. He struck after nightfall when the streets were still and law-abiding people were safely shut within their houses.

There were ten boys in Karl's gang. Stas's numbered only eight—nine counting Cort, whom Stas normally did not count. Stas's group were better fighters, but Karl's were bigger, bolder, and meaner. Stas decided that his best strategy was stealth. His gang approached Karl's corner from three different directions, using a set of agreed signals and a stolen alien timer for coordination. The street was lit only by the light of the large, white moon called the Hunter, now in crescent phase. The smaller moon, the Kiri, was not visible behind the larger.

Stas's gang were on Karl's quickly and silently. Three members of Karl's gang died, their throats slit in the dark, before they knew there was an attack. In the melee that followed, five more people died, two of Stas's and three of Karl's. Cort fought alongside the larger boys. In the dark, his swiftness and dexterity were assets, and so was his size.

When Karl's group broke and ran into the silent streets, Karl wasn't with them. Stas had captured his rival and bound him with alien ropes. "You drink my exhaust," Stas told Karl. His eyes glowed eerily, reflecting the handheld alien light the gang had stolen the previous week. In the dark night, the streets around them were silent.

Surrounded by enemies, Karl said nothing.

"You so slow and stupid," Stas said, "even my slave can burn you."

Cort looked up sharply.

Stas met his eye and grinned. "Now you see some light-speed action, Rat-butt. Burn your warp drives, runt."

With every member of his gang watching him, Cort took out his knife and moved closer to Karl. "Not while he's tied up, Master." The title was habit now and no longer had any meaning to Cort. "Not this way."

"Hear that, Slime?" Stas said to Karl. "He's garbage. He's a street rat, but he takes pity on you. Probably wants you to have a knife, too."

"Yes, I do!" Cort spoke eagerly. "He wouldn't give me one two years ago, but me, I don't want the signals telling I burned him unfairly. I can take him even-on."

"You're a big fool, Rat-butt," Stas said. "But this is your shift. Now we'll see what you're made of." He untied Karl's hands and returned his knife. "Now you fight," he told Karl. "We'll see what you're made of, too. You kill my slave, maybe I let you live to be my slave in his place."

"I'll kill him," Karl grunted. "Should've finished that two years ago."

Karl was bigger and stronger than Cort. Now seventeen, he had grown as tall as a starman, and he was as muscular as he was tall. But Cort had grown, too, and he had trained every day for the last eight hundred days for this moment. He was ready.

The two boys circled. Karl lunged, but Cort dodged quickly, slashing the older boy's arm as he moved.

First blood! The gang cheered, and Karl scowled.

Cort hoped his opponent would get angry. Karl would think less clearly if he was angry.

But Karl just circled warily, lunging once or twice when he thought he saw an opening, and carving a mark on Cort's arm once, almost on top of the scar he had left earlier.

"Come on, Rat-butt," Stas urged. "You going to circle around him all night?"

The comment made sense. Cort would have to do better than simple defensive maneuvers to win. But as Stas spoke, Karl attacked.

Cort ducked low and inside, cutting Karl across the thigh. Karl screamed and looked down, and in that moment, Cort had him. He ducked behind his opponent and held him, with the edge of his knife against Karl's throat.

"Drop your knife," Cort said.

With Cort's sharp blade already drawing a thin trickle of blood from his throat, Karl dropped his knife. One of Stas's gang picked it up.

"I want an apology," Cort said.

"I'm sorry." It was more a sneer than an apology.

Cort increased the pressure of his knife. "You know, I've been waiting for this apology for two years, and now I don't believe you mean it."

The blood flowed more strongly now. "Oh, Earth!" Karl swore. "I mean it! Earth, but I'm sorry! I'm really sorry! I swear I'll never do anything like that again."

"No, you won't," Cort said. He let up the pressure of his knife. "Because if I ever hear of you doing anything like that ever again, I'll come and I'll find you, and I'll kill you."

"Kill him now," Stas said.

But Cort shook his head. He remembered the soldier who had helped him after his first fight with Karl. *Save someone else's life sometime.* Karl's offense needed a lesson taught, but not death. "No."

"I'm ordering you, Rat-butt."

"No. No more, Stas. You've been a good teacher. The best. But it's over." He sheathed his knife and walked away from the corner, away from the gang, away from Stas, who had taught him, away from his vengeance. It was over.

Chapter 2

The Danger to Dilia

The following day, Cort took his father's knife down from its shelf and drew it carefully from the sheath. The knife had a savage beauty, crafted from some kind of petrified bone that had turned a deep brown over the years, slightly curved, almost as long as Cort's forearm, with a substantial weightiness. Its handle was wrapped tightly in red leather and decorated with feathers and red and white beads.

He turned the knife over carefully, weighed it and tested its balance, felt how it gripped his hand like the handshake of a long-lost friend. He touched the blade lightly, appreciating its deadly sharpness, and sliced it once, twice through the air. He nodded in satisfaction, re-sheathed the knife, and threaded it onto his belt.

He skipped school and went with Dilia out of the city. It was her day off from work, and she was caring for two children who lived on their street. She never asked for money from the children's parents, who were even poorer than they. It was just this kind of unselfish generosity that Cort liked about her, and now he hoped to make up a little for his neglect of the last couple of years.

They packed a light lunch and made a special outing of it. From a hillock at the edge of the fields outside the city wall, they sat with the children and ate their lunch. Afterwards, they watched the children play in the grass nearby. Below them, several people worked in the fields, breaking up clods of earth to make rows, and planting seeds from last year's crops.

"Sometimes I still miss my parents' farm," Dilia said wistfully.

Cort followed her gaze to the farmers, then touched her arm. "I'm sorry you lost it."

She turned to look at him. Her eyes were moist. "It's not your fault."

Cort was surprised that the long-ago loss still hurt her so badly. And there was nothing he could do to make it right. "I wouldn't let that happen to you. Never."

Dilia smiled and wiped an eye. "Cort, you were just a child!"

Taw, the little boy Dilia was caring for, ran up to them. "But he's a grown-up now. I'm four years old!"

"Yes, dear, you and your sister, too."

Cort laughed at the image of himself as a child running out into the field, brandishing his father's knife to threaten the soldiers who took her farm away. But he also remembered that time, two years ago, when he'd held off Karl and his bullies for long enough that the littler boy could run to safety. "I don't care how old I was," he said. "I would have helped you somehow. Maybe your mother wouldn't have died."

The little girl Tania had moved down the hill, picking the tiny flowers that grew among the grass. "Taw," Dilia said, "please go get your sister and ask her to stay closer." She turned back to Cort. "I don't think it would have mattered," she said, her voice so quiet it was almost a whisper. "I think she probably died of grief. After my father died, she was never really the same. I... I wasn't... enough for her."

Cort felt his throat tightening. He reached out to stroke her hair, but Dilia pulled away. "It was a long time ago," she said, "and anyway, the important part is that your mother took me in. We have a good home together."

A ground-shaking rumble announced the imminent return of one of the aliens' harvesting machines from the distant khenaran. Cort looked up, but it was not yet in sight. The twins ran to them. "What's that?" asked Taw.

Dilia pushed his hair back from his eyes and smiled warmly at him. "A harvester is coming, dear. And that will be a sight to see."

"Look!" said Tania as she came up behind him. "Flowers!" She dropped a handful of flowers over Dilia's hair.

Dilia laughed and gave her a hug. "Sit here, and watch."

The harvester came into sight, a flash of unnaturally bright orange in the woods beyond the fields, then another glimpse through the trees, and then the giant machine reached the edge of the woods. It was loaded to the top with huge logs of *khena* wood.

"The starmen say there's nothing on Earth like the *khena*," Cort said. "I guess that's the one thing we have here that they don't. They'll sell all that wood for a fortune back on Earth."

Dilia narrowed her eyes and tilted her head a bit from side to side. "Look how the wood glistens where the laser cut it, like living rainbows are swimming around inside. Like the wood is still alive somehow, even though the tree's been cut down."

Cort thought again of his father. "I can't imagine living among all those trees. It must be kind of like living in a forest of starships."

Dilia glanced up at the ship that towered over the base. "Only more beautiful. More alive."

Cort looked at Dilia, with her gray eyes and auburn hair that hung almost to her waist. Taw leaned against her, and Tania had left her drawing and lay with her head in Dilia's lap, half asleep. Dilia's figure was definitely becoming more womanly. For the first time, Cort saw her not just as his friend, but as a person who would fall in love someday, and marry, and have lots of beautiful auburn-haired children who looked just like her. His heartbeat increased, and he felt a warmth spread outward through his body. He wanted to run his hand through her hair, to draw her close, to... No, he wanted to give her the space to be herself and to find her own mate. "Yes," he said. "Beautiful."

An earth-shaking thud startled Tania awake. A khena log that was not quite secure in the grasp of one of the forklifts had fallen back to the harvester. Shouts rose, and then the grinding of engines as the forklift strained to get its blades under the log again drowned out all other sound.

"That was very loud," Tania said.

Dilia laughed, a merry sound that made Cort think of bells. "That's because it's so big. And if the pieces are so big, can you imagine how big the living trees are?"

"So big," Taw said, reaching upwards at a stretch.

"Huge," Dilia agreed. "I wish I could see them someday."

Cort watched as the log was loaded onto the forklift. "They showed holos at school. Even the harvester looked tiny beside the trees."

The four of them gaped at the neon orange harvester for a moment of silent awe. It was an impressive machine—three, four times the height of a man and armor-plated. Its total disregard of of camouflage shouted its invulnerability. But then, why camouflage the things? They were too massive for the natives to attack, and there was no hiding them; the ground itself shook as the giant machines came and went. And they were armed with laser weaponry that made the sidearms carried by the aliens—more powerful than anything the city folk could get their hands on—look puny. And as for knives like his...

Cort touched his father's knife on his belt. He couldn't imagine the bravery or desperation that had driven his father's people—no, his own people, ancestors and relatives of everyone living in the city—to oppose these monstrous juggernauts with only their spears and knives. But the opposition was so hopeless. So doomed. Cort swallowed a lump in his throat. "Those trees must be really something, to be so important to the people who live out in the khenaran."

"Khenaran?" Taw asked.

"The forest of khena trees. All of the Arantu used to live in the khenaran before the starmen came with their harvesters."

Dilia sighed. "It seems... I don't know, wrong somehow... to be the children or grandchildren of people whose homes were destroyed in this harvesting and never to have even seen a living khena. I'd love to go see the khenaran someday. "

Cort looked at her appraisingly. "It must be primitive, otherwise so many people wouldn't be coming to the city. I'd like to see the trees too, but I think we'll probably survive better by staying here."

She stroked Tania's hair. The girl was fast asleep again, with her head in Dilia's lap. "I want to learn everything I can about... well, everything, the khenaran included. I wonder what it's like to live there."

"Me too," Taw echoed.

"The khenaran is a long way from here," Cort said to him. "Before the aliens came, the whole world was forest, and that's why we call it Aran. But the aliens have been harvesting for generations. Now, Dilia and I would have to walk for months and months just to get there, and who knows how we'd survive. And meanwhile, who would care for you and Tania when your parents work?"

Dilia laughed. "Not today! But maybe someday."

"Someday," Taw repeated. He snuggled against Dilia and closed his eyes.

To Cort, Dilia said, "Maybe after you finish school, you could get a job on a harvester, and I could go with you. Then we could see the khenaran together."

And help the aliens cut the forest down. Not what he wanted to do with his life. Cort watched a giant four-prong forklift wrest its tines under another of the logs and move it from the harvester to a gravlev. "I'd rather get some other job."

Dilia tilted her head and raised an eyebrow. "Why? What job do you want?"

"If I keep my grades up, I'll qualify for almost anything when I finish school. Soldiering for the starmen pays well, but I think I'd rather be a technician up in the starbase. There's too much resentment between the city soldiers and the ones on the base. I don't want to spend my whole life fighting."

Dilia tossed a loose strand of hair behind her back. "Aren't you being negative today! No harvesting, no soldiering. So, what do you want to do?"

Cort glanced over his shoulder at the walls of the city with the starbase rising above it. At the far side of the base, a gleaming starship towered. "I'd like a job where I can come home every night and make sure my mother is safe. Maybe I'll work at the power station. I think that would be interesting work, and not dangerous, like soldiering." The alien power plant drew energy from the planet's mantle, with rods drilled deep through the solid rock that surrounded the magma below. Heat was sucked up from this almost limitless reservoir and ran generators that powered not the city, no, with its narrow, crooked streets and one-room houses, but the base itself and its mysterious technology.

"I'm focusing in the engineering track, with all the math, physics, geology, and engineering courses I can take, and I'll keep studying Starrish language and culture, too. If I work for the starmen, maybe you and my mother and I could all go see Earth one day." And maybe they'd even find his father there. "That would be something, wouldn't it?"

Dilia smiled at the thought, a faraway look in her eyes. "Oh, yes, everyone dreams of going to Earth. There would be so much to learn. But I don't know of anyone who actually went there. Do you?"

Cort tried to think of someone—not counting his father, of course—but he couldn't. "No. I guess not. But I'd even rather run one of those forklifts than work on a harvester. I don't think those harvesters are good jobs. Lor's father works on one of them, and he's gone for months on end. Sure, he probably sees the khenaran, but so what? He never gets to see his own family."

Dilia hadn't known about the harvester jobs, or she would never have suggested it. She bit her lip. "I wouldn't like you to be gone for a long time like that." First her father, then her mother, and then Cort. Could she and Mara even survive without him?

She shivered and wrapped her arms around her chest. "I'd like to have a family sometime... Children... But if you can't find a job that pays well enough, I could... I mean, I could keep working at the store, and if that's not enough..." She glanced at the children, who were both asleep. She lowered her voice. "Sometimes women have a kind of special arrangement to work up at the base. There's a customer in my shop who does that, and she always has a lot to spend. She has beautiful clothes, too. If we need more money, maybe I could—"

Cort drew back. "No. I don't want you to ever have to do that."

"But why? If it's that or you working on the harvesters?"

"Do you know what they do, up there? What that 'special arrangement' is?"

Dilia looked away. "The women don't say, directly, but yes. I'm not a child anymore. I'm just saying, if I had to..."

"You will never have to," Cort said. "I will study hard and do well. And you're going to find someone and marry and have lots of pretty children like Taw and Tania."

Find someone else? Dilia didn't know whether to feel hurt or relieved. But it probably would be best if she didn't start thinking about marrying Cort. He was more like a brother to her. "That's sweet, Cort. Thank you. I do want to contribute too, but I promise I'll find some other way. Okay?"

"Good," he said grimly.

"Unless I'm abducted, of course."

"What?"

Abductions were rare, but rumor had it that the prettiest girls were taken by Sleb and the other power brokers in the city and sold to the starmen. No one knew what happened after that. There were stories, of course, each wilder than the next: The girls were drugged and used for sex. They were killed. They were shipped back to Earth and sold as slaves.

Lots of rumors, but no one knew because the girls never returned to tell. Dilia lowered her voice. "Women and girls are abducted sometimes, you know. They vanish."

She watched to see Cort's reaction, but he was studying how the workers coiled the lithe young branches of the khena and tied them with red ropes of some strong alien fiber. After a long silence, he said, "Lots of people vanish, Dilia. Men and boys, too." He touched the hilt of the bone knife, making Dilia think about Cort's father. And hadn't her own father vanished, too, at the end, assumed dead? "But a lot of it is exaggeration. It's always, 'I heard from someone that her cousin knew someone who...' Do you yourself actually know someone who was abducted?"

She checked that the children were still sleeping, then sat silent for a long moment, watching as the workers loaded the coils onto a gravlev platform and guided it toward the city gate. "Yes."

He turned to her, his features shocked. "Who?"

"Someone who used to come into the shop. Minna. Her sister told me. Do you think Inei-Taru ever comes to help the people who disappear?"

Inei-Taru. She hadn't meant to ask that. She knew these were children's stories. Stories where Inei-Taru with his animal sidekick would help people in trouble. Stories where he got the better of the overmen and sometimes even of the aliens. Stories that grew in the retelling. Impossible stories, and yet, they were stories that people continued to tell because they wanted to believe them.

Cort was silent until Dilia met his gaze. His jaw was set and hard. "Dilia," he said. "I don't know about Inei-Taru, but I swear to you I will never let anything like that happen to you, not while I'm around. And if they take you when I'm gone, I'll go after them and find you and bring you back."

She looked away. "No one comes back."

He gently touched her chin and turned her face back toward his. "I will bring you back. No matter what."

It was the most wonderful thing he might have said. Dilia wanted to hug him, but her lap was still full of sleeping children. "It's probably silly of me to worry, but the other day a couple of Sleb's soldiers were in the shop, and they heard me talking Starrish to an alien who was looking for a souvenir. After the alien left, one of the soldiers told the other one that I spoke Starrish well and that would make me very valuable. I didn't like how they looked at me."

The equipment below them roared and whined. Cort fisted his hands. "I want you to quit that job," he said. "First thing tomorrow."

Dilia was sorry she'd brought it up. "But Cort, it pays well. How else will I pay for my share of the food? And what if we can't afford to pay for your school?"

"I'll steal more. We'll manage somehow. I'm not joking, Dilia; I want you out of there."

Dilia knew that Cort's advice was sound, that she should quit her job at the shop near the gate to the base. But because she could speak Starrish, her salary at the shop was good, and there were occasional tips from the aliens. The only other job she had any experience with was childcare, and no one would ever make a living from that.

Weeks passed. Dilia put the conversation with Cort out of her mind, but she became increasingly aware of the way the aliens looked at the women in the shop—as if they too were merchandise, souvenirs they could purchase if they wanted. And she didn't like some of the things she heard them say when they thought the shop staff wouldn't understand. And some of the Arantu soldiers were the same way. Some mornings, it was an act of courage just to go into work.

The morning the starbase commandant visited the shop was different, though. Four Arantu soldiers in the maroon uniforms of those working for the aliens came marching into the shop, their backs straight and heads high. The three customers who were in the shop—two family members of some rich kingpin, and an alien looking for souvenirs to bring back to Earth—stopped their browsing to watch. The soldiers ushered them all out of the shop, leaving only Abu the proprietor, Dilia, and one other employee.

"Any of you street scum speak Starrish?" the leader of the squad asked, and without waiting for an answer added, "I didn't think so."

Dilia knew she should stay silent, but she was proud of her education and glad for a chance to show it off. "I speak a little." Her voice came out ragged at the edges, tinged with fear.

"Good," the leader said. "You stay." His eyes settled on Abu. "You the owner?"

"Yes, my lord." Abu's voice sounded all jittery, as if his heart were beating in his throat instead of his chest.

The soldier barked a brittle laugh. "Not a lord, Shopkeeper. Just a sergeant. The lord will be here in a minute. You stay, too." His eyes moved to the other woman—a girl from the other side of the city, Jemi. He looked her over appraisingly, and Jemi shrank under his gaze, hunched over, head tucked low, with her arms folded protectively over her chest. "Go home," the sergeant said. "Your work is finished for today."

Jemi and the four soldiers arranged themselves, two outside the shop door, and two inside.

A few minutes later, two more soldiers came in, not Arantu but actual aliens. They wore uniforms of some alien material, all shiny and thick, a shade of red so bright it almost shone by itself. Behind them came the alien commandant. He wore the red uniform under a cape of red and an equally unnatural yellow, and on his chest were ribbons and medals of all sorts, too many to count in a quick glance—and Dilia was afraid to do more than glance at the man. The alien soldiers were all tall, taller than most Arantu, but the commandant was the tallest of them, and spindly like the rest. He looked to be of about middle age, as far as Dilia could tell, but his short hair was so pale it could almost have been white. Or maybe it *was* white, for the lines in his face suggested that he was older than the alien soldiers she had seen. Even his eyebrows and eyelashes were pale. He scowled and spoke an order in clipped Starrish: "Wait outside." The Arantu soldiers left the shop, so that only Abu, Dilia, and the three alien soldiers remained.

The commandant's expression of vague annoyance didn't change as he turned to Abu. "You speak Standard?" he asked in Starrish.

Abu knew a little Starrish; in his business, he had to. "I speaking Standard, yes."

The commandant's mouth curled downward as if he'd just tasted something disagreeable, and he gave a significant look to one of the soldiers, who laughed obediently. His scorn was obvious. He might as well have said, "Stupid natives!" out loud.

How dare they! Dilia's heart began pounding, and she felt her cheeks grow warm. *Stupid aliens, always selling us short!* "Perhaps I could help you, sir." The words came out before she had a chance to think. And after all those years of studying Starrish with Cort, she was confident she could speak it well.

The commandant turned and seemed to notice her for the first time. He wore an expression that might have been appropriate if he'd just heard the countertop speak. Then he seemed to see Dilia, really see her. He assessed her from top to toe. "Yes," he said, drawing out the word. "Perhaps you can."

Dilia helped him buy a couple of handwoven rugs with traditional Arantu patterns. He paid quite handsomely for them without negotiating, and he gave Dilia a tip, too. The tip alone was enough to pay Cort's tuition for an entire month.

After the aliens left and the store closed, Dilia rushed home. She could hardly wait to tell Mara and Cort about meeting the alien commandant, who had no sense of the value of money.

With part of her windfall from the commandant's tip, Dilia decided to buy fresh produce for a celebration dinner. She met Mara after work the next day, and they went to the market together. Coming home, they found their street full of soldiers—Sleb's men, in their dark green uniforms. They exchanged a glance. Should they go home? Or leave and come back later? But the soldiers ignored the two women. They seemed to be busy examining the condition of the houses. Since Sleb owned all the houses on the street, the soldiers' actions, though unusual, didn't seem strange.

The two women went into their house, only to find four soldiers inside. Dilia drew in a sharp, frightened breath and clutched Mara's arm. Cort hadn't come home yet; every afternoon after school he hung out with a group of boys—a gang, actually, though he'd tried to hide that fact from Dilia and his mother. Dilia didn't like this gang, but today she was glad Cort was with them. If he'd been home, there would have been a fight, and what chance would Cort have against four trained soldiers?

The soldiers looked the two women up and down, their eyes full of lust and caution, as if they'd like to touch the women, or more, but they didn't dare. Then the leader nodded toward Dilia and said, "Take her."

Mara made a noise that was half sob and half cry. "No!" She took hold of Dilia's arm, as if by sheer will she could anchor Dilia to the floor so that she could not be moved.

One of the soldiers said, "Step aside, woman."

Mara held her ground.

The soldier hit Mara, a solid punch in the stomach. Mara let out a whoosh of air, and she fell.

Another soldier grabbed Dilia's arm and pulled her toward the door. Dilia dragged her feet, crying, "No! Leave me alone!"

With one hand, the soldier held Dilia's upper arm so tightly she thought it might bruise the bone. He pulled his other hand back, fisted. "You want a bruise on that pretty face?"

Dilia was too terrified to speak. She shook her head.

"Then move!"

Still crying, Dilia allowed the soldier to lead her away, his hand still tight on her arm.

They took her through the streets to Sleb's compound, to a room with walls and shiny tile floors of bright white, and a steaming tub of water. A woman with unnaturally yellow hair and cold eyes stood with her arms folded across her chest. She wore three gold bracelets on her left arm and one on her right. It could be real gold, the kind the aliens valued so highly. Her gold earrings were embedded with pale stones that glistened when they caught the light. She shook her head and clucked her tongue, as if Dilia was the sorriest sight she'd seen all week, and then she uttered one word: "Bathe."

But Dilia didn't want to take off her clothes in front of the soldiers, who watched with more interest than a stranger ought to have in a modest girl. She took a step farther into the room, away from the soldiers.

The woman, following Dilia's gaze, said to the soldiers, "Get out. This one's not for you."

The soldiers left.

The woman stood and watched Dilia, her arms still crossed, her face a mask, but she rubbed the thumb of her right hand over her fingers again and again as if she were counting out coins, seemingly unaware she was doing it. Her bracelets jingled softly. "You're lucky, you know," she said. "The commandant himself expressed interest in you. Play your cards right and maybe you'll get to go to Earth with him when his shift here is done."

Go to Earth! Dilia's heart leapt. How Cort and she had dreamed of that! *But oh, not this way.*

And what would Cort say when he came home and found his mother hurt and Dilia missing? What would he do? Once, he'd said that he'd come and rescue her no matter what. The thought made her feel warmer inside, but then she remembered how many soldiers were around in their street, and here, too. She hoped Cort wouldn't do anything foolish.

She hoped that—and yet she didn't. More than anything, she wanted to be rescued.

The yellow-haired woman watched her bathe with a cool detachment, saying only, "Remember to wash your hair."

When Dilia left the tub, the woman inspected every inch of her body for any residual dirt, then nodded her satisfaction. She ran a hand lightly down Dilia's cheek, her neck, her shoulder. Her bracelets made a soft jingling sound as she moved her hand. She rested her hand on Dilia's shoulder and then shook her head slowly. "You are a pretty one," she said. "Too bad you won't be staying. I'd keep you around longer if I could."

Dilia figured that the woman must be either Sleb's wife or an important person in his household. She took a chance and made an offer. "If I lived at home, I could visit you every day if you wanted."

The woman barked a short laugh. "Not a chance of that, Sweetie."

Dilia swallowed and plunged on. "I could teach you some Starrish. I know math, and I can handle money. And I know how to cook really well."

"And that's not all you'd be good for." The woman did not sound like she was joking. "But you're already spoken for—and you'll do well enough up there. Now get dressed."

The yellow-haired woman laid out a red dress of a soft Starrish material, along with clean undergarments. Dilia was afraid to ask what had happened to her own clothes, but from her years in the shop, she had an idea what these new ones were worth. And she knew what their value meant: There was no way she was going to get out of this.

Chapter 3

Dilia at the Base

It was already late afternoon when Sleb's soldiers brought Dilia up to the starbase. The gate was still open, but several new soldiers had just arrived from inside—alien soldiers with their lasers and their bright red uniforms. They began engaging in the formal ritual of handing over command to the night watch, six soldiers approaching the gate, the same number retreating, with salutes and one-syllable commands shouted louder than necessary. Sleb's soldiers hustled Dilia up to the commander of the outgoing alien soldiers. Her heart was beating faster than the rhythm of the soldiers' marching boots, and she could feel her throat tightening along with the closing gate.

The leader of Sleb's men talked in a low voice with the alien soldier, and the alien handed him something in a pouch. It looked heavy. Money, Dilia thought. The alien coins that the starmen brought from Earth, and a lot of them.

Sleb's soldiers left through the gate just before it shut with a boom, closing Dilia away from the world she knew. An alien soldier with cold blue eyes took rough hold of Dilia's arm.

For a moment, she couldn't breathe, and then her breath came so fast, she couldn't catch it. Her skin crawled at the feel of his fingers. Dilia pulled her arm away.

The soldier laughed and said in Starrish, "Feisty little bitch, aren't you?" Then, in strongly accented Arantu, "You no want me touch, you come with, understand?"

Dilia didn't trust herself to speak, much less to let the soldier know she understood his language. She just nodded. Feeling more alone even than when her mother had died, she followed the soldier deeper into the base as the sky darkened to night.

The soldier led Dilia to a large building surrounded by gardens. It was low and rambling, an irregular shape that suggested many connected rooms, each of which might be almost the size of a house in the city below. A low hissing noise accompanied a strange breeze that seemed to be seeping from the ground all around them. Dilia remembered Cort saying something about the aliens' air being different. What had he said? Earthmen and Arantu looked a lot alike, both human, but the Earthmen's lungs were smaller. There was more of something in the air on Earth. Oxygen. Here on Aran there was not quite enough of it for the aliens. Maybe they were adding this 'oxygen' to the air around here. Maybe other things, too. Maybe one of these things was causing her strange feeling.

"Commandant house," the soldier said. He spoke Arantu with a strong accent that somehow, Dilia now thought was funny. She barely managed not to giggle out loud. Given her situation, she was feeling unaccountably good.

Inside the house, the feeling was more pronounced. She was led to a room the size of her entire house, a room that contained only three chairs and a table. The walls on two sides were lined with cabinets, and the remaining walls were decorated with pictures that she recognized from Cort's schoolbooks as scenes of Earth. The scenes were pretty, with jagged purple mountains topped with white. Dilia had learned from Cort's textbooks that such landforms existed on Aran, too, but somewhere very far away, farther than anyone from the city had ever traveled.

A person walked into the room. For a moment, Dilia was unsure whether the newcomer was male or female, Arantu or alien or... something else altogether. Like the Arantu and the aliens, the stranger had a human form, but with short-cropped hair and skin of a darker, richer brown than any Dilia had ever seen, contrasting sharply with a white coat over the same kind of red uniform all the alien men wore.

"You may go." She spoke to the soldier in a husky, but feminine voice, in Starrish. "Close the door behind you."

"Yes, ma'am." The soldier saluted, turned sharply toward the door, and stiffly strode out.

Female, then, despite wearing the hair style and uniform favored by the male aliens. Unlike the wealthier Arantu women such as Sleb's wife, she wore no cosmetics. Only her voice—and the slight lift of breasts beneath her jacket—gave her gender away. Dilia wondered how many of the starmen might actually be women.

"I am Doctor Abeni Inowa. You can call me Abeni. Do you speak Standard?"

Dilia hesitated. But, unlike the guard who had escorted her here, this woman seemed friendly enough. "Yes. My name is Dilia, and... and I would like to go home."

The dark woman continued speaking in Starrish. "Hello, Dilia. I'm sorry, I can't help you with going home. I'm just a doctor."

The fact that she spoke Starrish and wore the aliens' uniform suggested that she was from Earth—or might she be from some other planet that Dilia didn't know about? She stood no taller than Dilia, who was short, even for an Arantu. Most of the starmen towered over her.

"Are you from Earth?" Dilia was surprised at her own boldness, but Abeni just laughed and said, "Yes."

The doctor's easy laughter encouraged Dilia. "You don't look like the other Earthmen."

"Darker-skinned and shorter, right?"

"And you're a woman."

"Ah. Well, believe me, if you traveled around Earth now, you'd see a wide variety of racial types. And there are plenty of Africans and other Blacks in the service, too. Even here on the base. And women, too. It's not that unusual. You probably just don't see a lot of Earthers down below where you live, so maybe you haven't noticed."

"Maybe," Dilia said, "but I think I would have noticed *you*."

Abeni drew a deep breath and let it out in a long sigh. "No, I haven't gotten down into the city much. Funny, isn't it? I always dreamed of traveling to the stars, and now that I'm here, I'm busy on the base all the time." She opened her comm. "What about you? You speak Standard very well."

Dilia felt her face grow warm, but she couldn't help smiling a little. "Thank you. I've studied it for many years."

"You're well schooled, then?"

Dilia bit her lip and looked away.

Abeni didn't seem to notice. "On Earth, a person with a good education can go far. A woman like you or me can do any job, if she studies hard. There's no reason why not."

"I don't want to go far, Abeni. I just want to go home." There was a catch in her voice.

Abeni looked around, then picked up her medical case from the floor nearby, where she had put it down. "That's not up to me, I'm afraid. All I've been asked to do is examine you."

"For what? Why?"

Still not looking at Dilia, the doctor brushed her hand over her chin. She put the case on the nearby table and began laying out some instruments. "Shall we get on with it, then? It's not going to hurt."

Dilia took a deep breath, hoping to calm herself. She thought about studying on Earth as she watched the doctor preparing her instruments. She wondered what the commandant had in mind for her, and whether she might one day fly on a starship to Earth, the way Sleb's woman had said. Of course, Cort had talked years ago about going to Earth together if he got a good job at the base, but that was just talk. Idle dreaming. Dilia had never imagined that *she* might be the one who got a good job at the base, or that it might be a place where a woman could do a man's job—could do any job she wanted.

Did she want to do a man's job? She wasn't sure. She'd always thought she wanted to raise a family and care for people, but there was something appealing in the alien woman's quiet competence, a presence that Dilia thought she'd like to have, too. "You're a doctor, right? You help make sick people better?" she asked.

"Yes, that's right."

"Is that a job for women, on Earth?"

Abeni looked at her with surprise, and then she smiled. Her smile lit her face in a way that left no doubt that she was not only a woman, but very attractive. "I'll bet the commandant won't know what to make of you. He's probably never met a native woman who can talk back to him before. The answer to your question is that both men and women can be doctors, on Earth or here at the base. Now, open your mouth and say, 'Ah.'"

Dilia obeyed. She thought that if she ever did work at the base, or go to Earth, being a healer would appeal to her, as long as she could still have a family. "How do you become a doctor? I would like... to do something like that."

Abeni laughed. "Years and years of schooling," she said. "Regular public school, like you, and then university. Then medical school and a residency. If you want to go to the stars, like I did, there's an additional fellowship for that, too." She took Dilia's hand and clipped a small instrument onto her forefinger. It beeped, and Abeni nodded, seemingly pleased with the result. Then Abeni paused and looked more closely at Dilia. Her expression seemed sad. "You'd have to go to Earth to do all that studying; it's not possible here. I don't think that's what the commandant has in mind for you."

Dilia's stomach clenched. She wrapped her arms over it, trying to stay calm. Though she feared the answer, the question could no longer be avoided. "What *does* he have in mind for me?"

The doctor busied herself breaking a seal on a small vial and inserting it into something that slightly resembled a weapon. "This is just an inoculation," she said in a crisp, all-business tone.

She took hold of Dilia's arm and placed the device against her skin. It discharged with a faint "fthwt" sound, and Dilia felt a tiny pinch. "Ow! What's in—inocu—?"

"Inoculation." The doctor pronounced the word carefully. "It will protect you against diseases." She looked away, as if something interesting had started happening in the cabinets to her right. "And against an unwanted pregnancy."

"What? Why would I have..." Dilia let the sentence die as she realized exactly why she might have an unwanted pregnancy. She stood quickly from the examination seat. "I have to get out of here. Please. Help me. I want to go home."

There was genuine pity in the doctor's eyes. "I'm sorry. I have no authority on the base; I'm just a doctor. Most of the other native women I examine want to be here."

"Not me!"

"I'll... I'll tell the commandant, of course. If this is some kind of misunderstanding, I'm sure he'll clear it up. And meanwhile, of course, I'll check in on you often and make sure you're all right."

"But—"

"Look, maybe... since you speak Standard so well... maybe he has something else entirely in mind for you. Talk with him. I'm sorry if I've caused any misunderstanding. I really am. I will check on you again tomorrow." Abeni turned and left the room, closing the door quietly but firmly behind her.

A moment later, the soldier who had brought Dilia here returned.

Dilia thought about trying to escape; there was only the one soldier, after all. But this was an alien soldier, and he had a laser holstered on his belt. And even if she did manage to escape him, where would she go? The gate to the base was closed, and everyone knew that the wall around it could not be climbed; it could not even be approached without injury because of some kind of force field the aliens had installed. No, she'd have to find someplace to hide on the starbase, and then...

Dilia yawned. She suddenly felt very tired and a little confused. Had there been something in the inoc—inoculation the alien doctor had given her? Or was whatever the aliens added to the air really getting to her? She stumbled, and the soldier took hold of her elbow to steady her. She pulled away and forced herself simply to concentrate on walking in the direction he indicated. He accompanied her down a long windowless hallway, brightly lit by alien light fixtures spaced along its length. She was definitely feeling dizzy.

The guard motioned her into a room, also windowless but well lit. A man stood within.

"Commandant," the guard said, saluting with a motion of his hand.

"Dismissed," said the commandant; and the guard left.

The room was more than half the size of Dilia's entire house, yet it seemed barely big enough for the three pieces of furniture—a chair, a table, and a bed—that it contained. Dilia had the sudden idea that her house was very small, and the thought made her giggle. Was the air even worse in here? Or was a drug in the—whatever it was called—starting to take greater effect?

The alien commandant looked her up and down the way he had at the shop, as if she were merchandise that he would now need to find a place for in his house. "You're actually very pretty, now that they've cleaned you up. What's your name?"

She was afraid, but she remembered Abeni's advice: talk with him. "Dilia. May I ask, sir, what's yours?"

He drew back as if startled. Then he laughed. "My God, I've commanded this base for eight years, and in all that time, I don't believe a single native has ever asked my name. I think I'm going to like you. Let's drop the 'sir,' shall we? You can call me Karim."

"Karim." The name was soft and pleasant. It tickled her mind. She suppressed a giggle, then felt dizzy. "I'm sorry, I am not feeling... very well. Do you think I might go home now?"

The smile still lingered on his face, but something about it hardened. "No, Dilia; I'm afraid that's not possible. You have important work to do here. But of course you may lie down for a while first, while you adjust."

She nodded, swaying on her feet. Important work! Perhaps she and Cort would be going to Earth after all! When she stumbled, Karim put his arm around her, pulling her a bit closer than might be absolutely necessary to steady her. Too close, but Dilia did not object. She was grateful for the support.

But as he lowered her onto the bed, he did not let go. With one hand he held her arm so that she could not turn away, and with the other, he pushed aside her skirt.

Dilia had a good idea of what was coming. She tried to remove his hand with her own as she turned aside. But she seemed to lack any strength. "No. Please." Her heart pounded, and her head swam. "I... Please, I need to..." What was the word he'd used? "Adjust. I need... time. To adjust. Please."

Incredibly, slowly, he let her go. "All right, little Dilia," he said. "You rest tonight. Tomorrow, we'll talk some more." He put a strange, twisting emphasis on the word "talk."

He turned and left the room. Dilia was aware of the door closing as a distant sound already half in a dream.

Chapter 4

The Danger to Cort

C ort came around the corner onto his street, only to find it blocked by soldiers wearing Sleb's uniforms. It wasn't uncommon to see soldiers in the street, of course. They were always on some errand or another, but they generally didn't block it entirely. "Street's closed," one of them said in a gruff voice. "Find another way."

Sixteen and just finishing his next-to-last year at school, Cort was eager to get home and work through a set of challenging physics homework problems with Dilia. But he was curious. "What is it?"

The soldier's stance widened slightly, and he placed his hand on the holster of his stunner. "Street's closed. Move along."

A neighbor a bit bolder than most, an old man with a curved spine and wrinkled face, opened his door and beckoned Cort inside.

"What's happening?" Cort asked as he ducked through the doorway.

But the neighbor shrugged. "Does anyone ever know what it is, until after it's over? And maybe not even then. Just wait here. Later, we'll find out."

It didn't take a diploma to appreciate the neighbor's logic; Cort wouldn't be able to get past the soldiers without a fight, and it would not be a fight he could win. Cort could take any opponent in a knife fight, but he was no match for twelve soldiers with stunners. Not even close. He waited, anxiety building within him like hunger.

After the soldiers finally left, Cort inched to the corner, and saw the door to his house hanging open. His heart raced into doubletime. He ran down the street, then hesitated at the doorway. A muffled sound came from inside the house. Was his mother or Dilia wounded? Could there still be a soldier inside? Hand on the hilt of his knife, Cort entered the house.

After the bright sunlight outside, Cort saw nothing in the dark room. He blinked twice to adjust. His mother sat in the far corner, turned toward the wall. Her hair was disheveled, her head in the crook of her arm. She made a low, keening sound Cort had never heard before. Crying. His mother was crying.

"Mama?"

She shook her head.

He knelt beside her and touched her back. "What is it, Mama? What happened?"

For a few moments, she could only sob quietly, first without turning, and then in Cort's arms. Cort felt that his heart might break, without knowing why.

Then he guessed. "Is it... Dilia?"

His mother nodded.

Cort understood. A chill like ice slid down his back. His worst fear, realized.

He swallowed and said, "I'll get her back, Mama. Somehow, I'll get her back."

But his mother took his hand. "No, Cort." She wiped her tears and added, "I couldn't bear to lose you, too."

"I'll be careful," he answered softly, "but I have to try. I have to. I couldn't live with my-self if I didn't." Then, even more softly, as the ice in his spine changed to anger, he added. "I'll get her back. By Earth, I swear it."

Cort walked to Sleb's compound. If he couldn't find Dilia there, he might at least find out where they had taken her. Built in a prestigious position on the hill next to the starbase, the compound fronted on a wide garbage-strewn dirt road that was a main thoroughfare of the city. There were people still about, and a small gang of older men was scanning the passersby for likely victims. In the still air, the area smelled of garbage and sweat.

Like the starbase, the slum-lord's compound was surrounded by a high wall. The gates of Sleb's compound that fronted on the road were shut and no doubt guarded inside by Sleb's soldiers. Not the right place for a stealthy entry.

A distant boom announced that the starbase's gate was closing. Time was growing short. Perhaps Dilia had already been taken to the starbase, out of Cort's reach. No, he had to hope she was still here. Cort studied the compound from the street. The walls were high, but perhaps they could be climbed. He leaned casually against the wall, trying to look like he might be waiting for someone, hoping not to arouse any notice from the passersby. The wall was cold to the touch, its stones smooth and fitted so close together that he couldn't even get a finger between two of them. It was impenetrable.

There had to be a way in. Cort began methodically to survey the compound from all sides.

Only two sides of Sleb's residence faced onto streets. On the other two sides, the compound backed onto the walled compounds of other wealthy people. If he could get into one of these, he might find a way into Sleb's compound from an unanticipated direction. Cort followed streets and alleyways, but found no way he might enter any of these other compounds, either.

As the sun was nearly set, Cort arrived on a hillside behind the entire area, by the wall of the city. Weeds choked the foundations of what had once been a building, maybe more than one, now in ruins. He had spent an hour reconnoitering but had found nothing, an hour wasted, when every minute might count. Cort sat on a building-stone to consider his options.

The first Cort heard of the old man's approach was a discreet cough less than ten feet away. Cort jumped up and whirled around, his knife ready. He stood for a moment, on the verge of an attack, examining the stranger. The old man held his arms out away from his body, hands open to show he was weaponless. He smiled in a friendly way. "Nice knife," he said.

"My father's." Cort walked around the old man looking for a weapon or for something of value worth stealing from the fellow.

"From the forest," said the old man. His white hair was somewhat disheveled, almost hiding a blue crystal embedded in the skin near his hairline. The crystal might be valuable, but more likely, it was a fake. It was probably not worth the wound he'd have to inflict on the old man in order to get at it. Even in the waning light, he could see the man's clothing was poor, but it was city clothing, a plain, thin shirt that might have once been white, and ill-fitting brown drawstring pants. Like many of the poorest people in the city, he was barefoot.

Cort grunted his agreement. He had just about concluded that the fellow had nothing of value, but it didn't hurt to ask. "You got anything worth taking?"

"Just advice, young man." The old man smiled—an engaging smile that held nothing back. City clothing or no, he spoke with a forest accent. He sat on the building stone next to the one where Cort had been sitting. Cort sheathed his knife and returned to his seat, and the old man added, "Good advice."

Cort found he liked the fellow. He returned the smile. "I could use some good advice."

The old man looked out over the view of the compounds below, and Cort's gaze followed his. An alleyway between the two rear neighbors led to a small gate in Sleb's wall. The gate was closed. Beyond the wall, the rooftops within the compound showed a complex arrangement of buildings. "High wall," the man said, "but you could probably climb it. The stones back here are more roughly finished than the ones facing the street."

Cort turned to look at his companion, speechless. In profile, the old man's nose was sharp, his cheekbones pronounced. The setting sun glinted almost purple off the strange crystal.

"The problems start when you reach the top." The man gestured toward the top of the wall with a movement of his chin. "Can you see how sharp the stones on the top are? When you step to the other side, you'll be nicely silhouetted against the sky, if anyone is watching."

The old man met Cort's gaze. "The problem is, you don't have any way of knowing who's on the other side watching. The place is crawling with soldiers."

How could the old man have known what he was contemplating? Had it been that obvious? But Cort understood good analysis when he heard it, and he wanted to hear more. "What do you recommend?"

"You need a kiri," the old man said.

Cort didn't think he'd heard right. "What?"

"A kiri." Cort's companion spoke as matter-of-factly as if he had said something obvious, like "Air to breathe." But seeing Cort's incredulity, he muttered, "City born," as if it were a curse. Then he added, "Do you know what that is?"

"I know..." The conversation had gone so quickly from the insightful to the preposterous, that Cort was hard-pressed to keep up. "Of course, everyone... The Hunter and the Kiri, the two moons. It's a story about an animal companion that communicates telepathically somehow with a hunter and helps him, but in real life—"

"It's not just a story," the man interrupted. "In real life, in the khenaran, hunters still have kiris, some of them. You've become a hunter, young man, and the task before you is far from easy. You need a kiri."

Cort shook his head. "Even if... even if it's real, what I need to do... I don't have time to go off into the forest and try to find out how to get a kiri. I have to get inside there now. Today." In fact, it was already beginning to get dark. Time to go.

The old man sighed. "Then climb the wall back here," he said. "Wait until dark. Be careful going over the top. Stay as low as you can. Jump down as quietly as you can." He shook his head. "But there are too many soldiers. You have no way of knowing where they are, but they will find you. And you don't know where you need to go once you get inside. Perhaps what you are seeking isn't even there any longer."

Climbing slowly to his feet, the old man concluded, "In truth, if you are serious about your purpose, you don't have time for anything else *but* to get a kiri. But I suppose you will have to find that out in your own way. Good luck, young man. Be careful." He began picking his way slowly down the hill.

Cort turned to watch him. "You, too," he said. "Get home before dark."

The old man didn't look back. Cort watched until he disappeared around a corner.

After dark, Cort descended the hill and walked quietly up the small alleyway. It had been hours since Sleb's soldiers took Dilia from the house. Would she still be here? Cort swallowed hard and noticed that his fists were clenched tight. He loosened them. Where else could she be?

When he reached the wall, he tried the gate, careful to avoid making any noise. But the gate didn't move. It was either stuck or blocked or barred from the inside. From this close, the wall was daunting, more than twice his height. Despite himself, Cort worried about what the old man had said. His heart pounded, adrenaline flowing. He tightened his jaw and took a deep breath. Moving to the left of the gate, he felt along the stone wall until he found a spot where the stones were rough and uneven. He began to climb.

The light that spilled over the top of the wall from within didn't reach the outer surface of the wall. Cort climbed by feel alone. The ascent seemed to take forever. When he finally attained the top and reached for a better handhold, he felt a stab of pain. He pulled back sharply, almost losing his balance, and barely managed to keep from swearing aloud. He searched again for a handhold. He was more careful this time, feeling along the top of the wall until he found a spot free of the sharp rocks cemented to the surface. He thought again of the old man he had met earlier. So far, the man's advice had proved accurate. Cort hoped that he was wrong about the soldiers.

Cort pulled himself up to the top of the wall by holding onto the very edge. In the middle, jagged rocks formed a treacherous surface. Cort peered over the wall. He looked into a small courtyard lit by two lamps of alien manufacture that cast a weird blue glow. Around the courtyard were low windowless buildings, probably storage or utility sheds.

No one was in sight. Cort felt a bit giddy and almost laughed with relief, but then he realized that the danger was far from over.

He got a knee and then his feet onto the wall's edge. He stepped carefully over the sharp surface on the top of the wall and began lowering himself down the other side. Hanging from his hands, Cort dropped to the ground below. One foot twisted and gave way beneath him. When he stood again, his ankle protested with pain, but it did not give way.

He breathed a sigh of relief, and slipped into the shadow of one of the buildings.

If only he knew where Dilia was! He hadn't fully comprehended, when he'd been outside, how much of a problem the compound's size would be. Dilia could be anywhere. Cort took a deep breath and made himself think. Probably, she wasn't here among the sheds and storage buildings. Cort's best chance of finding her probably lay in capturing someone—whether servant or soldier—and getting them to talk.

Ten minutes later, Cort reached what appeared to be the living quarters of the compound. From deep in the shadows, he looked across an open courtyard at a two-story building with windows, some lit. This building seemed as good a place to start as any.

The open courtyard was a concern. Two soldiers walked back and forth along its border to Cort's left. To his right, the buildings on his side went on for some distance, and the detour around would be a long one. Perhaps he could slip quietly across the courtyard without attracting the soldiers' attention. He waited until they were on their way to the far side, so that he would be behind them. Then he started across.

"Halt!" The command came from behind. The two soldiers to Cort's left turned quickly, raising their weapons.

Cort's heart pounded. He looked around wildly for some way out.

Two other soldiers, directly behind him, aimed their weapons at him. Ahead, another soldier, similarly armed, came out of the lit building. The weapons they carried weren't lethal; only aliens carried the lasers that could burn a hole the size of a grown man's fist right through a person's chest. Still, the stunners that the aliens allowed to the soldiers of the city could inflict serious pain.

There was no escape. As ordered, Cort halted.

"Drop the knife and raise your hands slowly." The soldier spoke in a bored voice, as if he arrested intruders every day. And maybe he did.

Cort barely controlled the panic that rose in his throat, but he did as instructed, laying his father's knife down carefully.

The soldiers surrounded him, and the one who had given the order picked up the knife and tucked it into his own belt.

Cort felt like he might be sick.

"What's going on here?" A man about two doorways wide squeezed out of the doorway to the house ahead of him. Light-haired, his skin shiny with perspiration, the man was dressed in silvery alien silks embroidered with gold. A servant followed him, carrying a lantern.

"An intruder, Master Sleb," said one of the soldiers.

"Every day, something!" Sleb struck the open palm of his left hand with his right fist. "Today, two of them!" Sleb peered at Cort, who stood motionless with his hands raised and half a dozen stunners aimed at him. "What were you after, boy?" the kingpin asked. "My rumored fabulous wealth?"

Cort found that his mouth had become exceedingly dry. He had to work at answering. "No, sir," he managed. "I came looking for my friend. A girl." Remembering his manners, he added, "Sir," then, "Please."

"The boy wants his girlfriend back," Sleb commented to no one in particular, as if he were remarking on the weather. Two soldiers laughed nervously. Sleb signaled his servant to move the lamp closer, and studied Cort's features, as if he were considering Cort's sanity or trying to read his mind. Then he sighed. "Take him to the prison," he said. "Tomorrow we'll execute him, along with the other one."

Cort stiffened. Sleb had taken his dearest fried Dilia from him, and he'd taken the one possession Cort valued—his father's bone knife. By all of Earth, there was *no way* Sleb was going to take his life, too. Not without a fight. His hands tightened to fists.

Several of the soldiers moved to a more ready stance, hands near their stunners. Two drew their weapons.

Oblivious, Sleb turned and went back toward the building, the servant with the lamp scurrying behind him."Move," ordered one of the soldiers. Three of them now aimed their stunners at him.

Cort drew in a breath, let it out, and unclenched his hands. With the kingpin gone, instigating a fight with the soldiers would be pointless. Better to survive, if he could. Better to come back and try again to rescue Dilia.

A soldier took firm hold of Cort's arm.

Cort shook off the offensive touch, glaring at the soldier. But he said nothing. He'd made his choice. He went where they led him.

After passing several buildings, Cort was led finally into a large, rectangular building near the wall he had climbed to enter Sleb's compound. The doorway led into a hall illuminated by a single pale alien light. To Cort's right, a door opened to a more brightly lit guardroom, where two soldiers sat at a table, playing a game of cards. Their laughter echoed from the stone walls, as one of the soldiers leading Cort took a set of keys from a hook on the wall. Beyond the guardroom, the hallway was flanked with four more doors, two on each side. Each door consisted of firmly joined vertical iron bars. The soldier in front of Cort unlocked one of the barred doors. He pushed Cort inside, slammed the door, and locked it.

Cort stumbled into a windowless rectangular cell with rough stone walls. Iron rings were set into the walls in places. In one corner of the cell, a hole in the floor seemed to provide the only sanitation, and from the smell of the place, it wasn't enough.

Against the wall opposite the door, a man sat on the floor. When Cort's eyes met his, he nodded slightly. Cort had seen savages before, but not such recent arrivals as this man must be. Newcomers from the forest usually got rid of their outlandish skin clothing as soon as possible, but like this man, they could still be identified by their golden eyes. If newcomers survived the first few difficult weeks in the city, their eyes grew brown or hazel or, rarely, even gray, green, or blue. After a few months they looked like the rest of the city population.

Cort had heard of the forest skins, of course, but until now he had never seen anyone wearing them. He couldn't take his eyes off the strangely garbed savage. Cured animal skin had been roughly sewn into pants and a vest of sorts that was slung off one shoulder. The skins were decorated with beads and feathers in attractive patterns. The man's hair was long and appeared to have been tied back rather than combed. An assortment of feathers, thongs, bones, and other objects Cort couldn't immediately identify were woven into that mass of hair. The man had a flat, round face and high cheekbones and seemed about the age that Cort's father would have been, had his father lived. He sat perfectly still and alert.

Embarrassed that perhaps he shouldn't have stared so openly, Cort attempted a conversation. "Just get here from the forest?"

"Today," the man said glumly. "And you were born here?"

Cort smiled, crossed the cell, and sat down beside the other. "Confirm," he said. "Name's Cort."

"Cort." The savage rolled the name around in his mouth, trying it out. "My name is Neder-talerit. I understand that you city people prefer shorter names. Call me Neder." He spoke in the odd, formal, old-fashioned manner of the forest people. "Do you have a longer version of your name?"

Cort blushed, then was angry at himself for being ashamed. This man of all people would not find the name primitive. "Cort-anaran," he said. "After my father."

"Cort-anaran?" Neder rolled the name around in his mouth. "Corodh-an-Aran?"

The strange, soft *dh* sound didn't exist in Starrish, and so had been nearly extinguished in the language of the city, a dialect of Arantu heavily laced with Starrish words. But the name didn't sound wrong. Who was to know? In any case, what difference did it make? Cort shrugged. "Could be." He was silent for a moment. Had his father rolled the soft *dh* sound when he pronounced his name? He felt a sudden surge of sympathy for the older man imprisoned with him. "Bad piece of luck for you, to dead-end in this place your first day in the city. How'd it happen?"

"It's a long story, and one that would probably bore you. You city people have no doubt often heard the like."

"I'm not scheduled for lift-off any time soon," Cort answered. Seeing Neder's blank look, he paraphrased, "I'm not going anywhere." The savage was probably right that his story was common; disappearances and casualties among the new arrivals were high because they didn't know how to survive in the city. But Cort had never talked to an arrival as new as this one, and he was interested. And he wanted to put his own failure out of his mind for a short while. Afterwards, he'd be able to think more clearly. Afterwards, he'd start trying to figure out how to escape. But for now... "I'd like to hear it," he said.

Neder focused on a spot somewhere near the center of the cell. "I had two sons..."

Chapter 5

Escape

Neder sighed deeply, a long, sad sound. "Two sons," he repeated, "and now I have none." He had lived in a village that was almost a month's journey from the city, deep in the great khenaran. His only children were two sons, twins. As they grew to young adulthood, Neder's sons grew tall and handsome and strong. One took an interest in plants, and became adept at finding herbs for seasoning and for healing, as well as the rare berries and fruits that people enjoyed, and in growing some of the roots that were one of the mainstays of their diet. The other son wanted only to be a hunter.

Hunting (Neder explained) is not an easy profession. His son was perhaps not patient enough. There was an accident The son died. He was a likable and kind person. Everyone mourned him—but his brother Culan was especially devastated. Nothing that anyone in the village said or did could bring the surviving twin out of his grief. Months passed. If anything, Culan's grief only deepened. He stopped foraging in the khenaran. He no longer brought home the bright, sweet berries that had made the children happy. The fields he had once cultivated grew wild again. He began avoiding the sympathetic looks of others in the village, sitting alone in the forest for hours at a time.

Then one day, Culan disappeared altogether. The truth was that no one noticed right away. The young man spent so much time alone in the forest that a disappearance of a few days was not unusual. But after a week, Neder understood that his son had gone. He tracked Culan to the very edge of the khenaran, where the primeval trees gave way to the scrub wood that grew where the aliens had finished harvesting.

For another two weeks, Neder hesitated. He knew now without a doubt that Culan had gone to the city. But he could not decide what he himself should do. On the one hand, he wanted to find and talk to his son, to try to persuade him to return home. But on the other hand, he understood Culan's going to the city as an act of desperation, one from which perhaps there was no return.

And Neder himself had a strong loathing of the place. His emotions were a barrier to thinking clearly.

In the end, Neder's desire to find his son prevailed. Swallowing his loathing and (he admitted) his fear, he set out for the city, moving quickly. He traveled for half a month through the scrub woods, a place that he found unpleasant compared to the khenaran he had left behind. But compared to the city, the woods were like home.

Neder arrived at the gate around noon. The harvesters were out and were not due back for several more days. No one was leaving the city, and only Neder was going in. The bored guard took the time to talk with the newcomer, and Neder asked where he might find his son. In his own village, the question would have been perfectly reasonable, but in the city, most people are strangers. The guard laughed at Neder's naiveté, but not unkindly. "You probably won't find him, old man," he had answered, and then added, "but then again, if he's dressed like you are, I guess he'll stand out in a crowd."

Neder wasn't sure then what the guard meant, but it didn't take long to find out. The stares he drew as he walked down the street were uncomfortable, and mostly not as friendly as the young guard's. Neder's desire to avoid this unpleasant attention fought with his need to go where there were people, so that he could find his son.

But Neder didn't find his son. Culan found Neder. The young man had noticed a thickening of the crowd at one corner of a public square and hoping to find an easy mark or a pocket worth picking, had gone over to see what was happening. To his amazement, he found his own father in the crowd. He drew Neder into a quieter street.

At first he was annoyed that his father had followed him. But he seemed to understand how great was the effort Neder had made, traveling so far, and into such a foreign place, and so he welcomed his father.

Cul—as he now called himself—introduced Neder to a group of young men that he had recently met in the city, men that he called his friends. Neder struggled with bewilderment and even grief as he learned that his son now made his living by theft and assault.

Neder's voice broke as he told the story, and Cort touched his arm sadly. "It's how we live. Does it seem so bad to you?"

Neder replied only, "How can people live by profiting from violence to their neighbors?"

Cort had no answer. He had never thought about it, never considered any alternative. For the first time, he felt he had been judged and found wanting.

Cul's gang, Neder continued, was planning a raid on Sleb's compound.

"What?" Cort asked in disbelief. "What kind of fool would do that?"

"Newcomers, Cort," Neder answered sadly, "with dreams of getting rich quickly."

At first, Neder had tried to dissuade his son from going. He had not argued that the place was too well guarded and the risk too high, though he might have, had he known then what he knew now. Neder argued simply that it was wrong to take from another what was not freely offered.

Embarrassed, Cul had answered his father sharply. Almost, almost Neder had turned to go (how he regretted now that he had not!), but he felt unsure of his own position. Things were different in the city, Cul had said. Perhaps it was so. Reluctantly, Neder went with his son and the other young men.

The rest of the story was almost too painful for Neder to tell. Of course they had been intercepted. It had been foolish to dream that they had a chance of success. Luckily, the soldiers were still far off when the gang realized that they had been spotted. They turned and ran, but one young man was hurt badly by a blast from a soldier's stunner. Only Neder stopped to help. To Neder's intense disappointment, Cul didn't even turn around. Those who could, ran away. The soldiers captured Neder with the wounded man. They killed the wounded man at once, and Neder had been put into this prison to await his execution in the morning.

"Neder, what that gang did makes good sense," Cort said. " Anyone who stayed would have been caught and killed. Isn't it better for as many people as possible to get away?"

"It's not right," Neder insisted. "We should help our friends. Maybe if they had all stuck together, they could have saved their friend. Do you really think not?"

For a moment, Cort didn't know quite what he really thought. The ground seemed to shift like sand that was slipping out from under him. He pressed his hand to the floor for balance. "I don't know, Neder. What I said is true in the city. Everyone knows it. Everyone acts on it when they have to. But then, if I really believed it, I wouldn't be here, either."

"Ah!" Neder broke into a wide grin. "I knew it! You are a true human being—not like those others. From the moment you walked in here, I felt that you have a heart."

Cort's eyes stung, and he put his face in his hands. "No," he answered, looking up again. "Even in the city, we love our friends. Maybe I'm just a little more stubborn than some people. Neder, there's a girl who is like a sister to me. Maybe more than that. Sleb abducted her. I mean to get her back."

"How can you?" Neder was referring to Cort's imprisonment, and his execution that was scheduled in the morning, but Cort was thinking beyond the immediate situation. Listening to Neder's story had helped him clear his mind about his own predicament. Now it was time for action."I met an old man who said that I needed a kiri. Does that make sense to you?"

Neder thought for a moment. "Yes, I think so. If you don't know where your friend is. If she's well guarded and hard to reach. Yes, it makes sense, if you can find a way to get out of here."

"There are really kiris, then?"

"Yes, of course. There are kiris of power, such as wolves, and kiris of subtlety, poisonous serpents no longer than one joint of your thumb, and everything in between. Don't you know of them here?"

Cort had heard stories, of course, but like everyone in the city, he'd dismissed them. He wasn't sure how to answer.

Neder pushed back the hair that fell along the left side of his face. "Look. Can you see this?" Even in the dim light that glowed from the hallway, Cort could see the glistening of a deep red gem near Neder's hairline.

"What is it?" Cort asked.

"You don't recognize it at all?"

Cort shook his head.

"I use it to communicate with my kiri."

"You? You yourself?"

"Yes, Cort. I'm a hunter. Or was."

"Could you help me get a kiri?"

Neder sighed. "I don't think we're going to have time. I believe your neighbor Sleb has plans for us in the morning."

Cort had the beginning of an idea for escape. The chance of success was low, but better than not trying at all. If he threw away this second chance, Sleb would not give him a third. Cort turned over how he felt—in theory—about leaving Sleb's compound, knowing that Dilia might still be there. He wanted to try again to find her, but he'd already given it his best shot and failed. He needed to do something different. He studied Neder thoughtfully—the man's exotic appearance, the red gem at his hairline, his claim of being a hunter and having a kiri. Cort made up his mind. "If we could get out of here, would you help me?"

Neder turned to look at Cort. "You would come to the khenaran?" he asked.

"I'll come."

"It's a journey of weeks to my village and then back again."

"I said I would come. What choice do I have?"

Neder hesitated. "My help may not be enough."

"Why?"

"There are others who decide these things. I would be lying if I said that my influence is great." Neder paused, his eyes moving back and forth as if he was thinking through something complicated. "Still, it's something. I will help you as I can."

Cort nodded. "Thanks, Neder. Now…" He stood and stretched. His bones hurt from too much sitting. "Oh, that floor is hard! Let's hope the lock is not that hard." Cort walked to the door and bent over to study the lock.

"Do you have a key?" asked Neder.

"If only." Cort squinted at the lock. He couldn't quite see into the inner mechanism, but the lock seemed to be an old type. "It doesn't look like it would be hard to pick." He suddenly felt apologetic—as if there was something wrong with picking locks. Abashed, he turned to smile at Neder. "One of the things we city spawn learn from our elders. Unfortunately, they took away my knife, and I can't do it with my bare hands."

"They took my knife, too," the hunter said.

"But I'm wondering if you might have something worked into that hair-do of yours that might do the trick."

Neder reflexively touched the tangles of his hair. "What sort of thing?"

"Something long and thin and hard. I'll have to put some pressure on it, without its bending or breaking."

"Like this?" From the braids at the back of his hair, Neder pulled a long, thin bone and leaned forward to hand it to Cort.

Cort didn't even try to imagine why a person would work such an object into his hair. Instead, he studied it thoughtfully, turning it over and flexing it in his hands. "Confirm, my goodman. This is stellar." Seeing Neder's blank look, Cort shook his head and said, "You're going to get the street out of my talk, aren't you? My mother would like that. I said yes, it's perfect." He was in high spirits. "I'm going to get us out of here, my friend."

Neder stood and came closer to watch. "You're going to get the door open," he amended. "We're both going to get us out of here."

"Confirm," Cort agreed, but his attention was already on the lock.

The bone turned out to be an excellent tool, better than his knife with its wider blade would have been. Cort felt the tumblers slide open one after the other and had the door unlocked in just a few minutes. "On-screen, Neder. Look." He swung the door open.

"Excellent," the hunter said, smiling. "Now we shall have to pass by the guards' room quietly and invisibly. I can do this. The guards are stupid to light their own room so brightly, leaving in shadow the hallway they are supposed to guard. You must follow me exactly."

Cort returned the smile. "The helm is yours," he said.

Neder crossed the hallway so that they moved along the wall adjacent to the guards' room. If a soldier came out, he would be more likely to look across the hall than along the wall. When they reached the doorway, Neder stopped. Shadows flickered in the bright light from within. Four voices laughed and argued, apparently preoccupied over some kind of game.

Neder lowered his hand toward the floor, a signal. Cort understood and sank to his knees. Neder did the same. The two prisoners half-crawled, half-slithered across the light that tumbled from the door. When they reached the shadow on the other side, they stood again. Their eyes met for a moment. Neder smiled and nodded. Neither of them spoke a word.

The door to the outside was closed. Cort took the lead, silently opening the latch. The door was unlocked, but it opened outwards. The creak of its unoiled hinges was masked in a burst of laughter from the guards' room, but anyone outside who might be nearby would be alerted.

Cort's breath caught. He waited a moment, but could hear nothing. He glanced at Neder, who shrugged. Afraid to open the door wider, Cort shimmied through the narrow opening. No one was in sight. Cort signaled to Neder, and the hunter also slipped out. Cort drew a deep breath and closed the door.

The sound of the unoiled hinges was loud in the quiet outside air. In instant reaction, Neder moved quickly and silently to the corner of the building and peered around. He signaled with a nod and a motion of his hand that no one was there.

Heart pounding, Cort crossed the open yard in front of the building to reach the wall of the compound. The stones of the wall were as uneven on the inside as on the outside. Freedom was almost within reach. Cort took hold of a projecting edge and started to climb.

But Neder pulled at his shirt. When Cort looked back, the hunter shook his head. For a moment, Cort's need to flee warred with his sense that the hunter knew how to escape better than he did. His hands trembled as he descended the two steps he had taken and followed the hunter around the side of the building. Neder had found a dark corner where a shed of some kind abutted the prison building. He pressed himself into the shadow, pulling Cort after. Then, indicating Cort's light shirt, Neder moved aside, indicating that Cort should hide behind him, deep in the shadow of that corner. "Don't move," he whispered.

They weren't a moment too soon. The door of the prison burst open, squeaking its protest. A soldier shouted, "They're gone!" Lights in the compound blazed on, throwing into even darker shadow the corner where the fugitives hid. They pressed back as far as they could.

The four guards ran out the door, fanning out. Two ran by Neder and Cort without seeing them. Their shouts echoed off the walls, and before long, a dozen soldiers were assembled in the open area in front of the prison. Cort could see only a few of them; the rest were hidden by the bulk of the building, but he could hear their voices, louder even than the beating of his heart.

"...probably over the wall and long gone." Two latecomers trotted by the fugitives' hiding place. "No," the other answered. "I heard the door close, and I'd swear there wasn't time for that before we came outside." He slowed to peer into the shadows where the fugitives were hiding. Neder was perfectly still, and watching over Neder's shoulder, Cort didn't even dare to breathe.

"You'd be surprised how fast people can blast off when they're running on fear," the soldier's companion said. "Hurry up, we're already late." They joined the other soldiers in the front of the building.

"Attention!" a voice shouted. The other voices dropped to a buzz, then nothing. "We're going to conduct a thorough search for the escaped prisoners. If you see them, use your stunners immediately. We want these prisoners recaptured at all costs. Master Sleb desires to make an example of them in the morning. Now, I'm going to divide you into search parties for a thorough search of the compound. Look in every building. I will lead a group that will search outside the compound in case they managed to climb the wall. They can't be far. For those who capture the prisoners, there will be a reward."

The buzz of conversation that accompanied this announcement was quickly quieted. Soldiers were given search assignments, and the sound of marching boots heralded each group's departure. Several groups strode briskly past Cort and Neder's hiding place, but they looked neither right nor left as they hastened to their assigned search locations.

Although it was beyond the building's corner, Cort heard the heavy bar being removed from the gate in the compound wall, and a troop of soldiers marching out. At last, the stillness was broken only by the pacing of a pair of guards back and forth in front of the prison building.

Cort took a step, but Neder held him back. They waited for what seemed an eternity to Cort; then, with a firm hold on Cort's sleeve, Neder glided silently toward the open yard in front of the prison.

They started across the yard. Two guards were walking away from them. Neder crossed the yard behind the guards with a careful pace that seemed to Cort to be measured—not so fast that the sound or movement would alert the guards, but not so slow that they would be caught in the open when the guards reached the end of their path and turned around again. Aching to run, Cort held himself to Neder's pace and tried hard to walk as quietly as the barefoot hunter. His fear-fueled hearing magnified every footfall of his sandaled feet.

They crossed the yard while the guards were still walking away, but in a moment now, the guards would turn. Neder stopped at the gate and looked carefully. Then he slipped outside. Cort let out the breath he didn't realize he was holding, and he followed.

Neder was nowhere to be seen.

A hand waved from behind a narrow jog in the wall of the compound behind Sleb's: it was Neder. Quickly, Cort joined the hunter. Again, Neder positioned Cort behind himself, whispering the words "Be completely still" in Cort's ear.

The wait seemed endless. Cort was tired. He no longer had a clear sense of what they were waiting for. Only the hunter's completely alert stillness continued to warn Cort of danger.

Voices echoed down the alleyway. Then a troop of at least twenty soldiers marched briskly past the two fugitives and into Sleb's compound. The gate was shut, and the bar slid loudly into place.

Neder stepped into the street, and gratefully, Cort followed.

"We should find a place to hide until morning," Cort said. "The streets are dangerous at night, even for people who are armed. And we have nothing."

"Where?" Neder asked.

Now Cort was leading again.

"There's an empty area up the hill." Cort gestured to his left. "I was there earlier today. I think it may have been built up once, but now it's just ruins. There'll be places to hide. I left after dark, and no one was there."

Neder nodded. "Try to keep out of sight."

Cort dodged behind the rubble. The Hunter moon had risen and hung low, a golden half-orb in the east. The Kiri moon could not be seen, but there was enough light for Cort to pick his way among the ruins, moving higher and closer to the city wall.

"Here!" Neder called softly.

Behind some of the building stones, a weed-filled depression in the earth suggested the outline of what might have once been a store-room—or a prison. There was room for both of them out of sight from any passers-by. "It's good," Cort said.

They settled into the depression, hidden by the piles of rubble. The night's stress had taken its toll. Cort felt unusually tired. He stifled a yawn.

"You can sleep," Neder said. "I slept most of the afternoon in that prison, and I'm not tired. I'll watch."

Cort thought about objecting, but he was too tired to argue. He accepted Neder's offer. "Thanks. But wake me if anyone comes."

"I will," Neder said. "Be sure of it."

⁂

"Wake up."

The words were spoken softly, but Cort was alert at once, half on his feet.

"I don't think these people are a problem, but you asked me to wake you," Neder said.

The sun shone brightly. The sky was clear and blue, and the Hunter moon hung low in the west, barely visible in the daylight. Cort crept to the spot where Neder knelt behind a building stone and watched the street below. Two scavengers had left the street and were rummaging among the stones. "You're right. They're no danger. They might have found us, but they would have been more afraid of us than we would have been of them." He looked around. "How'd it get so late?"

"You must have been tired."

"I didn't mean to sleep this long." Cort shook his head, angry at himself. "The streets are safe enough by daylight. Let's move." He stomped away from Neder for a moment of privacy, and instinctively reached to touch his knife as he returned. The sheath, of course, remained empty. "Oh, Earth!" Cort grumbled. "My father's knife. Those garbage slime over there"—he gestured with his head toward the wall of Sleb's compound—"took it."

Neder glanced at the empty sheath on Cort's belt. "It's from the forest."

"My father was from the forest."

Raising an eyebrow, Neder asked, "What clan?"

"Clan?" Cort frowned. "How should I know? Does it matter?"

"Everyone has a clan," Neder said patiently. "Keep down, would you? That shirt of yours stands out."

"Ease up, Neder. They'd have to be scanning from the rooftops to..." Cort looked again at the compound in the distance. "You don't suppose...?"

Neder shrugged and gestured downward with his head.

Cort dropped below the line of building stones. He was impressed with the hunter's constant awareness of possible dangers in his environment. "Sorry, I wasn't thinking."

Before he headed out to the forest with Neder, Cort had to stop at his home. His mother would be nearly frantic with worry. Especially after Dilia's abduction, he wanted his mother to know that he was all right. Also, he had to say goodbye, as Neder had said the trip to the khenaran and back would take weeks.

Would he lose a year at school? He took in a deep breath and let it out slowly, seeing his plans all pushed back, maybe gone. But there was nothing to be done about it.

And who would lead his gang while he was away? Tark, probably. Tark was tough, tracking to become a soldier. He'd do fine. The gang would stay together.

Cort touched his empty knife sheath. When he got home, he could pick up the knife that he still kept there, the knife that he'd used as a boy before he'd allowed him-self to carry his father's knife.

The two fugitives crept out of the field. When they reached the street, Cort set a relaxed pace, but he watched everywhere. Weaponless, he needed at all costs to avoid recapture.

Four times, they nearly encountered soldiers, and twice, the soldiers were Sleb's. Each time he or Neder spotted soldiers, they detoured, or hid and waited until the soldiers were gone. The morning was late by the time they finally turned onto Cort's street.

Cort knew at once that something was wrong. The look on Neder's face confirmed it.

Densely packed with small one-room houses, Cort's narrow street usually bustled with people coming and going from just after sunrise until almost sunset. But now, the street was deserted and quiet—too quiet. So quiet that Cort's heartbeat pounded a drumming alarm in his ears. He picked up his pace and said to Neder, "I don't like this."

Before the hunter could reply, two soldiers came out of Cort's house.

Neder grabbed hold of Cort and pulled him into the narrow space between the nearest two houses. When Cort opened his mouth to protest, Neder covered Cort's mouth with his hand, and held him tightly. "Calm," he whispered close to Cort's ear. "Use your head. You have no weapons."

But Cort had to get to his mother. Blood rushed wildly in his ears, and he couldn't make sense of the hunter's words. He struggled against Neder's tight grip.

"Do you want to die?" Neder snarled in Cort's ear.

Slowly, the word "die" unfurled into a meaningful concept. He remembered his and Neder's own danger. He took a deep breath and stopped struggling. "I'm okay."

Neder watched Cort's eyes intently.

Cort sighed and looked away, his panic fading. Only then did Neder release his hold.

Cort nodded. The hunter was right. They had to wait. Any other action would lead to capture and death.

"Let me try something," Neder said. From his belt, he unwound a long leather strap. It was unevenly shaped, with a kind of pouch in the middle. Then the hunter looked around the alley where they hid and found a stone about half the size of his fist. He placed the stone in the strap's pouch and, holding both ends of the strap, crept to the corner of the house behind which they hid. Cort moved to follow. Without looking around, Neder seemed to know, for he signaled Cort to stay back. A moment later, he whirled the strap around his head, then let one end loose. Cort barely heard the muffled thud that followed.

When Neder signaled for him to move forward, Cort looked around the corner with frank curiosity.

"Not entirely weaponless," Neder said quietly. In front of Cort's house, a soldier lay still on the ground. He was bleeding from a wound in his forehead where the stone had hit him. A second soldier ran from the house to kneel beside his fallen comrade. He touched the other's pulse, then looked around nervously. Neder pushed Cort back and reloaded his sling. "There were four of them," he said. "Now there are only three."

The second soldier drew his stunner, flicked off the safety, and shouted, "Come out, if you want to save her! Do you hear me?" He turned, stunner aimed at about chest height, looking first up, then down, the street, then back again. He never glanced past the corners of the houses.

Neder backed away from the corner, frowning a warning. "Your choice, Cort," he said quietly. "But I think we might be better off fighting from here. If you go out, they will kill you, and you will still not save your mother."

Fear gripped Cort's stomach, but he fought it off and shook his head. "No, I have to. If I don't try, and they kill her, I'll never know whether I might have helped her." But he couldn't move. What if Neder was right?

"You have five seconds," the soldier announced.

Cort swallowed hard. He felt cold all over and wrapped his arms across his chest. "I have to try. I couldn't live with myself otherwise. I guess I'm a misfit here after all, what you called 'a true human being.'"

Neder put an encouraging hand on Cort's shoulder and squeezed slightly. "You do what you must."

"Five... Four..."

"Don't stay here, Neder," Cort said. "Save yourself."

"Three... Two..."

Cort stepped out from between the houses and into the street, holding his hands up and outward to show that he was unarmed. The scene in the street was almost too difficult to look at. A soldier held Cort's mother, with a knife at her throat. She was bruised and bleeding. Tears seeped from her eyes, and her clothing was torn. She looked at him with recognition and with anguish and tried to take a step toward him.

The soldier holding her pulled her closer, and a slight trickle of blood ran down her throat where the knife rested. Her eyes widened in fear.

Two soldiers immediately advanced on Cort, one leveling a stunner at his head, while the other systematically checked his clothing for weapons. "What'd you use to kill him, punk?" asked the soldier who had searched and found nothing.

"A stone," Cort said. "Just a stone. I don't have any more." He couldn't tear his gaze away from the pleading in his mother's eyes. His throat was tight. "You want me, not her. Let her go."

What happened next, happened almost too quickly to follow. The soldier who held his mother pushed her forcefully back into the house. Then he took a rod from his belt, an instrument of alien manufacture. He aimed the rod in the doorway, and a moment later, the house exploded in flames.

"No!" Cort threw himself at the soldier with the flame-thrower. The flame-rod clattered to the ground and rolled into the burning house. The soldier drew his knife.

The one who aimed a stunner at him should have had him then. There should be a searing pain in the back of his skull or between his shoulder blades, a great shock of agony that would throw him writhing to the ground.

But the soldier with the stunner crumpled and lay still.

Where had the fourth soldier gotten to? Cort's back tingled with dread of the shot that might still be fired at him.

He ignored it. The knife was a more immediate threat.

With one hand he tried to pry the soldier's fingers loose. With the other, he gripped the hilt of the knife, twisting to free it. The rolled over and over, fighting for the knife. The soldier was more solid and muscled, but Cort was a street-fighter filled with urgency and rage. They struggled, entwined. The heat from the burning doorway was intense enough to singe, but Cort didn't let go. Seizing an opportunity, he bit the soldier's arm hard, drawing blood. The man cried in pain, but maintained his grip on the knife. They rolled again, and then the soldier was on top, pushing the knife down toward Cort's throat.

It was as if he were thirteen years old and fighting Karl all over again. But this time, Cort was prepared. He wrapped his ankle around his opponent's leg and pulled him off balance. As soon as he had leverage, Cort pushed at the man. As the soldier rolled, Cort twisted the knife from his hand.

The soldier broke free and ran.

Cort sat back and for a stunned moment watched him go, and then the man rounded a corner.

Too late to throw the knife.

The fourth soldier was nowhere in sight. Cort was alone in the street, heat scorching his back. Flames and smoke poured from the small house. His mother! She must still be inside.

Cort tried to force his body into that inferno, but he couldn't do it. His brows and lashes burned. His tears vaporized before they left his eyes.

"No one's alive in there." Neder held Cort's shoulders, pulling him away.

Cort turned and sobbed against his friend's chest. "I wanted... to... save... her..." Cort gasped for breath. "I only... wanted..."

"I know." Neder folded his arms around Cort. "I know. You're a true human being."

The fire roared behind Cort's back. A few of the braver neighbors came out into the street. Some brought buckets of water to help put out the fire, or to stop it from spreading, but the flames were too hot and had spread too much already.

"Come on, now," Neder said. "We have to go. I killed another soldier, but the two that ran away will bring a lot more soldiers back here in a few minutes. Can you walk?"

Cort nodded, and allowed Neder to lead him away. Reflexively, he put the soldier's knife into his own empty sheath, barely noticing that it was shorter and narrower than the missing knife that belonged there.

His mind was numb. He stumbled after Neder for several blocks simply because there was nothing else to do. A troop of Sleb's soldiers approached, and the two fugitives hid until they passed by. At a fountain, Neder washed Cort's face and told him he thought the burns would heal. Cort's shirt was torn and scorched, and Neder helped him remove it, giving Cort his own leather vest.

As they approached the city gate, Cort was overwhelmed with the enormity of the void behind him and the unknown path before him. His chest felt hollow. He touched Neder's shoulder and asked hesitatingly, "You still... want me to come with you?"

"Do you still want to?"

Cort nodded. "All I have now is Dilia." If that.

The hunter smiled and said, "I'm proud to have you accompany me, Cort."

They walked side by side to the city gate, and the bored young guard, a native in the uniform of soldiers working for the aliens, with short-cropped sandy hair and green eyes, looked up. "Eh, back so soon, old man? I see you found your son after all."

Neder nodded, returning the guard's smile. "I found him," he answered, "and not a moment too soon."

"So it appears." The guard waved them through the gate. They headed north across planted fields until they came to the fringe of woods that marked the end of civilization as Cort knew it.

Cort looked across the fields at the city behind them. His whole life had been contained within those walls. Beyond the city rose the Earthers' base, and beyond all of it, a starship gleaming in sunlight, like a promise of hope. Dilia was still there, somewhere. He clenched a fist and silently swore he would come back to find her and free her, no matter what.

And then he turned and followed Neder into the woods.

Chapter 6

Departure

Dilia woke the next morning feeling sick to her bones. She tried to sit up but dizziness overtook her, and the accompanying nausea brought up bile from her stomach.

"Take it slowly." Abeni sat next to her. In one hand she held a pan in front of Dilia, and with the other hand, stroked her hair. "You're all right."

Dilia took a deep breath to calm her stomach. "No. I am not all right. *This* is not all right."

The doctor's jaw tightened, her mouth thinning to a hard line. "I know. Do you think you could hold down a little water?"

Dilia's mouth was dry and tasted sour, and she was still dizzy. But she did feel better. "Yes, a little, thanks. I'd like that. And then I want to go home."

Abeni poured a glass of water from a pitcher by the bedside and handed it to Dilia. "Rinse your mouth first, and spit it out into the basin." She indicated the pan she held. "I'm sorry, but you would need *his* permission to leave. No one else here has that authority."

Dilia did as ordered, then sipped the water. Was there a message behind Abeni's words that she wasn't understanding? No, she understood well enough what Abeni was saying, but she didn't want it to be true. "Look, last night..." She looked around at the windowless room. How much time had passed? "Yesterday. Earlier. What he threatened to do to me. He forced—"

The doctor put a finger to her lips. "Shh. That's over now."

Dilia's breathing quickened. "No, it's not. He said he'd be back tonight."

"That's not a surprise. Look, let me get rid of this basin. It smells awful and won't help your stomach settle." Abeni took the pan to the door. She said a few words to someone—a soldier, no doubt—outside, and handed the person the pan. She returned to her seat, her expression grim. "I'd help you get out if I could, but it's not possible. There are guards at the gate. No one gets out without a pass from the commandant. Without that, I can't leave the base, even by myself. They would never let the two of us through. And besides, even if we could get you out, we have to consider what he'd do after that."

After? "What?"

"He'd get you back again if he wanted, or he'd get hold of some other pretty girl. Or two. He'd demote me, too, but that's the least of it. He might possibly arrange to punish you, and your family, too, for your disobedience. You have a family?"

Dilia's parents were long dead, but Mara and Cort were her family now. "Yes. I do." Cort! He had said he would rescue her if this ever happened—but that had been, what, two years ago, and neither of them had had the least idea what would actually be involved. Would he come? Would he even try?

"Well, you don't want to put them in danger, do you?"

Tears welled up in Dilia's eyes, and she couldn't hold them back. "No, but I don't want to do *this* anymore, either!"

The doctor's eyes softened. "No, of course not. I'm so sorry. I'd like to examine you, if it's all right with you, just a quick check. If he hurt you last night—"

Dilia drew back, pulling her blanket more tightly around herself. "No, he didn't, not last night. But he's going to hurt me. That's what he said!"

"He said it?"

What had the commandant said, exactly, when he'd tried to lift her skirt? He'd twisted the word "talk" until it seemed to have a sinister meaning, but then, he'd also given her the night to recover. "Well, he implied."

"You two talked?"

"A little."

Abeni's eyes widened and she leaned forward. "That's a little more than I've heard of him doing with anyone else. Maybe you should try to keep him talking. If he interacts with you, maybe he'll be less likely to see you as someone to be used."

Dilia drew in a deep breath and let it out slowly. It all seemed so hopeless, but what choice did she have?

The doctor reached out and touched her hand, which still clutched the blanket tightly. Dilia made her hand relax.

"I can help make it easier for you, um, medically," Abeni said. "I'll give you something that you can use… before… so that you won't be aware, won't remember. And I can check you after to make sure you're still okay."

Dilia tried to picture this proposal. "So, I would use this medicine and, what, go unconscious? And then in the morning, you would come in and examine me and tell me whether he did… anything?" She frowned. This didn't sound at all appealing. "How would that work, if I'm supposed to be trying to talk with him?"

"Oh." Abeni nibbled at her lower lip. "I guess it might be either-or. But try talking first. It's always better not to medicate if you don't have to. And I will be there to help, if things go wrong."

If things go wrong. "If I get hurt."

"If it involves any blood or broken bones, I can keep you in the infirmary for a while until it heals. You'll be safe while you're there. And of course, I'll report all this when I get back to Earth, but my tour isn't over for another year, and then it takes twelve years… planet time… Look, I know all this isn't much, but it's all I can think to do. Really, talking is your best option. In my experience, despite his… proclivities… the commandant is not an unreasonable man."

Dilia had a sudden welling of vertigo, as if she were standing on a ledge only centimeters wide at the edge of a bottomless pit, with her back against a smooth wall. Nowhere to go but down, her familiar world lost to her forever. Her breath came too quickly, and her heart pounded.

If there was no one to help her—if Abeni could not get her out of here and Cort could not rescue her—then she must find a way to help herself. "I understand." She tried to make herself speak calmly, but there was a tremble in her voice. "I appreciate your help, really, I do." She swallowed. "But let me ask you something. Is there something you could give me... some medication... that might make me... unattractive to him?"

Abeni seemed to consider. "Like something that would make you smell bad?"

Dilia giggled. She knew she was overreacting to the humor in the idea, given the seriousness of the situation. This wasn't like her. She wondered whether there was some lingering effect of the inoculation she'd been given, or that whatever-it-was in the air, or perhaps just a reaction to yesterday's events. It was hard to make herself stop laughing, but the idea also did merit consideration. "I'm sorry. I never thought I'd actually *want* to smell bad. Do you have anything like that?"

"Nothing that would act right away, unless you count eating garlic."

Dilia hadn't heard of "garlic," but she was game. "Is that something you starmen do?"

Now it was Abeni who laughed. "Sometimes. It's tasty. But it's possible the commandant might like garlic. He might like it a lot, I don't know. Then you might smell delicious to him."

Dilia wrinkled her nose. This didn't seem to be going anywhere, but she had another idea. "How about some kind of medicine that I could give to him, that would make him have less desire for me, regardless of whether he likes garlic?"

"Aren't you being creative! Yes, such a medication exists, but it would be very dangerous for you to attempt to administer it. If he notices you doing it—and how could he not?—he'd have you punished. Or worse. Honestly, he could probably get away with—" She lowered her gaze and continued in a soft voice. "—doing away with you." Another pause. "And when he considers where you might have gotten such a thing, it would not go well for me, either."

The doctor stood and started pacing the small room. "It's hard, being a doctor, and having to watch this kind of thing. I can tell him you're experiencing intense gastrointestinal stress and ask him to wait a night or two. It'll probably work. No one likes being vomited on. But that's only a delaying tactic—at best."

Dilia's heart lifted, and the world seemed a little brighter. "Oh, Abeni, that would be wonderful!" A night or two just might give Cort a chance to find and rescue her.

"No guarantees, Dilia. The man has a mind of his own. I'm not going to re-up when my tour here is over. One year, and that's it for me. But for now, I report to him, and I have to follow his orders. We all do, here on the base."

"Even when it's wrong?"

Abeni drew in a breath and released it in a long, weary sigh. "I'll do the best I can for you, Dilia. That's all I can say. The drug that will make you more drowsy... You want it?"

Dilia sat up, and the room seemed to spin around her. The irony made her laugh. "I'm dizzy enough already! But seriously... yes. If that's all the help you can give, I'll take it." At least she didn't seem to be throwing up anymore.

Abeni straightened her jacket. "I really do have to go now. There are two people in the infirmary that need to be looked at, and I'm already late. I'll bring you that medication this afternoon."

Dilia drew in an involuntary breath, her stomach tightening. *Don't leave me alone here!* She stood up, suffering a new wave of giddiness. She reached for the wall to steady herself. "Do you think I might—that is, could I come with you?"

"Oh, you poor dear!" Abeni moved closer and gave Dilia a hug. "Do you think you can walk?"

"I will walk." Dilia let go of the wall and took a step, then another. The dizziness wasn't too bad, as long as she went slowly. "See?"

"Well, then, I don't see why you couldn't come. The commandant will be busy with his own work; he probably won't miss you during work hours. It'll be good for you to have something to do, take your mind off... things. But there have to be rules, understand?"

Dilia nodded. The motion made her vision spin.

"First, you must stay with me, or a guard, at all times. I don't want you wandering off by yourself, and I certainly don't want you trying to leave the base. Understood?"

"Yes."

"And if I tell you to do something, you have to do it, even if you don't understand why. No arguments, no questions. It could be something urgent. I promise that if you have any questions, I'll explain when I can."

"All right. I really appreciate this, Abeni. It would do me some good to have something I can do that's interesting, and where I can help other people, and maybe I can learn about medicine a little, too. It would make all this, well, not *worthwhile* exactly but at least worth something."

There was warmth in Abeni's eyes now. "I'm impressed! You'd like to learn some medicine, would you?"

"Oh, yes!" It was not a lie. It might even, almost, be worth the price, especially if Dilia could find a way to use her medical knowledge to protect herself, and maybe sometime in the future—that is, if she had a future—also to help others.

The infirmary was in a small building near the starship port at the top of the hill. In addition to the infirmary, the building housed a number of facilities, including the doctor's small office and her lab. Dilia had never seen a space quite like this. The room was dominated by a high table in its center with a counter that might be made of stone or concrete, its top crowded with large pieces of complicated-looking equipment whose function she couldn't imagine. Shelves with bins containing equipment and tools, along with built-in cabinets and files, lined the walls. Under the room's one window, a small desk and chair stood, its top surface clear but for a tablet and a small vase of flowers. The place had a slightly astringent smell, a faint hint in the air of something that, were it more concentrated, might make her gag.

Abeni looked at Dilia, frowned slightly, and then went over and opened the window. "I print chemicals and medications here sometimes. Sorry about the odor. Now, let's get you something appropriate to wear." From a cabinet, she removed a white coat like her own, and handed it to Dilia.

The air flowing in from outside was fresher. Dilia took a deep breath of it and put the coat on over her red dress, noticing for the first time how rumpled the dress was. "Maybe you could ask him to get me a change of clothes. Something more"—what was the word?—"appropriate?"

"*You* ask him, Dilia." Abeni's broad smile lit up her face. "I wish I could see his reaction when you do. He really is not going to know what to make of you."

Abeni made Dilia's predicament almost sound like fun. She would do it, somehow. She would talk with the commandant and win him over. She returned the smile. "So, tell me what can I do to help you here."

With thoughts about his mother and about Dilia whirling in his head, Cort woke that morning thinking he hadn't slept at all. But he opened his eyes in daylight. He'd been skeptical about sleeping out in the open when Neder had called a halt to their trek.

Cort had never slept outside of a house before, certainly never out in the woods. He'd never even wandered out of sight of the city's walls. Birds or insects—something—chirped and buzzed in the woods around, growing louder as evening descended. He had no idea what might be out there, but he hadn't wanted to look silly asking Neder if it was safe. He had to expect things to be different for the savages of the forest, among whose number he must learn to count himself, at least for now. As if understanding Cort's helplessness, Neder had shown Cort how to choose a level spot for sleeping, how to make sure there were no rocks, and how to make a cushioning pile of leaves.

But now, Neder was nowhere to be seen. Even the leaves Neder had slept on had been scattered back into the woods so that there was no clue where the pile had been.

Cort's heart raced. Had Neder abandoned him?

But no, Neder wouldn't do that. Neder was so... forest... he'd stayed with Cort when any sane city person would have run. Cort smiled, thinking of his new friend, who certainly would not have gone far. He walked to the nearby stream to wash his face and drink, and there he found Neder roasting a large bird of some kind over a fire.

"Hungry?" asked the hunter.

The roast meat smelled good. Cort nodded. "Yes. Thanks, Neder. Thank you for... everything."

"How are you doing?" The hunter's eyes, golden in the sunlight, were sympathetic.

"All right... I guess."

Neder swallowed and looked away. He shook his head, then met Cort's gaze. "I worry that I might have done the wrong thing in killing that soldier."

Cort had been thinking about little else while they were walking through the woods yesterday. He'd gone through the encounter with the soldiers at his house again and again, turning the incident over in his mind to see if there was anything he and Neder might have done differently to save his mother. But no, when the soldiers at his house didn't find him, they'd have assumed his mother was covering for him. They would have burned the house to make an example of his mother and him. And they would have brought his mother to Sleb, who would either use her or sell her to the starmen or execute her in Cort's place.

He'd hardly noticed the woods they walked through, stumbling on roots and rocks and rough ground. Thorny vines scratched his arms and legs, and he bled.

The sky had clouded up in the afternoon, and the rain ran down Cort's face like tears. And maybe there were tears too, mingled with the rain. An hour later the storm passed, and the sunlight slanted, as golden as Neder's eyes, through the trees. What had happened to his mother had been the inevitable consequence of his bungled effort to save Dilia.

"No, don't," he said to Neder. "My mother's death warrant must have been written when we escaped from that prison. What *I* worry about is that I may have done the wrong thing in *not* throwing my knife when I had the chance, at the soldier who ran away."

Neder's eyes were still filled with concern. "It's kind of you to say so."

"I mean it. I was thinking about this a lot yesterday while we were walking. They were planning to... to do what they did even if we hadn't shown up. For the house to go up in flames the way it did, they had to have soaked it in something pretty flammable, maybe even harvester fuel. There's not much flammable in the house. The fuel's expensive. Sleb must have ordered it done. I guess they wanted to send a message to me or anyone else that might think about standing up to them. The fact that we showed up when we did was a bonus from their perspective."

"I'm sorry about your mother."

"Thanks, I appreciate your sympathy." Cort's throat felt tight, but the last thing he wanted was to cry like a child in front of the hunter. He swallowed. "I tried, but I couldn't save her. I'll regret that... always. But right now, I still have a chance to save Dilia."

Dilia! Where would she be by now? Would he ever be able to find her? No, he must, he *would* find her. "The next time I go to rescue her, I have to succeed."

"It's a long trip," Neder said.

Nothing else mattered. "I'm ready."

Neder smiled. "Not before breakfast, you aren't."

Cort and Neder traveled for days through the woods that surrounded the city. The canopy was in places five or ten times the height of a man, and beneath it grew vines, bushes, and young trees fighting for space and light. There were narrow trails made by animals, and so there was hunting, and food. Though these trails were all but invisible to Cort, Neder found and followed them without hesitating. He walked silently and seemed never to tire.

Cort struggled to keep up with Neder's pace. Unused to long, steady walking, his legs ached. He worried continually about Dilia, about where she was and what might be happening to her, and about the amount of time this journey must take, when he would not be able to help her. He found it hard to concentrate on the trail. He stumbled frequently, slowing them both down.

After three days, the seams on Cort's city-made sandals began to split. Neder took out a bone needle and sinew to repair them, but he turned the sandals over and back, frowning. "What is this material? It's too soft for any real use. I'll do what I can, but still, you're going to wear right through these in a week or two."

"Too bad I didn't bring my spare pair."

Neder gave him a look as sharp as the needle poised in his hand.

Cort couldn't keep the corners of his mouth from tilting into a smile. "Don't you know, we city folk always carry around a spare pair of sandals just in case the regular ones wear out while we're in the middle of going somewhere, maybe shopping."

The hunter snorted out a laugh and returned to his sewing. "These are just about done, but I'd suggest that you start getting your feet used to walking barefoot."

Cort thanked his friend and took back the repaired sandals. He also took Neder's advice, walking barefoot as much as he could. His feet grew sore from stepping on stones and roots in the ground. He refused to complain, but more than once he gave up and put on the increasingly ragged sandals.

Sometimes, to Cort's relief, Neder called a halt by mid-afternoon and made Cort rest while he hunted.

They traveled among trees and bushes and vines and brambles for days on narrow paths that allowed no distant vistas and went on endlessly. They pushed aside hanging branches and stepped over fallen ones. Cort chafed at the passage of time, but his feet grew more callused and were no longer sore. "These woods are pretty much all the same," Cort said one day.

"Not if you know what you're looking at, they aren't," Neder said. "There are berries and flowers and edible leaves and tubers. I myself don't know half of them, I'm sure. My son Culan knows much more than I do."

"I'm grateful for the way you can find food and water, but I was talking more generally. I don't know how you can find your way around. I certainly don't see how you can live here."

Neder drew back, lips pressed tightly together. "I *don't* live here. I live in the khenaran. This... stuff... is just what grew after the starmen cut the khena down. I know of no one that lives here, though personally I would prefer it to the city."

"I'd prefer the city," Cort said. "At least there are things to do besides walking, walking, walking."

"Just wait, Cort. See how you feel once we reach the khenaran."

Two days later, the khenaran stretched out before them on the other side of a wide green river. The trees towered over the ones they had been walking through as an adult towers over a toddler. Cort guessed that they were perhaps thirty or forty times his own height, maybe more. The dark, shiny green leaves formed a wide canopy that let only filtered sunlight reach the forest floor, which was wide open beneath the trees and appeared to be carpeted with something like low moss or humus. The break between the scrub woods and the khenaran was sudden and complete. It seemed the aliens hadn't wanted to go to the trouble of crossing the river with their heavy equipment, but instead had turned their harvesting efforts in another direction.

And the river! Cort gaped. It was wider than the plaza in the center of the city where people gathered for celebrations and executions. It was wider, even, than the clearing just outside the city gates where the harvesters unloaded their cargo. And it flowed in a swift rush from their left to their right, as far as they could see in both directions, a perfectly, unbelievably huge quantity of water.

Neder's eyes glowed, and he shifted his weight from one foot to the other and back again, as if his feet were trying to move on their own accord. "Home!" He grinned. "Can you swim?"

"Swim?" Cort took his eyes from the vista to meet his friend's. "What's that?"

Neder looked at Cort with a funny expression, head tilted and eyebrows raised. Did he think Cort was teasing him?

But of course, Cort was not. "We drink water," he said. "from fountains and wells. We don't... swim, did you call it?"

"It's how you go through the water when it's too deep to walk," Neder said. "I take it that you can't."

Cort shook his head.

"The river's a little too wide here, and the current too swift, unless you're a really good swimmer. There are rocks downstream. You wouldn't want to be dragged into them. Probably the safest bet for you and me would be the ford about two days upstream. Swimming would have saved a little time, that's all. Also," he added with a smile, "it's fun. Ask one of the boys to show you when we get to the village."

They followed the river westward, upstream. Late in the afternoon of the second day, he heard a rumbling sound that increased steadily as they walked. Neder led Cort through the woods to cut across a spit of land that jutted into the river. When they emerged, they faced a wide waterfall that tumbled down a rocky escarpment into a deep, churning pool. The waterfall roared and whispered and glinted like gems in the sunlight.

Cort stared. The spume brushed his face like a caress. He had never seen so much falling water in one place. "I take back whatever I said about the forest being boring," he said at last. "I think now that I just didn't know enough about its surprises. Neder, will you teach me to swim?"

"Not here." Neder smiled, and his eyes softened. "It's too rough, and there are undercurrents. Upstream further, near the ford we can swim if you'd like."

At the ford, Neder taught Cort a few rudiments of swimming—enough that Cort could paddle around in the still, chest-deep water that pooled along the river's edge. Cort laughed with the pure joy of it. He had to show this to Dilia! His urgent need to find and rescue her returned in a rush. He waded and swam to where Neder waited on the other side of the ford, shook himself off, and said, "Let's go."

Neder was right about the khenaran, too. In a subtle way that Cort couldn't identify although he could feel it clearly enough, the forest was alive where the scrub woods were not. Not that there weren't living plants and birds and insects and animals in the woods. It wasn't that. It had to do with the sunlight and the air and the protective canopy of the trees overhead. Cort found himself brushing his hand against the khena from time to time, as if the contact were a communication.

"I can see why the people who live here want to stop the aliens' harvesting," he said, wondering at the courage it must take to oppose the monstrous machines with only a spear or a knife.

"Of course." Neder frowned. "Why do they do it, anyway?"

"Why?" Cort studied Neder's face, but the hunter was not joking. "Because the wood is really valuable on Earth. I had a teacher who said it's 'worth its weight in gold.' That's a saying in Starrish."

Neder looked more confused than before. "What's 'gold'?"

Cort shrugged. "Some kind of metal the starmen pay a lot of money for, for some reason. The point is that the khena are worth more. The trunks are harder than any blade, so hard they have to use monster lasers to cut them."

Neder drew in a breath as if to speak, probably to ask what lasers were. Cort rushed to continue. "The young branches have more tensile strength than the metal the aliens use to make their starships. They make bridges from it that go across chasms way bigger than the whole city. And they build buildings taller than their starships. The power station up at the base is built of khena because it's too tough to blast through."

Neder let out his breath, then said, "You'd think they could find some other way to do all that without involving us."

Cort had no response. He and Neder walked side by side now in the wide spaces between the trees. The soft ground muffled their footsteps, and the forest was filled with the songs of birds and the chittering and buzzing of insects. Golden sunlight sifted through the lacy green leaves high above to paint glistening multicolored rainbows on the tree trunks. A light breeze that smelled heady and spicy and pure dappled the ground with a constantly shifting pattern of shadows.

Cort's sorrow fall away like an unneeded cloak at the end of a rainstorm. At school he had studied all the statistics of the khenaran—the trees' height, the strength of the wood, the force required to cut through them—but now he wanted to know everything. It was not the statistics he needed but the experience of living there.

Neder answered Cort's questions when he could, and he laughed with delight at Cort's inquisitiveness even when he had no answer.

In the evening of their second day in the khenaran, Neder stopped early to make their camp. He'd found an area where the moss was especially thick, and where a cool, fresh stream provided ample water.

Grinning, Cort flopped down appreciatively onto the soft ground. He lay back to watch the shifting patterns that the breezes made of the tree leaves against the sky, but in a few minutes remembered that Neder would need help hunting or cleaning their dinner. He sat up again.

Neder was watching him, his eyes glinting with good humor. A sleek, slender brown animal coiled in and out between the hunter's legs, its dark, curious eyes intent on Cort.

Cort was fascinated with the animal's sinuous, graceful movements. Except for the game they had killed and the street rats that lived on the city's garbage, he had never seen a living wild animal. Unlike the rats, this animal seemed clean and intelligent, even playful.

"This is my kiri," Neder said. "She is a ferret. Are you familiar with the species?"

Cort shook his head. "Is she... that is, do I say hello? Will she understand me?"

"Not directly. You'd need a crystal like mine"—Neder touched the red crystal embedded at his hairline—"to talk with a kiri. But she'll sense your intentions clearly enough, and I can translate. Go ahead. Say hello if you want."

Cort knelt and held out a hand. "Hello," he said, hoping he didn't sound silly. "I'm glad to meet you. I hope to have a chance to know you better."

The ferret approached and sniffed at his hand. The whiskers on either side of her face tickled him as she sniffed. Cort smiled. Dilia would love to meet this creature. There was so much to share with her! The animal's eyes were very large for her face, and they were black with her expanded pupils. "May I..." Cort started to ask the ferret, then shifting his gaze to Neder, "may I touch her?"

For a moment, Neder's eyes lost focus. Then he answered with a smile, "You may."

Cort touched the ferret's head. Her fur was thick and soft. He moved his hand wonderingly down her back. In an instant, the ferret dashed behind a tree and was gone. Cort felt a pang of loss. "Did I frighten her? I didn't mean to."

"Not at all," Neder said. "She likes you. She thinks you're funny."

"Me?" Cort didn't feel particularly funny.

"Don't take it personally. She thinks almost everything is funny."

"I think she's beautiful."

The hunter beamed. "So do I," he answered quietly. "So do I."

A short time later, the ferret returned, carrying a dead quail in her mouth. As she dropped the bird at his feet Cort noted the sharpness of her teeth. "Thank you," he said solemnly. "I bet you're one incredibly good hunter." The ferret streaked off again.

"She is," Neder said, "and she knows it. She's not modest, and she intends to bring dinner for all of us. I guess I'd better start a fire."

Chapter 7

The Ways of the Khenaran

"Trouble," Neder said. He knelt, running his fingertips lightly over the moss, and shook his head slightly.

Cort looked around. They had been walking through the khenaran for three days, and this area didn't seem any more troublesome that any other. A breeze played with the leaves that arched above and rustled through a few clumps of nearby bushes. Golden sunlight shifted in patterns everywhere. He peered over the hunter's shoulder. "What is it?"

"Can you see how this moss has been stepped on?"

It was true. Areas of the moss were torn, and some of its delicate, tiny fronds bent and flattened. "What did it?" Cort asked.

"It's hard to tell from the print alone, but it's something heavy, that's for sure. The ferret says it's a boar. Her sense of smell is superb, so she would know." Neder brushed a strand of hair back and tucked it into a rawhide strip that was braided into his hair. "Wild foragers, even big ones, are normally quite shy and don't come this close to a village."

"A village?" Cort frowned, puzzled. He had seen no sign of human habitation.

"Yes," Neder answered, "only an hour or so that way." He inclined his head toward his right. "But the question is, why would it come close like this? Generally, the animals are leery of humans and stay away. I wonder if this boar might be wounded and looking for easy prey. Humans can be dangerous, but we're also very vulnerable. Especially children."

Cort shivered.

"If it's not wounded, it could be mad," the hunter continued. "Or, sometimes they just get mean. These tracks are new. I think we'd better warn the people here. Come on."

Neder led the way at a jog, which he kept up without even breathing heavily. He must have felt some urgency to be setting a pace that proved hard for Cort. But Cort was determined not to hold Neder back. He ran past his own shortness of breath and surprised himself by staying the distance. When they caught sight of the village through the trees, they slowed. The houses were built of skins and poles, with roofs made of layers of leafy fronds. They were as small as Cort's house in the city, though rounded where Cort's house had been square. Still, seeing people moving about and children playing in the grassy clearing transfused with sunlight, Cort felt as if he were on another world entirely than the one where he'd been born. Homesickness gripped him so intensely that he felt nauseous and leaned against a tree for support.

"Are you all right?" Neder asked. "Maybe I pushed the pace too hard. I'm sorry. You should have said something."

"I'm all right. I just... It's nothing, Neder. Shall we go on down?"

Neder examined his friend's face, and Cort forced himself to smile. Neder took a deep breath, then said, "Yes, of course." Cort followed him into the village.

"Strangers!" The child's shrill cry stopped half a dozen adults and twice that number of children in their activities. "Grandpa, strangers!" Two women who had been stirring a pot over a fire turned to look where the boy pointed. Another woman looked up from sewing beads onto a skin shirt. Two men stopped in the midst of a heated conversation to look at the hunter and his companion. An older man put down the wood he was carving and stood to walk toward them.

"We come in peace," Neder said to him.

"We greet you in peace, Hunter," answered the old man. "You honor our village with your presence. I am Okolo, seer and headman of this village, of the Fox clan. You are welcome here."

"I am Neder," answered the hunter, "born to the Wolf clan and adopted by Ferret. This is my friend and companion, Cort. He was born in the city and has no clan. Still, I ask that for my sake you welcome him as you do me."

Okolo studied Cort for the space of several heartbeats, long enough for Cort to become aware of how strange he must look to the headman. Though the village was only a few days from the forest edge, it was more than a week from the city. Judging from the growth of the scrub woods on the other side of the river, the aliens had not harvested anywhere near here for decades—probably longer than Okolo's lifetime. If like other forest dwellers, Okolo avoided leaving the khenaran, he would never have seen anyone with eyes as light as Cort's, or clothing as strange and impractical as Cort's ragged shirt and trousers. Cort held his breath, hoping the headman would find him acceptable.

Despite whatever misgivings Okolo might have about the clanless youth, though, it appeared that his duty was to the hunter. "You are welcome in this village, Cort."

Cort breathed a sigh of relief and answered, "Thank you." He could sense the villagers' eyes on him and not used to being a phenomenon, felt suddenly and unexpectedly shy. He moved slightly closer to the hunter.

Turning to Neder, Okolo asked, "Would you stay the night with us?"

"Yes, thank you," said Neder, "we'd like that."

From the slightly singsong rhythm of the interchange, Cort gathered that the question and the answer were a part of a ritual many times repeated, and he marveled that the community would open itself to a stranger. In the city, they could be starved, stabbed and bleeding on the street, and no friendly hand would be extended. No one would want to take the risk.

Cort looked around at the faces of these forest people. Everywhere, golden, yellow, or brown eyes openly returned his gaze. The people's hair ranged from a deep reddish brown to black, and their skin was clear and golden. In the mild climate, not much clothing was needed or worn. The people wore short trousers, the women's wider than the men's, with a sleeveless shirt or a vest above. The clothing was made of skins in a variety of brownish hues, swirled and patterned with earthtoned dyes and beads of bright colors. Alone in the city, any single one of them would have looked outlandish. But here in their own village together, they were as exotic and beautiful as rare butterflies.

Cort had no idea how to approach such people.

Neder excused himself from Cort in order to talk privately with Okolo. They went inside Okolo's house, leaving Cort on his own. Steeling his courage, Cort approached a youth who looked about his own age. "Hello."

The other looked him up and down and spat one word. "Clanless!"

"Is that a problem?" It had certainly never been an issue in the city.

"Who will befriend you?" asked the youth. "Who will stand by you in battle? What woman would have you for a husband?" A few other youths standing nearby came over to join him as the crowd dispersed.

"I have friends," Cort answered. He stood taller. "And Neder the hunter has already stood by me in battle." As for marriage... Cort was a long way from thinking about that. He had to rescue Dilia first.

"The hunter can do what he will, and no man will say he is wrong," the other responded. "He brings good fortune to the people. What do *you* offer?"

Cort almost said, *I will be a hunter, too.* But he was uncomfortable with the other youth's hostility and wanted to end the conversation. "I guess nothing," he said. "No matter what I answer, it would be nothing as far as you're concerned."

"Why don't you go back to the city where you came from?" asked another of the youths.

Cort's hand drifted closer to his knife. "Where I go is my own business." But he wouldn't stay here any longer than he had to. There were four village youths altogether, and none of them looked friendly. They all wore knives. One carried a spear. The odds were bad. Cort began backing closer to the nearest house, hoping to cover his back.

"You're not wanted here," the questioner said.

"What is this?" From the house behind Cort, Okolo returned, walking quickly, the hunter at his heels. "Is this the hospitality our village offers?" He glared at each of Cort's four young antagonists in turn, and four pairs of eyes turned to the ground.

"You shame me," Okolo said. "You shame this village." To Cort's astonishment, the old man knelt in front of him. "Cort, please forgive these foolish boys. Forgive me. Forgive all of us."

Cort was profoundly embarrassed seeing the old man kneel before him. His throat felt tight. He knelt also, and touched Okolo's shoulder. "Please, Okolo, it was just words. No harm has been done. There's nothing to forgive. Stand up."

Okolo turned to look at Neder. "Ah, Hunter, city-born or not, your companion has fine manners. Our village can learn from him." To Cort, he said, "I appreciate your graciousness." The old man stood slowly, first one leg and then with a weary sigh, the other. A pale blue gem at his hairline above the eye flashed in a ray of sunlight as he stood. He gave Cort a hand to rise also, and he turned to the four youths. "You cannot know the meaning of this young man's journey," he said. "He hardly glimpses it himself. But I say to you, you must welcome him as if the well-being of this village depended upon it. Is this clear?"

What did that mean? Was it some kind of a formality? Perhaps they were simply very good at formalities, these forest people. But the old man was frowning, and he glared fiercely at the youths.

Cort's former antagonists chorused, "Yes, Okolo," and "Sorry."

"Tonio," Okolo said to one of the four boys who had taunted Cort, "you will host Cort while I talk with the hunter. And he will stay at your house as if he were a brother of your clan. Show him around. Answer his questions, for he must come to know the forest and its people. Do you understand?"

"Yes, Okolo," Tonio said. "I'm sorry about what happened. It won't happen again."

Okolo smiled. "Good." He linked his arm through Neder's, and the two men again left the clearing.

Cort and Tonio's eyes met for a moment; then Tonio looked away, his deep brown eyes that had flashed with hostility earlier now calm. "I'm sorry if I was rude," he said. "Clanless or no, someone is watching over you, Cort."

"I'm sorry, too," Cort said. "But I really do want to know more about clans. I don't understand them at all."

Tonio shook his head in wonder. Three red feathers swayed in his nearly black hair. "Let's walk. Here, everyone will be listening. Would you like to go down to the river?"

"Sure."

Tonio led the way out of the village, with Cort at his side. "In our village," he began, "everyone is born into a clan. It's the same with our neighbors. I'd assumed it was the same everywhere."

"But how do you know which clan you're born into?" Cort asked.

Tonio drew himself up and smiled. He was shorter than Cort, and perhaps a bit younger. He probably didn't often have the opportunity to teach someone something, and his voice took on a didactic singsong. "Your mother has a clan, see? And your father, too. So if you're a boy you're in your father's clan, and if you're a girl, you're in your mother's."

"So if I were born in the forest and had a sister, I wouldn't be in the same clan as her, unless my mother and father were in the same clan."

Tonio blushed deeply and touched his own cheek, perhaps feeling how hot it was. He gave a nervous laugh. "No, no, no, Cort. Your mother and father couldn't be in the same clan. A person can't marry anyone that's in either his mother's or his father's clan, so that rules out marrying someone in his own clan, too."

Cort frowned. "But doesn't that kind of limit the options?"

"But marrying someone in your parents' clans would be incest!" Tonio said. "Like marrying your own sister or something! Besides, there are six different clans in this village—bear, wolf, fox, cougar, hawk, and ferret—and ten that I know of altogether, including the neighboring villages. So there's still a lot of choice."

"But what's the point?" Cort asked. "What purpose do the clans serve, anyway?"

"What purpose!" Tonio stopped walking. "I really can't believe you, Cort! Listen, clans are like family. I'm like, related to a third of the people in my village, and even if I go somewhere I've never been, I'm related to some of the people there, and I can stay with them. Everybody is always related to somebody."

This sounded good to Cort. "So then you don't have enemies?"

"No, we do have enemies." Tonio started walking again. Now Cort could hear the sound of the river in the distance. "Our village, for example, is friendly with the village nearest to us, but there's another village a few days more distant from both of us, and we're both enemies of that one."

"I don't understand. If you're related to them, how can you be enemies?"

"It's just different! Didn't you ever fight with your sister?"

Cort thought of Dilia and was suddenly sad. "No. I don't actually have a sister; it was just a question."

"But you fight with us," Tonio said, a bitter note to his voice.

"No, Tonio, I don't fight with you either. I just met you."

"You city people, I mean. Your aliens."

"Oh, the starmen. They're different. They're not us." Cort answered in casual dismissal. But the aliens were everything he had ever wanted to be. Suddenly he was not so sure. *They're not us.*

The river came into view. It wasn't wide and majestic like the one he and Neder had forded. This river was barely wider than a stream, and Cort could see the rocks in its bed. But it rushed with some force, drowning out the sounds of the crickets and birds in the trees. Cort knelt and put his hand in the surging river. The water was cold. He scooped some up and drank, and it was as good as it had promised to be. "But why are the clans animals?" Cort asked.

Tonio lay on the bank and drank from the river like an animal himself. He paused to ask, "What?"

"Why are the clans called after animals?"

"Oh, clans again." Tonio sat up. "Because legend has it that we and the animals were born of the same sky mother, and the clans express our relationship to them."

"Related? Can you talk with them, Tonio, like Neder does?"

"No, no, no. That's different. The hunter uses that red crystal in his temple to talk directly with his kiri. But the communication with the clan-animals is more, uh, spiritual."

Cort frowned. He didn't have any idea what that meant. "How do you communicate spiritually, then?"

"Oh, you know, you just have a feeling of kinship. It's not words or anything, if that's what you're thinking."

"A feeling of kinship... Do you think the animals feel that, too?"

"I'm sure they do."

"So a person in the wolf clan, for example, would never be hurt by wolves..."

Tonio let out a burst of laughter. Then he looked at Cort, squinting as if he was trying to read whether Cort was joking. "Oh, no, Cort, I didn't say that! But you're serious, aren't you? Listen, you have to be very careful around wolves. Anyone could get hurt."

"But maybe a person in the wolf clan would be less likely to be hurt by wolves," Cort said.

"That's it!" grinned Tonio. "That's the first thing you've gotten right so far! Because a person in the wolf clan would have a feeling about how to behave around wolves so that he wouldn't be attacked."

"No, I don't get it, Tonio," Cort sighed. "That's still not communication."

A ferret leaped from a bush to Cort's right. Was that Neder's kiri? The ferret streaked straight toward Cort, so that he reflexively stepped backward, almost landing in the racing river.

"What?" he asked, watching the ferret turn. Behind the small beast, the largest animal Cort had ever seen burst from the bushes. It ran on all fours, but its back still stood almost as high as Cort's waist, and it was thickly massive. The beast was covered in coarse, reddish brown hair. From its lower jaw emerged two tusks that curved upward, longer than Cort's knife, and wickedly pointed.

Without thinking, Cort drew his knife.

Tonio grabbed his arm and pulled. "Run!"

But running wasn't an option. Running from an attacker was death in the city, where a knife in the back was the likely result. Cort shook off Tonio's hand and stood his ground. He assessed the charging beast. He would have liked to hit the creature's throat, but it was too low to the ground, and its head was lowered belligerently. The beast's eyes were probably its most vulnerable spots, but they were small, moving targets. There was no other choice. Cort aimed and threw the knife.

The knife flew true, burying itself in the beast's left eye. Blood sprayed outward, but the creature never faltered in its mad charge.

Cort was doomed, but not without a fight. When the beast was almost upon him, Cort, heart pounding, prepared to grapple with the creature.

It veered toward his right. Following its movement, Cort saw from the corner of his eye Tonio fleeing. The beast was rapidly overtaking him.

Cort wasn't about to lose his new friend. He did the only thing he could, hurling himself at the creature as it raced by. The beast roared in rage, but its stride was broken. Cort struggled to hold onto its thick neck, now slippery with blood from its wound, as the creature shook its head and whirled to get Cort within range of its sharp tusks.

Cort's hands kept slipping, and he gave up trying to hold on. Instead, as the beast turned its head to gore him, Cort took hold of a tusk with one hand and the bloody hilt of his knife with the other. He pushed the knife further into the creature's eye. Blood spurted everywhere. Cort lost his balance as he slipped on the blood. He fell against the massive head and pushed at the knife with all the strength he could muster.

The beast fell to its knees, and then on its side. Slipping again, Cort managed to stay on top of it. The creature's stench filled the air: blood and musk, urine, perhaps. It kicked twice, and was still.

Cort felt weak and dizzy. He'd spent all the energy he had, and more besides. He lay on top of the dead beast until hands lifted him up. He turned to see a number of worried faces, Neder's among them. The hunter knelt beside Cort and asked, "Are you hurt?"

Cort shook his head. "I… don't think so. Just dizzy. I… I never saw so much blood."

"So much blood," echoed the hunter. "And you, are you wounded? How much of that blood is yours?"

With Neder's help, Cort stood. He was exhausted. He was sore in any number of places, but didn't feel the sharp pain of an open cut. He looked down at himself. He was covered with blood, sticky now that it was drying. "I don't think any of it," he said, "but I'm not sure."

His leg hurt and buckled under his weight. Had the beast kicked him while they were struggling? He allowed Neder to help him limp to the river. The hunter and Okolo helped Cort peel off his bloody and stiffening clothes and to wash the blood from his skin. "Here," the hunter observed, touching Cort's leg. A gash about four inches long ran down the side of his thigh.

Cort touched the spot gingerly. It didn't hurt any worse than the rest of him, not yet anyway. Just a flesh wound, but an ugly one. "It's not bad, but I wouldn't want it to get infected." Stas's death had left him leery of infections, and they were a long way from the city, where at least there might be a chance of getting some alien medicine.

"Clean it well," Okolo said, "and dress it with herbs. Infections are rare enough, if you take care of the wound." He paused, peering at Cort. "What? Are infections such a danger in the city, then?"

"They can be. We don't have any... herbs." There was so much he still had to learn about these forest people! "What was that animal, anyway?"

Neder's jaw dropped. "You don't know?"

Cort shook his head.

Neder glanced at Okolo, eyes wide, then turned back to Cort. "That, my young friend, was a boar, not exactly a creature I'd want anyone to meet alone. Maybe now you can understand why I was in a hurry to warn these people about him. Cort, this is an animal that we usually kill in groups of ten or twelve strong men with spears, not alone in single combat armed with only a knife. With a group, if the creature attacks one person, others can come from the sides and divert it, so that no one gets hurt. What you have done is quite unusual. Amazing, really."

"It speaks to the whynywir's interest in you," added Okolo, drawing himself straighter and folding his arms across his chest.

The whynywir? Cort had heard of legendary creatures called by that name, but had never treated the stories as real. Putting Okolo's odd declaration aside for the moment, Cort answered Neder. "Believe me, I would have waited for you if I could have."

The hunter laughed and tousled Cort's wet hair.

"Tell me about the whynywir," Cort asked Tonio over dinner. He had bathed, and his wound was dressed with a mixture of herbs that numbed the pain and (Okolo had assured him) promoted healing. Dressed now in forest clothing rich in beadwork of yellow and reddish ochre, deep blue and white, and seated in a place of honor, Cort felt relaxed enough to indulge his curiosity again.

Tonio rolled his eyes skywards. "I am certain," he exclaimed, "that I have been saddled with your questions as a punishment for all my past misbehavior, which I now rue completely."

Cort grinned. He had grown more comfortable with Tonio's banter over the course of the afternoon and evening. It was late by the time the boar meat was cooked, and the entire village had joined in the celebration. "When you finish answering that one," he said, laughing, "you can tell me why Okolo said the whynywir might be interested in me."

"Ah, that question is an easy one. The answer is that no one ever knows why the whynywir do what they do. But do you truly not know about the whynywir, or are you jesting with me?"

"Tonio, would I jest with you?" Seeing Tonio's doubting look, Cort laughed again. "No, I don't know about them. I mean, there are stories, of course. In the stories, the whynywir are wise, ancient creatures, older than the humans but decidedly not human, frightening sometimes…" He shrugged. "Really, Tonio, I don't know."

"But you *do* know!" Tonio responded. "I couldn't have described them better myself."

"But, Tonio, those are children's stories. No one believes them."

Suddenly serious, Tonio leaned forward and took hold of Cort's wrist. "Believe them! Have you seen the blue crystal in Okolo's forehead?"

Cort nodded.

"He is a seer. He talks with the whynywir through that crystal, as your friend Neder talks with his kiri though the red one. The whynywir are ancient and wise, just as you said. Through the seers, they guide us humans like…" Tonio faltered and shook his head. "I don't know a good analogy for you. Maybe like the aliens guide the people in the city?"

Cort tried to understand the analogy. He considered how the life of the city, from its clothing to its language to its deepest aspirations, was formed by the alien culture. But then he thought of Dilia, who might have been sold to a starman for profit. "Oh, I hope not, Tonio," he said. "I hope not like that."

⁂

After the communal dinner, the villagers went their separate ways. Neder stayed with Okolo, and Cort went with Tonio to the longhouse where the unmarried men lived.

Despite threatening to keep Tonio awake all night with questions, Cort fell asleep quickly. He slept deeply and without dreams until Neder came to shake him awake early in the morning when the sky was barely light enough to mark the small, round opening of the window above Cort's bedroll. Words weren't necessary. Cort understood the hunter's intentions. He pulled on his vest, buckled on his belt with his knife sheath, and slipped out of the house he had shared with Tonio and two other young men of the village.

"No fancy good-byes," Neder said.

But Cort, turning to look over the hunter's shoulder, saw Okolo approaching and said, "I think you're out of luck."

Neder turned. The old man was still bare-chested, and his hair was rumpled.

"I thought I heard you stirring, Hunter," said the seer. "I would have been most unhappy to wake and find you gone."

Burdened with necessity, Neder smiled and answered graciously. "I don't like fancy hellos or good-byes, Seer, but I would have been most grieved if I'd made you unhappy."

"Thank you, Neder," Okolo said quietly. He wasn't smiling. Cort was surprised to see Okolo's eyes moist with unshed tears. "I have a favor to ask of you, not for my own sake but for the wise ones."

"Of course." Neder's seriousness matched that of the seer. "Whatever is required."

"Only to take this package to the seer Tirei-sunar." Okolo handed Neder a small square package wrapped in deerskin and tied with a thong.

"Easily done; he is the headman of my village," answered Neder, tucking the package into the pouch that hung from his belt.

"Guard it carefully, Hunter. It contains both a red crystal and a blue."

Neder's eyebrows rose. "For Tirei?" he asked.

"I don't know for whom." Okolo sounded weary. "For Tirei-sunar, or for whomever he will be instructed to pass them to. I had hoped..." The old man left the thought uncompleted and sighed.

Had hoped... Cort suddenly understood that the seer had a son or a nephew or a grandson who would not now wear either of those crystals. His heart went out to the old man.

"What I hoped is of no importance. The crystals now pass to Tirei-sunar, and from there, wherever the whynywir instruct."

"I'll guard them; you need not fear for their safety." Neder spoke gently. "Perhaps the whynywir will also send another crystal to this village sometime."

Okolo smiled wanly. "Perhaps. Thank you, Hunter."

As he followed Neder into the forest, Cort turned for a last look at the little village where he had unexpectedly found a friend. The seer Okolo was still standing where they had left him, silently watching their departure.

Chapter 8

The Contract

Dilia's first day on the base passed quickly. With so much new to see and to learn at the clinic, she sometimes forgot entirely about her predicament for whole moments. But at the end of the day, a soldier came to the clinic to escort her to the commandant's quarters. She backed away, heart pounding. "I don't want to go back there."

"You must," Abeni said, sadly. "If you aren't there for him when he wants you, he may not ever let you come back here to the infirmary. But I saw him today, and I talked with him about you. I'm not sure, but I think possibly he might wait a day or two in order to give you a little time to... to... Well, let's try to set up a routine that maybe he'll buy into. Meanwhile, get a good night's sleep."

That night, Dilia sat awake in her room. She was shaking, but not from cold. She wrapped her blanket around her. She nibbled at her meal, but her stomach was clenched so tight it was impossible to eat. If the commandant came, what would she say to him that might make a difference? What *could* she say that hadn't already been said?

Dilia grew increasingly anxious, imagining the worst. But for two nights, the commandant did not come.

On the third night, he came to Dilia's room just as she was finishing dinner. He did not knock. The door simply opened. Dilia gasped, but he didn't seem to notice. Without asking whether he might come in, he entered the room. He was tall, even for a starman, and thin. His build emphasized the shallow chest all the starmen had, lungs too small to get enough of whatever they needed from Aran's air. No wonder they added so much extra oxygen and who-knew-what-else to the air! He wore a dark blue uniform so clean and pressed that it might still be warm from the iron. His expression was equally stiff.

"Hello, Dilia. Mind if I join you?" Without waiting for a reply, he sat at the little table opposite her. "Is the food to your liking?"

The food was actually quite tasty, though she wasn't sure what it all was, and it was served in an abundance Dilia had never experienced at home. But her heart was pounding, and she quelled a strong impulse to back away. "Y-yes, very much, thank you."

"I understand you're helping out at the infirmary. Doctor Inowa says that you're a quick learner."

"Thank you." Dilia took another bite and considered her words carefully. "I'm glad to be able to help out."

He made a noncommittal noise in his throat and looked at her assessingly, as if she were a shiny stone found in the street, and he was wondering if it might actually have some value.

"Look, I don't know why you brought me here"—she could feel herself blushing at the lie—"but I do have a good mind, and I want to use it to help people." She'd lost her appetite, and put down her spoon. "Why are you looking at me that way? That's not so hard to understand, is it?"

"It's not that." He took her hand.

Dilia wanted to pull her hand away, but she kept still. If this became a battle of wills, or of power, she would lose.

But he must have felt her tense up, for he let go of her hand. "I've just never encountered a native... except for some of the soldiers, of course... who even knew the language, much less spoke so articulately about wanting to learn a skill. You are a most unusual person." He leaned back and studied her again, this time with a warmer expression. "I like that."

Dilia didn't think she was all that unusual. The comment was belittling. She thought of Cort, who studied hard so that he could get a good job. Did he think they were all stupid? Before she could consider her words, she said, "I doubt you've met that many natives."

Karim recoiled almost as if she had slapped him. Then he laughed, a great, resonant bellow that must have carried to the farthest reaches of this house. "You're right!" he boomed. "I've met a few, but you, my little Dilia, are going to be a particular pleasure."

"What, do you think I'm your property, to take your pleasure of? I'm a human being, just like you. Is this the way they treat people on Earth?"

"Of course you are not my property, Dilia. How uncivilized! You are my guest, and I hope you will feel... most welcome." He put a sinister twist on the last two words, and gave her a smile that made Dilia feel like she was going to lose the dinner she'd just been eating. Maybe he'd never let her go home.

What a mess she'd made of this! No matter what she said or did, he just seemed more determined to keep her here, and to... and to... Dilia took in a deep breath and then let it out slowly. What were her options? She'd been a prisoner here for four days. If Cort was coming to rescue her, surely he would have been here by now. So, either he had tried and failed, or... worse. In either event, he would be no help. The thought made Dilia sad, but she couldn't think about Cort now. Whether he'd abandoned her or died, he was gone, just like her parents. She'd have no one to blame but herself if she never gathered the courage to keep trying to get home. "No, please. I mean, I'd be happy to get to know you better and to work with Dr. Inowa, but I want to go home in the evenings like everyone else. I have a family, and I miss them. That's not so unreasonable, is it?"

"Unreasonable?" His frown formed a deep crease between his eyebrows. "You signed the contract, so I really don't understand what your problem is."

This didn't make any sense. "Contract? No, I don't think I—"

Karim leaned forward, his frown now decidedly hostile. "Don't play coy with me, young lady. You know full well what I am talking about. You signed a contract agreeing to come live on the base, and I have a facsimile of it right here to jog your memory." He fiddled with his bracelet, unfolding something that looked like a comm screen. "Here. Look."

Dilia leaned closer to see and caught the unpleasant scent of the chemicals that might have been used in cleaning Karim's uniform. On his comm screen was a document full of almost illegibly small print in Starrish. It had a signature line with a shaky X scrawled on it, and a date stamped below.

"You see?" he was saying, "It's the date you arrived; everything is in order."

"But what's that X?"

"Where you signed, of course."

She drew a shaky breath. "No, Karim. If I'd have signed, I would have used my signature."

He looked at her, one eyebrow slightly raised, giving his frown a questioning look.

Did he think she was illiterate? "I can write, you know. Would you like to see?"

He turned his gaze away and preoccupied himself with folding the screen back into his bracelet. "Let's say," he said, "that I believe you. Then what is this document, and why was it delivered with you? I paid rather handsomely for certain... services... that you were to provide. I was led to believe you were willing to do so, and I have been more than patient with you."

Could it be true, that this was just some kind of misunderstanding, or worse, a fraud perpetuated on both of them by Sleb? If so, then she just needed to convince Karim, and he'd let her go. But what were the odds of that? Karim seemed determined to keep her here. Dilia shook her head, trying to think clearly. There was no point in being less than honest. It wouldn't hurt, and it might, just might, help. "I don't know anything about that document. I was ab—" What a time to forget a word in Starrish! "—taken forcefully from my house by Sleb's soldiers and brought here."

"Abducted," he said.

"Abducted."

"And you're saying that you did not sign this contract to provide services here."

"No, I did not."

"I paid handsomely for your... cooperation." He leaned forward and took her hand. "Could I, perhaps, offer you an inducement?"

Dilia wasn't sure what he meant by 'inducement,' but she could feel her eyes welling with tears. "I want to go home." Much as she didn't want it to, her voice quavered. "Please. Sir."

Pushing back his chair, Karim got up. He stood very straight, and the frown that had never quite left his face now looked resolute. "First, I must settle this matter with your man Sleb. I will need to investigate what he has to say about whether this contract was improperly made. And if it was, he must refund the payment involved."

"And then you'll let me go home, right?"

He gave her a curt nod. "If your story proves true. Of course. Earth law and common decency would require it. But meanwhile, you will stay here."

Dilia, too, stood. She had more reason for optimism now than since she'd arrived on the base, but still, Karim's response was less than she'd hoped for. "But—"

"Use this time to consider your options, Dilia. I can ensure that your family will be very well paid, and as for you... you will want for nothing while you are here. Tell me you will think about it with an open mind."

Dilia swallowed hard past a knot that had formed in her throat. She should be happy about this outcome. Why wasn't she? Maybe she just needed time to let it all sink in. "All right."

The commandant turned and left the room.

⁂

Each evening, Dilia waited tensely for the suddenly opened door, the unannounced visit, but Karim didn't come for almost a month. He couldn't have forgotten her. Perhaps he was staying away until he had news about the forged contract, trying not to put any pressure on her. She was grateful for his courtesy—and for not having to deal with his advances.

But how could it possibly take that long to investigate? Maybe Sleb had a way of avoiding the commandant, and maybe Karim was so busy with his other duties he didn't have a lot of time to keep looking for the dishonest kingpin. But when he did find him, surely this would all be straightened out. At least, Dilia hoped so. It would all be straightened out, and she'd be able to go home. Meanwhile, she resolved to make the best of her situation.

Abeni came for Dilia every morning, and they walked together to the infirmary. They put on their white coats, Abeni's over her uniform, and Dilia's over a silky dress that was one of the three such she'd been provided with. At first, Abeni allowed Dilia to read and study at her desk while she did her rounds. When her rounds were done, the doctor answered Dilia's questions and guided her study.

After a week, Abeni started allowing Dilia to come with her as she visited the sick people, instructing her to take notes while Abeni examined them.

Two soldiers were staying in the infirmary. One had recently arrived and was feverish with some infection he'd gotten on Earth or on the ship. He was fast asleep and did not stir as Abeni examined him. The other had broken a leg and two ribs in a fall from one of the harvesters. He made a whistling noise as the doctor and Dilia came to his bed. "Who's your friend here, Doc?"

Dilia drew in a breath, her face suddenly hot. This could only be trouble.

Abeni smiled and shook her head. "This is Dilia. And you'd better be polite, or I'll discharge you back to the harvesters."

"Hey, Miss Dilia," the soldier said, "you're right pretty. You want to step out with me, when I get out of here? They got music and some good booze over at the commissary."

Dilia drew back. "N-no. I—"

"She's staying with the commandant," Abeni said, giving the soldier a warning look.

The soldier seemed suddenly to have become a bit smaller, and farther away. "Sorry, Miss Dilia. Didn't mean nothing by it."

After that, no one who visited the infirmary mentioned the commandant, but they seemed to know of Dilia's association with him. They were uniformly distant and much too polite. They called Abeni "Doc," but Dilia was always "Miss Dilia."

No one but Abeni responded to any of her tentative overtures of friendship. Some days this was a relief. How many alien friends did she need, anyway? Karim was trouble enough—and where was the man? Other days, though, she felt listless and lacked all energy. She missed Cort terribly. The thought that he might be dead, might have died trying to rescue her, scratched at the doors of her consciousness, but she refused to let it in. No, by Earth and space, at least let him be alive and free.

When she was able to put her situation with the commandant out of her mind, Dilia enjoyed her studies, as well as helping Abeni while she made her rounds. She could imagine making a career in medicine. It was a fantasy, of course, but it brightened her days. The issue about the contract would be cleared up, and the commandant would offer her a job. She and Cort would both have good-paying work up at the base, and live happily together.

Of course, there were problems with this fantasy.

First, she had no idea if Cort was still alive. Even if he was, there was this inoculation thing she'd gotten that first day, that—what had Abeni said?—would protect against an unwanted pregnancy. But what about a wanted one? How could she ever marry anyone, if she couldn't have a child? No, Cort would want to marry someone else—but surely they'd still be neighbors and close friends. That, at least, wouldn't have to change.

The bigger problem was, how could she and Cort have any future at all together, even just a friendship, if she couldn't ever go home again? Could it really be taking this long for Karim to confirm that that supposed contract was a fake?

The commandant had been gone for almost four weeks—long enough that Dilia began to worry he might never come back, and there would be no one who had the authority to let her leave.

And then, one evening when she returned from the infirmary, she opened the door to her room, and there the commandant was. He stood straight and tall in his immaculate uniform, in the center of the room, waiting for her. Her heart tripped an alarm, and, hand to her chest, she took a step back. A corner of his mouth twitched into a hint of a smile. "Frightened you, did I?" He held out a hand to her. "Well, don't just stand there, come on in. Be a nice girl, and give me a hug." He took her hand, led her inside, and closed the door. Then he put a hand on her shoulder as if to guide her into an embrace.

Dilia stiffened, pulling her shoulder back. She looked away, into the corner of the room, anywhere but at him. "You were gone a long time. I... I thought..."

"Thought what, little one? That I'd forgotten you?" He let his hand drop. "You know I'd never do that. I was out inspecting one of the harvesting operations, that's all."

She took a step away from him. She raised her head and looked him in the eye. "I thought you might be investigating that fake contract."

For an instant, he looked at her blankly. Then he smiled condescendingly. "Ah, the contract. Yes, of course."

He hadn't been investigating it at all. He didn't even remember saying he would. What had she expected?

"These things take time," he said.

"I—I understand." She didn't try to keep her disappointment out of her voice. If she still wanted to go free, she'd have to find a way, somehow, to escape on her own.

He walked over to the bed and sat down. He patted the bed beside him. "Come, sit over here, and tell me all about how you're adjusting to life on the base. I understand you've become quite the little medical understudy."

Dilia stared at the spot he'd indicated, and her stomach turned. She took one of the small chairs from the table, turned it to face him, and sat down. "I like working with the doctor," she said. "I thought it might be a... a job I could do."

"You already have a job. Here." He patted the bed again and paused, giving her a significant look. "With me. I don't want to keep arguing with you about this, Dilia."

She swallowed. This was the last job in the world she wanted to do. "Just give me a chance! Let me work with Doctor Inowa, and if she says I'm good enough, let me go back to Earth with her for more training. Let me help with your sick and injured people. I could—" She took a deep breath and then plunged in. "I could live over there at the infirmary so that I could look in on the sick people at night when others are sleeping."

His low chuckle was altogether humorless. "You'll have to do better than that. *Yes* to helping the doctor, and then later on we'll see about maybe going back to Earth to study. *No* to sleeping in the infirmary. Nighttime monitoring is automated. You're staying here with me."

Dilia tried to tell herself that at least she'd gained something, but it did nothing to alleviate her nausea.

Karim took her hand again, firmly. "Come now, little one, it's not that bad. In fact, this could be quite pleasurable... for both of us, if you let it. I'm not an unattractive man, and I'm not unreasonable, either. Can't you find it in your heart to compromise a little? Perhaps just a small kiss, for now." He stood, pulling Dilia up as well. With his other hand, he brushed back her hair and looked long and deeply into her eyes.

Dilia tried not to cringe, not to pull back. What would it hurt to allow him this one small favor? But it did hurt. It twisted her stomach. She pulled away. "I—I'm sorry, but—"

The commandant sighed. "Other women of your kind have been more than happy for my attentions, and they have been well rewarded, too. But they meant nothing to me. You... You're different. I want to know you better. I want *you* to know *me* better. I won't force myself on you while you're not willing, and I won't hurt you. That's not the kind of man I am. All I'm asking is that you keep an open mind. You'll do that for me, won't you?"

An open mind. Dilia's throat felt so tight she couldn't speak. But he was waiting, gazing at her so intently it seemed he might pull her to him at any moment, willing or not. She mustn't give him a clue that she was planning to escape. She managed to whisper, "Yes."

He gave a single, curt nod of approval, turned, and left the room.

Dilia could not stop the tears that welled unwelcome from her eyes. She turned stiffly from the closed door, lay down on her bed, and wept.

Chapter 9

Neder's Village

"My village is just over that hill." Neder's gait took on an extra spring, bouncing on the balls of his feet. He and Cort had traveled for two weeks without stopping in another village or seeing another person, and now Neder was nearly home. They had kept to a brisk walk during most of the journey, but now the hunter broke into a long, easy lope without waiting to see if Cort followed.

Cort grinned and matched the hunter's pace. But as they reached the top of the hill, Neder stopped. It had drizzled in the early morning, a light, warm rain that made the forest greener and more richly colorful than normal, fading into softness in the distance. The rain had stopped about an hour ago, and a break in the clouds framed the village below in golden sunlight.

Between where they stood and the village, the forest opened up, and on a slight rise stood a man. He was of middle age, his black hair salted with gray. His vest was beaded in light and dark blue, and blue beads adorned the fringes of his dark pants. When he turned toward them, a blue crystal at his temple flashed in the sunlight. A seer!

The man stood straight and tall, his hands loosely holding a staff that extended from the ground to well above his head. Alternately rough and smooth, the staff had a slight bend as if it reached for something, and green leaves adorned a cluster of sprigs at its top. The wood of the staff gleamed in a rainbow of colors. It was the largest piece of worked khena wood Cort had ever seen.

Neder glanced at Cort, then nodded slightly as if acknowledging something someone had said to him. "It's Tirei," he said. "He's the headman of my village, and a seer. He's the one you'll need to talk with about becoming a hunter."

Neder set off down the hill. Cort followed him, his heart lifting, now that the end of his mission was finally in sight.

When they reached the older man, Neder introduced Cort. Tirei greeted him politely, and Cort managed a polite response, but he could barely tear his gaze from Tirei's staff, which seemed to glow with a special light. Seen this close, it was even more remarkable than from a distance, dancing with sparks of an inner fire. His hand twitched with the desire to reach toward it.

"It is living wood," Tirei said, following Cort's gaze. "Would you like to touch it?"

'Living wood' was a good name for it. Colors and patterns swam like fish in its translucent grain. Cort didn't trust himself to speak. He swallowed hard and nodded.

Tirei spread out his hands on the staff to open a large space between them. "Go ahead," he said, with the kind of encouraging nod he might give to a small child trying something for the first time.

Cort stretched out his hand and took hold of the staff, then gasped in astonishment. The wood seemed alive in more ways than one. It was as if the staff had actively taken hold of his own hand. It was warm, and Cort could feel its strength. Vitality flowed down his arm and seemed to send sparks inward to his heart. He felt he had the power to do anything, to rescue Dilia, to succeed. His other arm felt weak by comparison, and so he placed his other hand on the staff just above the first. The feeling was utterly exhilarating.

"How do you ever put this staff down?" he said.

"It's not difficult," Tirei answered. Cort met the seer's eyes. They were a soft, light brown, and his expression was filled with something serious, like sorrow or sympathy. "With the staff of the living wood comes great responsibility. Sometimes it's good to put such responsibility aside."

As had happened too often since he came to this forest, Cort failed to understand. His face must have betrayed his confusion, for the seer added, "While we hold this staff together, neither you nor I can lie to the other, and we will hold onto it until the staff lets us go. Now listen to me. I am Tirei-sunar of the clan of the hawk, instrument of the whynywir, seer, head of this village, and the father of five. I have lived here my entire life. Now tell me about yourself."

"My name is Cort." Cort felt terribly self-conscious. "I am city-born and clanless." He lifted his chin slightly as he spoke, defying the seer to reject him. "I don't live in the city anymore. I don't know where I live. And, Tirei, even without the staff I wouldn't have lied to you."

Tirei nodded. "I know that—now. But without the staff, I wouldn't have been sure. Now tell me about your name."

"My name? But I already told you," he said. "It's Cort. I was named after my father."

"But 'Cort' is not a forest name," said the older man.

"No, I guess not. Why should it be? I'm not a forest person. His name was something else. Longer." Cort frowned, trying to get it just right. "Something like Cort-anaran—and so is mine. But no one wants to deal with a long name like that, so no one ever calls me that."

The older man's eyes went distant for a moment, as if he were considering something complicated. After a moment of silence, he asked, "Corodh-an-Aran?"

"What?" Cort tried to move his hands to a more comfortable position, but they were as stuck as if they had been glued to the staff.

"Could his name have been Corodh-an-Aran?"

"Yes, I guess that sounds about right. The way you forest people pronounce the old words is a bit different from how we say them in the city."

"More correct," said Tirei.

"I guess. Yes, probably; that would make sense."

"Corodh-an-Aran." The older man drew out the syllables like a benediction.

"Does it mean anything to you?"

"You don't know what it means?"

"Should I?"

The seer sighed. "'Corodh' is a fine old word but it's fallen out of common usage. You might say, 'justice,' but that's not exactly right. It has the flavor of being what one is meant to be, doing what one is meant to do, having what one is meant to have. The rightness of things, and also setting things right. A good word. 'An' and 'aran,' you probably know. Of the forest, or for it. This whole world."

"Setting things right for Aran? For our world?" The idea pleased Cort. He stood a little straighter.

"Yes, that's part of it. The forest being and having what she is meant to have. The one who makes sure that happens. Who sets things right for our world."

Cort smiled. "I like that," he said. Then, after thinking about it, he added, "Still, it's only a name."

"An ancient one," said the seer. "A good one. And why have you come here, Cort?"

"To become a hunter, like Neder."

Tirei raised a quizzical eyebrow and glanced at Neder. Standing at Cort's side, almost out of the range of his sight, the hunter nodded. "But why?" the seer asked.

"To save my friend Dilia, who is like a sister to me," Cort replied. "More than a sister. My father and mother are dead. My home has been burned down. But Dilia is in the city or on the base somewhere, captive, and I intend to rescue her. It'll be dangerous. I can't do it alone. I'll need a kiri." He swallowed and added, "Probably no one's ever hunted in the city before, but I intend to do it, and I'll succeed, too. And—I didn't know this at first, but now I do—when I've rescued Dilia, I want to bring her back here to the khenaran, and I still want to be a hunter then."

"This will be decided by the whynywir," said the seer.

It wasn't quite a rejection, but it was far from the agreement Cort would have liked. "I understand that, but you're a seer! You talk with them directly, so you must have some influence with them. Will you help me?"

Again Tirei exchanged glances with Neder. Then he gave Cort a slight, sad smile, suddenly looking weary. "I will do what I feel is right for you, Cort-anaran. For you and for all of Aran."

Cort accepted this response as positive. He would do whatever was necessary to convince the seer of the rightness of his mission. But when he tried to let go, the staff held him tight.

Tirei continued to look at him, one eyebrow slightly raised. "You have a question?"

Cort filled the embarrassing moment with the only thing he could think of. "Why is this called 'living wood?'"

"Because it lives." The seer shrugged. "This staff was freely given by a true tree to my grandfather before I was born. The wood was alive when it was given, and it lives still." Cort followed Tirei's gaze to the crown of lacy, green leaves at the top of the staff. "I believe," Tirei said, "that the staff will outlive me as it has my father and my grandfather."

In awe, Cort let go of the staff, and now, surprisingly, it let him. He reached up with a hand to touch the living leaves. The feeling of vibrating energy in that side of his body eased, and a wave of deep sorrow rolled through him, carrying him in its tide. He felt a strong need to comfort—whom? Or perhaps it was he who needed comforting. He could barely reach the bottom-most cluster of feathery leaves, and the feeling of grief weighed him down. He ran his fingers along the patterned wood, and wept.

The staff wobbled slightly as Tirei let go, and Cort tightened his grip. He felt weak with loss almost beyond bearing, grief that ripped his heart like a twisting knife. He leaned against the staff as he sank to his knees, his cheek resting on the warm wood. His tears fell on the staff and the earth around it, and he breathed in great, gulping sobs until at last the feeling faded, leaving him short of breath.

Tirei touched his shoulder.

Cort looked up at the seer. "What was that?" he asked. His voice was hoarse. "Why?"

Tirei didn't answer. He studied the staff, which Cort still leaned on. "Can you stand, Cort-anaran?"

Cort rose shakily to one foot, and then the other. As he did, the staff seemed to release him. He couldn't help but let go of it. When he stood, the staff remained, still and vertical, though no one held it.

Tirei brushed the earth with his fingers, frowning. "The staff is mine no longer. It has taken root." He looked up at Cort, shaking his head. "It's a mystery. How are you feeling?"

"Like the whole world just turned upside down." Cort attempted a fragile smile. "What happened?"

"Some kind of connection between you and the khenaran, a very strong one, to have planted the staff of living wood. Beyond that..." His head shaking turned into a rolling motion, a man face to face with the ineffable. "I've never heard of anything like it. I suppose we will know more when the time is right for us to know. Meanwhile..." He stood and clapped a hand around Cort's shoulder. "You are welcome in this village."

Tirei's smile broadened further as he turned to Neder and asked, "And what do you have to say for yourself, Hunter? You were hunting for your son in the city. Have you brought him back?"

"I found him, but he did not wish to return," Neder said. "I am resigned to this loss. But I have not returned empty-handed. You can see what kind of guest I've brought—a man with a good heart. Oh, and this, too." He took from his pouch the package that Okolo had given him. "The whynywir have sent this to you."

"Ah..." Tirei took the package thoughtfully. "Yes, thank you. I was expecting this. And what about dinner, Hunter? Have you brought us nothing to eat?"

"As for that," the hunter said, "the day is still young."

Neder's village was fascinating in its strangeness. Everything about it was different from the city—the way people cooked, how they ate and worked communally in the open, how much they shared. But after only three days in the village, Cort began to get restless. He couldn't stop thinking about Dilia. He needed to get back to the city and rescue her—but how? Even if he decided to leave the village, Cort could no more find his way back to the city alone than he could go to Earth without a starship.

For the third time in as many days, he sought out Tirei, and he found him sitting outside the doorway of his house, sharpening his knife on a stone.

"When?" Cort asked. "When can I do the hunter ceremony? When can I get a *kiri*?"

Tirei looked up at Cort with a thoughtful expression. Then he went back to sharpening his knife. "When I decide. You must learn patience, Cort."

"But when will you decide?"

Tirei sighed. "When I am ready. When the whynywir give me permission. Here, have a seat." He felt the edge of his knife with his fingertips. "Now, tell me more about your father."

It was Cort's turn to sigh. He wanted to shout, *I already told you everything you need to know!* But nothing would be gained by offending the man who held the key to Dilia's fate and his own. "I never met him. All I know is what my mother told me. He came from the khenaran, that's all I know."

"In which direction from the city?"

"I don't know, Tirei. Does it matter?"

Apparently satisfied with his knife's sharpness, Tirei resheathed it. "You want to borrow my stone, while I have it out?" His eyes took on a distant look for a moment, as if listening to a voice Cort couldn't hear. Then he asked, "Was it a village that was destroyed by the tree harvesting?"

Cort instinctively touched the knife at his belt. He shook his head. "No thanks. It's an alien knife. Whatever they made it out of, it never seems to get dull. As for the village, I don't know... No, I don't think so, because if that were so, there would have been others with him. But my mother said he came alone."

"So in that case he must have come from some distance away."

"Tirei, I don't know." His voice came out more impatient than he'd intended.

The seer seemed not to notice. "What was his clan?"

"I've told you—we don't have clans in the city. If he had one out in the forest, my mother never mentioned it."

Tirei shook his head. "You city people lose so much... so quickly. When I try to imagine what it must be like, I cannot."

Cort smiled. "Most of us can't imagine life in the forest, either. Except for the people working on the harvesters, we seldom leave the city."

Tirei studied him in silence for a moment. "Very strange. Tell me, Cort, did you or your family have anything that belonged to your father?"

Cort sat straighter, lifting his chin. "His knife. It was mine until I was caught and thrown into Sleb's jail. They took it from me then. This is the sheath."

Tirei squinted at the sheath on Cort's belt, that now housed the alien Jerrald's knife. He made a noncommittal sound.

"Does it tell you anything?" Cort asked.

"It's well made, the stitching and the beadwork both. I don't recognize the pattern, but the whynywir might. Describe the knife."

A feeling flooded through him, as warm as joy. "Oh, Tirei, it was beautiful. The blade was made of petrified bone. It was wickedly sharp, and never needed honing. The handle was wrapped in strips of red leather; I don't know what was underneath, but it was shaped like it belonged in my hand. The leather was stamped with a pattern; maybe it had a meaning, I don't know. The ends of the handle were also beaded with red and white beads in a kind of herringbone design. There were feathers... Tirei, why do you care about this?"

Tirei studied Cort but said nothing for a long time. At last he said, "Because the whynywir want to know who you are."

"Then why don't *they* ask me?" Cort flashed.

"They *are* asking you. Through me."

Cort had reached his limit. "Just tell them I am who I am," he said defiantly. "A city boy. Clanless. Orphaned. The one forest object I ever had is gone. My best friend is captive among the aliens, and I need your help. I am asking your help. You tell them that."

Tirei closed his eyes wearily and sighed. "I *am* telling them, Cort. You'll just have to be patient with us."

When he wasn't fretting about the delay in his plans to become a hunter, Cort worried about Dilia. He'd been on the road for three weeks and languishing in Neder's village for five days. So much time had passed. Where was Dilia now? Still captive somewhere in Sleb's compound? Or on the alien base? Probably one or the other—unless they'd already sent her off on a ship to Earth. No, he had to assume she was still on Aran. Surely the aliens had enough girls of their own back on Earth. But who knew how the aliens in the enclave treated the girls they bought or stole? No one ever heard.

He walked to the hill where the living staff, now a slender rooted tree, grew. It was changing rapidly, as if making up for the time it had lost when it was a staff. In just five days, its branches seemed to have spread wider, and the hard bark with its deep subtle rainbows had begun hiding the flashing runes of the worked wood.

Cort felt a kind of kinship to that tree—as if it were his only living relative. He wanted to touch it, but when he brought his hand close to it, his stomach lurched, and he didn't dare. He didn't know if he could survive another round of unspeakable grief and loss.

"What are you doing?"

Cort hadn't seen Neder approach, hadn't heard him. He gave a start and then quickly folded his hand back into the crook of the other elbow. "Just burning my engines."

"What?"

"You know—standing here doing nothing, like one of these trees."

"Hmmph. Looks to me sort of like you're trying to touch that tree and also trying not to."

Cort almost reached out again, but he didn't want to end up drawing away. Again. In front of Neder. He kept his hands close inside his elbows. "That's about right."

"Well, you ought to do one or the other. Doesn't much matter which. But one way or the other, get past it."

"Thank you for the advice." His words came out more bitter than he'd intended.

"I was going to see if you'd like to come hunting with me, but if you'd rather stand around and stare at that tree, have it your way."

Cort's heart leapt. "Hunting? Sure! Right now?"

Neder smiled. "Yes, now." Then he patted his pouch and frowned. "No, wait. I forgot something. I'll just run back down to my house and get it. I'll be back in a few minutes. You wait here. See if you can make your peace with that tree... or something."

That wasn't likely. "Right."

Cort watched Neder go. Then he started pacing. The thing was, Neder was right. He should get this over with. He reached the crest of the hill and turned back. But the sense of loss had been so deep, so cutting. He never wanted to feel that way again. What if he didn't recover? He should just forget this crazy tree. He was now among other trees. He turned and headed back up the hill. His grief had felt overwhelming, but it was just an emotion. He'd get over it like he had last time. And worst case, Neder would be there in a few minutes and could get help if necessary. Looked at that way, this was an ideal time.

Cort stopped by the tree. He clenched his fists. "Earth and stars! It's worth the pain just to get over this!" He reached out and touched the tree before he had time to think better of it.

Nothing happened.

There was no surge of emotion. No pain. No energy, no tingling. The tree did not take hold of him the way the staff had.

The tree was just a tree.

Cort laughed with relief and wiped away a tear that was a release of tension. He ran his hand up and down the bark. Maybe it was just a tree, but by all the powers on Earth, it was *his* tree. He leaned against the thin trunk and waited for Neder to return.

They hunted together that day, but Cort was little help. "You move through the woods well," Neder said, "and you're good with that knife. But you need to learn to read the environment better. The wind, the terrain, disturbances in the brush. And you need to learn more weapons."

"All right." What else did he have to do with his time anyway, while those whynywir or Tirei or whoever made up their minds? "I'd like that."

"Tomorrow," said the hunter, "we'll work on the sling."

The thing Neder had used to kill the soldier. Cort might need that. He nodded grimly. At least, while he waited, he'd be doing something useful.

"What are they waiting for?" Cort asked Neder the next day as the hunter showed him how to use a sling. "What's going to be different tomorrow or the day after? Why don't we just get this over with?"

Neder looked up, but his hand, apparently intent upon its own business, continued to fish through the stones in his pouch. "This is not something to be done lightly."

"I'm not doing it lightly. If you think that, you don't know me."

The hunter raised an eyebrow. "And neither do the whynywir. Can you blame them for wanting to be sure?"

"What are they looking for?"

Neder shrugged. "Who ever knows about the whynywir? Ask Tirei. Now, do you want to learn how this sling works, or don't you?"

"But, Neder, they've asked me every question three times. When are they going to make up their minds?"

The hunter pulled a stone from his pouch and set it into the pocket of the sling. Then he put down sling and stone, and he turned toward Cort. "Did I ever tell you how my son Sarel died?" he asked.

Sarel. The one Neder never talked about. Cort shook his head.

"He wanted to be a hunter, as you do." In that moment, Neder looked much older. "And he was good at forest lore, too. Not like you." Neder smiled, softening the criticism, but Cort took no offense. It was true. "He was impatient for the ceremony, as you are. In the end, Tirei and I gave in to him when perhaps we shouldn't have. The kiri can be unkind, Cort. Aran can be unkind. There is no room for weakness. The ceremony changes everyone. It destroyed him."

Destroyed! Cort's stomach tightened. If he were to die... what would happen to Dilia then? Even Neder and Tirei would be hurt. "Neder, I'm sorry." Cort reached out to touch the older man's arm, but Neder sat impassively. "I shouldn't have criticized you. You were being cautious. I never thought what it must be like, having the responsibility of someone's life on your conscience. I'm grateful you're willing to consider me at all. Come on, show me that sling again."

Neder picked up the sling and resettled the stone in its pouch, but Cort caught Neder's wrist. "The thing is, I don't have a life anyway. I'm a city boy stuck out here in the forest, where everything I've learned is meaningless. My parents are dead; if I go back to the city and Sleb catches me, he'll kill me, too. If Dilia is dead... Neder, can you understand?" His voice broke, and he swallowed. "I have nothing left to lose."

Chapter 10

The Ceremony

C ort dreamed the ground shook as harvesters advanced. The shaking didn't stop, and it turned into a hand shaking his shoulder.

"Wake up, boy," Neder said. "How can you hope to become a hunter when you sleep like that?"

It was still dark. Cort groaned and rolled onto his side, facing away from the disturbance. "Go away."

"Fine," Neder said, his voice as indifferent as a shrug. "But never say that we didn't give you a chance to become a hunter and gain a kiri. Know that we made you this offer, and you slept through it."

Cort's heart skipped a beat. A kiri, today! He sat up, throwing aside his cover. "What?" He'd been working on his hunting skills with Neder for two days now, so busy during the day trying to improve his skills that he'd hardly had time to worry about how long he'd been here, waiting. Evenings were harder, thinking of Dilia, wondering how she was doing, if she was even alive. And now, suddenly, the day had arrived.

"Prepare yourself, Cort," said the hunter. "This day will you gain or lose what you've been seeking."

"I'm ready! I've been ready for days." Cort stood, stumbling a bit as he grabbed his short leather pants.

"Ah, no," Neder said. Cort couldn't make out Neder's expression in the dark, but he could hear the smile in his voice. "One moment you're asleep, moaning 'Go away,' and the next moment you're fluttering around the ceiling like a trapped bat squeaking, 'I'm ready, I'm ready.' This is not how a man meets his fate. A man takes the time to get up and wash and dress, and then walks to meet his fate with calm dignity. Now compose yourself. I will meet you in front of Tirei's house when you are prepared." Neder walked out.

Cort groped in the dark for his vest. His fingers fumbled as he dressed, clumsy in his haste. Dilia! Finally, he would be able to rescue Dilia!

Ten minutes later, dressed at last, and his heart still pounding, Cort found both Neder and Tirei standing in front of Tirei's house. Each carried a leather pack slung over one shoulder, and when Cort arrived, Tirei wordlessly offered him a pack of his own. Cort took it and then followed as the two men turned and headed out of the village into the khenaran.

Cort allowed his pace to match the other two men, and after a while, his heart slowed to the steady rhythm of his footsteps. He was burning with questions: Where were they going? How was it going to work? Would he get his kiri right away? Did they know what kind of animal it would be? But something about the silence of Tirei and Neder left no room for interruption. Cort tried to concentrate instead on the path they were taking through the khenaran, but after about an hour, he knew that he would be hopelessly lost if he had to find his way back alone.

After another hour, he ceased to speculate and wonder about the future and allowed his feet simply to walk as he took in the wilderness around them.

They walked silently for several hours more. At noon, they reached a spot where a large five-fingered rock of gray granite thrust upward from the ground like a hand reaching for the sky. The palm of this stony hand curved around a sheltered area where the rock was covered with velvety green moss. Here Tirei-sunar led the little party and lowered his pack to the ground. Despite its mossy softness, the stone radiated a chill that made Cort shiver. Neder begin to gather fallen wood for a fire, and Cort went to help him. Tirei kindled the fire as the two younger men continued to bring branches. They worked in silence.

When the fire was burning strongly, Tirei poured liquid from a small skin flask into a cup, stirred it briefly, and set it near the fire. Then he sat down. Neder sat to one side of him, and Tirei indicated that Cort was to sit on the other.

"Are you completely certain, Corodh-an-Aran, that you wish to become a hunter?" asked the seer.

Cort nodded. His voice came out a little hoarsely. "Yes."

"There will be danger," Tirei said. "After today, there will be no backing out, but now you have time to reconsider."

Cort thought the warning a little silly. If Tirei didn't know by now how much he wanted this... But he was struck with the formality of the situation, and so he answered formally, "I'm ready."

"Today I will cut you to affix the gem. The gem allows a Hunter to talk with his kiri, but you will not hear anything at first. Your mind does not know the way of the hearing. The voices in the gem will be just meaningless noises, and your mind will block them out, like the wind in the trees, like the river flowing over the rocks. Later, when the wound heals a bit, we will continue with the ceremony, and you will have to overcome the animal that will be your kiri. Are you ready, Corodh-an-Aran?"

"Yes, I am."

"Do you want to know about the pain?"

"I want to do this, no matter what the pain."

A slight smile formed on Neder's lips, but he remained silent. Tirei stirred the cup of liquid again, then picked it up gingerly by its brim. "Drink this," he said. "It will ease the pain. Be careful; it's hot."

Cort accepted the cup and brought the liquid to his lips. It was almost too hot to drink. He blew on it, then took a tiny sip. The stuff was impossibly bitter. He opened his mouth to complain, but the serious expressions on both men's faces stopped him. A bitter draught was a small price to pay for what he wanted. Best not to speak of it. Cort sipped again, then quaffed the hot liquid as quickly as he was able. Whatever was in it made his vision swim. Everything around him looked familiar, yet strange.

Tirei bent close to the fire. He ran the blade of his knife back and forth through the flames, heating it. The fire seemed to be dancing, a lithe and sinuous dance. It was beautiful. Cort was tempted to reach out to touch the fire, it seemed so soft, but his arms seemed to lack the muscles necessary for movement. He felt a light touch on his shoulders. It tickled, and he laughed. He turned to see that Neder had moved closer and taken hold of both his shoulders.

"Lie down and be still," Neder said. "I will hold you."

Cort leaned back, aware of Neder's hands lowering him slowly to the ground. The tree branches above swayed gently against the sky.

"Do not move," Neder's voice said, behind him. "If you value your life, you do not want to cause Tirei's knife to slip." The words had no meaning. They seemed to float gently upward, until they dissolved in the net of overhead branches.

Then Tirei's face loomed over him, blocking the view. Cort blinked, mildly annoyed. He felt pressure and heat against his scalp as Tirei did something with the knife just out of the range of Cort's sight. The knife tickled. Cort wanted to brush it away, but something held his arms. Neder. There was an intense pressure where the knife had been, and then the two men moved away.

Cort closed his eyes. He was suddenly tired. He slept.

In the deep gloaming, Cort woke. His head felt strange. He tried to touch the spot where it throbbed the most, and discovered that his head was wrapped in a velvet-soft thin leather strip. At that throbbing spot, something was packed inside the leather next to his head. It itched. Cort felt for the way to unwind the wrapping, and then he remembered what had happened—earlier today? Yesterday? Cort sat up, his blanket falling to his waist. It was cold. The fire had died to a faint glow. Two huddled masses marked where Neder and Tirei slept. Yesterday, then.

When Cort stood, the motion and sound were enough to wake Neder, who jumped to his feet and was at Cort's side before Cort had walked three steps. "How do you feel?"

"All right. A little dizzy, I guess. I'm thirsty. My head itches." Cort's catalog of woes brought a smile to Neder's lips, and Cort smiled, too. "Do you think I can take the bandage off and scratch it?"

"Maybe to the bandage," answered Neder. "We'll have to ask Tirei when he gets up." He glanced at the older man, who moaned and turned over. "It won't be long now. And no to the scratching. Would you like some cold water?"

"That sounds good. What was in that drink Tirei gave me yesterday, anyway?"

"Pain-killer." Neder stooped to pick up a skin of water.

Tirei stirred and sat up. He rubbed his eyes.

"Here," Neder said. "I filled this just last night."

"It tasted awful." Cort took a deep drink from the skin. "This is delicious." He drank again.

"The purpose is not to please your taste," Tirei said. "The drug did its job, and the gem is implanted. That's what's important. How do you feel?"

"I was a little dizzy at first, but I feel better now. When can we do the ceremony?"

"Not today," Tirei answered firmly. "You need a little more time to heal."

Hearing of this further day of delay, Cort felt his chest tighten. He frowned and couldn't keep a whining tone out of his voice. "My head itches."

"It's supposed to itch. That means it's healing. I packed into that bandage herbs to speed the healing. You must leave it alone. Rest today. Maybe tomorrow we'll continue."

There was no use in arguing with Tirei. Cort wandered into the forest nearby. He followed the sound of water rushing over rocks, until he found a splashing, clear, cold stream. He sat at its edge and tried to "hear" with the gem. But he didn't have any idea how to begin. Nothing seemed any different. Yet, the more he listened, the more Cort did hear. Not the words or thoughts of the animals that could be kiri to him, no, but the sounds of the forest.

Cort followed the stream for a while, and came upon a large dhelo in a clearing, its antlers gracing its head like a candelabra. His eyes met those of the dhelo, and neither Cort nor the animal moved. There was something deep in that contact, as if the khenaran itself was watching him. Cort felt as if he might project himself through the creature's eyes into its soul. As if the khenaran was taking him in, and he belonged there.

After a long time, the dhelo slowly lowered its head in Cort's direction, acknowledging him, and then walked off.

It was dinnertime before Cort returned to the camp, hungry and tired and wondering whether the future might be bringing him far more than he'd bargained for.

The next morning, Cort woke feeling both nervous and buoyant, with a knot in his stomach and an expectant smile on his face. Today was the day he'd finally become a hunter!

Tirei and Neder returned Cort's cheery "Good morning!" with solemn, silent nods. Cort was tempted to make a joke about their silence, but he thought better of it, and merely grinned as he waited.

Tirei unwound the bandage from Cort's head and nodded his approval. Then he applied a brownish liquid to the area. Cort reached up and wonderingly felt the hard crystal affixed at his hairline. The skin in the area was tender.

Tirei gently removed Cort's hand.

Still not a word had been spoken.

Tirei mixed herbs from his pouch into a liquid that he boiled over the fire while Neder sat at his side. The hunter seemed perfectly at ease, sitting calmly, his legs crossed, his hands on his thighs.

Cort tried that position for a while, but he couldn't get comfortable in it. He stretched and shifted, and fidgeted and shifted and stretched again as the sun climbed the sky.

Still, neither Tirei nor Neder spoke, and Cort didn't dare speak either.

No visible signal passed between the two forest men, but at noon Neder stood and, without any apparent stiffness, walked over to his pack. He brought out smoked meat and a skin of water, placed them in front of Cort, and spoke. "Eat."

As Cort ate, Tirei took the liquid off the fire. He let it cool until Cort had taken his fill of food and water. Then he and Neder sat in front of Cort.

"We say, Corodh-an-Aran, that this drink wakes the crystal," Tirei said. "But this is not exactly so. In truth, the drink wakes your mind to the crystal. The crystal is just an instrument, but the awakening is permanent. It is your mind that hears. After you drink this, you will be forever changed. Are you ready?"

"You know that I am," Cort said, but the knot in his stomach grew tighter.

"One of the kiri will come," Tirei continued, "but you will have to prove that you are worthy. You will fight. If your will is strong enough, you will win. If you lose, you will likely die, and if you do not die, you will go mad, for the crystal takes its price. Again I ask you, Corodh-an-Aran, are you certain of this decision?"

Cort drew a deep breath and let it out slowly. "Yes. I am."

"Be strong, then, and win. May the forest grant you favor."

Tirei offered the drink, and Cort extended his hand to take it. But Neder put his own hand on Cort's wrist. "Take my knife," he said. "It's a hunter's knife, lightweight and sharp and well balanced. May it serve you well." He handed the knife to Cort.

It was a gift beyond measure, the visible talisman of a spiritual event, and the symbol of the love a father might have for his child. Cort's throat tightened. He tried to speak but couldn't He swallowed and managed a hoarse "Thank you." Cort had never known his own father, and until this moment had never truly understood what he had missed. He threaded the knife's sheath onto his belt.

"I believe that you will win, Cort," Neder said when Cort had finished with the knife. "I wouldn't have brought you here if I didn't believe that."

Cort smiled at his friend, then took the cup.

Unlike Tirei's previous brew, this liquid was smooth and sweet. Cort savored it as he drank. It warmed him inside. He felt alert, but calm. Tirei was saying something, but Cort found it hard to make sense of the words. "The dizzying effect will last for only a few hours, no later than sunset..."

Effect of the drug? But he wasn't dizzy, only...

Neder looked at Cort with concern, then spoke to Tirei. "Are you sure you didn't give him too much?"

"Neder, I know how much to make."

The words made no sense at all, but that didn't bother Cort. It was the tension in their voices that he found hard to take. He stood up and moved farther from the fire.

The forest was lovely and calm; Cort felt better there, away from the other men. Taking a deep breath of the pure air, he tasted the light spicy scent of the khena trees. The voices of the forest were clear and understandable: insects buzzing their contentment, birds chirping a warning, alerting others to his passage. He reached the clearing where yesterday he had seen the dhelo, and four alandhal barely larger than city rats bounded away on powerful hindlegs, their tufted tails flying, their fear palpable. He crossed the clearing, looking for and finding a narrow trail, and he followed it. The path led among boulders, downward toward a stream that Cort could hear but not see.

A bobcat hissed from a boulder in front of Cort, a small female with powerful haunches. *So you want to become a hunter.*

"Yes, I..." Cort began, but the sounds were all wrong. He tried again, finding and using the crystal. *Yes, I do. Can you help me?*

Can, yes, the creature said. *Any of us can. But personally, I think you are a rather pathetic offering, and I would like to change your mind.* Before Cort could frame an answer, the bobcat gathered her haunches and sprang at Cort, claws out, teeth bared, aiming for his face.

Cort's streetfighter instincts were swift and sure. He lashed out with his right arm, striking the bobcat across the throat with the stiffened edge of his hand.

The creature scratched Cort's arm as she fell, but the leap was broken.

Cort threw himself on top of the fallen cat, rolling her onto her stomach. The bobcat yowled and raked her claws back toward Cort. She couldn't reach, but still, she struggled.

Cort gripped her throat. *I didn't deserve that.*

There was a moment of silence, and Cort could feel the bobcat gathering her powerful haunches under herself, her muscles tense and hard.

He tightened his grip.

The cat let out a strangled sound, something that might have wanted to be a growl. She wrestled against him, raked a claw toward his arm, still not reaching.

At last she gave up the fight, struggling only to draw breath. *Peace, Hunter. Let me go. I will attend you.*

Cort let out a breath of relief and sat back, allowing the animal her freedom.

I wouldn't have guessed it of you, Hunter, said the bobcat.

Cort smiled. Hunter. He was a hunter.

The bobcat led Cort farther into the forest. They walked together for a while, but then the cat bounded off to chase an alandhal that started from a bush as they drew near.

Cort walked on by himself. Something glittered in the path, and he bent down to look.

A squawk of rage tore in his ear, and the wind of wings brushed his hair. A hawk, its wingspan as long as Cort's spread arms, circled around to attack again.

What is this? Cort asked.

I will not attend you! screamed the hawk, gathering speed.

That may be, but you won't hurt me, either. Cort ducked to one side as the feathered attacker roared by. He reached out to grab it, but the bird was too fast.

The hawk circled again. *I'll have your eyeballs!*

Cort stood his ground as the great bird plunged at him, talons first. This time, Cort caught one of the hawk's legs, and he swung the bird to the ground.

The hawk scrambled to its feet.

Cort was faster. He caught the hawk's wings as they flapped hard to take to the air again. *Hollow bones,* Cort told the bird. *Lightweight so that you can fly, but so easy to break. Shall I break them?*

The hawk resisted no longer. *No, Hunter.*

Say please.

Please, Hunter.

And you will attend me?

So the forest wills.

Cort relaxed. He sat back and let go of the hawk's wings.

That hurt, complained the bird, shaking itself off.

Cort smiled. *I'm sorry about that. I didn't mean to hurt you, but I wasn't going to give you my eyeballs for dinner, either.*

Ah, yes, the hawk said. *Eyeballs. There was that. And would you like to look at the world through mine?*

Through your eyes? Can I do that?

Watch. The hawk shook out its wings, and with a bound, took flight. Higher and higher it circled. *Close your own eyes, Hunter. Look through mine.*

Cort did as instructed, and gasped with amazement as he watched the khenaran spinning beneath him. Instinctively, he reached for the ground and tried to grab hold of it to keep from falling. He felt at once dizzy and elated. The view was different not only in its perspective from hundreds of feet in the air, but also in the most minute clarity of its detail. Cort doubted that he would see as much detail in the clearing where he sat if he opened his own eyes and looked, as he now did looking down from above at the tiny figure that was himself.

The hawk dove.

Cort cried out, digging into the earth at his side with all the intensity his fingers could manage, ripping at his fingernails. But he didn't open his eyes until the great bird alighted at his side.

What did you think of that, Hunter? asked the hawk.

Cort's heart was still pounding. *It was... staggering. It was wonderful. I want to do that again—often.*

The bird preened its feathers. *I'm sure you'll find the opportunity,* it replied. *I will help you when I can.* The hawk took to the air again. Cort closed his eyes and followed its flight until it was beyond the horizon.

Thirsty, Cort followed a trail that led out of the khenaran toward a stream he could hear splashing among bushes and thick, leafy trees below. He could just see it through the undergrowth when he felt a weight upon his shoulders. Thick ropy coils descended on him, looping from a branch just overhead, glistening gold and green and amber where the sunlight fell upon them.

The serpent tightened around his chest, his arms, and most threateningly, his neck.

The pressure was intense. Cort struggled to pull air past his throat. He tripped over the creature's tail, now seeking a hold on Cort's legs, while he tried to get a fingerhold under the coil around his neck. His nails scratched his own skin, but he managed to work his fingers around the serpent, giving himself some breathing room.

It didn't help. Though Cort squeezed the creature as hard as he could, he didn't seem to affect it. The coils around his chest squeezed so tightly he could barely force his lungs to take in air.

He fought panic, tried to make himself think.

There was only one chance. He had to find the serpent's head.

He saw it, not far from his own face. Its eyes were golden and expressionless; its mouth seemed oddly to be smiling, jaws wide, the grin of a death's-head.

His lungs vainly tried to suck in air.

Cort freed his hand from the coil at his throat. He lunged for, and caught, the serpent's body close to its head. If only he could get his other hand free...

But he could not. And his chest was burning with want of air; the edges of his vision were buzzing black.

His grip on the serpent started to loosen, his strength gone.

A glint caught his eye—sunlight on water.

Water.

Two could play this choking game. Cort began rolling toward the stream. The downhill slope gave him momentum. Rocks bruised his tumbling body, but he took some satisfaction that they must also be hurting the creature that was squeezing his life away.

With a splash they were in the water. The stream was ice-cold, rocky, and shallow. Cort rolled just enough to hold the serpent's head underwater.

Shall we see who dies first? Dizzy from lack of breath, Cort wasn't sure it wouldn't be him. But if he did pass out, he would fall on top of the snake, probably taking it with him.

I yield, Hunter. I will serve you. The serpent's voice sounded—even in his mind—like a hiss, like the wind in dead leaves. Its coils loosened around his body, and Cort drew a deep, half-choking breath.

Chapter 11

Cort's Kiri

The wolves attacked at sunset, when Cort was hungry and tired. He'd been fighting all day, ached from an assortment of scratches and bruises, and felt depressed. He had taken over a shallow cave and established a camp, and was waiting for the bobcat to return with an alandhal or other dinner. He felt the wolves' approach before he saw them—a sense of the mounting excitement of the chase. Cort prepared. He took hold of the spear he had made by tying his knife to a long, straight branch. Backing against the rock wall, he waited.

The wait was short. A pack of yellow-eyed wolves raced around the rock and halted just out of range of the spear tip. They circled hungrily.

Come on, then, Cort said. *What are you waiting for?*

Will you throw it? snarled a wolf, feinting an attack.

Cort's adrenaline shot through his veins. He lunged, drawing the wolf's blood. *I'm not that stupid.*

The wolf howled, and again the pack circled. *You'll have to do better than that, if you want to call yourself a hunter*, said a wolf.

But Cort recognized the bravado of the pack. It wasn't so different from a gang. He watched, lashing out when he saw an opening. One wolf fell, bleeding from the neck. *No, you're the ones that will have to do better than that*, he said, *if you want to call yourselves wolves. I've got all night.*

He studied the animals as they circled, until he felt sure he knew which one led the pack. It was grizzled and older, but also larger and more strongly muscled than most of the others.

Keeping an eye on the pack, Cort paid special attention to the leader. Again a wolf attacked, and again Cort defended. Years on the streets of the city had made him quick. Years of training with Stas had made him agile. He swiped his spear, cutting the wolf on the side of its neck. The animal yowled and retreated. *Perhaps you can hold us off,* conceded the leader, *but you will have to do more than this if you expect us to attend you.*

There was something about how the creature said that last phrase. Cort felt confident at that moment that the wolves would attend him, though he didn't dare relax. He smiled grimly, and lowered his spear, moving his hand closer to the blade.

You've made your last mistake! gloated the leader, and sprang at Cort. Cort could have taken him in the belly then, but his goal was not to kill the beast. He stepped to the side.

The heavy wolf frantically attempted to change course in mid-air, and landed off balance.

Smoothly and quickly, Cort attacked the wolf, grabbing it around its chest and holding his knife steadily at the animal's throat.

It would definitely be a shame to have to kill such a fine animal, Cort mused. The wolf struggled in his arms, but Cort held firm.

You kill me, and the pack will attack you in that instant, the pack leader threatened.

This was pure gang bullying, and Cort knew how to handle it. *So many of us would die,* he said. *Attend me, and I will let you all live.*

I will not! growled the animal.

Then maybe your successor will. Cort pressed the knife harder at the animal's throat. A tiny rivulet of blood trickled down its neck. *Or maybe he will lead the pack away to safety, and your death will be for nothing.*

The pack leader did not answer.

Who will succeed this wolf? Cort asked the pack. *Agree to attend me, and I will kill him for you.*

Hold, Hunter. The pack leader sighed. *I will not have you sow dissension among us. It is the one thing a wolf pack must not have. We will attend you.* Not a wolf objected. The frantic circling stopped as the pack awaited the hunter's decision.

Cort lowered his knife.

The pack leader rose to his feet, shaking his fine coat of fur. He walked slowly back to the pack, his tail down, seemingly exhausted by the struggle. A younger, bristly wolf advanced to meet him. *I challenge you, old one,* growled the younger wolf.

The leader growled back, but Cort cried, *No!*

This is not your affair, Hunter, said the pack leader.

It's my affair because I'm the one who injured you. Cort turned to the challenger. *In two days, when the wound I gave him has healed, you may fight if you want, but not now.*

The challenger's yellow eyes assessed the young hunter. *I will wait the two days.*

The day after tomorrow, Hunter, you must come hunt with us, said the pack leader. *At the end of the hunt, we will do what we must.*

Cort agreed, and the wolves left calmly at a slow trot, in marked contrast to their arrival.

He felt lonely when they were gone. He missed the camaraderie they shared with one another, that he'd had with his gang in the city. He missed Dilia, Neder, even Tirei. He wondered if he should have gone with the wolves, but he was even more tired than he was lonely. He found a relatively smooth, mossy spot just inside the cave's mouth and settled down to sleep, only to realize that he'd left his spear outside. Sighing, he got up and went out to get it.

Something zoomed out of the darkness, biting or scratching Cort's ankle deeply as it raced off again. The attack was all the more vicious because he hadn't expected it.

"Ow!" His voice echoed strangely from the rocks. He huddled against the rock wall. He tried to examine his ankle, but couldn't see much in the dark. However, the feel of his warm blood flowing was unmistakable. *I'll get you for this,* he swore.

The pronouncement was greeted with amusement. *You'll have to be quick—and see well in the dark. You'll never know where I'll be coming from.*

It was true. The moon hadn't yet risen, and Cort could barely make out anything among the dark trees. Only the rock seemed slightly paler than the dark forms around him. *Who are you?* he asked.

More amusement.

Despite himself, Cort smiled.

Ferret, came the answer.

Cort remembered the playful, loyal creature that attended Neder. Of course, this wouldn't be the same one, but he was still well disposed toward the small hunters. *I don't want to fight you,* Cort said. *Can't we just work this out somehow?*

Are you afraid of me? asked the ferret coyly.

It was a good question. The ferret had already succeeded in hurting him more than the bobcat, hawk, serpent, and wolves combined. Another few blows like that last, and he'd be in danger from blood loss alone. And darkness and stealth were in the ferret's favor. Cort's heart pounded.

Yes, he answered truthfully as he began to unlash his knife from the branch that had served as a spear-pole. *But I've been afraid before. I would fight you despite fear.* A knot resisted his prying fingernails. *That's not why I don't want to fight you.* There! He had it. The knife came free in his hands.

The ferret streaked toward him, but Cort was ready. His knife flashed, and the small creature quickly veered away, unable to harm him, but deftly avoiding Cort's knife.

Purely defensive, said the ferret. *You'll have to do better than that. Why don't you want to fight me, then?*

Because I like you.

Nothing moved in the forest. Even the insects were silent. Cort strained to see where the ferret might be, but he saw only blackness. Could ferrets climb rocks? Cort shivered, and pressed his back closer to the wall.

The silence was ominous. Cort wondered what the ferret could be planning.

Why do you like me? asked the ferret. *I have done nothing to earn your favor. Face it; in the dark a human is no match for a ferret.* With amusement, the small creature added, *Maybe not in daylight, either. I could be ready to strike from where you least expect it, even now.*

The words were frightening. Somehow, Cort managed to press even more closely against the rock. *Attack me, and I'll kill you if I can,* he said.

What? I thought you liked me. The ferret seemed genuinely hurt.

Liking has nothing to do with it. Cort forced his fingers to relax where he gripped the knife too hard. He was sweating, and the pounding of his heart threatened to mask any noise the creature might make in its approach. *I like you because of how you seem to be enjoying yourself and me and everything about this situation. I like you because you're a ferret, and I like ferrets. But I'm also afraid of you right at the moment because you're a ferret, and you can be deadly dangerous.*

In both those judgments, you show good sense, said the ferret with a hint of self-satisfaction. *Is it true that you humans are almost blind in the dark?*

Cort looked around again. He could barely distinguish the horizon that separated the deep black of the forest from the starry black of the sky. *Yes, it's true.*

Then how can you hope to fight what you cannot see?

Because I must, Cort said. *And, ferret, because I want you for an ally. I guess you ferrets can see quite well in the dark?*

Close your eyes and look, Hunter.

Cort thought that perhaps he had misunderstood, or perhaps the ferret planned some devious trick. Sensing Cort's reluctance, the ferret added, *Go ahead and close them, before I change my mind. They are useless to you anyway.*

Cort closed his eyes, and the world around him exploded into shape and substance. It was lit with an eerie, pale light that was different from, yet like moonlight. Cort could see each line of bark, each leaf, each etched vein of rock with a clarity that would have been beyond him even in the daylight. From a perspective just a few inches off the ground, he was looking at himself not even four feet away. The view threw him off balance. Had his back not been braced against the wall, he would have fallen. Instinctively, Cort opened his eyes and looked back in the direction from which he had, just a moment ago, been watching himself. He could see nothing. He closed his eyes, and there was the world again in all its eerie detail.

You would have been hard to fight, Cort conceded. *What an advantage!*

Yes, I think so. The ferret was clearly having a marvelously good time.

So why did you give in?

Hunter, it was because you asked. And you asked so nicely.

Cort took, and let out, a deep breath. Then he carefully sat down. *I need to look at this wound*, he said.

I really got you good, didn't I?

Yes, ferret, you really did.

The ferret bounded over to Cort's side and allowed him to see the wound through its eyes. A deep gash ran across the side of Cort's ankle, more likely a scratch than a bite. When Cort wiggled his foot to check its range of movement, blood gushed out of the wound, but the foot moved freely. Despite the blood, Cort decided that the wound was superficial.

The ferret helped Cort find his way to the stream and watched with interest as he washed the wound and bound it with a strip that he cut from his clothing. Then the little creature helped him see his way back to the cave and, admonishing him impishly to be careful in the dark, left him to try to get some sleep.

But sleep did not come. Although he was exhausted, Cort was too tense to sleep, too afraid of the next attack that might come in the darkness. When the moon finally rose, he took his knife and went out of the cave, searching the forest for anything else that might be preparing to attack him in the night. In the moonlight, the forest was still. Deep under its leafy canopy, where the moonlight penetrated only dimly, Cort could make out nothing. An attacker could easily be lurking. But he could do nothing except fantasize about the situation; he turned to go back into the cave.

Thus it was that the great owl was able to swoop silently down upon Cort from behind.

Cort fought the owl, and exacted its promise to watch over him that night as he tried to sleep. But he was still too tense, and sleep did not come.

The next day, Cort fought a pair of cougars and a fox. In each of these battles, Cort overcame his opponents, but always he paid a price. By the time the sun disappeared behind the trees, leaving the forest in somber shadow, Cort lay exhausted on the moss of the forest floor, wounded, battered, his clothing torn, no longer caring whether his next opponent took him from behind or not. He had neither eaten nor slept since the morning of the previous day, and his energy was spent.

A bobcat padded up to the supine hunter. *Get up, Hunter. Please,* she urged.

Go away. I need to sleep. He didn't move, didn't even open his eyes.

Yes, you need to sleep, agreed the little cat. *You also need to drink and eat. Come with me; there is a stream not far from here.*

Go away.

The bobcat industriously began licking Cort's face, as if he were one of her kittens. Her tongue felt at once scratchy and rough and tender and tickly and soothing. Cort smiled. Then he opened his eyes. *What do you want?*

I brought you some food, Hunter. She stopped her licking to fetch a piece of meat, already torn into a small piece, and pushed it toward Cort's mouth. He accepted the offering. It was ragged and raw and slippery with the little cat's saliva, but the smell of the fresh meat made his stomach rumble. He put it in his mouth and began chewing. The meat was tender; its blood, satisfying. *That's good*, he said. *Thank you.*

There's more. When Cort didn't complain, the bobcat brought a small pile of meat to him. She sat silently as he ate, but as soon as he'd finished and his eyes started to close again, she nudged his cheek.

Now what?

You need to drink.

I need to sleep.

Yes, Hunter, that too. But drink first. Come. I will show you.

Cort groaned and sat up. Slowly, he stood. The bobcat padded away, looking back over her shoulder, and Cort followed. The stream wasn't far. It was just a trickle, but it was cold and clear. The bobcat crouched at the stream's edge and lapped the water with her tongue. Cort lay down on his stomach beside her and used his hand to scoop the water into his mouth. After drinking his fill, Cort rolled over without getting up, and fell asleep beside the little brook. He was dimly aware of the bobcat's presence as she guarded him that night, and he slept without waking until long after dawn.

When Cort opened his eyes, the bobcat was nowhere to be seen, and he was surrounded by wolves. The air was thick with their scent, and Cort felt their hunger deep in his own gut. Hunger for food, yes, and even more so for the chase and the kill.

Are you ready, Hunter? asked the pack leader.

More than ready, he was eager. *Do we hunt today?*

So you have promised.

Then that's what we'll do. Cort stood carefully. His entire body ached from the previous day's injuries, but the pain had lessened. He washed and got ready, taking the time to examine his cuts, scratches, and bruises. One arm was stiff, with a large bruise near the elbow. All the open wounds were already healing, especially the big gash on his ankle that had so worried him. Not a bad morning. Good day for a hunt.

As the wolf pack fanned out, searching for game, Cort stayed with the leader. The wolf's easy lope, seemingly so effortless, went on for mile after hungry mile. Suddenly, a small dhelo buck leapt from a thicket in front of them and ran toward them, followed closely by the wolf that had flushed it out.

Yours, if you want him, Hunter, said the pack leader.

Without a word, Cort drew his knife and threw. It landed true in the frightened animal's throat, and the buck fell as he ran. The wolves swarmed over the animal, biting and tearing pieces according to some order known only to them. They made room as the pack leader approached, and none argued as he offered Cort the heart.

It was bloody and still warm. It would not have been his choice. But he understood that the wolf offered more than just food. It was an honor bestowed only to members of the pack, and he accepted it. The sense of belonging, the warmth of brotherhood was deeper even than in his gang in the city. He cut the organ out with his knife, then cut it in half and offered half back to the pack leader. The wolf ate it greedily, but Cort found it tough. He chewed for a long time before he could swallow; then he cut himself a piece of more tender meat from one of the animal's haunches.

In the afternoon, full and content, the wolves napped. Cort slept too, curled up among the warm, furry bodies like another pup in a litter. Before sunset, they hunted again, and the honor of the kill went not to Cort nor to the pack leader, but to one of the younger wolves in the pack. They ate until it was too dark to see. Any challenge to the pack leader's authority seemed to have vanished. Cort slept with the wolves again that night.

The next morning they were up with the dawn. Cort rose and stretched, feeling the stiffness of old aches and healing wounds and a day spent running. He could do this forever, this running and hunting and living in the great forest. The spiced scent of the khena mingled with the musky smell of his pack-mates, and it was all good, life as it should be lived.

But... there was Dilia. He would not forget his purpose. *I have to go back to the other humans,* he said to the wolves.

Yes, answered the pack leader. *It is fitting. Your friends left the ceremonial place in the afternoon before yesterday, but this is not important. We are as far from there as from the village. We will travel with you, if you wish.*

Yes, of course. In truth, Cort was happy for the guidance of someone who knew the way.

They hunted again as they traveled, and it was only natural to stop to enjoy the kill. Cort reserved one dhelo, a small doe that he could carry across his shoulders, to bring back to the village. This slowed the pace. It was mid-afternoon by the time the village came into view.

Cort watched the village for a few moments, searching for words or concepts or ideas that would serve him, some way to come back from the wild place he had been inhabiting. He understood now that the crystal he'd been so avidly seeking was not only a gift but a danger, for the bond the crystal forged went far deeper than mere communication. It would be possible—no, easy—never to come back at all, and this would not serve him, or Dilia, or the kiri that had named him Hunter.

He turned to say good-bye one last time to the wolves, but the pack had already melted back into the forest.

Even after just two days with the wolves, Cort felt the shyness of a wild creature near humans. He wasn't ready. Maybe he needed a few more days alone in the khenaran, the enveloping, nurturing forest.

No, after a few days he would need another few days, and then another. Did some hunters go completely feral and never return? The idea enticed him like the promise of a free trip to Earth, but it was not for him. Not yet. Every day he delayed was a day he might be too late to rescue Dilia.

He took a deep breath and walked toward the village

A boy playing in front of his house was the first to see the returning hunter. His eyes widened. He dropped the stick that he was trying to fashion into a spear, and ran off calling, "Neder! Neder, come quickly!"

When Neder saw the young hunter, his eyes lit up and he rushed toward him. "We were worried, we expected you back two days ago. But you're all right?"

Cort could find no words. This was too soon, too sudden. He took a step back, ready to bolt into the woods.

Neder halted and held up both hands, palms out. He took one careful step forward, then another, slowly closing the gap between them. And all the while he spoke soothingly as he might to a wild creature, until he was close enough to touch.

"Welcome home, Hunter," he said quietly. "I hope you will stay with us a while." Formal words, a ceremony to bridge the gap.

Cort nodded. He pulled the formal response up from some recess of his memory. *I brought*— No, not like that. He had to find speech and use it. "I... brought..." The shape of the words seemed strange in his mouth. "I brought... this..." He shifted the dhelo on his shoulders. "...for you."

Neder took the doe from Cort's shoulders onto his own. "We thank you, Hunter. The village thanks you. Tonight we will feast in your honor." He smiled and indicated the village with a tilt of his head. A few people had gathered. "Will you come with me?"

"Yes." He recollected his friend's name and spoke it. "Neder."

Neder waited patiently as a moment of silence stretched into two, then four.

It was hard to form the concepts, the words—but less hard than a moment ago. "Thank you. I'm... glad to be here."

The two hunters walked together into the village, stopping only to hand the dhelo to a villager who would help in its preparation. "There's Tirei," Neder said, and indeed the old man was walking toward them. "He'll want to see you."

"Yes. I do." The approaching headman smiled, then squinted at Cort and wrinkled his nose. "You're covered with blood and dirt. Your clothes are torn. And you smell like... a wild animal. Let's get you bathed, eh, and some fresh clothes? Did you know your eyes have turned completely yellow? I'm surprised they're not slitted into the bargain."

So many words! Cort had almost forgotten they could be fountained like this, and he laughed. The two older men relaxed.

They came to the stream near the village, and Cort removed his clothing, torn and bloodied beyond repair, and waded in up to his waist. "Cold!" He shivered exaggeratedly and ducked under. When he came up, he wiped the dripping water from his face and pushed back his wet hair. "That feels... good," he said. "Thank you."

The smell of cooking drifted to them on the breeze. Cort's stomach growled. Tonight he would eat his meat cooked with vegetables and herbs, as humans do. It was good to be back.

"Who were you hunting with?" asked Neder. "Wolves?"

"Yes. How did you know? Have you hunted with wolves too?"

Neder shrugged. "Just a guess. From your... condition. No, I haven't done it myself. My kiri is a ferret, you remember."

"Oh, you should try it! I mean, the ferret is really wonderful, of course, but the wolves..." He shook his head and laughed with the joy of them.

"Don't let it go to your head," Neder snapped. "You're lucky, with the wolves, but it takes a lot more than a kiri to make a real hunter." He turned and walked back toward his house.

At a loss, Cort exchanged a look with Tirei. "I didn't mean to make him angry."

"It's not you that he's angry with. Seeing your success with the wolves, he's remembering his son. It was wolves that killed Sarel, and Neder still blames himself. He'll get over it. He'll be back in a little while. Meanwhile, let's get you dried off."

Cort stepped out of the cold water, shivering. He wrapped himself in the soft fawnskin Tirei handed him. "Tirei," he asked, "when Neder said that his kiri is a ferret, did he mean that the ferret is the only one?"

"Yes. That's the normal situation."

"I have a ferret kiri." When Tirei raised an eyebrow, Cort added, "Also a bobcat, a pair of cougars, and a few more, too."

Disbelief flared in Tirei's eyes, but seeing Cort's earnestness, he drew in a breath and then nodded. "I see."

"Is it unusual?"

"Very. Bobcats, of course, are not uncommon. Cougars are rare, like wolves, especially a pair of them. But all of these together... I've never heard of such a thing."

Cort frowned. "What does it mean?"

Tirei watched as Cort dried himself. "You look much better," he said. "Most of that blood was just on your skin. I don't know what it means, but the forest will reveal its purposes in its time."

Cort thought about that as he dressed in the new clothes Tirei had brought. "I'm going to have to tell Neder," he said at last.

"Break it to him gently," the seer said. And then he spoke the young hunter's name as if it were a benediction: "Corodh-an-Aran." He looked at Cort with a gentle sympathy that suggested Cort had no chance of ever leading a normal life. It made Cort's blood run cold, and he shivered.

"Is it that bad?" Cort searched the seer's eyes for some glimmer of hope but saw none. "What does it mean?"

"I don't know, Cort. One kiri, that's normal. Two, all right. But how many did you reel off? Six? Seven?"

Heat rose to Cort's face. He hadn't mentioned the hawk, the owl, the serpent... and were there others? He looked away, saying nothing.

Tirei shook his head, a man face to face with an inscrutable mystery. "I just don't know."

⁂

After a day of recovery in the village under Tirei's ministrations, Cort felt healthy enough to start his journey back to the city. His minor cuts and bruises were well on their way to healing, and Dilia was again foremost in his mind. The following morning, he gathered his few belongings and sought out Tirei and Neder.

"So, you are on your way," the seer said. "I expected as much. May your journey be safe and successful."

"Good-bye." Cort hugged Tirei, who stiffened slightly, then relaxed. "I can't thank you enough."

"No thanks are due," the seer said, giving Cort a pat on the back. "It is my duty to assist anyone who is as ready and eager as you. With the whynywir's permission, of course."

"Well, then thank them for me, too." Cort turned to Neder. "Thank you, too, my good friend," he said.

"No thanks are due," answered the hunter, echoing Tirei. "Good luck with your girl. We'll expect to see the two of you back here."

"If it's possible, I'll do it. I can't complain any more about not having a kiri."

Neder folded his arms across his chest and said nothing.

Cort had meant the comment as a joke, but he'd hurt his friend. He touched Neder's shoulder. "I didn't mean that... the way it must have sounded. Please come with me."

They'd been over this a dozen times, and Neder's face reflected his oft-repeated decision. "No. I'm finished with that city. I'm not going back. This is your work, not mine."

"But then, who's going to teach me to be a *real* hunter?" Cort couldn't keep the smile out of one corner of his mouth. "I could use the help."

"Get your dozens of kiri to help you. If you practice your woodland skills on the journey, there's hope you'll be a real hunter someday yet." Neder's expression was still sour, but his eyes softened with laughter.

Cort saw the twinkle in Neder's eyes, and he grinned. "I'll try, Neder."

The hawk guided him. The fox and the bobcat brought him food. The playful ferret appeared and disappeared from time to time to tease and cajole him and play hide-and-seek among the trees, a game the ferret never tired of playing, and never lost. As he defeated Cort, the ferret taught him, and Cort grew in skill as the days passed. He learned to move quickly and quietly, to gauge the direction of the wind, and to blend into the landscape among the trees. He also practiced using the sling that Neder had given him, and several times killed an alandhal on his own.

Cort felt guilty for the travel time he lost while he learned the ways of his many kiri. Every hour he delayed increased his worry for Dilia. But if he needed a kiri or two to rescue Dilia, then surely he also needed to understand how best to work with them.

The first nightmare came just two days away from Neder's village. Cort dreamed that, in the flames of their burning house, he could hear his mother crying, "Cort! Cort! Save me! Please! Come save me!" Her voice twisted with urgency.

But smoke choked his nostrils, and the intense heat of the flames was like a wall. He cried out to her and pushed against that wall, but he could not penetrate it, could not save his mother from the fire. He woke sweating and gasping for breath. The eastern sky was slightly lighter than the west. Cort didn't try to go back to sleep. As soon as the hawk returned, he was on his way.

Two days later, he dreamed that Dilia was chained to one of the great trees of the forest, and the harvester was approaching, the growling of its motor growing louder and louder. She turned to him, tears running from her eyes. "Help me," she whispered. Cort moved to reach her, but he, too, was chained. The machine was so loud that Cort was certain it was about to come into view. He was sick with urgency and helplessness. He woke troubled and unbalanced.

He determined to make do with only about four hours of sleep, four exhausted, dreamless hours—but still he dreamed.

Cort dreamed again of the fire. The smoke smelled of burning flesh. The heat of the fire singed his hair, melted his skin, threw him back from the doorway.

Afraid of his dreams, he began to postpone going to sleep and slept as little as he could.

As if aware of the hunter's wakefulness at night, an owl appeared and began teaching him. Cort sat, his back propped against a tree, his eyes closed, watching the forest through the owl's eyes as she hunted her prey and taught him to recognize the sounds and smells of the night.

Chapter 12

Dilia Attempts to Escape

F or Dilia, the mornings were the worst. Every morning, when she woke, she felt dizzy and exhausted. The bed, with its soft covers, invited her to stay and sleep all day, and she didn't have the energy to refuse. But Abeni took to coming in the morning to rouse her, to help her bathe and groom herself and get dressed. Abeni would then help her traverse the distance from the commandant's residence to the infirmary, and the walk in the fresh air invariably made Dilia feel better. Once in the infirmary, Abeni would open the window by the table where Dilia sat and studied, as wide as the weather permitted. Usually, by lunchtime, Dilia felt almost entirely well.

Dilia threw herself into her study of the native plants, and evidently Abeni considered this good for her. She lent her a tablet from the infirmary and helped her to download the data that had been collected about Aran when the people from Earth first arrived, and all that had been gathered since. She even let Dilia take the tablet back to her room in the evenings, but Dilia had trouble breathing in the room. She was usually so tired by dinnertime that she seldom used the tablet there.

Dilia had been feeling weak and sick for a week now, maybe two. Maybe longer. It was hard for her to keep track of the time. It had been a long time, in any case, long enough that living on the aliens' base had begun to feel like her normal life.

"Are you feeling up for a walk?" Abeni asked. It was a rare quiet noonday, when the infirmary was completely empty of patients. "I think the fresh air will probably be good for you."

"Oh, yes! I'd like that. There's been a breeze here all morning, and I'm feeling fine."

They strolled the perimeter of the base, close to the wall, but not so close as to penetrate the invisible forcefield just inside it. A slight breeze blew across the base from the woods beyond, fresh and clear, with no hint of the staleness in the commander's house or the antiseptic cleanliness of the infirmary, and not the least familiar smells of cooking and garbage that permeated the city below. Dilia breathed deeply and smiled. It smelled to her like a new beginning.

They walked to the uppermost corner of the base, the port where the aliens' starships took off and landed. The port was seldom empty. There was room only for one ship, but Dilia remembered from Cort's lessons that incoming ships often waited in high orbit until the berth opened up. Harvesting, she'd learned, was constant and efficient. Cort and she had worked a problem set where they'd had to calculate the cost of a single hour's delay in getting the khena wood back to Earth to be processed and sold. The cost of the next ship idling in orbit for a few days was miniscule in comparison.

The ship here today was being loaded and would soon depart. Its silver skin shone in the sunlight, towering over the staging facility, where gravlevs heavy with khena wood still waited to be loaded. Two other gravlevs were filled with luggage, and several people waited nearby.

"People going back to Earth. They're lucky. Their tours are over." The longing in Abeni's voice was unmistakable.

Dilia turned to look at her, but Abeni's gaze was fixed on the scene. "I have six more months here," Abeni said. She took in a deep breath, then let it out with an audible whoosh. "Then it's home to Earth, and away from..." She let the sentence drop, but her hand made a small sweeping motion that might have encompassed the base, the city, and all of Aran.

All at once Dilia felt a deep empathy for the alien doctor. They both ached to go home. But Abeni would have been away for two years, the length of her tour. And because of the relativity of space travel, she would arrive back on Earth twenty-six years after she left. Her classmates and friends would now be parents or even grandparents, and there would be things on Earth changed beyond her recognition. "Oh, Abeni, this must be so hard for you! I can't even imagine... all the years..."

"They pay me very well," Abeni said. "I'll be able to retire in comfort when I return, if I want."

"So, it's worth it, for you?"

Abeni put a hand on Dilia's shoulder and gave it a little pat. "I thought when I did my fellowship and enlisted, that it would be worth it, yes. And it might have been, under other circumstances. But as it is..." She shrugged.

"As it is, yes," Dilia echoed, feeling a sudden sadness about her own situation. "Abeni, could you tell me more about that innoculation you gave me the first day I was here."

"Oh, that." Abeni studied the ground in front of her. "Prevents you from getting certain diseases. Nothing to worry about."

"You said, 'Unwanted pregnancy.' How does that work? Forever? Or only for now?"

"Nothing is forever," Abeni said. "Even this base may not be here forever." She frowned and took a step away. "Look! What's this?" She stooped down and plucked a small flower.

Dilia's heart sank. There could only be one reason Abeni didn't answer her question, the effect must be permanent. She felt tears burning at her eyes.

But Abeni was holding out the flower and smiling. Perhaps Dilia was mistaken. Perhaps the doctor thought she *had* answered the question. *Nothing is forever.*

Dilia took the flower. It was actually a small stem of flowers, only about ten centimeters long, with eight tiny dark red buds. The bottom two had already blossomed into pale lavender flowers. The holo image she'd studied had been larger, and there were more flowers. But of course the image was probably magnified, and this stem was only starting to bloom. "Dewdrops!" she said. "Right?"

"Why, I don't know. You've studied the native plants a lot more than I have." Abeni took out her comm, keyed in a few commands, and pulled out a holo image. "Dewdrops, it is. Good job! Useful, according to native lore, for stomach and digestive tract disturbances."

Dilia felt a surge of excitement. "Can we use them?"

"Wouldn't hurt to try a little, if we get someone with an upset stomach."

"I brought a bag we can use to gather some. Let's see what else we can find."

They studied plants along the perimeter of the base for the rest of the afternoon, and when they returned to the infirmary, they had identified six different plants that were thought to have some medicinal value.

A knock on Dilia's door shortly after her return to her room signaled the timely arrival of her dinner. She grimaced. Why couldn't they at least let her eat dinner with Abeni? In the infirmary, or in the officers' dining room, or anywhere but here?

She took a deep breath and turned to face the door. "Come in."

But it wasn't dinner. The commandant came in and closed the door behind him. "Sit down, sit." He sat down on the bed as usual and gestured to the space beside him.

Dilia ignored the gesture as she always did. She pulled up a chair and sat across from him.

But this visit was somehow different. Karim bent over so that he rested his elbows on his knees and covered his eyes with the palms of his hands.

Dilia bit her lip, thinking. Something was clearly bothering him. He must have wanted to talk with her, or he wouldn't have come here, would he? Was he waiting for her to ask? She steeled her courage. "What is it? What's the matter?"

Eyes still covered, he shook his head. Then, slowly, he took his hands away. "I have a headache, that's all. Long day, lots of problems. Nothing you'd understand."

Now, that was condescending! Dilia felt her cheeks grow hot, and she pulled back as if he'd slapped her. "How do you know? Try me."

"One of the harvesters has broken down, and they're going to have to fabricate the replacement part. It will take four days to get the part out to where the harvester is, and another day to do the repair. At best. So the harvester is going to be almost a week late meeting the ship that is expecting to be loaded up the day after tomorrow, delaying take-off by that much, and so on, rippling down the schedule." He rubbed his hand over his face.

It seemed that once he got started with this tale of woe, there would be no stopping him. But Dilia didn't want to stop him. She much preferred letting him talk to her about his problems over enduring his advances. "I'm sorry."

He grimaced. "That's not the worst of it. There's a visitor aboard that incoming ship. Someone important, a person who will be able to carry a first-hand report of the incident back to Earth. And he has the ear of the higher-ups. He'll report that I should have planned for this, should have had the spare part on board. I don't think he can get me fired, but this is definitely the kind of thing that could affect my standing when I get back home. Aren't you glad you asked?" He let out a low moan. "And on top of it all," he went on without waiting for Dilia's response, "I have a splitting headache."

Dilia considered. Surely he would have gone to the infirmary today if his headache was so bad, but he hadn't. Perhaps he already had whatever medication Abeni would give him, from an earlier visit. But clearly, if he had taken it, it wasn't working. Did he know that she had been studying the native plants? Probably. Maybe he was here because he wanted to try something different, but what would happen to her if it didn't work? The aliens looked human enough, but there were physiological differences. What if something about the native plants made him sick?

No, what kind of healer would she be if she didn't try something? "I can't do anything about your harvester scheduling," she said cautiously, "but I might have something that could help with your headache."

He smiled, just a wry quirk at the corner of his mouth. "A nice massage, maybe?"

It had become a game, a not-quite-playful ritual they'd gone through many times, and it no longer frightened her as much as it used to. "Now, Karim, you know—"

He made a placating motion with one hand: calm down.

She continued before he could speak. "But I could make you a little tisane. There's a plant that my people use to ease headaches. Maybe it would help you too."

"Right. That, and some reason, no doubt, why you have to go back down to the city for one thing or another to make it work."

Her first thought was an angry one. Did he think this was just some kind of a ploy? Her fists clenched. "No!" On the other hand, she rather wished she'd thought of something like that. He wasn't that far off the mark. "No," she said more calmly. "It's just an herbal cure. Why not give it a try?"

He studied her face, looking, she imagined, for some clue whether he could trust her. She must have passed, for he smiled and said, "Why not indeed?"

He never took his eyes off her as she poured hot water over the freshly picked leaves and buds, but he hesitated to drink the tisane.

"Oh, by all the stars in the galaxy! You are going to give *me* a headache, and then I'll drink this myself! I am trying to *help* you, not harm you!"

He nodded slowly. "Abeni says you would make an excellent doctor." He quaffed the liquid. "Let's have dinner, shall we?"

Dilia drew back.

"Oh, for Earth's sake," he said. "Just give me a little companionship, would you? I've had a tough day. We'll eat together, and then you'll give me a friendly kiss goodnight, and I'll leave. All I want is a fair chance."

A fair chance, this was not, whatever he might think or say. Dilia wanted to tell him that if he really wanted something fair, he would let her return to her own home. But because she was in his power and this was not fair, she kept silent.

The next day, Dilia's mind was in a turmoil. Karim's headache had disappeared by the time the dinner arrived. He'd been jubilant, declaring her his "savior" and promising that her remedies would be made available in the infirmary from now on.

By making herself so useful, she had completely outwitted herself. If she'd ever had any hope that Karim might eventually let her go home, she no longer did. She would die of old age before Karim ever let her off the base. Her only consolation was that he now allowed her to walk outside every day, though only on the base, to search for the medicinal plants she'd identified. There was plenty of good, fresh air outside, particularly away from the more densely built areas of the base.

A soldier from among Karim's personal guard accompanied her on these forays. These soldiers were invariably taciturn, responding to Dilia's attempts at conversation with a grunt or a nod, or a "Yes'm" or "No'm." They never relaxed, and they never smiled. Dilia tried to pretend that they had been assigned to protect her from some danger she couldn't imagine, but she knew the truth. They were there to prevent her from trying to escape.

Dilia went in different directions each day, hoping to see some opportunity that might allow her to escape the base. On her third day of this activity, she noticed next to the wall a small clump of plants with tall branches covered in tiny leaves, called "haleya" in the data she'd read, and potentially useful to relieve muscle cramps when worked into a salve. It was a good excuse to get a closer look at the wall, and she started walking in that direction.

"Stop!" The soldier's loud command conveyed both authority and something else. Fear?

Dilia's heart gave a loud thump. She stopped. "What's the matter? I'm just going to look at that plant—"

"Two more steps," said the soldier, "and you'll fry. And I'll be demoted for it."

"What? Why?"

The soldier exhaled a sharp, scoffing breath. "See that box over there?" A black box, a cube maybe half a meter on a side, was mounted on a concrete pad about a meter inside the wall. "And there?" He pointed in the other direction, where a similar box sat. "Force field relays. No one can get within a meter of the wall and live."

Dilia's gaze shifted from one box to the other. Further along the wall, she could also glimpse a third box through the plants that grew wild here. "I can't... go near the wall... anywhere?"

Grim faced, the soldier shook his head. "The force field runs from the gate along the whole length of the wall and back to the gate again. Continuous. Gate's the only place you can get near the wall."

Dilia nodded solemnly. She tried to match the soldier's neutral expression, but her heart sank. If what he said was true, her best idea—no, her *only* idea—for how to escape had proved infeasible. "I guess I'll have to look for haleya plants somewhere else." She made her tone as nonchalant as she could. "Let's head over to the area near the port."

The soldier gave his assent, and they walked back into the more densely settled part of the base on their way up to the port.

The weedy clearing near the wall gave way to gardens and individual houses built mostly of concrete or stucco and painted white, with dark gray roofs. A few small vehicles of Earthish manufacture were parked along the roadway they followed, but the road was empty of traffic. In about ten minutes, the buildings had grown denser, offices or workplaces of some sort, perhaps. A cross street opened up a short block away to some kind of square, where a lot of people had gathered. A few more walked by Dilia and the soldier, on their way to or from the square.

"What's this?" Dilia asked.

"Central plaza," said the soldier. "Fourth day market. You won't find any plants there. Keep moving."

The idea of going to a market reminded Dilia of the countless times she and Mara had gone together. Back home. She stumbled. How was Mara? Did she miss Dilia? And Cort. Dilia wished she could find out somehow whether he was all right. This not-knowing was almost as bad as not being there. Her throat tightened, and she felt the sting of new tears. No, not in front of the soldier, she wouldn't cry. Quickly, she wiped the tears away.

<hr>

Five days later, the ship that had been docked at the port since Dilia arrived at the base, took off. With the same antigrav thruster technology that powered the gravlevs, it was almost silent. She'd been transfixed by this event since childhood, but she'd never seen a lift-off so close up. Sunlight glinted off its silvery hull as it rose. Going to Earth. She and Cort had once dreamed of being on such a ship—but no longer. She let out a deep sigh and turned her gaze again to the ground and the plants that grew there.

The following day, a new ship arrived. Karim had mentioned that this ship had waited an extra week or so in orbit because a harvester had been late. It was carrying some kind of special person with high connections on Earth, and Karim had been afraid of a bad report.

Funny, the commandant, of all people, worrying about a bad report, but of course he must be accountable to someone on Earth, and they would want their shipments on time. Dilia wondered what this high-ranking person from Earth would be like. She imagined someone stiff and pompous and unlikeable. She hoped she didn't have to meet him.

In fact, Dilia did not meet the newcomer that day, but Karim came to her room the next evening.

"I could use a hug," he said.

Dilia backed away.

He put both his hands up, shoulder height, palms out. "Just joking."

But of course, he wasn't. Not entirely. She attempted a smile that he might interpret as, "Yes, I knew that."

"As you know," he went on, "I have a visitor." He looked away, frowning. "The last thing I need right now, but I need to treat him well. Tour of the base and so on. He's expressed an interest in the natives, so I'll have to take him out into the city as well, and all the security that will entail."

The city! Dilia brightened. "I could translate," she offered.

He smiled and shook his head. "No, my little Dilia, what you need to do is just stay out of sight. No infirmary duty tomorrow, understood? Maybe you could just go gather your little plants out there in some remote part of the base all day, okay?"

It didn't seem like a bad way to spend the day. Better than translating for some pompous official, actually. "Okay."

"I'm afraid my personal guard will be busy with me tomorrow, so you'll be on your own. You understand, don't you?"

She did, and it was a relief. One day to explore on her own. But she didn't want to appear too eager. She made herself hesitate as if she was uncertain, then said, "The company is nice, of course, but I'll be all right."

"Of course you will. I'd feel better if I had a guard protecting you, but I'm sure you'll be perfectly safe. Just don't go near the barracks."

Dilia nodded. "Don't worry. I'll stay away from the barracks. There probably aren't very many plants around there anyway, with everyone tramping back and forth all the time."

He laughed and gave her a hug without asking permission. Dilia stiffened. In truth, the greatest danger she faced on the base was Karim, and he'd be busy tomorrow. Perfectly safe, indeed.

Karim sighed, shook his head, and let her go.

The next day, a soldier came to escort Dilia from the house. He led her upstairs, and as they passed the room Karim used as an office, Karim called out. "Corporal!"

The soldier stopped and drew himself up to attention. "Sir!"

Karim was standing by his desk, and next to him stood another alien, a man Dilia didn't know. He was taller than Karim, and thinner. His hair and eyes were a light color, and he smiled at her when their gazes met. So this was the new arrival that Karim had fretted about. He didn't seem so bad to Dilia. No worse than any other alien.

"And who is this?" the stranger said to Karim.

Karim looked at him and scowled. "Just one of the natives on the base," he said, making a dismissive motion with his hand. To the soldier, he said, "Get her set up, and then I want you right back here, you understand?"

"Yes, sir," said the soldier.

"Set up for what?" the new alien asked.

Karim shook his head. "Nothing important. You and I have a busy day. Let's go over the agenda."

The soldier led Dilia outside and walked with her up the hill until the buildings on the base gave way to an untended area near the wall. Then, with a stiff nod, he returned back toward the commandant's house.

Dilia walked along a slope just inside the force field, looking for the various plants she had identified as potentially useful. But she couldn't concentrate. If Karim wasn't going to let her visit the city as a translator, when she spoke Standard better than any other Arantu he knew, he would never, *never* let her go home. She might just as well go back to her room at the commandant's house, lie down on the bed, and just wait for... wait for... nothing.

No! Dilia clenched her teeth. She would *not* give up! There had to be a way to get out of here. Karim had agreed to let her wander the base in her search for the plants she'd learned were medicinal. Better yet, for the first time, neither Abeni nor a soldier was accompanying her. She was alone and free on the base. Maybe what that soldier told her last week was wrong. Maybe there was a place where the wall had an opening, perhaps a place that some kind of animal might have burrowed through, or that a tree root had lifted up. And if the wall had been damaged, perhaps the force field next to it was weakened as well. She resolved to search the entire perimeter of the base, no matter how long it might take. But where to begin?

Movement and bright colors at the gate below caught her eye. A number of people carrying satchels and baskets heavy with goods were entering from the city below: vendors for the fourth-day market. Sentries were checking each of the bundles, but the search was perfunctory. There were no weapons, only goods for sale, and judging from their indifference, the sentries knew it.

Dilia had had no reason to go near the gate while out looking for herbs. Wild plants didn't grow in areas where the soldiers trampled around, and she wouldn't have been allowed near the gate in any case. Now, though, with Dilia's reinforced determination to leave, and no one to watch over her, she had to consider the gate . Maybe there would be fewer soldiers at the gate because they would be busy with the commandant's visitor. In that case, all she had to do was wait for the right moment, and then she could just slip out the gate.

But no, sentries were still posted there. She could see them. How could she get past?

Suddenly, Dilia knew. She knew exactly how she might get past the sentries at the gate. And the best part was there was no need to hide. She could leave the base today!

The little plaza between the commissary and the enlisted soldiers' dining hall where she'd seen the market last week was a pleasant place despite being paved over with cement. Dilia paused just before its entrance, looking around.

There were benches along the walkways, and flowers blossomed at the plaza's perimeter. The builders had left open squares here and there in the plaza, and these had been planted with trees—not the giant khena of the wild forest, but smaller, ornamental trees whose names she didn't know. If they were native to Aran, she might recognize them from her studies, but she didn't. Perhaps they had been imported from Earth, trees that seemed exotic to her, but might be familiar and comforting to a lonely Earther far from home. Could these Earth trees have any medicinal value, as did so many of the plants of Aran? Dilia shrugged the question away. It didn't matter. She would be leaving the base. Today! She would never see these trees again.

Sure enough, the Arantu people she had seen entering the gate had come here with their baskets and their bundles, and they had set out their wares on cloths on the pavement: fresh fruits and vegetables of all sorts, in abundance. Handicrafts there were, too, weavings made of rushes and straw and colored with dyes made from native plants, and wood carvings from various types of wood scavenged from the nearby trees. A couple of ambitious men had brought bottles filled with home-distilled spirits, a highly alcoholic amber-colored liquid in which floated impressively ugly and fierce-looking insects and serpents no wider than her fingers but half as long as the distance from her hand to the elbow, coiled inside the bottles in sinister spirals. Those would fetch a handsome handful of tiyus from the aliens.

Indeed, several aliens had come to the little plaza to peruse the natives' wares, off-duty soldiers as well as a few civilians. Probably officers' family members, some with a small child in tow. Dilia thought of Karim and wondered if he had a wife here on the base. No, surely not, or he wouldn't be so interested in Dilia.

A pair of soldiers were on duty by the main street that led from the gate to the plaza. Another pair walked the perimeter of the plaza. The soldiers were conspicuous in their red uniforms, but seemed relaxed, interacting informally with the people coming and going.

What if one of these aliens recognized her from the infirmary? Dilia's heart beat faster at the thought. But so what if they did? She was doing nothing wrong.

Not yet, anyway.

Dilia waited until the roving soldiers were on the far side of the plaza, out of sight behind the impromptu market. Then she made herself take a deep breath and walked into the plaza.

She spotted an old woman, her shawl wrapped over her shoulders, who was selling the kind of homemade remedies that people in the city used when they couldn't buy or steal the more effective medicines the aliens had. The woman, with her herbs, would be a perfect explanation for Dilia's presence here. She went over to the woman. "May I sit beside you?"

The woman looked her up and down, pausing when she saw the bundles of freshly picked herbs in Dilia's basket. She shrugged. "Suit yourself. Is that worrinot you've got there?"

"What, this?" Dilia folded her legs and sat beside the woman. She touched one of the bundles of herbs she'd picked. The database she'd studied had identified in the plant a chemical compound that was a relaxant. It might be useful to ease someone's stress-filled mind. "I'm not familiar with that name. Did you call it 'worry not'?"

The woman picked up the bundle and nodded. "Worrinot. I could use some of this. Where did you find it?"

"I..." Dilia swallowed. She didn't want to reveal that she'd been gathering plants on the aliens' base. "I'd rather not say."

"I understand." The woman chuckled. "Protect your gathering places, and all that. Well, I'll buy some from you. How much are you asking for it?"

Dilia laid some of the bunches of herbs from her basket out in front of her, trying to look like one of the merchants, and giving herself some time to think. She turned to study the other woman. The woman looked friendly enough, openly waiting for an answer. Her eyes were surprisingly dark for a city resident, but she wore city clothing. If she'd come from the forest, it was probably a long time ago.

Dilia realized how little she herself looked like a city resident, wearing the bright-colored alien clothing that had been given to her. The more she looked just like the others, the better. "I'll trade it for that shawl of yours."

A look of surprise flashed across the woman's face. "What, this rag?"

Dilia gave her a smile. "I'm chilly, Grandmother. And besides, I know where I can go to get more, um, worrinot."

"Done!" said the woman. "And don't call me 'Grandmother.' Makes me feel old. Name's Lana."

"Mine is Dilia. Pleased to meet you."

Dilia used the old shawl to cover her bright green dress, and the two women chatted amiably as the aliens passing by examined their wares. Most did not even glance at the women's faces. They were not very interested in the plants Dilia had gathered, calling them "weeds" in the Starrish language they assumed none of the natives understood. But the concoctions Lana had put together in embroidered sachets and small clay jars were popular with the aliens. It wasn't long before some of the city dwellers began packing up their mostly empty baskets and bags.

"Time to go," Lana said, standing up. "It's been a good day for me." She looked over the piles of herbs still sitting in front of Dilia. "Too bad you still have so much left."

"Oh, don't worry." Dilia was beginning to get nervous, but she tried to sound light-hearted. "I can always make use of them." She gathered the now-wilted bundles back into her basket and stood.

"You wouldn't be interested in selling some of those to me, would you?"

That was a good question. Would it be better for her to have an empty basket, or a nearly full one? "Maybe some." A deal was quickly struck, and the two women joined the group of people heading toward the gate. Dilia's heart picked up its pace. She felt cold and pulled the shawl more tightly around herself.

One by one, the city dwellers passed through the gate. Lana and Dilia were near the end of the line. The sentries seemed bored with the stream of natives. They were looking at their comms more than at the people passing by, but they maintained serious expressions and glanced up now and again.

Dilia walked past, close on Lana's heels. Her heart was pounding so loud she feared the sentries would hear it. She could see the dirt street and the walls of the rich people's houses on the city side of the wall. She could barely breathe, her chest felt so tight.

"Miss Dilia!" A man's voice, one of the sentries.

Dilia gasped. She picked up her pace, pushing past Lana.

"Stop that woman," the sentry shouted. "She's not to leave!"

She was breathing rapidly, her heart pounding. She attempted to hide from sight by pushing between two of the city men who were leaving, but they shoved her roughly away.

Two alien soldiers appeared from just outside the gate, peering at the departing city dwellers. Seeing the soldiers, the city people started to run toward the city, away from the base. Caught up in the widening panic, Dilia ran, too.

She was out of the gate! Free!

A hand grabbed her arm roughly, making her stumble. Her knee scraped the ground. A second soldier took her other arm, and Dilia was caught. She struggled back to her feet, trying to get her ragged breathing under control.

"Aw, Miss Dilia, why'd you have to go and do that?" The soldier was young and dark-haired. He seemed genuinely sorry, his eyebrows gathered in, shaking his head. "How're we gonna explain it to the commandant?" He looked familiar. He must have been in the infirmary sometime, to know her name.

She said nothing.

"He been treating you bad?" the soldier asked. "I would've stepped out with you myself, if I could've. I would've treated you real nice, Miss Dilia."

Now she remembered. He was the one who'd asked her out her first or second day in the infirmary, before Abeni told him who Dilia was. It seemed like a lifetime ago.

And it would be the rest of her life ahead. A life sentence, and no way out.

She felt numb, her muscles almost too weak to support her. "No," she said. "He treats me okay. I just want to go home."

Chapter 13

Cort Reenters the City

After traveling for a week and a half, Cort reached the river that marked the edge of the khenaran. Here, he hesitated. He didn't want to leave the forest, which felt like home more deeply than the city ever had. A breeze wafting across the river seemed to carry the stench of decline and decay. And death.

He touched the nearest khena, and its bark was warm, inviting. It seemed to call to him, *Stay, stay.*

The ferret came to bid him good-bye.

Come with me, he begged. *It isn't for long. Don't leave me alone.*

But the small hunter twined around Cort's legs, breathed an apology, and left.

The fox did the same.

Wolves howled in the distance but didn't come close.

Cort gathered his strength at the edge of the river. He knew he must go, and the sooner the better, but he could not make himself cross. Had his father felt like this, when he left the khenaran for the city?

That night Cort dreamed that he was helplessly sinking into the ground, suffocating, while some terrifying danger approached above. He woke in a panic, his heart pounding. He clenched his teeth, more determined than ever to find Dilia and save her. He got moving quickly, crossed the river, and before the sun had completely risen, headed into the scrub woods that surrounded the city.

The hawk and the owl continued to fly high and to guide him, but they never landed near him. They never landed in the scrub woods at all.

Only the bobcat stayed with him.

A week later, Cort and the bobcat reached the city. They stopped within the border of trees, at the edge of the cleared area around the wall.

Cort had been gone for more than two months, and the place now seemed strange to him. He was taken aback by the size of the city with its wall, as if he were seeing it for the first time. The wall—easily six times the height of a man—was interrupted by a gate, a jutting kind of doorway with two bored-looking guards stationed on its roof. Wall and gate alike were constructed of concrete that would not burn and could not be pierced by forest weaponry—sling, blade, or bow. But the concrete was rough-surfaced. Cort wondered if it could be climbed. On the mountaintop above the city, the walls of Hsu-Lin Base rose even higher, shining unnaturally white in the sunlight. Beyond the walls of the base, the piercing tip of a starship thrust toward the sky.

Had this place actually once been his home? His muscles were tense, his heart quick. He unfisted his hands and flexed his fingers, feeling like a spy infiltrating an enemy fortress, a man who would try to blend into a strange place but would never belong there.

Hunter, are you going in?

He looked down at the bobcat by his side. *Yes. I have to.* He was growing more nervous by the minute. No more delay; the sooner he went in, the better.

Then I will see you again on the inside.

Cort nodded. *Thank you. Be careful. Stay safe.*

The small animal responded with wordless amusement and loped away.

Cort straightened his vest and, head high, marched toward the gate.

Two guards monitored traffic through the gate. The older one, so fair he was sunburned, patted Cort down, looking for weapons.

"Another savage from the forest," he said, while the younger guard recorded the entry on a tablet. "He's clean," the first guard continued. "Only a personal knife."

"Well, he's probably going to need that." The younger guard yawned, scratched his head, and finished entering his data.

Cort knew the young guard, though not well. He had been two years ahead of him in school. "Talis, is it? How you doing?"

The guard looked up from his tablet and surveyed Cort from the top of his braided hair to the toenails of his bare feet. He scratched his head again, as if the motion would stimulate his brain. "I know you?"

"Roger that. Two years behind you in school before I left. You would have just graduated. Name's Cort."

Talis squinted at him skeptically. "I knew a Cort. Gang leader. Just disappeared."

Cort grinned. "That's me."

The guard relaxed, at last recognizing him. "You gone native. Look at you. Hair, clothes, all different. Never would have had you on my screens. What's the idea?"

"Life's pretty good out there in the forest. Maybe you should try it." He winked, turning the comment into a joke.

Talis laughed. "Ain't for me, shipmate. And maybe ain't for you either. I can't help noticing you come back."

"We'll see. Could go either way."

Talis had what anyone in the city would consider a good job, working as a soldier for the aliens. He would be paid well, and his hours would be reasonable, with little risk of actual danger. Once, Cort would have envied Talis his job. But now, he could hardly imagine it. The sooner he was out of city again, the better.

The city seemed shabbier to him. Downright dirty. And the streets were narrower, the filth harder to avoid. How had he never noticed this before? Nothing green grew here; the dust in the streets clung to the walls of the crooked low buildings and clogged the lungs. It smelled of garbage—and worse.

The bobcat loped out from a narrow alley as Cort passed. A light layer of dust clung to her once-sleek fur, suggesting that she'd somehow squeezed through a crack in the wall. Cort didn't ask how the little animal had found him again. He was grateful for her company as he sought out his old friends.

No one hung out at the gang's normal corner. What was that about? Then Cort realized that school was still in session. He'd forgotten the rhythm, the routine of school and street-corner tyranny. He hid in the deep shadow of a recessed and locked warehouse entrance, and he waited.

A gang of children not more than ten years old robbed an old woman as Cort watched, and he did nothing to stop them. He felt bad for the woman and thought about stepping in to break it up. But he needed to stay hidden until his old gang appeared. Besides, stepping in might do more harm than good: the woman was not in personal danger, and the children were practicing the skills they needed to survive in the city.

The children vanished when the older boys arrived, all of Cort's old friends. Tark began making assignments. He had grown taller in the weeks since Cort left, and he wore the tight curls of his blond hair cut so short and soldierlike that his scalp showed through. Cort smiled. Good for the gang—Tark was the logical choice to be leader. Cort stepped out from where he was hiding. "Greetings, my goodmen."

The gang members looked uncertainly from their former leader to their current one. "Cort?" Tark asked. "That you, my goodman?"

"None other."

"Hey, my goodman, had me darksided," said Tark. His words were friendly enough, but Cort didn't miss the coldness in his eyes and the hand hovering near the hilt of his knife. His wariness was understandable: Cort had taken leadership of the group from him once before. "Gone native?"

"You might say." Cort smiled, holding up his empty palms. "I see you goodmen are earning your ticket to Earth." And he added to the bobcat that waited just around the corner, *Stay close.*

"We've been making ends meet without you, Cort," Tark said. "We grieved you in the beginning, my goodman, but now you'd just be extra weight."

Cort had hoped his old gang would just fall in line and agree to help. But that was apparently not how this was going to play out. No surprise. He was prepared to prove himself to them again. "Extra weapons, not extra weight. I can still outshoot you if I want to." Cort drew his knife slowly—a personal challenge, not an invitation to a melee—and raised his eyebrows with what he hoped was an inviting smile. "Care to check it out?"

Tark drew his own knife.

"Easy, Cort, my goodman," interrupted Lor. He too had grown taller since Cort left. He was almost as tall as Cort now, and his hair curled wildly in an unkempt dark halo around his face. Lor had always been one for compromises. Cort used to see that as a weakness, but now he appreciated Lor's talent. "Keep that stunner on safety. We just wanted to know your mission. Right, Tark?"

Tark nodded, but kept his knife in hand, and his eyes never left Cort.

"Perfect logic, Lor, my fr—my goodman." The street slang didn't roll off his tongue quite as easily now. "I don't aim to vaporize you. I just need your backup firepower for one quick job, and then I'm out of the vision screen. Tark is captain, same as always. You read me?"

"No static," Tark agreed. "But we need to see the map before we agree to the trip."

Cort nodded. "Sleb's men took Dilia, and I'm going in after her. I can take Sleb, but I need a diversion. You'll organize the diversion."

"Sleb!" gasped Nal, a third gang member. "We heard he got you and your girl, too. But going after him? That's suicide. No one gets past his guards."

"That's where you come in," Cort said. "I want the soldiers out of his house tonight. Get some other gangs to help if you can."

"Like to help you out, my goodman," said Tark, "but when we run a risk, there has to be some reward. The greater the risk, the greater the reward."

"Agreed, my goodman. What would you like from our friend Sleb? Gold? Weapons? I'll get them."

"I'd need some proof of that, my goodman, or I'm likely to conclude that your thrusters ain't balanced. Sleb ain't been penetrated yet. Why should I believe you can do it now?"

Cort had expected it to come down to this. He painted a cold smile on his face. "The forest is an amazing place, my goodman. I have weapons you've never dreamt of."

Tark raised an eyebrow. "Proof," he said simply.

Cort sheathed his knife, took off his belt, and handed it to Lor. "Hold this," he said. Cort turned back to Tark, who hefted his knife from one hand to the other and back again. "Now you have a knife and I don't, Tark, my goodman. Take me, and you command the ship. Lose, and tonight it's my command."

"I also get your knife," Tark said. "*If* I let you live."

Cort wondered that he had never been bothered by Tark's obvious mean streak. He met Tark's greedy eyes, gold staring into green, until Tark blinked and looked away. "You have to win first."

He dodged Tark's quick thrust. "Too predictable."

Tark attacked again, and Cort grabbed his wrist, using the leader's own momentum to throw him to the ground. Cort shook his head sadly. "I don't even need my kiri for this, but I want to show you why I can beat Sleb." *Are you ready, bobcat?*

Ready, Hunter. This is too easy to be much fun.

As Tark stood up, growling angrily, Cort said, "Don't red-out your screens, my good-man. Anger never helped a fighter."

Tark let out a cry of rage and slashed at his foe.

Cort danced nimbly aside, and the bobcat leapt out of the shadows onto Tark's back, digging her claws into his shoulders.

The boy screamed and dropped his knife, reaching uselessly behind himself to try to dislodge the cat with its sharp claws.

Cort picked up the knife and spoke calmly. "Surrender, my goodman."

"Get it off me!" Tark howled. He dropped to his knees, still grappling behind his neck. His neck and hands were both bleeding, his eyes were filled with terror, and was that the smell of—? Yes, it was. Tark would have a hard time living this down. "Get this thing off me!"

Cort looked at each gang member in turn, and each nodded to him. He was the leader again. *Thanks, my friend,* he said to the bobcat. *That should do the trick.* He took his own knife back from Lor.

The bobcat leapt away and disappeared into the shadows.

Tark touched the back of his neck, winced, and then examined the blood on his hand. "Could have been worse. What was that?" The fear in his eyes lowered to more manageable levels, but it didn't go away. Tark's eyes darted from side to side as if he no longer quite trusted the solid world around him.

"My kiri," Cort answered. "They're real, Tark, my goodman, not folklore. And with this kiri, I will vaporize our friend Sleb, and you will share in his wealth. Shall it be gold, my goodman, or weapons?"

Tark bit his lip and looked around at the others. "Both are good..."

"Then both you shall have." Cort grinned, a heady mixture of adrenalin and anticipation. "But I'll need a cosmic disturbance. Can you ready your systems?"

Tark fell into line. "All systems go, Cort."

"Nineteen hundred hours," Cort added. "I'll count on it."

He turned to go, but a hand on his shoulder stopped him.

"Wait." It was Lor, whose brown eyes searched Cort's face, looking for—what? Some sign of friendliness? And there was something else in them. Worry? "I'd like to go with you."

Lor had never been a particularly bold fighter. Cort didn't understand why he would take the risk. "Why? You got it easy enough here. Stellar gang. Good prospects. You come with me tonight, it could blast all that."

"Negative. My father got injured, his last trip on the harvester. Ejected from the crew. Ain't no money now to finish school." Lor's eyes were pleading. "No school, no prospects. Nothing to blast. I'd rather take my chances with you in the forest than stay here."

"Tonight won't be easy, Lor. It'll be dangerous."

"Then we'll be safer if there are two of us."

Cort tried to read Lor, but all he could see was desperation. "If I take you with me, I'll be counting on you."

"I won't let you down."

* * *

"I'm not very good at this yet," Cort said. He picked a smooth, round stone from his pouch and placed it in the pocket of his sling.

He and Lor watched and waited in the shadows near the door to Sleb's compound. Several squads of soldiers had run out to answer one emergency or another, emergencies that Cort's gang and their allies caused near Sleb's properties throughout the city. Two soldiers still guarded the gate.

Cort twirled the sling, aimed, and let the stone fly. It hit the nearest soldier on the head, and the soldier collapsed. "Lucky shot," he muttered. He drew a deep breath and loaded another stone into the sling.

The second soldier knelt by his companion, who was either unconscious or dead. By the time the second soldier conceived the idea that he, too, might be in danger, Cort let the second stone fly. It flew over the soldier's head and clattered on the wall behind. Cort swore silently and reloaded the sling.

The soldier drew his stunner as Cort released the third stone. It struck the soldier squarely between the eyes, and he, too, collapsed.

"Lightspeed, my goodman," Cort breathed, racing for the gate. Lor followed on his heels.

They dragged the two soldiers around the side of the wall, out of sight. One had been hit on the back of the head and appeared to be only unconscious. The other sported a bruise between the eyes and was not breathing. Without a word, each of the youths undressed a soldier and donned his uniform.

"Better than knives," Lor said as he donned his jacket. "No blood, no mess." His sleeves were too short. He tugged at them, but to no avail. Then he looked at Cort and laughed. "Your hair..."

Cort smoothed his unruly hair back.

Lor's eyes widened at the sight of the glittering red gem, and he gasped. Then he shook his head. "No, the other way was better."

The living soldier stirred and moaned.

Cort let his hair fall loose and quickly buckled the soldier's stun-gun at his own waist. "Blast off," he said.

Lor and Cort walked through the open gate as if they belonged in Sleb's compound and knew where they were going. In truth, Cort knew the place well. He had spent the afternoon watching as the bobcat slunk through the compound. He'd marked the buildings, the places where the off-duty soldiers stayed, the patrol routes of those on duty. He'd also studied from the hawk's viewpoint the organization of the buildings within Sleb's walls, and he knew where Sleb was. "He's in the compound, over here," he said, leading Lor down a path to the left.

A pair of soldiers passed on a crosswalk in front of them, engaged in intense conversation.

Cort and Lor slowed slightly so that they wouldn't come too close, then continued on their way. Cort led the way inside the building he had in mind.

He was on his own. No kiri had mapped out the building's interior for him. Cort paused to listen, then followed voices down a corridor to his right, Lor close behind. Cort peeked into the open doorway beyond which the voices emanated.

The room was lit with the bright, steady light of expensive alien lamps, its floor covered in carpets of Earth manufacture. Piles of fabric, also from Earth, lay on chairs and on the rugs. A middle-aged woman with pale hair argued with two men over the price of this fabric, jabbing softly at it with blood red fingernails.

Unseen, Cort backed away. Silently, he shook his head, then returned down the corridor.

A soldier stood stiffly in the entry hallway, saluting as four more soldiers entered the building.

Cort's heart began racing. He held his breath, and, pushing Lor behind him, shrank back into the darkened doorway of an unlit room. He drew his knife.

The groaning of the stairs under heavy footsteps announced Sleb's arrival a few seconds before he came into view. "Report," he ordered.

"Sir, there have been attacks and senseless vandalisms all over the city. We're still gathering data, but what we have so far suggests that you may be the main target; most of the properties being vandalized are yours."

Cort couldn't see the soldier who was describing the situation, but as he watched, the kingpin clenched his fists, and his face brightened to red. "Whoever's doing this, I want them caught," he said. His voice was authoritative, menacing. "I'll hang them."

"Yes, sir. I've sent out all the troops I can spare already, and we are doing our utmost to capture the criminals."

"You'd better capture them, Captain. Spare nothing, or it's you I will have the pleasure of hanging. Do I make myself understood?"

"Yes, sir. I assure you it will be done, sir."

Sleb nodded curtly, and the soldiers left the hallway. Sleb stood watching until they were gone, then turned and puffed his way back up the stairs.

This was good. The house would be lightly guarded for their exit—and now Cort knew where Sleb was. He waited until the sound of the kingpin's heavy footfalls faded, then crept cautiously back to the entry hall. It was empty. Cort and Lor silently climbed the stairway.

Upstairs, the stair landing led to a wide carpeted hallway. On one side was a railing that overlooked the entryway below. Three doors faced this hallway. Only the farthest was open—probably the room where Sleb had gone. Cort led the way to the farthest door.

Inside was a wood-paneled room, with shelves full of artifacts and books. A desk dominated the center of the room with a grouping of several chairs upholstered in a rich, red fabric nearby. Sleb, alone, poured himself a drink from a bar that was built into the far wall of the room.

The carpet muffling their footsteps, Cort and Lor stepped inside. As Lor closed the door, Cort advanced quickly on the kingpin. How satisfying it would be to slit the man's throat! His jaw clenched so hard it hurt. This hatred he felt for Sleb wasn't good; it could affect his judgment. Cort shuddered and took a deep breath.

By the time Sleb figured out that he had company, Cort's arm was around his chest, his knife at his throat. The 'kingpin's glass fell to the floor. "Not a sound, slime rat," Cort hissed. "I'd sooner kill you than get a ticket to Earth."

A ticket to Earth, of course, was what everyone in the city dreamed of. Cort could feel the man shaking. His threat must have terrified the kingpin as much as the knife drawing a trickle of blood at his throat.

"What do you want?" Sleb asked, his voice quavering. "Ease up, won't you? We can talk reasonably here."

"Can he talk reasonably, City Boy?" Cort asked Lor, smiling grimly.

Lor picked an apple from a bowl of fruit on one of the small tables in the room. It was a Starrish fruit, preserved forever as fresh and firm and juicy as when it had been picked, perhaps decades ago, in some alien orchard, priceless.

"I don't know, my goodman," Lor replied. "Ask him and we'll see." He took a bite of the apple. Wiping the juice that ran down his chin, he added for the kingpin's benefit, "My goodman there is a savage, so he probably cuts people for fun, you know. Eats their eyeballs for breakfast. What you got here?"

As Lor began studying the objects on the shelves, Cort said, "I'm looking for a woman."

"Ah!" The kingpin's face brightened. "I can get you women. Pretty, soft city women. As many as you want."

"I said 'a woman,' slime rat. You weren't listening. I have very little patience." Cort leaned closer to Sleb and whispered, "I'm a savage, you know. I collect the ears of people who don't listen."

"Please!" Sleb's voice rose to a squeak. "Whatever woman you want! It may take a little time, but..."

"Cort, look at this," interrupted Lor. "He's got a knife collection. I think I recognize your old knife."

"Take it," Cort replied. "Take as many of them as you can." To the kingpin, he said, "Her name is Dilia."

"I don't... I don't know any of the names..." When the man swallowed, Cort could feel the added pressure against his knife, and there was a tiny trickle of blood.

"Think hard. You also captured a young man looking for her. Burned the mother in her house." A flush of heat swept through Cort at the memory, and his hand shook. Earth, but the soft flesh of the kingpin's neck was tempting! Cort pressed harder, and the blood that flowed was a pleasure he didn't want to acknowledge.

Sleb emitted a sound somewhere between a gargle and a squeak.

Reluctantly, Cort eased the pressure. "Speak, Kingpin," he said, "but I will know if you are lying. I collect the tongues of liars."

"I remember the girl," admitted the kingpin. "Long hair. Auburn. Very pretty. Worked in a shop not far from the base. She was nothing but trouble to me, though. A fighter. She's... ah... she's gone now."

"Where?"

The man was rigid, so tense he shook, the acrid smell of his sweat strong in the stale air of the room. "I don't run a brothel; I sold her. Please... Let me find you another woman."

"Where did you sell her?"

Sleb's shaking eased and he relaxed a bit, perhaps with some hope that he might yet survive. "To the aliens, of course. So many men up there, so few women. They pay well for pretty girls, sometimes."

"Which alien?" Cort demanded.

"Do you think you can break into the base the way you broke in here?" asked the kingpin in a surprising burst of anger. "They don't need guards; they use technology. It was the commandant himself, but what difference does that make? She's gone, that's all. Look, I'll give you the girl's sales price if you just let me live."

Cort was curious about this. "How much?"

Sleb hesitated, then licked his lips and looked away "A hundred alien gold."

Sold her and lied about it! Cort was livid. Despite himself, his right hand moved, slicing a neat line just skin-deep on the kingpin's neck. "You got write-only memory? You forget what I do to liars?"

Sleb swallowed with a hesitation that spoke of fear. Fear that the knife would cut deeper. Fear of tasting his own blood. Fear of dying. "Five hundred."

"Tell my goodman there where you stow it."

Sleb directed Lor to a key in his desk drawer, then to a safe built into the wall behind a row of books. When Lor opened the safe, he let out a low whistle. "Enough alien in here for a ticket to Earth," he commented. "Maybe two."

"Take what you can carry, my goodman, but no more. After this, we need lightspeed. Slime rat here is happy to pay."

"Hey!" protested the kingpin, but then he thought better of it. "You going to let me go, right?"

Letting the kingpin go was not what Cort wanted. He would rather slit the man's throat and leave him here to bleed out, but it had been Sleb's soldiers that saved his life as a child. There was a debt to pay. "Maybe I will," he said, "after you help us get out."

They left Sleb bound and gagged in an alley not far from his house. He would live, if his own men found him before one of the local gangs did. Cort figured that it was an even chance. It was the most he could bring himself to give the man, and he did it over Lor's objections.

They met Tark and the others at the gang's usual corner. Cort distributed the gold and weapons among the gang members, keeping for himself his father's knife and the five hundred alien that had been Dilia's purchase price. If Cort's leadership of the group had been in doubt before, it was in doubt no longer.

But Cort had no future in the city, and he knew it. If Sleb lived, the kingpin would stop at nothing to hunt him down. And even if Sleb died, Cort figured that after tonight the odds were high that the aliens would be searching for him.

Looking from one face to another of the boys who had been his closest friends, Cort realized that even if Sleb and the aliens were not problems for him, he didn't want to live in the city any longer. He was a hunter. The forest was his home now.

"Tark, my goodman," he said, "you've done an Earthworthy job. Sky-high. Couldn't have had better backup. But now I'm solo again. It's Hsu-Lin Base for me, and from there I won't be back. You be captain again, my goodman. You're most worthy for certain."

"You buy that ticket to Earth?" asked Nal, one of the gang members, referring to the large amount of currency Cort had reserved for himself. Several people laughed, but the comment made Cort angry. This wasn't about personal gain. The laughter stopped when his friends saw he wasn't laughing.

"I buy back my girl, my goodman," Cort replied quietly.

Tark nodded. "You still need backup? You lead us into the base, we go."

It was a generous offer, but Cort shook his head. "Negative, my goodman. I got no programming for getting in. Even less for getting out again. I'm solo." Then he thought of the risk he was taking and added quietly, "Maybe I am buying a ticket to Earth at that." He was using the expression's other meaning: for most city folk, the only way out of the slums was death.

Tark nodded. "Safe journey, Cort."

"You, too, Tark, and all my goodmen," Cort replied.

He turned to go, but Lor put a hand on his arm. "I'm cruising with you, my goodman, remember?"

"No, not this time." Cort shook his head. "Solo is solo."

It was an unfortunate turn of phrase, for it gave Lor an opening. "'Solo is solo,'" he quoted the old saying, "'but two covers your back.' If you can get in, so can I. Let me help you, Cort."

"You're missing some data, my goodman," Cort said. "I'm not coming back here. I'm not a city boy any longer. Read the output screen, Lor. I survive tonight, I'm heading to the forest."

"You're the one that should be reading the output!" retorted Lor. "I told you, there's no life for me here any more. Fuel tank's empty. You can be a forest boy, then maybe I can too. Besides... you think my life is worth much here in the city after tonight? Sleb survives, I'm history. Rather do it on my own terms."

Cort looked at Tark, who shrugged. But still, he wasn't sure whether Lor would be a help or a liability.

Lor clutched at his arm. "If you think there's a chance Dilia's still alive in there, if you think it's a chance worth the risk, then I want to help you." He lowered his voice. "I always liked Dilia. She's one stellar girl. She's never mean to anyone, always ready to help. Nice to little children and old folks, too. I always hoped, when I get a girl, she'll be a lot like Dilia."

Cort couldn't help smiling. "Thanks, Lor, that's fleetworthy. I can't promise anything. I don't know what's going to happen. But you can come... for now."

Chapter 14

Cort Gets on the Base

The smooth reinforced concrete wall that surrounded Hsu-Lin Base loomed above Cort, silhouetted by the alien lights that burned all night long in the starmen's compound. He stared at the gate that led from the city to the base, wishing there was some way through it, but the gate had been shut tight since just before sunset.

"Not going through there," he said to Lor.

"Not tonight," Lor said.

People could, and did, get into the base during the day—if they had legitimate business there, if they had a permit from the commandant, or if they were accompanied by one of the starmen's soldiers. Or, rarely, if they worked in the compound and had one of the strange alien IDs and their handscan matched the starmen's database.

Cort had none of these things. He'd lived all his life at the foot of Hsu-Lin Base and had never been inside.

He'd circled the wall, of course. All the boys had. They'd followed the curves and angles of the wall across the uphill edge of the city, followed it to the very cliff edge of the chasm that ran steeply down the hillside and through the city. They'd crossed where the chasm became shallower in the more level terrain and was slowly being filled up with garbage and other detritus, until it leveled out enough to be built upon. They'd picked up the wall on the other side of the chasm and followed it back to the gate, an impenetrable barrier that divided the world into "them" and "us," the ones who could return to Earth and the ones who yearned to go there but never would.

Now that the gate was shut, there were no guards in evidence. But Cort knew, as all the city dwellers did, that a small patrol of starmen soldiers made the rounds inside the walls all through the night. Additionally, an alien forcefield surrounding the base provided an invisible fence that kept intruders out more certainly than any physical wall patrolled by squads of soldiers might have done. Day or night, any attempt to pass through the forcefield would be fatal.

Cort had to find a way around it.

If he didn't get into the enclave this night, he might be able to smuggle himself through, or bribe a guard, the next day. Lor had been right about that. But with Sleb's soldiers about, the risk would be much higher.

"There's one place in the wall I want to try," he told Lor as they followed the base's perimeter along the deserted alleys of the city. On one side of them were dark, windowless buildings, the backs of warehouses. On the other side, the base's concrete wall, over four meters tall, protected the people of the city from the devastating forcefield that was Hsu-Lin Base's true defense.

"In the *wall*?" Lor asked, his voice rising to a squeak of incredulity, "You'll fry, my goodman; you will fry."

"I think maybe not. Here, look at this." They were in a narrow street abutting the wall of the base and flanked by warehouses, deserted at this time of night. The warehouses, too, were walled. Cort jumped to reach the top of the wall surrounding one of the warehouses and pulled himself up. Lor followed. From this height, they could see, but barely, over the base's wall. "See the energy repeaters for the forcefield?" Cort pointed at two dark boxes a meter on a side that sat on concrete pads half a meter inside the base's wall. "All around, they're spaced like that—maybe six meters apart. Except in one place. You know where the chasm is? The space between the energy repeaters on either side of the chasm is longer than fifteen meters."

"But that's because there's nowhere to put a repeater in the middle of the chasm! And besides, no one could scale the cliff there anyway, so what's the point of it?"

"I'm going to scale it."

"You better run some high-level diagnostics, my goodman."

"Maybe so, Lor. But the bobcat has already been in and out of Hsu-Lin Base twice that way, and I think I can make it in, too."

Lor heaved a weary sigh that seemed to say, *The things we adults have to put up with.* "You mean *we*, my goodman. *We* can make it in."

Cort felt a surge of warmth toward Lor and turned to look at him. He'd never had a brother, but from time to time he'd imagined having one. A fine, brave, loyal brother who stood by him through every danger. Someone like Lor.

But no, this was one place Lor couldn't go with him. "Lor, you're my true goodman, and no doubt. But the bobcat will help me know the best path to climb, where to find each handhold and foothold. You won't have that kind of help. So when I said *I* can make it in, I meant it. Me, not you."

Lor swallowed. He looked almost ready to cry. But—thank Earth!—he didn't argue. "What can I do then? How can I help?"

"Wait outside for me. Get some food and water. Good shoes for yourself, if you're serious about coming into the forest with me. Maybe some clothes for Dilia, in case I find her. Lor, my goodman, I don't know what we'll need. Just make a good guess, and meet me outside the city gate tomorrow morning as soon as they open it."

Lor looked at the open area where energy repeaters generated their deadly field that kept the aliens safe from the planet's natives. He looked back at Cort, then away. "I'll do that, my goodman," he said. "Keep your shields up, Cort."

The two friends dropped lightly back to the dark alleyway. Cort put a hand on Lor's shoulder. "Of course I'll be careful. I've come too far to fail now. You put your shields up, too, my goodman. Stay out of Sleb's crosshairs. Rendezvous tomorrow."

"Tomorrow," Lor agreed, and he disappeared into the darkness of the city at night.

⁂

The wall spanned the chasm near its upper end. Below, the chasm tumbled down the hill and into the city, defining a gap where nothing was built. Nothing that lasted. In heavy rains, the chasm flooded. Rockslides from the chasm's sides were not unusual. Even hikers were at risk from the instability of the loose rock that formed its floor. By contrast, the canyon walls were made of a single large rock that looked like it had been split in the formation of the world by a lightning bolt hurled by an angry god. It was so smooth and sheer that no one even imagined it was climbable.

The bobcat knew better, though she had a strange idea of what constituted a foothold. More than once, Cort found himself hanging from a toe on a thin ledge, and the bobcat would say, *That's it!* The handholds pointed out by the little cat weren't much better. Cort hung on by will as much as by muscle.

Slowly, he inched up the wall at the end of the chasm. The muscles in his arms burned. His feet cramped. Time existed only in the space of moving one hand or one foot three inches upwards or sideways. He followed a zigzag path, going now up, now sideways, once even downward again. As he struggled to find each next step the burning in his hands and feet started turning to numbness, an even greater danger.

At last, his fingers felt the top edge. It was the best handhold in the whole climb, and there was even a tiny shelf where he could rest the toes of one foot, relieving some of the pressure from his aching hands.

Next came the hard part.

Cort had studied the wall from below with the little cat, and they'd noted that the top of the rock was almost—but not quite—level. One of the great rock's natural depressions might barely allow a person to shimmy under the main energy field as drawn in a straight line from one repeater to the next. The bobcat had done it easily. Twice.

But Cort was considerably larger than a bobcat. And he would have to work his way leftward about fifteen feet to reach that spot, hanging by his hands alone.

He reached out to his left, took hold of the rock, and let his feet swing loose. His fingers screamed protest, and he let out an involuntary moan.

Quiet, hissed the cat. *Two people approach.*

What?

Two male humans, dressed alike. Bearing weapons.

He could hear them now, talking amiably.

His complaining fingers were threatening to let go. He couldn't hold on this way until the guards passed. With another groan—silent, this time—he inched back to the place where he could put his foot down and ease the weight from his hands.

The guards were speaking Starrish. At this time of night, of course they would be aliens, and that meant they would be carrying lasers. "...going home in two months," said one.

"Well, but it's two months here and then twelve years on the ship."

"Not in perceived time."

"Not in *your* perceived time, but in hers."

"All the more reason she should have waited. I'll come back to her young and vigorous, while she'll..." The voices faded into the distance.

Cort took a deep breath and let it out. Time to go.

But his hands refused to move.

He clenched his jaw until it threatened to split his teeth, cursed the pain, made his hand take the next hold, and swung off his resting foot. Hand by hand, he inched leftward. His fingers refused to curl, but somehow he made them. *How far to go?*

Patience, said the bobcat.

He made his left hand move once more. Then his right.

You're at the spot, Hunter. Be careful now.

As if he wouldn't be careful! But Cort could barely hang on. With an effort greater than any so far he pulled himself up, until the front half of his body lay on the cool, smooth rock. Then he began wiggling forward, keeping as low to the ground as he could.

His head began to tingle. As the tingling spread to his shoulders, Cort felt pain in his head. His heart thrummed an electric alarm. He had no idea how strong the field still was at this spot, or how much time he could spend in it before it did permanent damage.

He scrabbled desperately along the rock, resisting the urge to stand and run. Standing would be certain suicide. He thought of Dilia and slithered along the ground through the fence. The line of pain passed over his back, his buttocks, his legs.

He was through!

Cort rested for a moment, his cheek on cool, soft grass. But when he closed his eyes, the owl that flew high above showed him how exposed he was in that bare spot. And the soldiers had already started back. Alien soldiers who carried deadly lasers.

Cort took a deep breath and stood. He looked around, blinking away a momentary blurriness as he adjusted to his own night vision, so much less sharp than the owl's. There was barely enough moonlight to see by.

Hsu-Lin Base—at least the part of it Cort could see from here—was not like the city. In the city, the buildings were packed closely with jumbles of narrow streets, and no one person knew the way through all of it. But here, there seemed to be a small compound of widely spaced houses, each large enough to shelter a half dozen city families. There was more to the base than this—barracks for the soldiers, storehouses, places for mechanical equipment—but these were not visible where Cort stood. Around the houses were lawns and gardens and fountains, beautifully elegant open spaces that offered no haven, no places to hide. There were only a few streets; these were paved and, like the gardens, immaculately clean.

No haven was necessary. The owl confirmed that no guards, no one at all, roamed the spaces among the houses of Hsu-Lin Base.

In the gardens of the base, a quiet hissing muted any noise that might have drifted up from the city below. Cort almost stumbled over one of the air outlets before he understood the source of this soft sound. Near the outlet, the air smelled neutral, mechanical. It lacked any perfume of flowers or pungency of the living earth. And it felt different—a heady mixture of gases rich in oxygen and other trace compounds designed to bring the air to closer approximation of the aliens' home planet.

Suppressing a chemically-induced feeling of euphoria, Cort continued on his way. He knew where he was going. On more than one sleepless night, he had sailed the sky above the base with the owl's eyes, just as he had used the hawk to view the alien enclave by day. One house seemed larger and finer than the others, with more people coming and going. Cort was willing to bet he'd find the commandant there.

He knew what the commandant looked like. At the beginning of every school year, the commandant came to address the assembled students, urging them to study hard and do well. Every student could recognize the man, though he was seldom seen in the city except on the most formal occasions. Cort remembered the commandant as a particularly stern individual, pale-eyed and pale-skinned even by alien standards.

Like all the students, Cort was in awe of him.

He followed a paved path along darkened gardens, avoiding the areas where light spilled from a window or from a fixture highlighting a flowering shrub. Within ten minutes, he arrived at the large house he'd identified as the commandant's.

A glance through a lighted window showed that his deduction was correct. Inside, two aliens were talking in what appeared to be a living room. The room shone with a diffuse light from no obvious source—perhaps the walls themselves. One of the aliens was the commandant. Cort didn't recognize the other. The commandant was not in uniform; he wore brightly colored clothing of alien material that hung loose and looked comfortable. His guest wore clothing of a similar material, but in a more subdued tan color. Cort was struck by how pale both aliens were—light blond hair, pale skin, blue eyes, as if they had been grown in a cave. And their lanky tallness seemed to confirm the cave-grown hypothesis; they were like plants that needed more light.

Cort went to the front of the house. The door was closed. He looked around, but there was no sign of danger, and no way to tell if any danger lurked. He could see no sentries, but he couldn't rule out the possibility that they might be patrolling a loop in this residential area and might return here at any minute. Surely the aliens relied on more than their energized perimeter for protection! A quick check through the owl's eyes revealed a patrol of two sentries at the far side of the base's residential area, just turning a corner to head back toward the commandant's house. They'd be here in five minutes at the most.

It was so quiet, he could hear his heart pounding.

Cort was good at picking locks, but the security here was sophisticated. There was no obvious lock to pick. A security panel by the door did not show whether the system was armed. If it was, just trying to open the door might set it off. On the other hand, the commandant was at home and had company. This might indicate that the security system was unarmed.

The sentries were approaching, almost here. What choice did he have? Cort tried the door. Surprisingly, it opened. He slipped inside and closed the door.

He stood in a darkened vestibule. A door to the living room opened to his right, and the vestibule narrowed to a sort of hallway ahead. Other rooms opened to the left. All of these except the living room were unlit, and no people were in sight. Other than the sound of quiet conversation from the living room, there was no noise in the house. No sign of anyone in the house except the two men.

He was as out of place here as a wolf in a khena tree. He would have no place to run if any of the base's soldiers came after him. His heart pounded. But there was no going back. He put his hand on the hilt of his knife and took a step forward, toward the living room.

No, it was better not to appear threatening, not when a simple discussion might be all that was needed. He made himself let go of the knife. Holding his hands out and open in a peaceful gesture, he passed through the empty entryway into the living room, blinking in the bright light.

The two aliens looked up when he walked in, their conversation forgotten. The stranger's words fell away into silence, and his gesturing hands dropped to his side.

The commandant touched something on a table at his side, but it wasn't a weapon. "Who are you?" he asked in Starrish. "What do you want?"

The strong speech Cort had prepared, stating his demands, flew from his mind in the presence of the most powerful man on the planet. He swallowed hard but couldn't shake the deference toward alien authority that had been drilled into him in years of schooling. He bowed slightly and then answered in the same language. "My name is Cort. I have been told that a friend of mine—a girl—was sold to you. I have come to get her back." He tried, but couldn't help adding, "Sir."

A gruff voice behind him said, "Raise your hands and turn around slowly." It was one of the aliens' soldiers, here in the house after all. He held a laser aimed at Cort.

Cort's heart began pounding again, and he flushed with heat. It was one thing to be avoiding the soldiers, knowing what a laser can do, but quite another to be no more than three meters from the wrong end of a laser in the hands of a person who clearly was ready to use it. Cort had seen an alien laser burn a hole right through a man once, when he was nine years old, and the image of the stinking, burned corpse was still vivid in his mind. No way was that going to happen to him. He raised his hands. They were shaking, but he didn't turn, not yet. This was his only chance to talk with the commandant. "I mean no violence, sir. I didn't raise a weapon against you, and I have the money to pay you."

"Take him away." The commandant made a dismissive gesture.

"Wait." The second alien put a hand on the commandant's arm and shook his head slowly. "I'd like to talk with him, first."

The commandant shrugged.

"What makes you think this man"—the alien indicated the commandant with a tilt of his head—"is holding your friend?"

Cort glanced over his shoulder at the alien guard, whose unswerving laser was still aimed at his back. "I talked with the man who sold her to him. I believe he was telling the truth. He said this man paid five hundred gold for her. I've brought back his money."

The two aliens met glances. The commandant looked away.

Encouraged, Cort continued, "Ask him. Her name is Dilia."

"Is this true, Karim?" asked the alien.

The commandant drew himself up, standing stiffly. "Many of us buy the services of some native girl from time to time, but never against their will. It's a mutually beneficial arrangement. These natives will do anything for the opportunity to live on the base. You'll get used to the idea when you've been around a while. I resent the implication that I have purchased the girl like... like a commodity."

But that's just what he must have done! Cort glanced at the second alien, who was frowning. Maybe not all the aliens approved of this behavior. Maybe this one didn't approve. That might work to Cort's advantage. His heart beating faster, he said to the commandant, "Then you won't mind her leaving." Cort glanced back at the soldier holding the laser. No sense in taking chances. He added, "Sir."

The commandant's companion laughed. "The boy has a point, Karim. I suppose you'll have to ask the girl."

The commandant glared at the other alien, his face reddening. He clenched his right hand into a fist, but he did not respond. Instead, he stood and walked past Cort to the doorway. "Wait here."

Cort's arms had started to tremble, and they weighed more with each passing moment. "Sir, may I put my hands down?"

The commandant frowned.

"I'm unarmed, except for my personal knife. I could have threatened or harmed you before he came in." Cort inclined his head toward the guard. "But I didn't."

"Search him," the commandant said.

The guard dutifully patted at the few places where a stunner might have been hidden in Cort's scant forest clothing. "No weapon but the knife, sir. There's a small sack of something heavy on his belt, but it's not a weapon."

"Money," Cort said. "Enough to repay you for this… misunderstanding."

The commandant raised an eyebrow, and from the slight tilt of his head seemed to be considering Cort's offer. Or perhaps just wondering where, and how, a forest savage might have come across that large a sum. "We'll see," he said.

"Sir, shall I take the knife?" asked the soldier.

The commandant looked from Cort to the other alien and back again. His features twisted into something that might have been a smile—for an alien—but on a regular person would convey considerable malice. As if he might be hoping that Cort *would* do something that would justify killing him. "No," he said. "I think we can trust him, don't you, Lennard?"

The man called Lennard opened his mouth to say something, but the commandant didn't give him the opportunity. To the guard, he said, "Come with me."

Alone with the stranger, Cort allowed his arms to drop back to his side. The movement gave him a moment of dizziness, and he blinked to clear his swimming vision. It must have been the strange air. He fought off the giddy feeling.

"Come on in," said Lennard. He seemed in good spirits. "Karim there would like for you to slit my throat. He and I are… not friends. Then of course he'd have a reason to slit yours. Two problems removed at the same time. But we're not going to play that game, are we? Have a seat." He indicated the chair nearest to where Cort stood. "I don't believe we've been introduced. My name is Lennard."

"Cort," said Cort, selecting a chair nearer the alien.

"Yes, yes, I know. You said that. Forgive my ignorance, Cort, but I've only been here a short time. You look… different from the other natives I've met. Do you live out in the forest? And if you do, how did your Standard get so good?"

Lennard had stood up for Cort in his exchange with the commandant. Cort didn't see any harm in answering a few of his questions while they waited. "I used to live in the city until recently. I attended the school, studied engineering. I used to want to work here on the base."

"Used to? But no longer?"

"No. No longer. The man who..." He had to search for the word. "Who abducted my friend... He's a very powerful man in the city. It wouldn't be safe for me here any more. I have friends, a place to live, out in the forest." Of course that wasn't the only reason, but how could he explain to an alien about the kiri?

"But that's a shame!" Lennard's blue eyes were sympathetic.

Cort looked away. "Not really. It was a..." Another word not found. "...a piece of good fortune, as it turned out. If only I can free my friend."

"Yes," Lennard said. "It comes down to that. And you should know that if in fact your friend has been abducted, Earth law is on your side."

The idea that there was any Earth law, much less that it was on his side, was funny. Was Lennard toying with him? Or was that an effect of something in the air? Lennard looked so perfectly serious he could have been a caricature of an alien. Cort suppressed a laugh.

Lennard smiled and shook his head. "It's true, Cort. Bringing news of that law is one reason I came here. Your commandant and I were just talking about that. The legislature has passed strict regulations regarding interference with the native populations on any of the colonized planets. In fact, we no longer allow settlement on planets with intelligent native life, although, naturally, New Richmund—Aran, as you call it—and the other planets that already have settlements are exempted from that part of the law. So, you see, we will be happy to return your friend to you—if, in fact, she wants to go."

Fighting intense drowsiness, Cort tried to focus on what Lennard was saying. Happy to return Dilia? The commandant hadn't seemed happy, not at all. He'd seemed angry. Cort couldn't think of what to say or to ask. The best he could manage was a nod. Lennard leaned forward and studied him closely. "Are you well?"

"I..." Cort shook his head. "I think it's the air."

"Stuffy in here, isn't it?" The alien smiled agreeably. "But we Earthmen need a little more of a few things than your planet naturally provides—notably, oxygen. Still, I'm sure we'd both feel a little better with an open window." He got up and opened one of the windows.

A fresh breeze came into the room. Cort took a deep breath of it, and then another. He began to feel somewhat better.

"Are you planning to take your friend back to the forest, assuming that she wants to come with you?" Lennard asked.

"Of course she'll come with me."

"To the forest?"

Cort nodded, then stood and walked over to the open window. Small lights illuminated the gardens of the base. Beyond, reflections of those lights glinted on the silver skin of the starship that would never carry him to Earth. "To the forest," he said. And no regrets.

"I can help you," Lennard said. "If she wants to go with you like you said, Karim does not have the authority or the right to hold her here." He swallowed and shook his head slowly. "The idea is repulsive, and I won't let it stand."

Cort wasn't sure what the alien could do, but he wasn't going to turn away any help that was offered. "Thanks, Lennard."

"Now I have a favor to ask of you."

"Of me?"

"Yes. It's not a precondition or part of a bargain or anything, but I'd like you to take me along to the forest, too. If you would. Please."

Cort again thought that the alien must be toying with him. He turned to look at him, frowning in puzzlement. "What?"

Lennard's intense blue eyes met Cort's. There was a communication in them, though of what, exactly, Cort wasn't sure. The earnestness, perhaps, of a person who at last has found within reach the thing most denied him. "I want to go with you to the forest."

"But why?"

"Does it matter why?"

It was a good question. Cort wanted to be with Dilia again more than he wanted anything—didn't he? But he had to consider the damage the aliens could do. Had already done. "Yes," he answered reluctantly. "It matters. I don't want you teaching my people any of your alien..." Again, there was no word. "...ways," he finished lamely.

Lennard laughed heartily. "Would it be so bad?" He met Cort's eyes and must have seen the seriousness in his grim expression, for he continued rapidly. "I don't want to teach anyone anything. I want to learn. I'm a xenologist. Do you know what that means?"

Cort shook his head, willing to listen.

"It's someone who is trained to study alien cultures. I want to learn everything I can about how your people live when they are not, ah, influenced by our 'alien ways,' as you call them. You'd be surprised how little we know about you back on Earth. I have a research grant, trip fully funded, yet I've been unable to find anyone that actually knows anyone who lives out in the, ah, wild. Until you, that is. Your people in the city don't seem to venture outside the walls, and as far as I've been able to discover, absolutely no one lives in the woods hereabouts." He made a sweeping gesture with his hand. "And the forest of khena trees, what you call the khenaran, right? That's quite a distance away, and I can't find anyone that even knows the way."

"But you don't speak our language!"

"Yes, I do." Lennard spoke in passable Arantu. "A little. I am studying. How are you? My name is Lennard."

Cort laughed.

Lennard's hopeful expression collapsed, and he switched back to Starrish. "Was it that bad?"

"No! No, not at all. I was just surprised. But how can you have any influence over the commandant's decision? He's in charge, isn't he?"

"Yes, he is," Lennard said. "But I'm his equal in rank, and I have a significant advantage over him: my commanding officer outranks his. Furthermore, I have a prepaid ticket back to Earth. That means that any unfavorable report from me will have a bad impact on him when he gets home, and he'll have no way to counter it."

"But why—?"

Lennard laughed. "Would he let your friend go? Because my round-trip ticket gives me a power over him that I probably don't deserve, and I've been making his life miserable this last week or so. He'll probably be so glad to get rid of me that releasing your friend will be a small price to pay. He'll be praying every night that I get killed by some kind of native poison dart or something." His smile changed to a frown. "You people don't have poison darts, do you?"

"Not that I know of. But there will certainly be dangers."

"You'll take me, then?"

Cort couldn't see any reason why not. Besides, he was beginning to like this alien—although of course that might just be the effect of the air. Slowly, he nodded. "Help me," he said, "and I'll take you."

Dilia moaned in her bed. Karim had kept her locked in for, what, three days? Four? He no longer allowed her out, not to hunt for herbal plants, not even to the infirmary. To teach her a lesson, he'd said.

She was losing track of time.

Not just time, she felt she had lost everything. Cort had not come, and she had not managed to get free. Who knew if she even had a home any more to go back to? Worst of all, if she'd understood Abeni right, she would never be able to have children. What was there to live for?

Dilia had never felt this listless. It must be the air here. In the past, she'd always been able to get out and go to the infirmary where the windows could be opened, but here, it seemed there just wasn't enough good air. She needed to get up, to walk around, and then maybe she'd feel better. Maybe she'd be able to think of some kind of plan. By Earth, she'd settle for just one small window she could open.

Her dinner still sat on the table. She hadn't been hungry, but she'd made herself eat a few bites anyway. That had been hours ago, and the food was beginning to develop a distinctly unappetizing smell. Why hadn't the soldier come to take it away?

As if in answer to her thoughts, there were footsteps in the hallway. The door opened.

At first she didn't recognize the person who stood in the doorway—and then she did. "Karim!" All these days, weeks, and she'd never seen him out of uniform before.

"Get up," he said. "I need you upstairs." He spoke harshly, maybe a little too loud. Could he still be angry at her for trying to escape? But that was days ago! She wished she could think more clearly.

A soldier was standing behind Karim. She frowned. What was this about? She struggled to sit up, feeling dizzy and weak, but she managed to stand. She took one shaky step forward, then another. Once she got moving, it wasn't too bad.

Karim led the way. The soldier stood back as she left the room, then fell in behind her.

Following Karim, Dilia started up the stairs, but she stumbled on the first one. She silently cursed the air in this place, that made her feel so faint. The soldier caught her before she fell, but she shook the man off and took a tighter hold of the railing.

At the top of the stairway, she stumbled again, and the soldier took firm hold of her upper arm as they followed the commandant into a large room, obviously a living room of some sort. Two people stood looking out an open window, an alien and... an Arantu from the forest?

"Plotting behind my back, are you?" Karim said to the two men. His voice was full of malice. Dilia shivered.

The men turned. The starman was Karim's new visitor, and the native looked familiar. He looked like... Cort!

This had to be a hallucination. She felt faint.

"Oh, absolutely!" The alien stranger laughed heartily. "At every opportunity."

The native—yes, incredibly, it *was* Cort—looked past the commandant, and his eyes met Dilia's. He straightened and started to smile. But he looked at the soldier who still gripped her, then back at Dilia, and the smile vanished.

"Dilia!" Cort leapt forward, scowling in anger, his hand reaching for his knife. "What have they done to you?"

Dilia cried out, "Cort!" She tried to pull away from the guard, to run to Cort. But the guard tightened his grip, squeezing her arm so hard it hurt, and pointed his laser at Cort. "Stop, or I'll shoot."

Chapter 15

Travel Through the Woods

Caught between his desire to take Dilia from this man, to talk with her, to help her, between his desire... and his fear for both their lives, Cort stopped. He considered his chance of drawing and throwing his knife before the guard could fire.

Nonexistent.

He silently called his kiri. *Bobcat?*

Hunter, I am just outside the window where you're standing.

Ah. Good. Actually, it wasn't good. The first alien the little cat would reach would be Lennard, who was probably not a threat. And Cort and Dilia and the little bobcat would all be dead before any of them could harm the guard or the commandant. *Wait there.*

Dilia seemed only slowly to become aware of what was going on around her. She focused on Cort, lifted her head, and gave the kind of smile that might accompany a pleasant thought of something far away. She spoke with difficulty, as if making her lips move were an unfamiliar activity. "Cort! I knew... you would come."

He ached to take her in his arms, away from the alien soldier, away from the commandant's house, away from the city. But he didn't dare to move for fear she would be hurt—or worse.

"As a matter of fact," Lennard was saying. Cort looked from Lennard's face to the commandant's, and there was no affection on either of them, though they both smiled. "I believe this young man and I have reached an understanding that will be greatly to your liking. He has agreed to take me, along with his friend here, back into the forest where he came from. So I can begin my study, and you will have me out of your hair."

"The girl is mine," replied the commandant. "You have no right to bargain with what is not yours." But his voice was uncertain, and his eyes flicked from Lennard to Dilia—who was trying to pull her arm away from the guard—to Cort, and back again.

"There, there, Karim," Lennard said soothingly, patting the commandant on the shoulder and seeming not to notice when the other man flinched. "She's not really *yours* per se, is she now? She's just staying here with you for a while. But surely you can find so many other young women in the city, all eager, as you say, to live here on Hsu-Lin Base. It seems such a small price to pay, considering the benefits we *both* will gain from the arrangement." He paused, as if giving the commandant time to think through his argument, then added, "Especially considering the questionable legality of what has happened to this particular young woman, if indeed she was abducted before she, ah, came willingly to you."

The commandant glared silently at his unwelcome guest. "Very well," he said at last. "To be clear—I've done nothing illegal, but you're right, who knows what kind of... unfortunate business... might have happened to her before she came here. As you say, it's a small price to pay." He turned to the guard and said, "Let her go."

The guard holstered his weapon, and released his hold on the girl.

Dilia walked unsteadily toward Cort, her features somehow full of both suffering and relief. Cort raced to her side. Dilia sighed and eased herself against him, resting her head on his shoulder. The feel of her skin against his, the solidity of her body in his arms was almost overpowering. For a moment, he forgot the danger they were both still in. He just wanted to go on holding her.

"When will you be leaving?" the commandant asked. He stood stiffly, the line of his jaw tight, and the coldness of his pale eyes anything but friendly.

"Uh... tomorrow?" Lennard answered with the uncertainty of a person who had had no opportunity to make plans.

"Tonight," Cort said. "Right now. Get your things, but no more than you can carry. I'll wait outside."

"Tonight!" The commandant laughed, a condescending tone that left the unspoken "stupid savage" hanging between them in the air. "In that case, I'll wish you the best of luck, Lennard." His tone was laced with the conviction that Lennard would need more luck than he was likely to get. "I'll take that money you brought, young man, and then my soldier here will see you out the gates." The commandant nodded toward his soldier, who stiffened, face neutral, and said, "Yes, sir."

As Dilia leaned on him, Cort's anger grew. His breathing quickened. *Let it be only the air. If he's damaged you in some way, I'll kill him. Even if I die doing it.* He moved to pick Dilia up, but she pulled away from him. The effort he was making to hold in his anger made his hands shake as he handed the leather pouch to the commandant. Then she sighed and seemed to relent, putting one arm around Cort's neck.

The soldier moved aside as Cort and Dilia walked out the door.

A warm breeze carried a vague scent of garbage from the city below. The air jets quietly hissed their subtle poison, but the air was still much better than indoors. How had he ever thought he wanted to work on the base, in the power station that fueled all this? He touched Dilia's cheek and whispered her name.

Dilia looked up at him and smiled and said, "Cort. I... was waiting for you. Can we go home now?"

Dilia was in high spirits from getting outdoors again, and—wonder of wonders—with Cort at her side. Her eyes widened at the sight of the thin-limbed alien carrying his huge pack. He looked like some kind of giant insect, all bulbous body and long, thin limbs. She burst into laughter.

Cort was laughing, too. "That's too much, Lennard," he said. "Take half that much, no more. Less, if you can."

Lennard's face fell. "But..." Whatever he'd been about to say, he must have thought better of it. He removed and opened the pack and began taking items out.

How many changes of clothing had the man packed? More than Dilia had owned in her entire lifetime.

"One set of spare clothing will be enough," Cort said.

"What about winter?"

"What about it? You will find a way to get clothing in the village if you need any."

Lennard nodded, and took out much of what he had packed. "What about food?"

"You starmen eat our food?"

"Why, yes, I..."

Cort folded his arms over his chest, looking just like his mother when she was angry. But he was smiling. "Then why are you packing food?"

Lennard laughed. "I don't know," he admitted sheepishly. "I guess my daypack will do." From his large pack, he took out a smaller one. He put a few things into it, slung it over his shoulder, and announced, "I'm ready."

Dilia didn't have a pack. Was she ready? She looked down at what she was wearing. Her dress flowed from shoulder straps to a wide hem mid-calf. It was bright red and so thin it revealed the lines of her body beneath. It would be worse than useless once off the base, and the night air was a bit chilly. "I think I could use some different clothes. And—oh dear, my shoes."

Cort looked her up and down. "Yes, you're right," he said. "Lennard, can you arrange something?"

Lennard spoke to the soldier, who went inside the house.

The soldier returned with a soft, gray cloak, which Cort put around Dilia. He helped with her shoes, and then he stood and lifted her to her feet. Still unsteady from days in the poor air, she leaned against him. They walked out openly through the base's gate, and heard it close with a loud thud behind them as they walked down the street of the city.

Unaccountably, Dilia started crying. "I've... I've... It's been so long, I thought I'd never—" She swallowed hard. "Thought I'd never be free, never see you again. Never go home."

Cort held her close. "It's going to be all right," he said, stroking her hair as if she were a small child. "It's going to be all right again."

Dilia wiped away a tear, feeling exhausted. "Are we going home now?"

"No, not home," Cort said. He bit his lip and looked down, and he frowned as if at a troubling thought. But when he looked back at her, his expression had cleared. "Better than home," he said, with some enthusiasm. "We're going to the khenaran."

"The khenaran, now, in the middle of the night." The idea was so preposterous, so unlikely, that Dilia laughed. Maybe it was just an effect of the chemicals in the base's air, but by Earth, it felt good to laugh again. "Cort, you're really funny!" She threw her arms around him in a hug, and he held her close. Then, trailed by Lennard and the commandant's soldier, they set off down the street, away from the base. But they did not go to the city gate.

* * *

"Lor, wake up!" Cort banged on Lor's door, and the noise carried up and down the silent street. Not a light was lit, and no one came to investigate the disturbance. Dilia stayed close to Cort's side, while the two aliens waited nearby. "Lor!" Cort banged on the door again.

The door opened a crack. Lor was barely visible within, looking from one of them to another. When he saw Cort, he threw the door open, and sheathed his knife. His curly hair was even more unkempt than usual, and he was only half dressed. "Cort!" And, with even more amazement, "Dilia! Cort, my goodman, you did it. You looking for a place to land?" Then his gaze rested on the aliens, and he frowned. "All systems operating?"

"All systems in prime condition, my goodman," Cort said. "This gentleman"—he nodded toward the soldier—"is going to let us out of the city. Right now, if you want to go."

Lor looked from Cort to Dilia to the two aliens, then back to Cort. "They'll be after you in the morning, won't they." A statement, not a question.

Would Karim come after them in the morning? No, surely he wouldn't be that desperate.

"You and everyone with you," Lor continued. "If Sleb's around come morning, my life won't be worth a slime rat's droppings here. I'm on this mission, my goodman, wherever you lead it."

Sleb? Dilia was confused. What did Sleb, of all people, have to do with it?

Lor's face lit up. "I packed some supplies. Let me just say good-bye to my folks." He closed the door.

"Lor's coming with us?" Dilia asked.

"Yes," Cort said.

"That's good," she said. "I used to like him. But why is Sleb after him?"

"I think Sleb could be after all of us," Cort said. "I'll tell you about it later."

A moment later, Lor returned. "Ready, my goodman," he said. He stepped into the street, a pack on his back. Lor's pack was bigger than Lennard's had been. Cort sighed, but Dilia just had to laugh. Cort would deal with it, surely, sometime when he wasn't in such a hurry.

Lor closed the door, and behind him, someone slid a bolt into place.

"Let's go," Cort said to the soldier, and the unlikely group headed toward the city gate.

It was a sleepy city guard that responded to the alien soldier's sharp rapping at the guardhouse. "Open the gate," the alien ordered.

The city guard rubbed his eyes and gaped. "Wha—?"

The alien soldier said nothing, but he drew his laser.

The city guard held up his hands, palm out. " Easy," he said. "No problem." He woke his comrade, and the two of them opened the heavy city gate, which rattled loudly in the still night air as it slid open.

Cort and Dilia and the rest of them passed through, as the alien soldier stood inside and watched them go. Then the two city guards went back inside, and the heavy gate rumbled closed. They were alone in the clearing outside the gate. Light spilled from the base above, and the full Hunter moon lit the area further. The fringe of scrub woods beyond the fields was visible as an uneven black border in the distance.

Cort surveyed their group. "I want to make some progress tonight before the moon sets." He looked particularly hard at Dilia. She lifted her chin and straightened her shoulders, and he gave her a smile. She felt she could walk for miles for a smile like that.

Apparently, he wasn't as happy with Lor's response. "We have to, Lor. I'm worried that something might go wrong. The commandant of the base"—he glanced at Lennard—"might reconsider. He might send soldiers after us. We need to put as much distance as we can between ourselves and the city." He touched Lor's shoulder and gave him an encouraging nod.

Lor looked away, swallowed, and said, "Confirm."

And last, Cort looked at the alien Lennard, who regarded him with disarming earnestness. Why were they even bringing an alien with them, especially this stranger? Then Lennard grinned happily at Cort and surprised Dilia by speaking in Arantu, "Ready?"

Cort returned the smile. "Ready," he said. "Follow me closely." He headed through the fields and into the woods.

They didn't get far. Much as she wanted to, Dilia couldn't move very fast. She was exhausted from her experience on the base. Lor constantly strayed off the path, which was narrow and barely visible in the darkness; and the alien's breath came rasping and loud, the desperate sound of a person struggling to breathe the planet's natural air. Cort's sense of urgency was palpable, though, and no one complained.

When the moon dipped below the treeline, Cort called a halt, declaring that they'd made good progress. He found a fairly level spot where they might camp and helped each of them find a comfortable spot to sleep.

⚜

Dilia woke before sunrise. She was chilly. She sat up, pulling her gray wrap more closely around her. Last night was a blur, but today she felt much more clear-headed. And here, right next to her, lay Cort. He was tossing restlessly, perhaps dreaming. She was with Cort, out in the woods, free of the base. She felt like a weight she hadn't known she was carrying had been lifted.

Cort moaned. He turned and opened his eyes. He looked drawn, older, worried.

"Are you all right?" Dilia asked.

"Just a bad dream. I'd like to get started, though." He sat up.

Dilia nodded solemnly. She wondered why they were on this trek and not going home, but Cort was already preparing to move on. Perhaps they could talk once they got on the way. "I'm ready," she said. "Mornings were so hard for me, there. Some days, I could barely get up. But today, I feel great." She took a deep breath. "This fresh air is wonderful."

Cort looked at her with such tenderness she thought her heart might melt. "That's good. You seem better. There were days I thought"—he swallowed—"I thought that no matter how hard I tried, I might never see you again. And now, here you are."

Dilia thought about her time at the base, about wanting, trying, begging to go home. About wondering whether Cort was all right, whether he was even still alive. All those weeks. "I feel the same way. Being there was like... It was like a bad dream I couldn't wake up from." She thought about her failed attempt to escape and being held prisoner in the commandant's house. And then, when she'd all but given up hope, Cort had come for her. But what were they doing out here in the woods with Lor and this alien? "Cort, why aren't we going home?"

"I'm so sorry," Cort said. "I wish I could have come sooner. I tried to rescue you the day Sleb captured you, but I couldn't. Sleb's men caught me and threw me into his prison. I managed to escape that night with Neder—you'll meet him later—and we went back home just in time to see..." Cort looked away from her, his eyes moving as if he silently reviewed the scene he was describing.

Dilia waited, afraid to interrupt him, not daring to breathe.

"I saw Sleb's soldiers leaving the house and setting it afire." Cort spoke in a rush now, as if it wouldn't hurt so much if he could do it quickly. His voice was choked up. "I tried to save her, Dilia, I swear I did, but I... couldn't. It went up all at once. They'd used some kind of alien flame-thrower. Maybe harvester fuel, too. It was so hot. She was inside, and I... just... couldn't get in." He looked back at her, his eyes pleading. "I couldn't save her."

A wave of sorrow engulfed Dilia, hanging heavy in her heart. Tears welled from her eyes. "Oh, Cort, I'm so, so sorry! I'm sure you did everything you could, and I'm glad you took me away from there. I don't think I could have borne going back."

He looked away. "I still have dreams sometimes."

"No wonder!" Dilia touched his shoulder. "I'm amazed you escaped Sleb and found me. How did you ever do it?"

The sorrow seemed to fade from Cort's face, and he smiled. "That's a long story, and one I'd rather tell after we're on the way. I want to get as far from the city as we can, as soon as possible."

When Cort smiled, Dilia felt as if the sun had just risen.

Dilia watched with interest as Cort set about organizing the group for a long trek. He started with Lor's pack. Lor suffered the ordeal patiently, despite—or perhaps with the help of—Lennard's friendly jibes and jokes about his own pack. Lennard's Arantu was surprisingly good, and he soon had them all laughing.

The trail through the woods was still narrow, and so the group was forced to walk single file. Cort led the way, Dilia kept close behind him. Lor brought up the rear, but he kept looking around and wandered off the trail twice. After the second time, Cort asked him to trade places with Lennard. The short-of-breath Lennard then brought up the rear, pretending he knew what, if anything, to watch for.

"This is going to take days, isn't it?" Dilia asked. She knew the khenaran was far away, of course, but she'd never thought about it in terms of days of walking.

"Weeks," Cort said. "Are you managing all right?"

Dilia looked around. The woods were filled with a variety of plants. Many, she recognized from her studies, more and different ones than were growing on the base. This was going to be interesting. "Oh, yes," she said.

"We'll take it easy," Cort said. He pitched his voice a bit louder, including Lor and Lennard in the conversation. "If anyone needs to stop and rest a bit, just let me know."

At the end of the day, Cort found a good place to camp, a small clearing in the woods, not far from a stream of clear water. Dilia glanced over her shoulder to where Lennard and Lor, both exhausted, sat by the stream. She put a hand on Cort's shoulder and guided him toward the woods, away from the others.

"What?" he said.

"Do we really need to bring Lennard all the way to the khenaran? I like him, but it seems... wrong somehow." She looked again toward where they left the others. Neither of the two had followed them. The sky had turned gray, threatening rain, and a wet breeze rustled the leaves of the trees.

"Why?"

Dilia took in a long breath then let it out with a loud sigh. The exertion of dealing with this topic was almost too much for her. "He's an alien, that's all. Every time I look at him, I think of Karim, the way he kept me there against my will, and he lied to me about it. And he was so... so..." She shuddered. "I don't want to be reminded. I don't want to remember."

"Dilia, dear..." He put his hands on her shoulders to hug her.

She stiffened but didn't draw away.

Cort let his hands fall back to his side. "Be reasonable, Dilia. Lennard is not the commandant, he's a regular person and a good companion. You said yourself that you like him. Besides, he helped me get you free. I owe him for that—*we* owe him."

Her fists clenched, and her lower lip trembled. "I *hate* those aliens. I hate all of them. Karim—what he did. He had no right. And even Abeni. She acted friendly, but she innocu—She was not my friend. She did whatever he told her to do."

"Not Lennard," he insisted. "Lennard's not like that. He's a good man, Dilia."

"He reminds me—"

"What happened to you is horrible, but you're going to have to stop letting everything remind you of it."

"I don't let everything."

Cort looked away. "I know. I shouldn't have said that. But you flinched when I touched you now, and I guess it kind of slipped out. I'm just glad you're here, with me again."

"Oh, Cort, I'm sorry." She rubbed her hands over her face, as if she was trying to wipe the memories away. "I didn't mean to, but sometimes..."

He put a finger to her lips to silence her but stopped just short of touching. "Don't say it. You just need more time." She was shaking her head, but he plunged ahead. "I'll be here for you no matter how long it takes."

"No," Dilia said. "Don't. I'm not worth it. I'm not worth anything any more." Tears ran down her cheeks, dripped from her chin, broke her voice into helpless sobs.

He pulled her close and held her until the rigid tension in her body dissolved, until her sobs turned into gasping breaths, and then until her breathing became even again. He wiped the tears from her face.

She looked up at him and laughed a small, hesitant laugh, then reached up and gently stroked his cheek. "You idiot," she said, at once disbelieving and affectionate. "You complete idiot."

She went down to the stream, edging past the alien, and washed her face. She felt a lot better, determined not to burden Cort any further with her troubles.

She busied herself with gathering soft leaves they could sleep on, and Lennard, concern clearly written on his face, began helping her. Nearby, Dilia saw some edible berries she recognized from her studies. "Aliceberries, and they're ripe!"

"What?" Lennard asked, reaching for his tablet.

Dilia laughed. "Aliceberries, but don't write it down, Lennard. That's the Starrish name for them. I learned it from the database at the infirmary. I don't know the Arantu name, but supposedly they're quite tasty."

Lennard looked disappointed. He put down his tablet. Then he brightened and picked it up again. "No matter. I'll make a note to ask someone sometime, when we have a chance."

Dilia gave him a smile, realizing she had something in common with this alien: they both wanted to learn more. "I'd like to know that, too."

"There's more than just berries for dinner," Cort said. He gestured with a tilt of his head toward the edge of the clearing. A bobcat stood in shadow, something lying on the ground in front of it. "Fresh meat, too. Time to start cooking."

Cort began teaching Lor how to build a fire. Then he paused, watching Lennard jot notes on his tablet. "There's going to be an exam, Lennard." Cort gestured toward the tablet. "On Arantu fire-building methods. Take good notes."

The alien grinned. "I'll be ready—and I'm also studying for the exam on berries. You can put me to work, too, you know. I'd like to be useful as well as studious."

***

As the days passed, the group made slow but steady progress.

With the help of his kiri, Cort made sure the group had meat, and Dilia took more and more responsibility for gathering and preparing wild fruit and greens. Ever more adept, Lor took responsibility for their campsites; he set them up, made the fire, did most of the cooking, and without asking what needed to be done, broke down the camp in the morning. Lennard helped however he could, but by nightfall he had little energy.

One evening as they made camp, Lennard asked Dilia quietly, "Can we talk in private?"

Dilia gestured his assent, and walked several paces away from the others. "What's up, Lennard? Is something bothering you?"

"No," Lennard said. "Something's bothering *you*."

Dilia looked away, off into the woods that faded into twilight. "I just wish we were there already."

"Yes, of course. Don't we all—but you, how are you doing?"

Anger flashed in her like heat, like lightning. "I'm all right, no thanks to your commandant. I didn't exactly enjoy my time on your base."

"No," Lennard said. "I imagine you didn't. I won't make excuses. It's... despicable. We like to think we are civilized. I think we *are* civilized, mostly. I hope you can believe that. Every generation, we get better, but still... sometimes someone does something like this, and..." He shuffled his feet a bit, as if there might be some more comfortable position, but he couldn't find it. "I am ashamed for him. For all of us from Earth. I want you to know."

"Thanks. I know it's not you, Lennard."

Lennard nodded. "I'm not making any excuses for him or for any of them. I just... I thought if there's anything more I can do to help..." His words hung in the air between them.

Lennard had been helpful when the others were confused, energetic when they were tired, cheerful when they were depressed. As the twilight turned to night, an insect nearby began chirruping, and others followed, so that the woods were alive with sound. Dilia's anger had vanished. "If I think of anything, I'll let you know. Thanks for the apology."

Chapter 16

Jerrald and the Soldiers

Hunter! The hawk called from high overhead.

Cort looked up but didn't see her through the canopy of tree branches. They had been traveling a long time. The journey had gotten easier—Lor now kept to the path, and Lennard didn't wheeze as much, and Dilia let him hold her hand—but still, he ached to be back in Neder's village. *Hawk! How far to the khenaran, do you think?*

No more than a heartbeat, answered the swift bird. *But at your pace, at least five days. Six. More. And you are leaving a trail so clear a blind owl could follow it in the daytime. You will not make it to the khenaran before the others overtake you.*

What? Cort stopped walking. The others, following, stopped too. *Who?*

A large group, said the hawk. *Soldiers, and an alien with them. They are tracking you. The alien seems quite good at it, too—for a land creature.*

How many are there, hawk?

Many. More than six. Six seemed to be the limit of the bird's ability or interest to count. *Many more.*

Cort told his party to take a short rest. He sat down and said to the hawk, *Show me.*

The change in his vision was sudden and dizzying. He was soaring high above the woods, looking down. He saw his group and himself far below, and many kilometers behind, following them, another, larger group. He counted thirteen people, twelve in uniform following one who was not.

How do you know one of them is an alien? he asked the hawk.

He felt a prick of revulsion and realized it was the hawk's feeling. *He moves differently. It is the one that also looks different.*

Cort returned to his own vision and shook his head to clear it. "Lennard," he asked. "Do you know of any reason why someone would be following us?"

Lennard seemed genuinely puzzled. "Who?" he asked.

"An alien, with a party of soldiers. Twelve soldiers."

"Are you sure? How do you know?"

Cort felt suddenly proud of his kiri and of the life he'd taken up, and the feeling crept into a brief smile. "Oh, yes, I'm sure. Also, the alien seems to be a good tracker."

Lennard scratched his head. "I suppose it could be Jerrald. He's head of security. I've heard that he's quite a tracker and enjoys it immensely. Sometimes he goes out with the tree harvesters just to keep in practice. I don't know why he'd be following us, though. Maybe just for the practice?"

"With soldiers?"

Lennard shrugged. "Protection? Or maybe Karim changed his mind?" He shook his head. "But that doesn't make sense. I don't know, Cort, but I don't like it."

Satisfied that Lennard was not party to whatever was going on, Cort nodded. "They're closing the distance between us," he said. "I want to move faster. Much faster. Do you think you can?"

Lennard's face expressed all the misery of days of long travel in oxygen-poor air. But he straightened his lanky frame and lifted his chin. "If Jerrald can do it, so can I."

Moving faster was difficult. Though no one complained, they all struggled to keep up with Cort. And Cort, growing increasingly anxious, struggled to slow down enough for them. Dilia stepped on a thorn, not a major injury, but she favored her cut foot. With the increased speed, Lor fell behind and lost the path several times, and the group had to stop and wait for him. Lennard managed the best of the three of them, gasping for breath, but keeping doggedly in Cort's tracks.

At the end of the second day of their forced march, there was no mistaking how exhausted Cort's three companions were. Cort couldn't ask them to keep up the pace any longer. He abandoned his hope of getting them to the shelter of the khenaran, where several of his kiri could help if necessary, but now he needed another plan. *How close are we to the khenaran?* he asked the hawk who had been his guide.

About two days away, answered the hawk. *Or three. You have made good speed. For ground creatures.*

And the ones that were following us?

No more than two days behind. They still gain on you. Do you want to see?

Yes, please.

Cort moved away from the group's little camp and sat with his back against a tree. He closed his eyes and was instantly viewing Aran from above. Though the sun had set, he could see every tiny detail. He saw his own group—Lennard, his breathing still ragged, talking quietly with Lor, while Dilia sat on the other side of the camp, her arms wrapped around her chest as if she were cold, or as if she held close some sinister burden. Cort saw himself sitting a short distance away. Then he turned his attention to the trail they had come down, and as the hawk soared, he saw a campfire. Around it sat twelve soldiers and an alien. The hawk was right. They were camped in the very spot that Cort's group had occupied just two days ago.

What on Earth or Aran could they want? Cort shivered. He had a strong feeling that there *was* an answer, and it wouldn't be a good one. It would chill him so deeply no campfire could help.

The next day, Cort was unwilling to push his group to move faster. Instead, he urged care on his friends to avoid leaving a trail. He followed a stream some distance, walking in the water, the others following him single file. But the stream wasn't heading toward the khenaran, where Cort needed to go. When he reemerged into the woods, the scrub bushes and vines were so dense that he had to keep to the path. And Lor, inept as ever, left a clear trail of broken branches and crushed vines.

That night, the alien and his soldiers had cut the distance between the two parties to one day. The next day, Cort opted again for speed.

By evening, the undergrowth began thinning out, and a few large trees dominated the scrub woods. They were approaching the edge of the khenaran. The ferret came to greet them.

Cort's heart lightened with the appearance of the small, playful beast. He led his tired followers after the sun set until, a few hours later, the Hunter moon set, too. Then they made their camp, too tired even to eat.

Only Cort stayed up. He flew with the owl that night, and learned to his dismay that their pursuers were only three hours behind. They could no longer outrun their pursuers, but he must do whatever was necessary to keep his friends safe. He made his decision. *Ferret?* he asked.

I am here, Hunter.

Tomorrow, I am going to send the others on ahead while I wait for the ones that follow.

The ferret wrinkled his nose. *They smell of hatred, Hunter. They intend you no good.*

Yes, I know. That's why I want you to lead the others. Take them to Neder's village if anything... if anything happens to me. Seek help from the people there, or the kiri.

Hunter, this assignment is no fun.

I'm sorry, ferret. But I need your help. You know they would never find the village, never even survive in the khenaran alone.

I cannot guarantee their survival.

The idea of his friends in trouble, of being unable to help them, brought a lump to his throat. Had he rescued Dilia from the aliens' base, only to bring her and Lor and Lennard into greater trouble? Cort swallowed. Perhaps the alien pursuer would be satisfied with him alone. *I know that, ferret. I'm asking you just to lead them. And to bring them food as you can.*

This will ease your mind when you face the others? asked the curious ferret.

Very much, my little friend.

Then I will do it.

Thank you.

Thanks are not necessary, Hunter. Another kiri comes, even now, who will offer you more than I can. But on this subject, the ferret did not know more. He could say only that the next day would provide the answer.

Dilia stood facing a khena tree, her hands caressing its rainbow-lit bark. She turned toward Cort and smiled and said his name. And she stepped backwards and melted into the tree. Somehow, the tree took on her appearance, with her graceful shape, and Cort felt a love toward the tree that was Dilia, as if it was a part of him. Then the harvester came, the terrible alien machine that cut through the rock-hard wood of the ancient trees. Cort screamed and tried to stop the machine, to tell the driver that the tree was a person, his friend, but he couldn't hear his own voice over the roar of the motor.

He woke terrified. The sky was light in the east. Cort didn't have to call upon the hawk to know that the pursuers were already on their way. Cort's stomach was in a knot, his chest tight. He didn't want to be separated from his friends, and he didn't want them to have to find their way alone. He didn't know whether he could protect them by confronting the alien pursuer, though he was determined to try.

Cort woke the others, who groaned and stirred reluctantly, as if their bodies were in rebellion from their minds and would not move despite their best intentions. When they were awake at last, Cort hesitated, searching one last time for any alternative. There was none. He steeled himself and spoke urgently to them. "Time is short. The people that have been following us will catch up with us today. I want you to go on ahead. We're only a day or so from the khenaran. I have a kiri, a ferret, that will lead you. Follow him. I'm going to try to stop the others. I'll catch up with you later."

At least, he hoped he would.

The first thing that went wrong that day was that the others didn't agree to leave. Lennard wanted to help negotiate with the other Earthman. Dilia fought back tears and begged Cort not to leave her. Lor pointed out that two sets of arms were stronger than one and said that he would die fighting.

"But I don't want anyone to die!" Cort exclaimed. "I'll just try to find out what they want. Maybe there's some simple explanation." He couldn't imagine what.

"Then let me help you," Lennard said. "I do have some authority among my people. It's the least I can do. Besides"—he gave an apologetic smile—"I'm pretty tired trying to keep up with all of you. I'd really like a chance to stand around and wait."

Cort returned the smile and nodded his acceptance. He turned to Lor. "Lor, my most true goodman, you are as brave and as steadfast as any. But if I am going to deal with this situation today, I need a calm heart. I don't want to lose Dilia again. The best way you can help me is to lead her away from... from whatever is going to happen here."

Lor shuffled his feet and seemed about to move on, and then he hesitated. "I'd do anything for you, my goodman, you know I would. And for Dilia, too. But we wouldn't get far without you. Besides, you'll need protection."

"I'll let Lennard stay, so there will be two of us, if only you will take Dilia and go." To Cort's great relief, Lor nodded. Cort turned to Dilia. "Go with Lor," he said gently.

Dilia swallowed and shook her head. Her eyes were shining.

Cort felt his heart would break if she started to cry. He took her hand. "I'm asking you. Please. It will help me."

The ferret came out from the woods and, as if understanding Dilia's need, ran a quick circle around her feet, then scampered to the start of the trail and stood there, waiting.

Cort smiled, his heart feeling a little less tight. "The ferret will guide you and hunt for you," he said to Dilia. "Just follow him. You'll be safe."

She looked at Lor, then Cort, and then the ferret. She narrowed her lips and raised her chin. "All right, Cort. If this is what you need."

Lor and Dilia quickly packed their belongings. Dilia touched Cort on his arm, then on his cheek, her eyes moist. "Be safe," she said, then turned and followed Lor and the ferret down the trail.

Long after the sound of their footsteps had melted into the background noises of the wind in the leaves and the insects and the birdcalls, Lennard turned to Cort and said, "So it's just us, my young friend."

Cort nodded but said nothing. He was watching in the direction from which his pursuers would arrive.

"I hope it's not Jerrald," said the alien. "He's a mean son of a... how do you say it? Slime rat?"

"Yes, slime rat," Cort said, noting that Lennard's Arantu was improving.

Silent and still, Cort and Lennard waited in the woods at the edge of their campsite as their pursuers approached. The alien entered the campsite, frowning, studying the ground. He was completely bald. His skin was tanned a deep, rich brown and shone with sweat. He wore clothing in shades of green and brown that blended surprisingly well with the shrubs and trees of the woods.

It was Jerrald. He looked up, and his eyes widened slightly when he saw Cort and Lennard. Then he smiled, an odd stretching of the skin around his mouth that left his light brown eyes completely untouched, and said, "Hello, Lennard."

His eyes, though, were evaluating Cort.

As the soldiers came up behind him, Jerrald gave them orders without looking away. "Company, halt. At the ready. Wait for my command."

"Hello, Jerrald," Lennard replied. "Surely you haven't come all this way simply to wish us a good journey—and with a troop of soldiers, too. Karim knows we left the city. We've done nothing wrong."

"*You* haven't," agreed Jerrald, but with a slight nod of his chin indicated Cort and said, "but *he* has."

Cort was surprised. "What?"

"Illegally entering Hsu-Lin Base. As head of security, I need to know how you did it. And, as you probably know, it is a punishable offense."

"But the commandant already let me go!"

"I don't give a bloody fart what the commandant did. Security is my responsibility, and I intend to enforce it. Speaking of which, where is the girl and your other companion?" Jerrald looked around the campsite, eyes narrowed with suspicion.

A green and gold and brown snake slid slowly from branch to branch in the trees overhead, blending almost perfectly into the dappled sunlight on the leaves, its movements following the sway of the breeze in the branches. Cort saw it and recognized it, and then he averted his eyes so that no one would follow his gaze.

Cort was still wondering what the alien had in mind, and how he could disentangle himself from this pursuit, when Jerrald drew his laser. "Answer me, boy!"

There seemed to be no harm in answering; the security chief could track them easily enough if he wanted to. "They're not here. They went on ahead."

"Fine. There'll be time enough to deal with them later. Now remove your belt—slowly, and let it drop to the ground. If you make any sudden movements, you're fried. Understand?"

Cort nodded. He considered trying to draw his knife and throwing it, but the odds were on the security chief's side. He didn't relish dying with a hole burned through his chest or guts or neck. He began unbinding his belt—slowly, as the alien had indicated.

"Come, now, Jerrald," Lennard interposed. "What's the meaning of this? You know that I have an approved project to study these people in the wild. This young man is my ticket in; I need him. If you arrest him now, I will make certain that the Legislature hears of this. They will be most upset."

"Oh, I am sure that they will be upset," mocked Jerrald, as Cort's belt, and with it, his knife, fell to the ground.

Again, Jerrald smiled his unsettling smile, and what gleamed in his eyes was a combination of malice and pleasure. "But not the way you think. They will be horrified to learn of your brutal murder at the hands of this savage," Jerrald indicated Cort with a nod of his head, "which unfortunately, we could not arrive in time to prevent. He was arrested and confessed to the deed—but was unfortunately killed while trying to escape."

I am ready to strike, Hunter, said the serpent.

Cort started. Mesmerized by the alien's speech, he had all but forgotten the snake. Despite Jerrald's malice, Cort hesitated to kill him. In all his street-gang activities, he had cut and wounded people, and been wounded in return, and had even at an early age seen death. But he had never killed a person. *Hold,* he answered without daring to look up, *until I give the word.*

But what was he waiting for, that he didn't already foresee? The words of the soldier who had saved Cort's life years ago floated into his mind. *Save someone else's life sometime.* He had to give the man a fair chance. "Look, what if Lennard and I go back with you to the city?

That should meet your needs, shouldn't it? I'm not going to murder him—or anyone, if I can help it."

Jerrald laughed softly, a chilling sound. "No, you're not going to murder him—I am. With your knife. Most pleasurably and most brutally. And every one of these men"—he nodded back toward the soldiers, their posture stiff, their expressions all painfully neutral—"will swear they heard your confession. And then these soldiers will bring you back to the city while I find your companions and decide how to dispose of them."

Cort shivered. He felt the man was capable of doing exactly what he said he would do. He was afraid as he had never been before, not even on the night that he fought the ferret in the dark. For the ferret was not evil, but this man...

He feared for Dilia even more than for himself. He barely heard Lennard saying, "Look, Cort, I'm sorry. I had no idea it would come to this. Karim must have wanted me out of the way more than I thought, and now I've given him this opening..."

Serpent, Cort said to the kiri, *the man has a weapon, and it is swift and deadly.*

As is my poison, Hunter. I am ready.

Poison! Cort remembered his own battle with the great snake when he was becoming a hunter, its coils more than three times as long as he was tall, and thicker and more strongly muscled than his thigh. The creature had dropped almost invisibly from a tree and wrapped itself around Cort, coiling ever tighter until Cort had thought he would burst. But the serpent had never bitten him. Had never given the slightest hint that it had any poison. With a rush of understanding, Cort saw that every one of the animals he had fought that day had given him the opportunity to win, had *wanted* to surrender to him.

Not so, the man he confronted now. This man would take pleasure in his slow, tortured death. And Dilia's.

Cort made his decision. To the serpent, he said, *Take him.*

The snake flashed from the branch over Jerrald's head with astonishing speed, and struck at the alien's neck.

Some of the soldiers cried out. Three turned and ran, but most stood watching with horror, or perhaps waiting for some order from their leader. But Jerrald ignored his soldiers. He whirled and fired his laser at the great, glistening, green-patterned snake; the hole he burned cut the creature near its head, and its long body fell to the ground. The head still hung from his neck. The alien's knees collapsed under him as he reached with his free left hand for the snake's head.

The snake's pain seared Cort's mind, fired nerves in his spine that made his legs go numb and his knees give way. *Oh, no, my friend!* He focused through the pain enough to draw his knife from his belt on the ground. *No, not this!*

Never mind, Hunter. It's a noble death, and I'm not sorry for it. Keep my skin to remember me. Do not waste the meat.

Seeing Cort take the knife, the alien Jerrald raised his laser and aimed again at Cort.

Time froze.

Cort froze. He could almost feel the coming burst of heat and pain.

A tremor shook Jerrald's hand. Despite the contortions of effort on his face, his fingers did not pull the trigger. Every muscle in his arm bulged, tight, and yet his arm dropped.

Jerrald fell to his side, paralyzed.

Cort ran to the fallen alien. Jerrald was still alive, watching helplessly, anger in his eyes, unable to speak. But it was the serpent Cort cared about. Gently, almost caressingly, he released the creature's head from the alien's neck.

In that moment, any one of the soldiers might have taken him, but it was as if they still waited for Jerrald's orders. As if they were in the thrall of a holo in which they played no direct part. Not one of them moved.

Serpent... I am sorry.

Do not be, sighed the serpent. *Another serpent will come to help you when you need it. This is my... privilege.*

And it was dead.

Released from fear, overcome with grief, Cort shook with anger at the cruel alien who lay paralyzed at his feet. "You think you're so smart, but you aren't. You wanted to know how I got into the base, but you never thought to ask how I knew you were following me.

"Think about it, Jerrald! You're the tracker. Did any of us ever double back? No! We were moving as fast as we could to get away from you. You know that, right? So on the day you were finally going to overtake us, how come I was waiting here for you? How did I know you were coming? The same way that I got into Hsu-Lin Base, Jerrald.

The same way I killed you just now. Because the animals helped me. Aran helped me. Did you even see the hawk flying overhead? I watched you from its eyes, watched you coming every day. They helped me, and they don't help you because I am part of Aran, and you and your people are not. You should never have come." Cort's voice choked with a sudden sob, and he swallowed to relieve the tightness in his throat.

If the alien understood Cort's outburst, he gave no sign. He no longer even blinked, though his lungs still fought the paralysis enough to make his chest rise and fall with shaking slowness. Soon, even that would stop.

Cort pried the laser out of his hand and stood up. He'd been aware of a rustling movement among the soldiers. Still in formation, they'd laid down their stunners and held hands in the air, palms outward. Their faces expressed fear, maybe, though that seemed improbable. Concern, maybe. Worry.

"Go home," Cort said. "Go back to the city. I didn't want to kill him, and I don't want to kill you, either." He felt the heavy laser in his hand and didn't want to raise it, didn't know if he could bring himself to fire it if he had to.

"Please," replied one soldier, the leader of the group from the sergeant's stripes on his uniform. He was a red-haired man with brown eyes and thickly muscled arms, ten or fifteen years Cort's senior. "We can't go back to the city. The commandant will believe that we turned on this startrash—" He jerked his chin toward the alien's body. "—and killed him. Our lives would be forfeit."

"Our families' lives," added a second soldier. "They will leave our families alone as long as they believe we are dead or captive with him." He indicated Jerrald with a tilt of his head. "But if we come back without him, they will think we killed him. The starmen will execute us, and our families, too. Please."

Cort remembered Dilia saying that the aliens had threatened her family if she tried to escape. He felt a welling of sympathy for these soldiers, who had families in the city.

"We can't live in the forest alone, either" said the sergeant. "We don't have the skills."

"Still, it would be better for us to try to make a living here than to go back to the city," said a third soldier.

"You are Inei-taru, aren't you?" the sergeant asked. "That's why the animals obey you. We are trained soldiers. Take us with you. Protect us, and we will serve you."

Inei-taru wasn't real. Or was he? "No," Cort answered. His anger was fading, leaving him feeling empty and tired. And what did he need a troop of trained soldiers for? All he wanted was to go on to Neder's village—his home now. "I'm just a regular person. My name is Cort. I was born in the city, like you, but I'm not going back there. I'm not rescuing anybody. I'm just going home to the khenaran." He hesitated, but his sympathy for these men, for their predicament, won out. "You can come with me if you want, but you'd better be certain about it. I'll try to help you find a place to live there, but it's a long way to the city if you change your minds."

The leader of the soldiers glanced at Lennard and smiled slightly.

Cort winced, remembering that some of the Inei-taru stories gave the hero an alien sidekick.

"As you would have it," said the leader. "Still, you are Inei-taru to us, and only death awaits us in the city. We'll follow you." The troop of soldiers murmured their agreement.

Cort looked from one man to the next, and each met his gaze with hope and pleading. "You'd better call me Cort," he said finally. "Not Inei-taru, or anything else. And you are...?"

"Aj," said the leader. "Formerly Sergeant Aj, of the Hsu-Lin patrol." And he introduced each of his men in turn.

Chapter 17

Into the Khenaran, Okolo's Village

Cort had little to say to anyone. He felt like he'd been run over by a harvester, with no feeling inside and little energy. He dragged Jerrald's corpse away from the campsite into the scrub woods. He returned to the clearing and sat, head in hands, staring at the serpent's sinuous body. If he had acted sooner, perhaps he could have saved its life. The responsibility lay heavily on him, but there was nothing to do now but to grant the loyal creature's last wishes.

The soldiers were staying well away from him, as if sensing his fraught emotional state. But there was work to be done. He turned to Aj. "Have your men make a fire for me, would you?" It would be dark by the time they cooked and ate a meal. There would be no catching up with Lor and Dilia this day. Cort sighed. "And tell them to settle in for the night."

Aj barked a few commands to his soldiers. Some of these went off to gather wood and started a small fire. Then they pitched their camping tents, fetched water, and generally exhibited the camaraderie and discipline of a group of professionals used to working together.

Cort set about skinning the dead serpent.

Lennard struggled to his feet, showing his exhaustion clearly. But he put on a smile, drew a deep breath, and approached the fire, where Cort was working. "Can I help?"

Cort had set the skin aside and was cutting the meat into chunks. He glanced at Lennard, but the sympathy in the alien's eyes was too much for him, and he looked away. "That's all right, Lennard." He put some of the chunks on the fire to roast.

Lennard touched Cort gently on the shoulder. "It's not your fault."

"I waited too long, trying to work things out with Jerrald. I should have given the serpent the command sooner. Maybe Jerrald would have been less ready."

Lennard pressed his lips together and shook his head. "Not Jerrald. It would have worked out the same for your serpent."

Cort sighed.

"The fact that you gave Jerrald time to change his mind speaks to the goodness in you, Cort."

"Naivete," Cort said.

Lennard let out a little breath of laughter. "It beats cynicism. Good people are always willing to see good in others. I really am sorry about the serpent, though. I see it meant a lot to you."

Cort finished putting the snake meat on the fire and began stirring it. "Thanks, Lennard."

"That smells delicious," Lennard said. "But you're not expecting us to eat snake meat, are you?"

"Are you hungry?"

Lennard's face twisted, looking like his stomach was not agreeing with him. "For snake meat? From a poisonous snake?"

"This is the only dinner there is, Lennard. I want everyone to have some. You too."

"I'll do it, if you want. But why?"

"Because the serpent wanted it."

"You have a special power to know what the serpent wanted?" Lennard spoke half in jest, but his hand twitched in a reflexive move toward his tablet.

Cort answered simply, "Yes."

They settled into a companionable silence. Then Lennard asked, "Do you think it would be all right if I... that is, do you think anyone would take offense if… Cort, I think I'd like to bury Jerrald—if it's not offensive to your people."

Cort shrugged. "I don't care. He's not part of Aran. Do what you want."

This seemed to spark the xenologist's interest. "You care a lot about what the snake might have wanted, but not about Jerrald. Yet Jerrald, with all his faults was, after all, a human being, and the snake was only an animal."

"The serpent was my kiri," Cort flared, suddenly angry. "He died defending me. I have an obligation to that serpent. And, yes, I do care about him."

"As if he were a person," Lennard observed.

"He *was* a person! Just not a human one."

"But, Cort, surely you know the difference between an animal and a human. A human can talk… reason…"

"Act nobly," Cort said, "and share friendship."

Lennard nodded. "Exactly."

"Lennard, the serpent—all the kiri—do all those things. They may not be human, but that serpent was as intelligent in its way as any of the people here."

"I understand you think highly of the serpent," Lennard said. "And he certainly did me a good turn, as well as you. But it's quite a leap from there to say that the creature can speak and… and all that. I'm certain I did not hear it speak."

Cort stared blankly at Lennard for a moment, and then he realized what the alien's problem was. "Of course you didn't! Because you don't have one of these. Look." Cort brushed back his hair with his hand to reveal the red jewel embedded in the skin at his hairline just above the ear. "I communicate with my kiri through this. You wouldn't hear anything. How did you think I knew we were being followed?"

Lennard reached out to touch the gem, and Cort let him. "Does it grow there like that? I never noticed it before. Does everyone have one?"

Cort shook his head solemnly. "No. It's implanted. Very few people have them." Then he became aware of the smell of burning meat. He wrinkled his nose. "Enough talk. Let's have dinner. Afterwards, I'll ask the soldiers to help you bury Jerrald if you'd like."

Cort couldn't stay with the others in their camp. It was too loud. The soldiers joked and bantered and reveled in the newfound freedom that had come unexpectedly upon them. Even their breathing sounded loud to him. Cort found a spot about a hundred meters away where the ground was carpeted with moss, and he made his own small camp there.

The first thing he did once he was alone was to check that Dilia and Lor were safe. He lay back and let the owl carry his sight far into the night, where he watched them sleeping quietly near the bank of the wide river that marked the boundary with the khenaran. He breathed a sigh of relief. Then he and the owl sped northwest across the miles to Neder's village, still far away, where no one stirred in the moonlight. If only they were there already! He sighed at the thought of how many days of travel remained. Then he left the owl to its hunting and fell into a tired sleep.

Cort dreamed he had sunk into the earth. All around him, the earth was red and soft and somehow nurturing. He luxuriated in its warmth. But something was wrong. In the distance a great machine rumbled. He could feel its vibrations through the earth, a distant humming at first, but it was coming closer. The machine was cutting the earth, and the earth bled. The rivers ran red with its blood. Cort tossed and turned in the womb of the earth, but there was no escape as the machine came closer. Now the noise of the engine was louder than his ears could stand. He screamed, but couldn't hear his own voice. The blade of the machine was about to cut into him—

When he woke, it was still night. Though the night was full of sounds—insects chirping, a breeze rustling the leaves of the trees, a small stream tumbling over rocks just at the edge of hearing—the silence was overwhelming. He sat up, tense with the threat of danger, until he understood that it had been a dream. Then he sank back down and touched his cheek to the moss that covered the earth where he slept. It was as soft as the finest Starrish silk. He was overwhelmed with grief for the mutilated earth in his dream, for the people and animals and trees that had been destroyed when the aliens and their machines tore up the khenaran. His sorrow felt like a weight in his chest, more than he could carry. He stroked the yielding ground as if it were a person, as if they could comfort each other.

There would be no more sleep this night. Perhaps only a person already helplessly awake could make out the slightly lighter color of the eastern sky, but it was enough for Cort. He'd been apart from Dilia only one day, but after the weeks of forced separation, even just one day was too much. Time to get moving. Time to reunite with Dilia and Lor. He woke the others. Within the hour, Cort led a troop of tired soldiers and one bemused alien through the gloom of the pre-dawn forest.

Cort could hardly wait to see Dilia and Lor again, so he set a fast pace, and he checked regularly on the two of them through the hawk's eyes. Following the river toward its source, Lor and Dilia had angled far toward the north, away from Neder's village. Cort didn't try to track them on the ground. Knowing where they were, and where they were heading, he cut directly through the woods, adjusting his own course from time to time so that his path would intersect with theirs, at times pushing through the undergrowth where a direct trail was lacking.

Behind him, the soldiers trampled a trail so beaten down that even Lennard had no trouble keeping up.

Cort overtook Dilia and Lor late that afternoon at a spot where the surface of the river was still and wide, almost like a lake. They had paused for a drink, but looked up when Cort called their names.

"Cort, my goodman!" Lor said.

Dilia stood and ran to him with a hug. "We worried about you when you didn't come last night."

The hug felt wonderful, and he prolonged it, holding her close. He wanted more of this new, physical level of their friendship and wondered whether Dilia did too. "I worried about you, too." He looked for the little ferret and saw him at the edge of the woods. *Thank you.*

"What's this?" Dilia asked, touching the snakeskin that Cort had draped over his shoulders.

"He's going native," Lor said, laughing.

Cort returned the jest. "Did that a long time ago. I'm just waiting for you to catch up."

"We're working on it," Dilia said with a smile, "aren't we, Lor? And here's the khenaran in sight on the other side of the river. Now we just have to get there."

There was a crash from behind Cort, and laughter. Dilia started, then gripped Cort's arm as the band of soldiers marched into the clearing.

"I was going to tell you," Cort said. He patted Dilia's hand. "They're friends. They'll be traveling with us. This is Aj." He made introductions all around, and the awkward, formal courtesy with which the soldiers greeted Dilia coaxed a tentative smile from her.

They were not far from a good ford. Everyone was eager to enter the khenaran, and so the group traveled into the evening, until at last Cort allowed them, wet and tired, to pitch tents and light a fire on the far side of the river.

The Hunter moon was full; the Kiri moon flamed red in front of it. Long after the others had gone to sleep and the fire had died down, Cort still couldn't face his dreams. When he heard the wolves howling in the distance, he set out at a steady lope and met the pack in less than an hour. They hunted in the night by moonlight, and Cort staggered under the weight of the dhelo he carried into the encampment at dawn, reeking of blood.

When he woke later that morning, Cort took stock of their situation. The soldiers were in good shape, having marched for days under Jerrald's leadership. Dilia and Lor could also continue, but Lennard was clearly exhausted. The alien wasn't complaining, but he looked more gaunt than ever, and he'd fallen asleep in his tracks the night before. Cort declared a rest day to give Lennard a chance to recover. And to give himself time to figure out how he was going to keep a group of sixteen travelers fed. To his surprise, a couple of the soldiers set about skinning and preparing the dhelo Cort had brought back to the camp. They talked and joked around and were generally too loud, but Aj kept them focused on their task. Cort resolved to teach the sergeant and maybe one or two others some basic hunting techniques. He considered engaging one of his kiris to help.

Dilia wandered into the khenaran and came back with an armful of leafy stems that she called "cress," promising that it was not merely edible, but tasty. She was smiling like a child with candy.

Over the next few days as they traveled, Dilia smiled often, and her laughter was like a stream splashing over rocks in the sunlight. She moved with a lithe step, sometimes wandering, as he did, into the khenaran. And she found things—berries and other fruits that she had seen the birds eating or that she knew from her studies, and flowers that she braided into her hair.

She was more like her old self with the others in the group. She spent patient hours telling Lennard about life in the city, drawing Lor into the conversation, too. And for the soldiers, who were surprisingly shy and deferential in her presence, she occasionally brought flowers.

Best of all, when they walked together, she held Cort's hand. After her experience on the base, Cort was happy simply to be a close brotherly friend to her, but he began to imagine more. He wanted to live his whole life with her. He thought about talking with her about their relationship, maybe even about loving her, but he reluctantly decided not to. Not now. It simply wasn't the right time for such a conversation. He wanted to be sure they had their old relationship intact before suggesting anything more. And he wanted to wait until they arrived in their new home, not while they were on this unsettled journey. Besides, he didn't want to put any pressure on her. She would come to it in her own time. Or not.

As the days passed, Cort's lack of sleep left him with less patience for the soldiers' constant chatter, for Lennard's endless questions, for Lor's bumbling. More and more, he traveled by himself, a little ahead or to the side of the group, with Dilia by his side. As soon as he was sure Dilia felt safe, he went off for an entire day with the wolves. But with fifteen mouths to feed, whatever game he caught disappeared quickly, and the need for food and water seemed endless. Even ignoring the nightmares, he hardly had time for sleep any more.

On top of this, a new worry began elbowing its way forward in his mind: too many people. Tirei and Neder would be expecting him to return with Dilia. Lor would probably be no problem either. They might be disconcerted by the alien, but Lennard had an easy way with strangers, and he'd likely make himself welcome. A dozen loud soldiers, though, with their military discipline, were another matter entirely. And how could Cort ask one small village to feed and house all fifteen new people?

No, the soldiers would have to start learning forest survival skills while they were still on the way. And the squad would ultimately have to be broken up.

Is that a village? Cort lay awake one night, allowing his vision to soar with the owl over the khenaran.

Yes, though not the one you are seeking.

I know that. Neder's village is still at least two weeks away. But this village is close. I could use a break. Maybe we could stop there. I wonder if they would be friendly. Could it be the same village where Neder and he had stopped when he first came to the khenaran? But there had been no sense of direction then, no kiri to guide him. He wouldn't know if it was the same until he arrived.

To a hunter, answered the owl, *all villages are friendly. I see dinner, Hunter; hold steady.*

The owl plunged dizzyingly through the forest canopy to seize an alandhal with its claws.

The next morning, Cort turned his party northwards toward the nearby village.

A number of people are approaching you from the north, warned the hawk soaring overhead.

I'm glad you're around. Show me. Cort halted his group and braced himself against a khena so that he could concentrate on the hawk's vision. He closed his eyes and for a moment experienced the giddy feeling of dislocation as the view from high above the trees wrapped itself over his senses, and the feeling of standing on solid ground whirled away dizzily.

There! Look! the hawk cried.

Perhaps ten men threaded their way single-file among the trees. They moved quickly but warily, examining the khenaran carefully as they passed. They all carried spears. They were too many for a hunting party, too fully armed for a welcoming party.

Cort frowned. What were they up to? And how could he avoid trouble between the two groups of armed men, his soldiers and these others?

Best to meet these people by himself, first.

He found a place where there was fresh water and announced that the group would rest for a few hours. Lor let out a loud exclamation of exhaustion and threw himself onto a mossy area at the base of one of the khena trees.

"Look, I'm stronger than you are!" Lennard teased. He pounded his chest and then broke into wheezing breathlessness. "I could go on like this all day! And all night!"

Lor grabbed the alien's ankle, toppling him to the ground.

"No fair!" Lennard choked out the words between coughing and laughter. "Now I'll never get up again."

Dilia smiled, watching them, and as always, Cort felt warmed by her smile. "There's something I need to do," he told her. "It will take a few hours, but I'll be back before nightfall."

A worried look flashed across her face and was quickly gone, her expression more neutral. But there was strain in her voice when she said, "Take me with you. You know I can keep up."

His heart melted, seeing that Dilia's painful experience at the hands of the aliens hadn't entirely healed. But he couldn't take her with him, not when he didn't know the strangers' intentions. "There are armed men approaching. I don't want to put any of you in danger." *Especially not you.* "I'll be back soon."

Her eyes flashed, a touch of her old spirit that he was glad to see. "Maybe I can help! If it's danger you're facing, I don't want you to be alone."

"Dilia, please. I'm a hunter. No matter their intentions, these people won't harm me. But the rest of you"—he tilted his head slightly to where the soldiers were noisily filling their canteens at the stream—"we don't know what to expect. It's best for me to go alone."

She bit her lip, then nodded slowly. "All right. I see. I'll just help everyone get settled down here, then."

Cort touched her cheek. He wished he didn't have to leave her for even one second. "I won't be long."

He angled his path to meet the strangers, choosing a path where his steps made clear footprints in crushed moss. No point in hiding, when they were heading to meet his group anyway—and when he was planning to take his group to their village. Better to show them who and what he was now, and deal bluntly with any potential hostility.

He passed a large rock outcropping, then stopped and carefully stepped back into his own footprints. When the path he had followed crossed back over the higher, drier, rockier ground, Cort veered toward his right and followed the rocks to the largest of them, which he approached now from behind.

Hidden from sight behind the rock, Cort waited. The men approached silently, but Cort followed their progress clearly enough from the vantage point of the circling hawk. They went by without seeing him behind the rocks. They did not look back as they passed Cort, though from that perspective he now stood in plain view.

"Look!" the leader called softly. Two of his fellows gathered around as he pointed toward Cort's footprints. "Someone has come by here."

"Two people," one of the others said, "one walking in the footprints of the other."

"I think not," answered the leader. "One person walking forward, look, to this point here." He pointed along the ground. "Then he stepped backward in his own footsteps. Look at this print here." Again, he pointed. "He didn't step exactly. You can see how the indentation is deeper at the heel when he walked forward, but at the toe when he stepped backward. I wonder where he went."

It was a good analysis. Cort smiled. He had learned something this day. He took a step forward and said, "Right over here."

The men whirled around, their spears leveled at Cort. Hostile eyes examined him from head to toe, taking in the glistening green snakeskin he had draped over his shoulder, the feathers and snake-teeth and bits of fur that he had twined with rawhide and snakeskin into his hair, and the bobcat that stood at the top of the rock behind him.

Cort recognized none of them.

"Ah... Hunter." The leader of the party lowered his spear, and the others followed his example. "We mean you no harm. You will be most welcome at our village, since you seem to be going that way."

Cort nodded his acknowledgment. "Thank you. I was hoping you'd say that. But you didn't come all this way, armed as you are, to welcome me. Is there danger? Who, or what, are you looking for?"

The man's face brightened. "Perhaps you have seen them. Our scout reported a troop of city soldiers not far from here. They have never come this far north before. We thought to discourage them."

"I've seen them, yes. They're with me."

"With you!" scowled another of the party. "Teha, he is no hunter but a scout for the city soldiers!"

The bobcat arched its back and hissed. Cort tensed and dropped his hand near his knife, readying for a fight.

"Whether he is a scout or not, he is a hunter," Teha replied, giving his companion a sharp warning look, "and to harm him will do ill to our village. The kiri will remember."

Cort relaxed slightly. Maybe this would work out He made a placating gesture. "Yes, I am a hunter, and I tell you that the soldiers mean no harm. Everyone in my group has left the city behind, looking for a new life in the forest. We've been walking a long time—weeks—and the group needs to rest. We would welcome your hospitality."

The men exchanged glances. A few shifted onto the balls of their feet, clenched their spears more tightly. But the leader was having none of their hostility. "We are civilized people, Hunter. You will all be welcome in our village. I am Teha, son of Okolo of the Fox clan."

"Okolo? The seer?" Cort was relieved to know that the village he was heading toward would not be an entirely strange one. "I met him once, some months ago, and I'm happy to return. But I don't think I've met you."

Teha shrugged. "People come and go, for one reason or another. I don't think I've met you either."

"My name is Corodh-an-Aran, or just Cort." He hesitated. The clan issue could be a problem. But it was better to address it up front, here, by himself, than with the city folk present later. He said, "I hunt with a fox sometimes, but I'm city-born and have no clan."

Teha's eyes widened slightly, as if he recognized something in Cort's introduction, but some of the men scowled and murmured among themselves, casting him glances that weren't friendly. They spoke so quietly that Cort couldn't make out what they said, but when one man reached toward the hilt of his knife, the gesture was unmistakable.

The bobcat rumbled a warning deep in its throat. Cort's heartbeat sped up, and he moved his hand back to where he could get at his knife quickly.

But Teha put a hand on the other man's wrist and glared a warning at him. "Peace, Hunter. I said you would be welcome, and so you shall, you and your party."

The other man dropped his hand.

"You wouldn't be the clanless young man who killed a boar near here some months ago, would you?" Teha asked, and then answered himself, "But no, he wasn't a hunter."

Relieved at the recognition but also a bit embarrassed, Cort said, "Yes, that was me. I wasn't a hunter yet, back then."

"Newly crystalled, eh? Well, bring your people to the village," Teha said. "I'll tell my father you're coming."

Cort hoped that the two groups of people would get along once they met. He returned to his group and got them moving again. It would be only an easy day's walk to Teha's village, half today and half tomorrow. The group was in high spirits, marching up the trail as noisily and obliviously as the others had been quiet and observant. Some of the soldiers broke into a marching song.

Alone among them, Cort worried that the comingling of the two groups might not go easily. The soldiers would have to learn the ways of the forest, even as he had—and there was no time to start like the present. He took Aj aside and told him of his encounter with the villagers. "They will welcome you," he concluded, "but some of them are uneasy. You might try to be a little quieter. Keep your weapons sheathed no matter what, and respond courteously, no matter how you are addressed. I want no trouble."

"We want no trouble, either. Who knows—this place might be a home for some or all of us. You can count on us." The former sergeant spoke to the others, and they fell into an uneasy silence.

Around noon the next day, they entered a clearing in the khenaran. It took Dilia a moment to realize that it was a village. Small dwellings with roofs and sides of grass, leaves, and woven woody material of some kind were arranged in no recognizable pattern around a central space. It looked nothing like the stuccoed houses and rectilinear streets of the city. Women and men working in small groups broke off their chatter and stood and stared as her party approached. She moved closer to Cort.

A man came out of one of the houses, an older man with thinning white hair, unkempt like Cort's. Given his apparent age, his steady stride surprised her. He scrutinized Dilia's group, his gaze shifting from left to right, then back again. Dilia tried to imagine what they must look like to him—the hunter, the alien, soldiers, a young man in worn city clothing, and she the only woman, all in all a most motley assortment of people.

"Cort?" The man peered more closely at Cort, then broke into a smile. "I should have guessed. You are welcome here, Hunter. In my name and the names of all these people"—he made a sweeping gesture that encompassed the entire village—"I welcome you and all of yours."

There was a moment of quiet talk among the villagers, some accompanied by scowls. One person spoke up. "Not all of them, Okolo. Not the city people and their soldiers. And surely not the alien."

Dilia moved behind Cort, her heart pounding. The soldiers, too, moved closer together at stiff attention, as if they had to pass muster—or to defend themselves. Lor lounged at the edge of the group, his casual posture in sharp contrast to the soldiers' but with his hand close to his knife. Lennard smiled and stepped forward, arms extended, palms up in an open gesture. He seemed the very embodiment of friendliness, more eager than afraid, he who had the most to fear of all of them. Had they come here only to die?

Cort drew in a breath and seemed about to speak, but Okolo forestalled him with a raised hand and a frown. "Every person in the hunter's party is welcome. *Every* person. That is the custom, and we will honor it."

Dilia didn't know what it was—perhaps her face or her stance reflected her fear—but something about her drew a resonant response from one of the village's young women. She was tiny—much shorter than Dilia—with richly black hair that was tied with a thong and hung, loose and thick, almost to her knees. "Poor dear," she said, taking Dilia's hand, "how long have you had to travel alone with all these men?" She glared at them as if each one had been guilty of the most heinous crimes. Or at least thinking about them. Despite the woman's diminutive size, her straight posture and firm jaw radiated strength. "Come," she said to Dilia. "You must need a break."

Dilia touched Cort's shoulder, longing to go with this other woman, but afraid of what might follow.

"My daughter Nel," Okolo said with a smile of parental pride. "I can vouch for her."

"I will show you everything," Nel said cheerily. She was practically bouncing on the soles of her feet. "Everything! Are you going to be staying here? Your hunter friend is so handsome."

Dilia almost couldn't follow the rapid shifts of Nel's conversation, but the comment about Cort's good looks made her blush. "I'd love to see everything here," she said. "We might be staying for a while, but I don't know how long. Cort's taking us to the village where he lives now."

She looked back over her shoulder. Most of the villagers had dispersed, back to whatever tasks they had been doing before the city people had arrived. A man took a seat at a large wooden contraption with many threads attached. A loom, Dilia realized. A small boy stood at the man's knee, watching as he began work. Cort was still talking with Okolo, but he looked over at Dilia and gave her an encouraging smile. Nel was right, he *was* handsome, so tall and muscular. She'd never paid much attention before to the way he looked.

Nel turned and followed Dilia's gaze. "Are you two married?" she asked.

"No!" Now Dilia was *really* blushing. "He's like a brother to me." Or was he more than that? No, the relationship with Cort was too good. Perfect, really. Besides, after what the aliens had done to her, she could never have more than a friendship with anyone. She changed the subject. "How about you? Are you married?"

Nel laughed. "I'm not in any hurry. Besides, the men here are all so boring. When I get married—someday—it will be to someone exciting and romantic. But I'm not in any rush."

Dilia smiled. "Well, then, we have a lot in common. I'm not in any rush, either."

Nel took Dilia by the elbow. "Come with me, I want to show you the fish pond, and the lilies, and the best spot to find worrinot. Are you interested in plants?"

"Oh, yes!" Dilia said, and she followed Nel out of the clearing.

Cort nodded to Dilia, feeling strangely empty when she followed the village girl away. Empty yet glad to see her making a new friend and to catch a glimmer of the self-reliant person he'd grown up with. He allowed himself to hope that Dilia might fit into this different life in the khenaran. To hope that they all might.

He felt so grateful for Okolo's warm welcome that he took the glistening green snakeskin from his shoulder and offered it to the headman. "I know so many city people all at once must be an imposition," he said. "I will hunt for us all, and I want you to have this, as well."

Okolo reached out and ran his fingers along the smooth skin. "It is… magnificent. A fine creature." He looked at Cort. "I am impressed that you managed to overcome it, Hunter."

Cort felt a wave of sadness. "I didn't," he said. "The serpent was my kiri. It died defending me."

"Oh, Hunter, I am so sorry. The ancient stories say that humans and kiri were all born, ages ago, from the womb of the sky mother. But hunters and their kiri are even closer to each other than people of the same clan. I know how hard the loss of a kiri is. Surely you wish to keep this skin for yourself."

"No, I want you to have it. Please, Okolo, this seems right to me." He took the snakeskin from his shoulders and held it out to Okolo.

"Then I thank you," Okolo said as he accepted the gift, "with all my heart."

"Where's Tonio?" Cort asked, looking around again to check whether he'd missed his one-time friend in the crowd.

"He's traveling," Okolo told him. "His mother's brother is not well, and she has taken him and the other children to her birth village to see him."

"Pity." Cort smiled and waved a hand toward his group of city people. "I was hoping I could rely on him to explain clans to these people here."

Okolo returned the smile, and the wrinkles on his face turned into a map of merriment. "I'll ask someone else to do it, if you promise to tell me the whole story of how you've turned into a hunter since the last time we met. Perhaps we can share dinner and talk then."

When Cort was assured that all of his party were settled in the village—the men with space in the longhouse shared by the village's unmarried men, and Dilia with Nel in Okolo's house—he took his leave of Okolo and went into the khenaran alone.

The afternoon still stretched before him. A pair of cougars, his kiri, greeted him within sight of the village, and Cort ran with them until they came to a rocky area where the khena did not grow. They climbed to the top of a flat rock, warm in the afternoon sun. An open meadow shone in the sunlight below them. Half a dozen dhelo grazed there, young bucks.

We are downwind, said one of the cougars.

I can circle around, Cort offered. *The smell will drive them toward you.*

We will take two of them, said the other. *One, we will share among the three of us, and the other you can bring back to the human place.*

It was like the cougars to plan things out. Cort smiled in pure enjoyment of them and agreed. For the first time in a long while, he allowed himself to believe that everything was going to turn out well.

Long after the other men in the longhouse had gone to sleep, Cort lay awake. The soldiers had spread out their bedrolls in the aisles, and the house held almost double the number of people it was built for. Cort slept next to the door, but the air carried the smell of too many people too closely packed. The sound of the other men's sleeping rolled around in his head like the rumbling of a distant storm and hung in his ears like an indictment, the only person who could not sleep. Proof of some essential wrongness in his nature, which demanded his punishment by nightmares.

Of course, sleep might not come in any case, but Cort reluctantly decided that he had a better chance out in the open. He tucked his bedroll under his arm and silently left the crowded house.

The khenaran was beautiful in the moonlight, all silver and black, and alive with the chirruping of nocturnal insects and the susurration of a slight breeze in the trees. The air smelled faintly of something heady and night-blooming. Twenty minutes from the village, Cort found a place where the moss was soft and the moonlight played in delicate patterns across the forest floor. He spread out the bedroll—an unaccustomed luxury from the village—and lay back, allowing the whispering air to stroke his face as he drifted to sleep.

Cort dreamed that he ran with Dilia through the scrub woods near the city. Sleb's soldiers were everywhere, and fear of them cut him like a knife. Heart pounding, eyes wide, he searched the woods, but there was nowhere to hide. No kiri came to guide them, and the soldiers were drawing closer. Dilia seemed oblivious to the danger. She stopped to show him a delicate flower that grew almost from the roots of one of the trees. He tugged at her arm, frantic with the need to protect her, with the futility of trying to hide as the soldiers' footsteps pounded closer.

The moon was close to setting. Three men slipped quietly from their homes in the village and met at the edge of the khenaran. One, the leader, looked at each of the others, straining to discern their features. Their grim expressions mirrored his own feelings, and he touched each one on the shoulder with a decisive nod. Then he indicated with his head the path into the forest.

Only a few rays passed horizontally through the leafy canopy of the great trees that whispered of the approaching darkness. The three men silently followed the narrow trail that led into the khenaran. They moved slowly and carefully, disturbing nothing. All three carried spears.

They stopped at the edge of the clearing where Cort's bedroll rested under one of the great trees, the shape of his sleeping form within barely visible in the fading moonlight. The men waited several minutes to be sure they had not awakened him.

The hunter did not stir.

The leader of the three decided that the time was right. He made a quick gesture toward the bedroll.

The other two men nodded their assent.

With a quick movement, each of the three jabbed his spear deeply into the sleeping hunter. Then they pulled their spears free. They didn't wait to assess the results—and what would there be to see but blood and a corpse? Besides, there was the danger that a kiri might at any moment spring from the trees. Quickly, they returned down the path toward the village. They spoke not a word.

Chapter 18

Changes

F ascinated, Cort watched his own murder. He shuddered, imagining how easily he might still have been lying in that bedroll, dreaming of soldiers.

But the owl had awakened him scant minutes before his attackers arrived. There had barely been enough time. He'd hurried to move a mass of damp and decaying leaves and moss, almost composted to earth, from a depression behind his tree into a pile under the bedroll. Hurried to tuck the bedroll around itself in the rough shape of a sleeping person. And hurried to hide behind the tree as the men approached.

He watched his murder from a branch above, through the owl's wide eyes.

When the presumed murderers left, Cort came out from behind the tree. Because he wanted to be quite sure of his attackers' identities, Cort followed the three men silently as they returned to the village. They spoke together in low voices for a few moments; then each went to his own house. One of the three returned to the longhouse where Cort had earlier been trying without success to sleep.

This, too, might have been a narrow escape. If he had actually fallen asleep in the longhouse, would they have had the nerve to attack him there, in front of possible witnesses? If so, he would probably now be dead.

He stood for a long time at the edge of the sleeping village. Had he offended the villagers in some way? He had to know. Whatever mistakes he might have made here, he couldn't afford to repeat them elsewhere. He still had to find homes for Lor and Lennard and a dozen soldiers.

But what could he possibly have done to have merited such a death? This surreptitious attack would not attract notice in the city, but it seemed out of place in the khenaran. Cort considered the possibility that these village men might have just placed themselves at his mercy.

The next morning, Cort returned to the village as the sun was rising. Okolo's wife and three other women already stirred a pot of hot cereal over a fire, as Dilia and Nel sliced fruit into a bowl. Dilia stood as Cort approached and took his hand affectionately, leaning into his hug. "What, did you go out into the forest to sleep?"

Cort nodded. "Couldn't sleep in the longhouse. It was better out there."

"I really liked staying with Nel. She's great." Dilia smiled at her new friend, who returned her smile.

One of the women offered Cort a bowl of the savory, steaming mush. The smell of it set his mouth to watering, and Cort accepted. He ducked into the longhouse to wake the soldiers.

Aj was already stirring, as were some of the others. Hopelessly tangled in his bedroll, Lennard slept deeply in his corner. Cort shook his shoulder, but the alien was oblivious. "Can you wake him?" he asked Aj. "There's something I need to do."

"No problem," answered the soldier, grinning. As Cort turned to leave the longhouse, the ex-sergeant leaned over the alien's ear and spoke loudly. "Get up, Starman!"

Lennard jumped, and every other man in the longhouse woke as well. Still grinning, Aj said to no one in particular, "It's time to get up already."

Cort stood outside the door of the longhouse, studying Okolo's doorway and waiting. Villagers, perhaps a couple dozen of them, came from their houses into the clearing. Some brought food, and others had bowls and implements, and began dishing out the breakfast. As Cort watched, the headman came out of his house. He wore in his headband two long, curved red and white feathers, and Cort was distracted by them for a moment, wondering from what kind of bird, and how far, they might have come. But the headman turned to speak to the man that followed him out of the house, and Cort recognized at once one of the three men that had tried to kill him last night. The man saw Cort, and his eyes widened a bit, then he looked away.

The time was right.

His heart thudding, Cort approached Okolo and knelt at the headman's feet. The conversation between the headman and the other stopped, and Cort heard the scuffle of feet as people drew closer.

"What is the meaning of this, Hunter?" the headman asked.

Cort's pounding heart was so loud he feared it might be audible to the headman. But Cort said nothing, hoping that one of the men from last night might come forward.

None did.

"Please speak to me," said Okolo, his brow creased in worry. "What's the matter?"

Cort let the silence draw out as long as he dared. "I'm afraid I've offended you in some way, Okolo, you or the village. I swear I meant you no harm. Please—tell me what I've done and how to set the matter straight."

"No, get up, Hunter. You have not offended us. Less than a year ago you saved one of our people from a savage beast. Maybe more than one person. And just last night, we feasted on your catch. Your presence graces this village. Get up. Get up, please. Just tell me what's the matter."

But Cort stayed prone, his head lowered, until the old man knelt at his side and tugged gently at his shoulder.

"Please, Okolo." Cort spoke almost in a whisper. He had to be certain that he had committed no offense, had done nothing the headman might be reluctant to mention. "I don't want anything between us. I would make whatever amends I can. But you know I am new to the ways of the forest. I need to know what I must do."

"I swear that you have done nothing to harm us, and there is nothing you need do to make amends. Has my hospitality been lacking in some way, to give you this impression? You must tell me, Hunter; I will listen to you. But first, please, humor an old man. My bones ache. Stand, so that we may speak together."

Cort grieved for the pain he was about to cause this kindly man, so much greater than any pain in his knees. But he stood, and then gave Okolo a hand. "If you're sure I've done nothing to give offense, then I'd rather not talk about it anymore."

"No, you must," Okolo said. "Whatever has happened to cause you such grief, I would know of it. This village owes you much. It is our obligation to remedy any deficiency in our hospitality. Please, Hunter, tell me what has happened."

A crowd had gathered, perhaps fifty or sixty villagers, but not a word was whispered. From the woods beyond, the yellow eyes of a pack of wolves also watched.

Cort looked down. The words of the story were suddenly hard to find. "Last night," he began, "in the dark," and paused.

"Three men came into the clearing where I had been sleeping." He swallowed. Though he was surrounded by people, he could hear the breeze in the trees. A baby cried and was hushed.

"They carried spears. When I didn't rise from my bedroll or respond to their presence, they stabbed my blankets with their spears, and then left the clearing. I could have killed them easily, Okolo, but I was afraid I had somehow given you offense where none was intended. I let them go."

Anger flashed in the headman's eyes. "Believe me, whoever did such a thing acted without my knowledge or consent. They have shamed the hospitality of this village, and I say that if you but name the men, their lives are forfeit."

Cort met the eyes of the tall man at Okolo's side, and the man glared back at him. Cort then scanned the faces of the crowd. Most were looking at him with open curiosity, but near the back of the crowd, he found the two others standing side by side. One man would not look at him, staring instead at something in the dirt between his feet. The other man glared at Cort, frowning, his clenched fist just visible. Cort gazed at him until he looked away.

"I can't name them," he told Okolo truthfully. *But I know well enough who they are, and they know that I know. Now we will see what they are made of and whether they are worth saving.*

With the slow movements of a person heavy of heart, Okolo knelt before Cort. "Then it is my life you must take, Hunter," he said, "for

I offered you the hospitality of this village, and I have failed to deliver it."

Swallowing a lump in his throat and stifling his strong desire to bring the headman again to his feet, Cort turned to the man who stood at Okolo's side. Again he met the man's eyes, wondering whether, and how long, he would let this charade continue. Cort said nothing, waiting.

"Enough!" the man cried angrily, glaring at Cort. "I have done this deed, and the hunter knows it well enough. I, and Keva and Nesula. He has caught us, and now he's toying with us, as a cat toys with a mouse. We have seen the wolves at the forest's edge. Our lives are forfeit in any case. Let us put an end to this game he is playing."

"You, Denra?" asked the old man. He struggled to his feet, accepting Cort's helping hand. "But why?"

Cort's chest ached, suddenly too small to hold his swelling heart. He hadn't expected that this would hurt Okolo so much, or that he himself would feel Okolo's pain so deeply.

"Why?" Denra spoke angrily, answering the headman but watching the hunter. "Because he is city-bred and clanless, that's why! Because it's an outrage that one such as he should have special privileges in this forest. Because already other city people follow him, and even an alien. Soon perhaps the khenaran will be filled with city people and aliens who don't know our ways, and we shall all pay a price for it. I thought this the lesser of two evils, and Keva and Nesula agreed with me." Chin raised, Denra proudly awaited the hunter's punishment.

Cort was at once pleased by the man's tough spirit, and cut to the heart by the truth of what he had said. Cort replied quietly, "City-bred and clanless I am, Denra. I've made no secret of it. Yet Aran has allowed me to be a hunter, and I intend to honor Aran as best I can. That's more than I can say for what you and your friends did last night. The people I'm with all want to be part of the khenaran and learn your ways. Wouldn't it be better to take us in and teach us, rather than try to kill us?"

Denra looked away, his cheeks flushed. He folded his arms across his chest, and his mouth turned down, hard. "Send in your wolves, Hunter. I am ready."

But wolves were not what Cort had in mind. "Is this man's life truly forfeit, Okolo?"

A glimmer of fear passed across Denra's face.

The muscles in Okolo's face were rigid, holding in pain like a dam that might break. "This man is my first grandson, the son of my eldest daughter, yet I say to you that as of this moment he and the others are no longer members of this village. You may take their lives in whatever manner you desire."

Cort's heart ached for the old man. He wanted to tell him that everything was all right as it was, that it didn't matter, that they could all forget about it and live life as they always had. But that would have been far from the truth.

"No!" One of the two men at the back of the crowd cried out.

"Nesula!" Denra shouted.

"He won't take me like that! He will not!" Nesula broke into a run, away from the village and the people of his birth, toward the khenaran.

Growling, several wolves emerged from the khenaran. The villagers backed away, giving Cort a clear view of the pack. In an instant, Nesula was blocked by the great, gray creatures, their sharp teeth bared threateningly. The wolves sensed the man's fear with excitement.

The wolves' wild emotion rose in Cort's chest, too, and the blood lust. Heat raced through his body; his breathing quickened. The joy of killing a terrified quarry! He fought it down, struggled to stay human, and soundlessly cried to the wolves, *Hold!*

No, this one is ours! answered a wolf. Nesula veered away from the wolves, but he wasn't as fast as they were. In an instant he was surrounded by the pack.

I say hold! Cort turned to Denra. "Denra, you must help your friend. Now. If he panics, I may not be able to hold the wolves back. Walk over to him as if he were surrounded not by wolves but by mice, and take his hand and lead him at a walk back here. Can you do that?"

The wolves growled and snapped at the hapless man's legs, but, miraculously, he did not run. Perhaps he simply couldn't find a direction to run to. He stood with his shoulders hunched and arms raised, protecting his chest and face.

Denra glared sharply at the hunter, distrust spread across his features, as if he was wondering whether this was a trick, if this was the way he would die.

"Do it!" Cort ordered, holding Denra's eyes. Then he spoke more softly. "Do it, and live, both of you."

Denra nodded, then turned and walked to where Nesula stood trapped by the wolves.

You will not harm them, Cort said to the wolves. *They are mine.*

You will owe us, Hunter, a wolf growled as Denra walked past him.

Agreed, Cort conceded. *I want no bad blood between wolves and humans. Tomorrow, we will hunt together.*

It is not enough! As the wolf spoke, Denra took his friend's hand. He sought and found Cort's eyes, and Cort nodded to him. Denra and Nesula started back through the circle of wolves.

I will say what is enough. Cort allowed the wolves nothing as the two men walked back toward the other villagers. *I will hunt with you for two days, but for the pleasure, not as a bloodprice.*

Denra and Nesula reached the circle of villagers safely.

Very well, conceded the disappointed wolf. *Two days.*

Don't sound so glum about it. Cort allowed himself a smile. *Two days of hunting is a pleasure I shall look forward to.*

To his surprise, it was Denra who responded to the smile. "So, then, Hunter, what do you have in mind for us? Apparently it is not being torn limb from limb in front of our families."

"No, I..." Cort looked at Okolo, an eyebrow raised in a question.

"You may do as you wish," Okolo said. If he still felt pain, it no longer showed on his face, and his voice was strong. "They are no longer of this village. They are welcome nowhere. Nor will they live long in the khenaran, not after today."

Cort nodded. He had a flash of memory—Sleb's soldiers saving him from Karl so many years ago. *Save someone else's life sometime.* "Then let them come with me, Okolo. I could use their help." He was suddenly struck with another idea. He hesitated, not sure if he'd be overreaching, then drew a breath and plunged on. "If I take them with me"—In his peripheral vision, Cort saw Denra shaking his head, and he ignored it—"would you trade three of my men for them? This group of city people is too big, I need to break it up."

Okolo nodded his assent.

Cort turned to Denra. "You and the other two come with me. We'll leave here this morning."

If Denra and his friends could teach the soldiers how to live in the khenaran, the soldiers could keep watch and make sure these villagers did no mischief while they traveled. Perhaps the soldiers would learn quickly, and a few could be placed here and there among the small villages of the khenaran without causing a major disruption.

Cort turned to leave, but the third man, Keva, stated, "I won't! I'm staying here. You can't make us leave, Hunter."

"Perhaps he can't—but I can," Okolo said. "This man helped our village, but you have shamed us all. You are no longer of this place. You are not welcome after the hunter leaves." The headman returned Keva's hostile stare with authority, until Keva had to look away. He turned right, left, but none of his neighbors responded to his beseeching gaze.

"You must go," one of the men near him said. "Those wolves—the hunter has saved us but he also has in his power to destroy us. Be a man, Keva. Do what you must."

"But why?" Denra asked Cort. "I'll go with you, if that's what you want, and so will my friends, once they think about it a bit. But after what we've done, why spare us? Why take us with you? What makes you think you can trust us?"

"I need help," Cort answered simply. He was coming to like Denra and hoped the willful young man might, in time, return the good feeling. "You happen to be the ones who volunteered. And I trust you, Denra, for Okolo's sake, and because you risked your own life to stand by your friend."

"Hunter?" It was a frail woman with a long, thick braid, who spoke in a shaky voice. She stood behind Denra, almost in the doorway of the house. She was almost still a girl, yet she carried a baby on her hip, and two small children clung to her dress. She seemed to draw on every bit of courage that she possessed, just to address Cort.

He nodded, but the fear in her eyes didn't lessen. Cort wanted to kneel in front of her to make himself less frightening.

"I am Denra's wife, Neila," the woman said. "I would like to come with him. If I may. And the children, too. I don't believe you will harm us...?"

Cort swallowed. A woman and her small children? He'd seen how he could use the men from the village to teach the soldiers, but this was more than he'd bargained for.

"I am grateful for my life," Denra said quickly. "It is enough. I do not ask this favor of you." His eyes were filled with longing despite his strong-set expression.

Cort looked for Dilia and found her with the group of women who had been cooking. She smiled at him, the slight, sad smile of a person who had been caught in a storm but is beginning to feel the rain might let up. How could he say no to that?

"Don't think I'm granting you any favors, Denra," Cort said. "But it will be good to have another woman with us... for my friend Dilia. You may bring your family."

Neila let out a sigh of relief. "Thank you."

Cort turned to the other two men, who watched with open puzzlement. "If you have family you'd like to bring, they may also come." It was only fair.

A female voice said, "I'd like to come with you." For a moment, Cort couldn't see who had spoken. The crowd shifted slightly, revealing Nel, Okolo's daughter.

Cort didn't want to cause Okolo any more pain. He shook his head and opened his mouth, the word "No" already full on his tongue and ripe to be spoken.

But Nel had turned to her father and beseeched him. "Please, Papa. I want to go with Dilia. She needs me, and I'll be fine with these people, and Neila will be there too, and she'll need help with the children. Then... later... I'll come home again, I promise. Please."

Still, he would have said the "No" that was on his lips.

He looked at Dilia, and the word remained unspoken, such was the longing in her eyes.

Tears stood in Okolo's eyes, a frown etched on his features.

Dilia's pain or Okolo's—Cort couldn't make such a choice. The "No" he wanted to say hung heavy in his mouth, unspoken.

Nel walked to Dilia's side. She took her hand and looked again at her father. "Please."

"You may go," Okolo said with the great weariness of a man who could deny his daughter nothing, not even a piece of his heart. Then he spoke in a voice booming with authority, a voice that seemed impossible to come from his frail frame, "Denra and you others, hear me! This man is *Corodh-an-Aran*, Avenger of the Forest. Our mother Aran has given him more and greater kiri than any hunter ever. I say to you that the khenaran still forms him, and he will stalk a quarry greater than any hunter before him has ever dreamed, greater than he himself may know. Go with him. Help him. Help Aran." Then, as if shaken by his own pronouncement and by his grief, the old headman turned to leave. He seemed as frail as a leaf that had fallen from its tree.

"Wait!" The word came out ragged, as if it had ripped itself from Cort's throat. "What does that mean—a quarry greater than, what was it, greater than I may know? What quarry?"

"I don't know." The old man seemed tired and worn as he faced Cort again. "Those were the whynywir's words, not mine. Sometimes they speak in riddles. Surely, if you don't know what they mean, neither do I. But still there's truth in the saying, Corodh-an-Aran. You must find your own way to it."

Cort stood and watched as the old man walked slowly, stoop-shouldered and head down, back to his house. His own heart had grown heavy with the weight of an unknown but formidable task that apparently had thrust itself upon him.

When Okolo had disappeared behind the blanket that hung in his doorway, Cort turned to the people in his party—Dilia, Lor, the alien Lennard, the soldiers, and now the headman's daughter, the three would-be murderers, and their families—as if seeing for the first time all the possibilities they held—and yet his future was closed to him. He refused to give in to despair. "Let's go."

It was mid-morning before everyone was packed and ready, and good-byes had been said, and tears shed, and eleven nervous villagers joined the troop of city folk that headed slowly northwestward under Cort's direction. Between the small children, who often had to be carried, and the starman still panting for breath, and a general uncertainty about the future, they moved slowly.

Cort found he had ample time that day to sit and allow the heaven-borne ground view of the hawk to take over his vision, and still he could easily overtake the large group. He'd have no trouble making small corrections in their course as they traveled toward Neder's village, weeks away. But how would the group manage while he was out hunting with the wolves? The person most capable of keeping them together and moving in the right direction was Denra.

"I need your help," Cort told Denra as the sun lowered behind the western trees.

"So you've said." Denra circled his heart with his arms, protective, indifferent.

"Can you keep the group headed in this general direction tomorrow and the next day?"

Denra narrowed his eyes. "Why?"

"Denra, I have... an obligation. I'll have to spend some time with the wolves. I, that is, I owe them..."

"For this morning?"

Cort nodded once, slowly. "For this morning, yes."

"And what was the price of two lives, Hunter?"

Cort decided to take a chance on the other man. "Two days of hunting. But it wasn't a blood price. I don't want the wolves thinking that people are fair game for them. It would be trouble, in the future."

Denra stared at him. "All right, fulfill your obligation. I'll keep the group moving for you." And almost, almost he smiled.

After Cort left, Denra faithfully kept the group heading in the right direction. To his surprise, the soldiers were no trouble. Whatever he asked them to do, they did competently and without complaint, and when they saw something they could help with, they volunteered. Denra's friends were another story. They watched him sullenly from under lowered brows, arms folded over their chests, though to their credit, they helped out with their own families willingly enough. Perhaps, Denra thought, it was their wives that kept the two of them in line. Well, whatever help was offered, he'd take it.

He was glad enough when Cort returned on the third morning, his feral yellow eyes gleaming in the sun-light. The hunter sat on his haunches and watched the group eat breakfast. He didn't touch any of their food, no doubt already sated; stains of the blood of his prey still ran down his neck and arms. He startled if someone came too close, backing away to the fringe of the trees and seeming to hold himself near the group by sheer will. He suffered their closeness, their attempts at conversation, their gazes, saying nothing.

Denra assessed the hunter's tough muscles and fluid movements, his easy stride as the group headed out and the hunter adjusted the course slightly northward. Denra kept everyone together, finding the easiest trail, but his eyes were mostly on the hunter, who loped in and out of view among the trees. He realized that Cort had taken on a big task, a task that kept growing bigger, like the khena trees in the forest. And Okolo had said that Cort's task would get even bigger yet. Clearly, Aran had in some way claimed Cort as its own even though he had no clan. If Aran favored the hunter, who were Denra and his friends to stand in his way?

The next time Denra had a chance, he took both his friends aside. "You remember what Okolo said about the hunter, right?"

Keva grunted. "Something about stalking big game."

"Not exactly. He said..." Denra closed his eyes, searching his memory for the exact words. "'He will stalk a quarry greater than any hunter before him has ever dreamed, greater than he himself may know.'"

"Yeah," Nesula said. "It was weird. And then he ordered us to help him."

Denra looked at each of them. "That's right. So, we have a job to do, but it looks like you two are still grumbling about it."

Deva and Nesula exchanged a glance but said nothing.

"Seems to me," Denra said, "that if Aran has some big job for the hunter to do, it might be a lot bigger than whether anyone has a clan or not. It might even be bigger than that whole city they came from. The way I see it, it just might be a really good idea to stop complaining and help in whatever way we can."

Nesula grimaced. But then he took a deep breath and said, "I guess you're right. My wife's been saying something like that, too."

Deva nodded his agreement. "I'm in," he said. "There'll be no end to the nagging otherwise." He looked over toward the group's camp, where a fire had already been built, and the delicious aroma of roasting meat wafted into the air. "Better get to work before the food's all gone."

Denra watched his friends walk back to the camp, where Cort handed them both empty buckets and pointed them toward the nearby creek. Denra wasn't sure whether he was jealous or sorry for the hunter, trying to absorb so much in so little time. But he no longer hated him.

Dilia had found some cress growing near the pond where they stopped for the evening. She washed it and set it out alongside the meat from Cort's hunt and boiled grains the women had brought. No one would go hungry tonight, which was quite a marvel, considering the number of people in the group. The four of them from the city, of course—at this point, Dilia counted Lennard as one of their own—plus nine of the soldiers, and now Cort's three "volunteers" along with their wives, two little girls and a baby, and Nel. Twenty-three people. It was like an entire small village on the move. Not entirely alike, of course, there were too many men and too few women and children, but still... How were they going to continue keeping everyone fed?

Dilia found Cort sitting alone at a slight distance from the others, and she joined him. "How far is it, do you think, to where we're going?"

"Neder's village. At the rate this group can move"—he gestured with his head toward the fire, where people bustled about getting ready to settle in for the night—"I'd say three or four weeks."

"That's a long time."

"Tell me about it." Cort sounded weary, like he'd been carrying a large weight for a very long time, with nowhere to put it down and rest. And that was probably true.

Dilia touched his hand. "Are you all right?"

"I could have run with the wolves a long time," Cort said. The light of the fire barely reached them but an occasional breeze brought the smell of smoke and cooked meat and sweat and dirt, and underlying all that, the sweet smell of the khenaran.

"I know." She smiled at him. "But you came back."

Cort shook his head. "Not completely. It's hard."

"I know," Dilia said again, softly this time, sharing the mystery of who they no longer were, of who they had yet to become. "We're both changing."

Cort sat silently, lingering on each detail of her. "Your eyes are hazel," he said. "There's not a hint of blue in them. You're not a city person anymore. And you're covered in flowers."

Dilia had twined flowering vines in her long hair earlier in the day; the flowers had wilted a bit, but the leaves still glistened, fresh and green. She carefully pulled loose one of the vines and draped it loosely around Cort's shoulders. "Now you are too."

He fingered the flowering vine. "Do you dream?" he asked.

Dilia shook her head. "Never. I don't think I could bear..." She pushed aside the thought of the children she would never have. She let her gaze fall to the ground and twined her fingers around and around the stems of the small plants growing nearby.

"I do. Nightmares." He looked at her, frowning slightly, his eyes full of concern.

"Tell me," she said.

"I don't want to trouble you. I know you have worries enough of your own. My dreams aren't that important."

But of course, if they weren't important, he wouldn't have mentioned them. "No, " she said, "you have to tell me, or otherwise I'll be worried about you, too."

He was silent for a moment, taking long breaths, his fingers twisting the vine he now wore. At last he said, "They're strange dreams. I dream about my mother. In the dreams, she's calling to me. I have to do something. There's a feeling of danger. But I don't know where it's coming from. I look around, and there's nothing but this terrible, urgent feeling of danger. But when I turn back, Mama's far away. Like she's being pulled away or something."

"That's only natural!" Dilia reached a hand toward him and gently touched his cheek. "Because she died."

"But you don't dream like that."

Dilia shrugged. "I didn't see it, like you did."

Cort swallowed visibly. "But that's not all. Sometimes I dream I'm sinking into the earth. And there's always a feeling of terrible, imminent danger, like an alarm ringing just beyond hearing. Some nights I can't sleep at all. When I was with the wolves, I slept."

"Oh, Cort," Dilia said softly. She tried to imagine what he must be feeling, but she could not. "Maybe you're changing too fast. Slow down a little."

Cort shivered. "I can't."

Chapter 19

In Neder's Village Again

The next day, Cort organized the soldiers into groups of three and assigned one of his "volunteers" and their families to each cluster. He called on the villagers to make the soldiers productive, to teach them as they would their own sons, the skills needed to live in the khenaran, and to do it as they walked on.

The villagers and soldiers alike took to their assignment with surprising enthusiasm, and even a degree of competitiveness. Lennard moved from group to group, always asking questions, always taking notes. And he was as curious about the women's work as the men's, a trait that endeared him to the women and earned him some good-natured jibes from the men. Lor took a cue from Lennard, moving from group to group and observing carefully. But he didn't go so far as to take notes.

Keeping everyone fed was a challenge. Cort hunted frequently, leaving Dilia in charge when he was gone, often with the ferret by her side. The small kiri did not complain that Cort hunted with larger animals, in fact, the ferret and Dilia seemed to enjoy each other's company even though they could not communicate directly.

In the evenings, Cort made a place to sleep slightly beyond the edge of the group's camp, where the fire was just visible through the trees, and the distant smells of smoke and cooked meat were overpowered by the light, spicy fragrance of the khena. Dilia moved her bedroll near his. Awake, he listened through the ferret's keen ears to Dilia's soft breathing, mingling with the susurration of the light breeze among the khena leaves.

He wondered occasionally, when Dilia was sleeping nearby, whether Dilia might pick one of the people traveling with them for her husband, and the thought made him sad, then angry at himself for feeling sad. He wished Dilia every happiness. Why, he himself, mightn't he... It was a thought he couldn't bring himself to complete. Her friendship was too important to him to risk her rejection.

In the mornings he watched from a distance as the group packed their few belongings, and when he saw they were ready, he headed out without a word. The group trailed behind him, reluctant to disturb him. Even the soldiers' sporadic outbursts into taunts and boasts and the occasional song trailed off into silence.

And as the group fell silent, the city people began to watch more, and to listen, and to draw closer to the folk from the forest.

Cort's vision was changing. To feed his large group, he hunted every day, and more and more, he shared the viewpoints of the animals that hunted with him. As night fell, he allowed the images from the sharp-eyed ferret to be superimposed on those of his own eyes. Sometimes during the day, he absentmindedly did the same. He no longer had to close his eyes to see as the ferret saw. The ankle-height perspective of the small creature at his side blended with his own head-height view of the forest to create a radically different perception, one that Cort increasingly enjoyed. And relied upon.

He no longer had to stop and concentrate in order to watch the slow progress of his small group from the map-like perspective of the hawk that flew high above them. Sometimes, the images of the terrain as seen from high above would float unbidden into his mind, and Cort began to integrate these, too, with his own vision.

The first time it happened, Cort lost his balance, stumbled, and fell.

The second time, he was able to sit down more gracefully, and he stared in wonder as Dilia asked, "Are you all right? Are you all right?"

"Oh, yes," he whispered to Dilia, who was both right in front of him and a tiny, crystal-clear little doll a hundred meters below. "I'm watching us all from..." He looked up, moving his eyes slowly, carefully, up between the tree branches to where the hawk circled. His dizzying perspective now showed him, and was, the bird high above. He pointed. "...from there."

Dilia looked at him, looked up and following his finger, caught a glimpse of the bird. She looked back at Cort, and her smile reflected the joy he felt. She sat beside him as the hawk glided out of sight. Then she let out a deep breath in a sigh. "I wish I could do that."

Far to Cort's left, and to his right, a pair of cougars guarded the group. Through two pairs of feline eyes, Cort saw each little, rustling movement in the vegetation, and the adrenaline in his body responded along with the cats'. In the hollows at the bases of the trees and in the tumbles and fissures of rocks, he was aware of the nests of potential prey—and dens of predators. At night sometimes, when the others slept, Cort roamed the forest with the great cats, knowing it as if for the first time.

The group reached Neder's village two days later. Introductions were made, and within a few hours, the visitors were settled among the residents of the village. Feeling responsible to provide food for the extra people he had brought, Cort went out hunting with Neder in the forest. Also, he simply wanted to share with his friend the pleasure of the hunt, each a companion to the other.

But Cort's nightmares were getting worse. "You sleep," he told Neder their second night out. "I just want to... sit here a bit." He settled at the base of a giant khena tree, and with his eyes he begged the older hunter not to ask questions.

"You cried out in your sleep last night," Neder said.

Cort shrugged.

Neder was persistent. "You got up and went out into the woods and didn't come back until almost dawn."

Cort looked away. "Doesn't sound like *you* slept too well either."

"I slept well enough. It's you I'm worried about. Talk to me, Cort."

Cort bit his lip, trying to think of what he should say and what he shouldn't, and how he ought to say it. He didn't want his friend to worry, but he couldn't think of any way to avoid the issue.

Neder waited through Cort's silence.

"I've been having dreams," Cort said. And he told Neder about them. "What do you think they mean?"

Neder shook his head sadly. "I don't know, but I think they're important. When we get back to the village, you should ask Tirei. He usually knows the answers to such things."

But when Cort talked with the seer the next day, Tirei didn't know. He studied with a frown Cort's gaunt face, the hollows under his eyes. "How long has this been going on?"

It was a good question. To Cort's sleep-deprived mind, the best answer seemed to be, *forever*. But he thought back carefully. "Not when I first came to the khenaran," he said. "I think it might have started with the staff of living wood. I mean, I know that wasn't a dream, but the feeling was the same, of utter, helpless loss. But the dreams themselves, maybe not until after I became a hunter."

"Did you have dreams like this in the city?" Tirei asked.

"You mean, before?"

"No. When you went back this time."

Cort shook his head. "I wasn't there for long enough. I never slept there. But it may have been worse in the khenaran than in the scrub woods. Why are you asking? Do you know what could be going on?"

"I am asking because the whynywir have asked me," Tirei said.

"Then do the whynywir know what's going on?"

"Probably," answered Tirei. "They understand so much. Perhaps they ask these questions to test a theory. Or perhaps to make you think." He heaved a long sigh and shook his head. "Who knows, with the whynywir."

Cort frowned, thinking. The conversation wasn't going anywhere. "Then what should I do?"

Tirei looked away, He sucked thoughtfully at his lower lip, then said, "The whynywir didn't say, but I think it might be useful for you to sleep here, in my house, for a while. Perhaps I might observe something that could be informative for them. Perhaps even helpful to you."

How many people had already watched him sleep, or wake from his nightmares? Dilia, certainly. Neder. Probably several of the people he'd traveled with. No one had had any helpful observations yet, but Tirei was a seer and a wise man. "All right. Thank you."

That night, Cort fell into an exhausted sleep.

He sank deep into the earth—but rest was impossible. The danger was too great. Huge, steel-girded machines ripped open the earth, moving closer and closer...

Cort woke with a cry of alarm, his heart pounding. At first, he didn't recognize Tirei's worried face hovering above him. "Nothing helps," he choked. "Nothing makes them stop."

"We'll find something," the seer promised.

But Cort didn't believe him. He didn't believe there was anything that could help him. He left that morning for the khenaran to look for the wolves because when he ran with them, he didn't think, he didn't worry, and he didn't dream.

Three days later, Cort returned, rested and bloody, carrying a dhelo across his shoulders. He was as shy as any wild animal near a human settlement. When a child ran up to him, he snarled and backed away. He might have bolted and run, but for the sight of Dlia, with Tirei behind her. Cort steeled himself and walked across the village's central clearing to the seer, suffering the curious stares of the villagers. He dropped the dhelo at Tirei's feet. He sought answers in the seer's gaze, but found only concern. And that—for the time, at least—was enough.

Cort slept in Tirei's house that night, fully, deeply, and without dreams.

The next morning, Cort felt more his normal self. He greeted Tirei with a hearty "Good morning!" He danced a small step as he greeted Tirei's wife Galeta and laughed when she scowled at him. He pulled at their daughter Lela's braids and returned her grin as she gave him a mocking shove.

Tirei seemed reluctant to disturb the young hunter's good mood—but several times he cleared his throat as if about to speak, then shook his head and gave Cort an apologetic smile.

As Cort finished his third bowl of warm cereal, Tirei said, "The whynywir want to see you."

Cort wasn't sure he'd heard right. "What?"

"They want to see you, Cort. In person. It's an honor. Only a few people make the pilgrimage, and I have never heard of anyone receiving an unsolicited invitation. It's a long journey, but you must go."

"Why would they want to see me?"

"I think it's about—" He seemed reluctant to name the thing that had so disturbed Cort before he'd left with the wolves. "About what we discussed before."

"But why can't they just ask whatever they want through you, like before?"

Tirei shrugged. "They want to see you," he repeated. "In person."

Cort mulled the idea over. Going hunting for a few days was one thing, but he didn't want to leave the village for yet another long journey. Didn't want to leave Dilia for, what, weeks? Months? And there were too many city people to stay for more than a few weeks in this one village. Who would hunt to keep them fed? No, the city people were his responsibility, and he still needed to spread them out and help settle them into other villages in the khenaran. "Is it far?" he asked, and then, "Can't they come here?"

"Yes, it's quite far." Leaning forward, Tirei added, "Cort, the whynywir do not visit the villages of men, and it is probably well that they do not. They know much, and their commitment to Aran is beyond question. But... they are not like us. They are much more alien in some ways than your friend Lennard, though without doubt the whynywir are of the khenaran and belong here. Humans have never been comfortable in the presence of the whynywir, and perhaps neither are they with us. No one questions the wisdom of their staying away."

"Stellar," Cort muttered. "Just stellar. Sounds like a great trip."

Tirei ignored Cort's city slang and his sarcasm. "Nevertheless, they probably know the answers you're seeking. Think it over, Cort. But don't take too long. Soon it will be midsummer. The journey is long, and by the autumn equinox, the mountains will be covered with snow and impassable."

Reading the seer's concern, Cort acquiesced. "All right. I'll think about it." Before he committed to anything, he wanted to talk with Dilia. And if things went the way he hoped they would, there was no way he'd be leaving the village for a months-long trip.

Dilia was working with Nel and a few other women planting a crop of turnia for late-autumn harvest when she saw Cort approaching.

Between his time hunting and hers helping in the fields, she hadn't spent time with him for days. She smiled and waved excitedly, then put down her trowel, stood, and joined him. "I'm so glad you're here! I was hoping to see you."

"Me?" he asked. "Or you were just hoping for a break from your planting?"

For an instant, she wondered if he was serious, but no, she recognized that joking twinkle in his eyes, and she smiled more broadly.

He returned the grin. "It's good to see you looking so happy."

"I like it here." She glanced back at Nel, who nodded. "Do you have time?" she asked Cort. "Nel and I have been exploring in the khenaran a bit, and there's something I'd like to show you."

"I'd like to see it," Cort said. "Now?"

Dilia looked at Nel. "Do you think we can? Or should we finish this first?"

"It's almost lunchtime," Nel said, "and we shouldn't be planting in the heat of the day in any case."

Dilia pushed back a stray lock of hair, then rubbed the back of her neck, suddenly unsure. "We can invite Nel, too, can't we, Cort? And maybe Lor, too? We could make a picnic of it."

"Of course," he said.

The four young people packed a lunch of leftover venison, carrots from the fields, and thinly-sliced turnia, and set out. Dilia led the way, happy to have a chance just to relax with Cort and their friends. The warm sunshine on her skin seemed to reflect the glow she felt within. Rain the night before had left the air fresh and the leaves glistening. She breathed in the spicy, clean scent of the khena trees and the underlying perfume of wildflowers. For a long time, the four walked in silence.

It was Lor who spoke first. "Hey, Cort, do you remember the time that Tark was late and Stas was going to punish him by making him spend the night outside the gates?" he asked as they descended a narrow trail that picked its way among rocks and thorny bushes full of unripe berries. It was the first that any of them had spoken in an hour.

Dilia frowned. "Who's Stas? I don't remember him." She bit her lip. Was her memory going bad? Did this have something to do with what the aliens had done to her?

"You probably didn't meet him," Lor said. "He was someone we knew from—"

"From school," Cort said, a little too quickly.

From that gang they'd belonged to, Dilia realized. The one Cort never talked about—as if he could keep from her what he'd been doing every afternoon. She turned to look at Lor. He'd been keeping smoothly and effortlessly to the trail, not nearly as bumbling as he used to be. His hair was longer, too, and he'd braided a feather into it. Lor was changing, becoming more attuned to the ways of the khenaran. They all were. "What, was he your gang leader? Do you think I didn't know? Go ahead, that's all finished now. You can talk about it."

Cort blushed. It was quite charming. The man was hard to resist even when he was embarrassed.

"Go ahead," Dilia urged, not quite managing to keep a bit of laughter from her voice. "Tell us about that time, if you remember it."

Cort turned his head, and for a moment his gaze was far away. "I remember. We all thought it was the most terrible punishment. We thought he would die."

Lor grimaced. "Or be kidnapped by savages or something. But Stas was probably joking, don't you think?"

"No, he was serious," Cort said. "It was all I could do to talk him out of it." There was something about the faraway look in Cort's eyes, perhaps sadness.

"So, what happened to this Stas?" Dilia asked.

"He died, must be two years ago now. Got injured, and the wound got infected, and we couldn't get hold of any of the aliens' medicine."

Dilia touched his arm. "I'm sorry," she said. "You liked him, didn't you?"

Cort made an assenting noise.

"I bet that wouldn't have happened if he'd been injured in the forest. Herbs are a lot better than those drugs you all tried to steal from the aliens."

"It's hard to believe we ever thought that way, isn't it?" asked Lor. "Now, leaving the city seems like a real opportunity."

"I'm glad you like it here," Nel said. She smiled at Lor, and the smile she gave him, and her appraising glance, lingered.

"It's wonderful here in the khenaran," Dilia answered, pushing on ahead. "There's so much to see and do and discover. Oh, look!" She pointed past the bushes to her right, and she waited for the others to catch up. A vine covered with delicate blue flowers climbed the trunk of one of the great trees, and among the flowers perhaps half a dozen blue-and-gold butterflies fluttered. Patterns of sunlight filtered by the tree's delicate leaves played over the vine. When the sunlight touched one of the butterflies, the creature's wings glistened like the living wood.

They watched the scene silently for a moment.

"That's beautiful," Cort said. "Thank you. I might have walked right by it without noticing. Do you know what they're called?"

Dilia stood a little taller, pleased by the compliment. Even prouder that she knew the answer. "People call the flowers *blue gems*. They make a tea from them that relieves muscle pains and cramps. Isn't that right, Nel? And what are the butterflies called?"

"*Gemsuckers*," Nel said. "Funny name, isn't it? But they really do drink the nectar of the flowers."

"You both know a lot," Lor said admiringly. "I'll never be able to learn all that."

"Oh, but you will," Nel said, smiling dreamily at him

Lor's face reddened, and he quickly looked away.

They ate lunch in the valley Dilia had in mind. It was filled with starflowers, tiny ankle-height plants covered by white flowers with a thick, heady perfume. Bees and brightly colored butterflies were everywhere, and the flowers were so rich that the insects completely ignored the human intruders. Cort leaned back, smiling as the breeze ruffled his hair. "All the forest is pleasant, but this... The air is so sweet."

Warmed by his enjoyment as well as the sunlight, Dilia beamed. "I was hoping you'd like it."

Lor flopped onto the ground near Nel and said, "I like it, too. People in the city don't know what they're missing."

Nel turned to look at him. "You think so?"

"I do." He blushed again and fell silent.

Those two clearly needed some time alone. Dilia met Cort's eyes. "Let's go for a little walk, just you and me." She gave Nel and Lor a look as loaded with significance as she could make it.

He followed her gaze. His eyes widened. "Oh. Sure." He stood and took Dilia's hand, and together they walked back toward the trees. "It's cooler here in the shade."

"Do you think he likes her?" Dilia asked as soon as they were away from the others.

"Lor? Nel?"

She laughed. "Well, I'm not talking about the alien!"

"Yes, I think he might."

"She likes him."

"Really?"

"Oh, Cort, can't you see it? Sometimes you're just impossible!" Dilia laughed. "I thought we might give them a little time alone."

He looked at her in a dreamy way, as if he was envisioning a bright and splendid future for them, a future he still believed was possible. "And maybe..." He hesitated, then swallowed audibly and said, "Maybe you and I too."

Dilia's heart lurched. She took her hand from his and wrapped her arms around her chest. "Yes, of course, but... it's different for us."

Cort crossed his own arms on his chest, mirroring her gesture. He wrinkled his brow. "I don't understand. How is it different?"

She looked down, unsure what to say or how to say it. "I think... they're kind of falling in love."

He looked at her in silence, studying her face as if it had suddenly become transparent, revealing the network of her arteries and veins. "But we're... no, wait." He took a deep breath and let it out slowly, as if he had just come to a momentous and difficult decision. "I know we grew up together like brother and sister. I hope we'll always be that close. But I've been thinking a lot while we were traveling, and I guess I've come to realize there's no one else for me but you." He swallowed hard, took another breath, and touched her shoulder. "Now that we're here together, I want us to be together always. It's you I love. I always have."

Whatever had gone wrong with her heart was getting worse. "I... love you too. But..." Out with it. She needed to let him know. "There's no future for us."

"Why not? Just because we're living in the khenaran now? We're the closest of friends, and haven't we always said..."

Dilia couldn't stop her silent tears. "We can still be friends, of course, always." Her voice was small, but it choked up her throat. "But I can't have children."

He took her in his arms.

Dilia thought it would be unkind to let him hold her, to let him hope. She should push him away. But somehow her arms seemed to have a mind of their own. Or maybe it was her heart. She unfolded her arms and put them around his neck.

"Why do you think that?" he asked.

She spoke into his shoulder, barely audible even to her own ears. "The alien doctor... said..." Her throat was so tight she couldn't squeeze out any more words.

He stroked her hair, her shoulder, her back. Then he asked, "The doctor said you can't have children?"

She swallowed past the knot in her throat. "She said... they fixed it... so I wouldn't."

His arms tightened around her, shaking with tension. He emitted a sound like a low growl, swallowed, and then said, "So you wouldn't... back then? Or forever?"

Dilia pulled back just enough to look at him. His face was red and contorted with anger. She gasped. "Oh, Cort, please don't be angry with me. I don't know. I asked, but..."

His expression softened at once. "It's not you I'm angry with." He brushed tears from her cheeks and spoke gently. "But listen. That's in the past. Let's not worry about it. No one ever knows if they're going to be able to have children or not, and not just because of aliens *fixing* things. There are lots of reasons. Of course I'd like to have children. We both would, you especially, I know. But I love you the same as always, regardless."

Something in Dilia's heart spilled up and over, tears too long held in.

"What—are you crying again?" Cort asked, his face etched with concern.

"Hush, tell me why."

She was crying and laughing at the same time. "Because I love you so much. You are so entirely too good to me." The tears were gone as suddenly as they had arrived, and so was the laughter. Dilia wiped her cheeks. "But, Cort... I can't have that kind of a relationship. I just can't. Not now. This is all"—she waved an arm expansively, including the khenaran, the village, his mother's death and whatever the aliens had done to her, her entire world—"an adjustment. I need... time."

"But you'll think about it?"

"Yes. Of course."

He hesitated. His gaze shifted away from her, looking from side to side as if to see something that might materialize in the air. He swallowed, then said, "I've been thinking I may have to go away for a while. I was considering not doing it because the journey will take a long time. A few months. I don't know, maybe more. But if you need time anyway..."

She couldn't imagine what he was talking about. "Where are you going? Surely not back to the city."

"No. I'm finished with the city." He told her about the whynywir, and how they had requested his presence. "Would you wait for me?"

"Yes, of course I will. I could use the time to think this through, and maybe you could use the time, too, to decide if you're sure—"

"I *am* sure!" he interrupted.

"Well, maybe I just need to know you have the time to be sure, whether you think you need it or not. And I need time, too," Dilia said. "So, yes, go see the whynywir. I think maybe that's best for both of us."

His eyes moved back and forth, as if he was watching some future scenario playing out in his mind. "I'm not sure I should. You're facing a big issue, and I don't want to leave you here alone."

Once he got an idea in his head, the man would never let go of it. He had to go see the whynywir, that was certain. Dilia would not let her own dilemma stand in the way. She put her hands on Cort's cheeks and brushed them along the sides of his head. Then she pulled him toward her and brushed his lips with a kiss.

For a moment, the birds seemed to stop singing and the world went very still. Dilia was dizzy with the enormity of what she'd dared.

Then Cort returned the kiss.

When she found her voice again, she said, "Go, Cort. You need to do it, and I will be here for you. I promise."

Part II:
Saving Aran

Chapter 20

Journey to the Whynywir

Cort was walking in the khenaran. The air was still, too still. He looked around, every muscle tense, but nothing moved, not even a leaf.

He saw Dilia up ahead. "This way!" she called.

Cort ran to catch up with her, but Dilia had disappeared. "Dilia?" There was no answer.

"Dilia!" His heart pounded. He had to find her.

He ran through the khenaran looking in every direction. There! She was walking among the trees ahead. He ran to her, but Dilia retreated until her back was pressed against one of the great khena trees, her gaze never leaving him, imploring.

Then she stepped back again and melted into the tree and was gone. No! Dilia!

Cort pressed his hand against the khena's smooth bark. It was warm and shimmered with rainbow colors just beneath the surface. He could feel Dilia's heartbeat inside. A vine of blue flowers climbed the great trunk. Then Cort heard the noise. A distant hum at first, it grew steadily. Cort knew the sound. A harvester. His stomach churned. "No," he moaned. "Not Dilia. You can't take her away again."

Somehow, he was holding a spear made of the tree's living wood. The life of the tree ran from the spear up into his arm. It buzzed in his veins like electricity. The noise of the harvester was a roar, but not as loud as the sound of the trees in its path crashing to the ground. Cort's throat tightened with determination. He gripped the spear and stood in front of the tree that was Dilia.

The harvester entered the clearing. It was huge. The roar of the machine was deafening. The giant treads on which it rolled flattened whatever was in their path. Even his spear of living wood would not prevail against the might of the alien machine. He shouted, "Stop!" but his voice was lost in the harvester's roar, and already the laser-amplified diamond blades were spinning, flashing in the sunlight, ready to cut Dilia down.

"No! Stop!" Cort lashed out.

"Wake up, Cort," Tirei said, fending off the blow. "Wake up. It's just a dream."

Cort groaned as he opened his eyes. Early morning daylight filtered into the house. Tirei knelt beside his bedroll, and Galeta and Lela watched intently from across the room. Cort had clenched his fists so tightly his fingernails dug into his palms. "The aliens were... the harvester..." He took a deep, shaky breath, all the air his lungs could hold, then let it all out, shaking his head. "It was so real."

Galeta offered him a ladle of fresh water. He drank it gratefully. "Thanks. I'm sorry I woke you up. From now on, I'll sleep out in the forest where I won't disturb anyone."

"That's not necessary," Tirei said, sitting straighter. There was a hint of formality in his voice. "I invited you to share my house, and I meant it. Tell me what you dreamed."

Cort took a deep breath, not wanting to remember, unable to forget. "It's always the same dream. A little different each time, but always he same. The trees, the earth. The harvester or something alien cutting into the earth. The danger—terrible danger. Tirei, what could it all mean? Why do I dream this way again and again?"

Tirei said nothing. But then, what was there to say?

"I have to go see the whynywir, don't I?" They both knew the answer.

"I think so," said the seer in a tone that suggested it was about time Cort realized this.

Cort sighed deeply, disentangled himself from his bedding, and stood. "I guess I might as well get started. The sooner I get there, the sooner I'll learn what these dreams are all about. Who knows, maybe the whynywir will even know how to make them go away." Cort attempted a smile. "You'll have to point me in the right direction, Tirei. I don't have any idea how to get there."

"That won't be a problem. People in every village will point you in the right direction, but the journey is long. The whynywir live high in the mountains, where the winters are cold, and the snows come early. I think you'll have time, but you mustn't tarry."

Cort shrugged, refusing to dwell on how much he'd miss this village and his friends. And above all, Dilia. "I'll leave today."

Tirei shook his head. "It's not that easy. You must go as a pilgrim; only this will ensure your safety among the whynywir. You'll need to wear a white fur, one you have caught and skinned yourself. It's a sign. As a hunter, you shouldn't have much of a problem. But there is a bigger thing." He paused, frowning. "Have you considered how you will talk with the whynywir once you get there?"

'Cort hadn't. He shook his head. "Why, no, I guess I just assumed... that is, they must have a language, right?"

"Yes, but not one you can share, unassisted." He touched the blue crystal at his hairline.

Cort's heart skipped a beat. His eyes widened. "Another crystal?"

"It's their wish, Cort."

"I'm not sure I like this."

Tirei shrugged. "It's your choice. You don't have to go to them."

"Yes, I do. I can't live with these dreams. They must know that. But I just feel so... *unequipped* to be a seer. I wanted to be a hunter, and it feels right, but this..."

"It's unusual," Tirei agreed. "But the whynywir are not whimsical creatures. What they do is for the best."

Cort looked deep into Tirei's eyes. "You believe this?"

"With my whole heart."

Cort swallowed. "All right, then. I'll do it."

Tirei nodded thoughtfully. "In that case, your next step will be to find yourself a white fur to wear, a pilgrim's fur. It probably makes sense to hunt a white creature before you start out. It shouldn't take you very long, and it'll be a lot easier when you're not carrying all the gear you'll need for the journey. Then when you have the fur, return here for the crystal."

A white fur. A lot of gear to carry. A new crystal. This was going to be more complicated than he'd imagined. Cort's heart gave a lurch, but he wasn't going to back out now. "I'll start today."

Find a white fur! What kind of an assignment was that?

Cort walked for days through the broad khenaran. A fox came and went, bringing him a quail or alandhal or other small creature from time to time, but none with any white fur. The hawk scouted from above, but if any of the forest creatures had any white in their fur, it was on their underbellies, invisible from above. How could he hunt and kill a white-furred creature when he couldn't even manage to find one?

He missed Dilia and Lor and Neder. He was surprised to realize that he missed Lennard, too. On good days, he even missed the troop of rowdy, high-spirited soldiers. Was this crazy assignment going to exile him from human company forever?

The nightmares continued. Afraid to surrender to sleep and often jolted awake in pain or fear, Cort seldom slept more than four hours in a night. He forgot how it was to feel rested. The sleeplessness and exhaustion kept him to his purpose even when frustration filled him with impotent rage.

Find a white fur indeed!

He traveled by moonlight when he could, as well as in the day. And so it was that one night, when the moon called the Hunter had reached full, and its small satellite, the Kiri, blazed red in the sky beside it, Cort entered a valley fringed on either side with tree-covered hills that were shadowed in deepest black. Clear of trees, the valley was luminous in the Hunter's fragile silver light. The air was still and filled with the sweet perfume of the low-growing white starflowers, fragrant and shining silver in the moonlight.

The starflowers reminded him of Dilia. He stooped down and plucked a small stem, and wove it into some strands of his hair. He missed Dilia intensely.

As he walked, the valley rose to a high, rocky outcropping. Cort climbed the rock, then turned to look back.

Entering the far end of the valley, glistening in the light of the Hunter, was a tiger, as white as the flowers, marked by only the palest silver stripes. The great beast was as silent as the moonlight and moved as gracefully as a dancer, its muscles knotting and unknotting with its long strides. Cort watched the tiger, enjoying its beauty and altogether unmindful of his own purpose, until the tiger had almost reached the base of the rock on which he stood.

The tiger looked up, and their eyes met. The tiger's eyes were silver in the moonlight. It seemed to be waiting for him. Cort touched the knife at his belt and prepared himself to kill the beast. He climbed down the rock.

The tiger was large, coming almost to his shoulder, and it must have been five or six times his weight. It gave off a musty, animal smell, not unclean but intense.

They stood and looked at one another for a moment, Cort's golden eyes, the tiger's silver ones. Cort drew his knife.

The great white beast knelt in front of him. *Hunter, I am ready.* It stretched out its throat.

Cort touched the tiger, felt the coarse, heavy fur of its shoulder, the soft, velvet fur of its throat. He tested the heft and balance of the knife in his hand—and could not make himself use it. He couldn't bear the thought of killing a creature of such grace and beauty. *Get up. Get up,* he said.

The tiger didn't move. *You need a white fur. I have come to provide it.*

Not this way.

The tiger stood. *How, then? Do you want me to attack you?*

Cort shook his head. He wasn't afraid of dying. Besides, if the tiger hadn't killed him already, it wasn't going to do so. *No. Maybe if you had attacked me to begin with, I would have fought you and never known, but now... No, I won't waste your life this way. Come with me.*

I am old. My joints ache. I desire this worthy death at your hands.

Cort hefted his knife, examined the tiger's throat, and tried to imagine making the cut. His stomach clenched, but he forced himself to picture it. The resistance of the tiger's skin as he pressed the knife against it, and then the sudden yielding. The pressure he would need to slit muscles and tendons. The great, pulsing spurt of blood from the jugular, its overpowering smell filling the air as the tiger died.

The joy of the kill. The heady pulse of adrenaline. Time would slow. He would feel the tiger's every faltering heartbeat in the hand that held the knife. Perhaps he would drink the warm blood as it flowed—he'd done that with the wolves, and it was good, and fresh, and right.

No, it was entirely wrong. He couldn't do it.

One does not cut down a creature that comes in peace. *I can't kill you this way. Come with me. If you can't make the journey, well, then we'll see. But if you can, you will be my living white fur.*

Such a thing has never been done. Who knows how the whynywir will take it?

But Cort smiled and replied, *I guess we'll find out.*

The tiger bowed his great, furred head. *Your will, Hunter.*

Tirei was not pleased, and he was blunt about it. "As a pilgrim, you have to wear a white skin, and that is absolute. If you won't kill the beast that has come to you for that purpose, then you must find some other."

They stood at the edge of the village, under the first spreading tree of the khenaran. When Tirei had understood that Cort was taking him to see the living tiger and not a skin, he had stopped, pulled himself to his full height with his arms crossed, and refused to go any further. "This is not a negotiable requirement. I will give you the blue crystal only after you show me the skin. The *dead* skin."

But Cort didn't think he would be able to kill any animal that came to him in silver moonlight and extend its neck for his knife. "Look, Tirei, I'll be bringing my white skin with me. That's almost like wearing it."

"It will not serve. Don't make trouble for yourself."

Cort hated making Tirei angry, and he tried to be conciliatory. "If there's trouble, I can deal with it when I get there. Meanwhile, I'll have a good kiri for companionship on the journey. That's worth something, isn't it?"

"You do not suffer from a shortage of kiri," Tirei observed dryly. "Go find yourself a skin, and then come back to me for the crystal."

"No." Cort crossed his arms and matched the old seer's stubborn posture. "The tiger has offered his skin, and I've accepted it. I just don't choose to kill the tiger to get it." They stared at each other in silence, neither willing to give in. "If this means you won't give me the crystal, I'm going without it. Just let me know."

"The whynywir are not like us, Cort. You will accomplish nothing without the crystal."

"But I will try. With it, or without it."

Tirei nodded slowly. "You could be quite possibly the most pigheaded young man I've ever met."

Despite himself, Cort smiled. "Does that mean you'll do it?"

"I'll let you know," Tirei said. He turned and left Cort standing at the edge of the khenaran.

Cort waited.

He and the tiger found a sheltered spot about an hour's walk from the village—far enough to keep the tiger safe from curious villagers, who would never have seen such a creature—and the villagers safe from the tiger.

Two days later, having hunted down a small, aged dhelo doe, they ate their fill and lazed in the afternoon sunlight. *Meat's tough*, Cort remarked.

Old and stringy, like me. The tiger let out a satisfied belch. *Good, though.*

Cort raised himself onto an elbow and scratched his chin as if considering the proposition. *You would not be good to eat*, he declared and lowered himself back to the ground, the matter decided.

Oh, I am very good, Hunter. And my fur is very white.

Stop that!

Suddenly, the tiger lifted its head. *What's that?*

What?

People are coming. Two people. The tiger groaned and hoisted itself to its feet.

Two? That would probably be Tirei and Neder. *No, don't go. Stay here with me.*

A few minutes later, Tirei and Neder arrived. "Are you ready?" Tirei asked abruptly.

"Ready!" Cort jumped up. "Yes, of course. I'm sorry if I was rude to you before, Tirei; it's just... I guess I've gotten somewhat attached to this tiger."

Tirei's eyes moved to the tiger, and he acknowledged it with a stiff nod. "This attachment will cost you dearly." He spoke softly and seemed weary rather than angry. "But that reckoning is yours to meet, not mine. I will give you the crystal."

"Thank you."

"Thank me later. Afterwards. If you still feel that way. Tomorrow morning we will go to the ceremonial place, and I will insert the crystal. It will take two days, much like the process for the red crystal. On the second afternoon, we'll return here, and you must be prepared to leave the next day. Travel quickly, Cort. The summer solstice is already here. Winter comes early to the mountains, and if you do not get there in time, snow will block your passage. There's no way of knowing whether you can use the crystal, though, until the whynywir choose to talk with you. You'll just have to go there and see."

※

The blue crystal was inserted without any problems, and Tirei declared the process a success. The day after they returned to the village, Cort went to Tirei's house. As he waited for the seer to come out, he nervously touched his temple, where the blue crystal was buried under a bandage. The spot was still a little numb, but there was no pain. He wondered if it would actually work.

Then he wondered whether the whynywir would want to talk with him if he wasn't wearing white. No, he refused to think about this. Any intelligent creature would see that he'd brought his white fur with him. Surely this would be sufficient.

Nervously, he checked the pack that Neder had given him. It contained dried food and thick, ankle-high boots and gloves made of skins that had been waterproofed and finished with the fur on the inside. He'd learned about snow in school, of course, and he'd felt chilly from time to time, but he could not imagine weather so cold that he would need clothing like this.

Tirei came out of his house, carrying a long cape made of alandhal skins sewn together. Brindle skins and tawny ones, but not a visible white hair on the whole cape. Not that that would make a difference—not unless Cort had killed the little white creature himself.

Tirei nodded approvingly. "You're ready for an early start. That's good. Travel hard and don't tarry. The summer days are long now, but you'll be lucky to reach the place before the equinox, and there could be snow, even by then."

"Yes, so you've said," Cort agreed amiably. "So can I take off the bandage?"

"I will do it. Here, take this." He handed the alandhal-fur cape to Cort.

"Thank you, Tirei." Cort was dismayed by the prospect of carrying the heavy cape, but he smiled gamely.

"Don't give it away, either. You'll be thankful for it later." Tirei unwrapped the soft skin that he had used as a bandage and gently brushed away the herbs he had placed against the wound to prevent infection. "It looks good," he said, "though you won't know for sure if the crystal works for you until the whynywir choose to address you. Assuming they do."

Cort touched the tender spot at his temple where the silent blue crystal protruded. "It'll work," he said. "It has to."

Tirei knew Cort well enough by now not to caution him further. He just smiled.

"Thanks for everything, Tirei," Cort said. "I guess I'll see you again sometime around the winter solstice."

"If you get there in time and get out again," Tirei said. "If not, it will be a year or more. But I will know your progress through the whynywir, if they're willing." His own blue crystal glistened softly. "Good journey, Cort."

Dilia was the last to whom Cort said good-bye, and that good-bye was the hardest. He didn't want to leave her, not ever again. He reminded himself that Dilia had wanted this time alone—or had she? Maybe she'd just said that in order to give him the freedom to go. But no, that was wishful thinking. Much as he wanted to stay here with her, it was too late to change his mind now. He straightened his shoulders and went looking for her.

Dilia was by the village's stream, harvesting wild cress. She turned and smiled as he approached. "Cort!" She looked him up and down, taking in the pack on his back and the fur cape over his arm. "Time to go?"

Heart in his throat, he said, "Yes, I'm afraid so." He paused, noticing again how she had blossomed in the forest. Her skin had color, and her eyes were clear and golden and free of pain and worry. "I'll miss you." It was an understatement, but sometimes all words fall short. Oh, by Earth and space and all the stars, he didn't want to be leaving.

Dilia touched his cheek. "Don't," she said. "You need to do this."

Cort opened his arms, and she leaned into them. Then she reached up and kissed his cheek gently, a sweet, loving, sisterly kiss that made him ache for more. "I'll be here when you get back," she said.

He laughed. "Oh, no, Dilia. Don't send me off with just a little peck on the cheek. I'm going to miss you for months. Give me a kiss to remember you by."

She drew in a breath and looked up at him. Then she pulled him close and kissed him deeply, a long kiss that seemed to last forever. Afterwards, she said, "You come back to me, Corodh-an-Aran. I want to give you more kisses like that."

Chapter 21

Sojourn

The journey was as long as Tirei had promised. Driven by his dreams, Cort pressed to make good time. The tiger was his only companion, for none of Cort's other kiri would go near the great beast, not even the bold ferret. Cort and the tiger traveled in great, easy loping strides. It seemed to him that he and the tiger belonged together, and so Cort avoided the villages of men, where the tiger would not go, except when he needed directions to make sure he was on course.

They came to a great river that rushed from the northwest, so wide that the opposite bank was just a bare darkening of haze. Cort didn't know whether or where there was a ford, or even whether the river might turn in such a way that he could go around it altogether. He was traveling mostly northward. He decided to follow the river toward its source for a while and to see what he could learn.

Three days later, Cort was no nearer to finding a way across. He burned with frustration. Every day wasted was a day longer before he could return to Dilia. But the river continued broad and swift, and it continued to force him farther west than he wanted to go. When he saw a small village on a bluff above the riverbank, Cort decided it was time to ask. He learned that in two more days' journey, the river would swing in a gradual curve toward the south. There was no choice, then, but to cross. One of the villagers, a man of middle age and a stout build that spoke of muscles and strength, offered to ferry him across on a raft.

"My kiri also," Cort said.

"Hunter," the villager replied, "it would be dishonorable to refuse." The man drew back, hand to his heart, clearly having second thoughts when he saw the great white tiger, who paced the riverbank and growled nervously.

But his concerns were nothing compared to the tiger's.

It took all of Cort's determination—along with an offer of the dhelo the tiger had killed but not yet eaten—to get both man and beast to agree to the arrangement. In the end, the tiger crouched low on the raft, wet with spray and quivering by Cort's side, as the villager poled the raft across the current. They reached the far side at dusk, but the ferryman would not tarry with them. He set his course back across the river and left Cort and the tiger, both of them wet and hungry, on the far side.

Never again, Hunter, growled the tiger.

Cort smiled sympathetically. *It wasn't so bad as all that.*

It was worse! Tell me you will find some other way home, for I will not come this way again.

Cort sighed. *I'll try.*

Shortly afterwards, their path began to climb. Within a week, they had reached the foothills of the mountains. The trees of the great forest began to thin, and finally, they left the khenaran behind altogether. The ever-increasing distance from Dilia gnawed at Cort's heart. One night they camped on a ledge, with the khenaran spread out below them as far as the eye could see. The sun was behind them, and there was a chill to the air. For the first time, Cort was glad for the warm clothing he had been carrying all these weeks.

Higher and higher they climbed. Cort unpacked the fur-lined boots Neder had given him. The slopes of the mountains were bare and rocky, and his shoes with their smooth soles slipped in ways his bare feet never would have. But they kept his feet warm.

They had not passed any villages since they'd left the khenaran, and Cort wasn't entirely certain they were still on the right path. The landmarks were consistent with what he had been told, but the blue crystal remained stubbornly silent.

It seemed impossibly cold. Even wearing every piece of clothing he possessed, and wrapped in the alandhal-fur cloak that Tirei had given him, Cort woke chilly. He began sleeping close against the tiger, like a littermate. He was glad he had decided not to kill the great beast, for he valued its companionship. And besides, the living tiger kept him warm far better than the mere tigerskin would have.

The air was humid and fresh. In the still air of the pre-dawn gloaming, soft white flakes drifted slowly down from the sky. Cort sat up and discovered that he was covered in white.

Tiger! What is this? Snow, do you think? He remembered his school lessons, the pictures of mountains on Earth covered in white, and Tirei's repeated admonishments to hurry lest snow block the path. But pictures and words fell far short of the astonishing reality of these cold, white, lazy, beautiful flakes, which turned to rain on his skin.

I'm certain I do not know. The great white tiger stood and stretched, reaching his front paws far forward. *But it's slippery*, he added, carefully shaking liquid off each front paw in turn. *If we are going to cross that ridge today, we should start now.*

The ridge was just beyond them—no more than an hour's walk in good weather, even at this high altitude. Had the night not been so dark, Cort would have crossed it before they camped. Now he was sorry they had not. He could barely even see the ridge in the thickening snow. He agreed with the tiger's assessment. Cort gathered his few things—his knife and sling and a bundle of meat left from yesterday's hunting—and wrapped the warm cloak around himself.

The snow made the climb difficult. Even the normally graceful tiger slipped and scrambled on the wet rocks. Cort had to concentrate to find each place to step. The occasional handholds he needed were also slippery. A slight breeze picked up and blew the snow in gusts. Inside his fur-lined-mittens, Cort's hands grew numb.

The top of the ridge took Cort by surprise. Because of his concentration on what was immediate-ly in front of him, he hadn't looked up in a long time. Before him, a valley spread out in all directions. Bounded by mountain ridges on all sides, the valley tilted upward toward the east, where the sun was just rising under a layer of dark clouds. The snow that still danced in the light breeze around Cort and the tiger caught the golden early-morning sunlight in glints and sparkles like tiny fireflies. The valley was green and still. Cort stopped walking, overwhelmed. For a moment, time stopped, and he simply looked, struck by the beauty of it. He wished Dilia could be here to see it.

Riding the air currents on giant wings, many large birds circled gracefully over the valley. They were feathered all in white like creatures of the snow. Four flew toward Cort and the tiger.

What have we here?

It was a voice like none Cort had heard before, echoing and resonating inside his head as if caught in a chamber too small for it. Unconsciously, he reached toward the crystals at his hairline and touched the familiar red one. But no, this voice came through the blue crystal. A whynywir's voice.

It could be a pilgrim, another voice like it answered, pushed at his mind, as if caged.

> *Not a pilgrim, he wears no*
> *white.*
> *It could be breakfast. (Now,*
> *that is a possibility.)*
> *((Looks tough, though))*
> *What is offered freely*
> *should not be refused.*

Cort could hardly follow the rhythms and ripples of the conversation, which felt at once as if many voices engaged in it, yet only one thread of consciousness owned it, like a chorus singing in multi-part harmony.

He had imagined the whynywir as essentially human, white-bearded and wizened little old men, perhaps, or a warrior race, muscled and towering above him, not at all as giant and possibly carnivorous birds. As they circled closer, Cort assessed their sharp talons. He caught a glint of dangerous-looking teeth inside one open mouth. Yes, they were definitely carnivorous.

Are you whynywir? he asked doubtfully.

Could he be a pilgrim, who does not know the whynywir? a voice chided.

(who wears no white)
But perhaps he imagines
that the snow will serve for
white
((he is cloaked in))
(until it melts)
((And then we will surely
have breakfast)) (soon,
soon)

The whynywir circled closer, snapping at him.

Cort drew his knife. *Whynywir or not, I will defend myself*, he warned. Then he remembered to add, *Besides, I brought a white fur. He's right here with me. So what if I'm not wearing it?*

The tiger, who had already started down the ridge toward the valley, turned. Seeing his companion's danger, he bristled and growled and headed back to defend Cort. *I am too old for this*, he said, but he continued to growl menacingly.

The rising sun ascended behind the clouds, and the ridge was plunged into cold shadow.

Your life is a small thing, said the whynywir.

(We are hungry)
Should we call you Pilgrim,
or not?
(what does it matter, once
the snow melts?)

One of the whynywir swooped closer, its golden eyes glistening in the sunlight, its great talons outstretched to grab him. Cort dodged and slipped in the wet snow, barely managing to lash out with his knife as he fell. His blade dealt the great creature a glancing blow, probably no more than a scratch.

The whynywir veered away, but circled around again. As it drew closer, the white tiger roared and leaped at the bird. In an instant, a second bird plunged upon the beast.

The tiger twisted aside. Four long lines of blood dripped red across its silver flank.

Stop! He clenched his fist hard around the hilt of the knife, muscles tight up to his shoulders. *He's been a true friend, but you...* Damned cold creatures. This whole pilgrimage thing was a terrible mistake. Good thing Dilia hadn't come with him. *This tiger and I did not come all this distance just to be your breakfast.*

He stood and turned his back on the whynywir. To the tiger he said, *Come on. We're leaving.*

The tiger's pain and puzzlement burned wordlessly through the red crystal.

Cort started back up the ridge, out of the whynywir's valley, and the tiger followed, its steps halting and slow.

Do you give up so easily, then? asked the circling birds.

> *Can such an insignificant*
> *thing stop you?*
> *(You*
> *Of all people?)*
> *((Corodh-an-Aran))*

The whynywir had used his name. That implied much, since he'd never introduced himself—but his anger had its own momentum. *It's not insignificant to me. Go away. Leave me alone. I want nothing to do with you.*

> *But truly, will you leave*
> *((You and the tiger)) (your*
> *questions unanswered)*
> *after you and he have*
> *traveled so far*
> *(to answer them?)*

Cort stopped and turned to watch the circling avians. He needed to understand his dreams, to do something about them. But killing the tiger—the price was too high. *I won't stay if you're going to kill him.*

> *It is the way of Aran,*
> *Corodh-an-Aran.*
> *One creature is made to*
> *kill another. (The meat is*
> *eaten.)*
> *((The bones return to the*
> *soil.))*
> *(Nothing is wasted.)*
> *Aran blesses us all with*
> *rebirth.*
> *((You humans would say*
> *there is love in it.)) We say...*
> *there is harmony.*
> *(It is complete.)*

He is my friend. It is the way of humans to stand by their friends.

Something like amusement filtered in through the blue crystal. Or contempt. Or maybe the kindly indulgence of parents toward a very young child. *Very well.*

> *(But know that the tiger is*
> *old.*
> *((Bony.)) (He will not live*
> *long.)*
> *((There is little meat on*
> *him in any case.))*
> *(And what there is will be*
> *stringy.)*
> *You may keep him with you*
> *if you wish.*

I do wish, Cort said.

But he will die anyway
((and soon.))
When he dies, you will keep
the skin,
(Corodh-an-Aran.)
((It is yours.))

Yes. Agreed, Cort said.

The skin is yours. But the
meat is ours
(and we will feast on it)

Cort grimaced. *Yes, fine. If he dies.*

Not if but when he dies.
((Soon.))

The whynywir flew off toward a cliff on the far side of the valley, and Cort watched until they were just small specks against the sky. He hadn't expected the whynywir to be so... alien. With the tiger by his side, he hadn't expected to feel so alone here.

A hot spring welled from the highest part of the valley, at its eastern side. It pooled into a deep, warm lake, from which a mist of steam rose like a beacon of warmth, a promise of survival. Cort worked his way down toward the lake, and the air became warmer as he went. The tiger limped unsteadily after him.

With a heavy sigh, the tiger settled near the warm lake, rested its chin on its forepaws, and indifferently allowed Cort to do what he would with the herbs Tirei had packed.

Days passed, a week, two, with no sign of the whynywir. Cort thought often of Dilia, so far away. He wished she could be here. With her natural curiosity, she'd probably discover a dozen things about this valley that he'd never noticed. And they'd be interesting things, but still... No, it was better that she stay far away from these dangerous whynywir.

The tiger's cuts healed with clean scabs, but the tiger had no strength. It no longer went into the woods with Cort when he hunted, and in any case there was no game of a size that might feed a creature as large as a tiger. Of the few alandhal and other small creatures that Cort could trap, the tiger ate little and grew thin.

The day came when the great beast no longer lifted its head. *I would like to die now, Hunter. Surely you need me no longer.*

Cort's heart surged with pain, with loss. *Oh, Tiger...*

Do not grieve. I will be reborn a tiger. There is no better life.

In that case, I'll come and visit you.

Yes. I would like that. Though I will be a young cub, and frisky. You may not recognize me.

I will know you, Tiger.

And I, you. I am sure of it. You will keep the skin, yes?

Yes, I will. I promise.

And the meat... Let the whynywir have it.

As you wish, Tiger.

Yes, I wish. It is the way of Aran.

After the tiger died, Cort dragged the heavy body some distance from his campsite by the lake, jaw tight, holding back tears. Grimly, he set to work skinning it. Several whynywir circled high overhead. He paused to look at them, his fist so tight around the handle of his knife that his knuckles were white, as if the great avians were somehow to blame for his friend's death. A light snow fell, numbing his hands and chilling his heart.

As Cort worked, the clouds slowly dissolved into small cumuli. Though the air was cold, the sun was strong. Cort could feel its heat on his back as he cut away the tiger's skin with his knife. The snow melted quickly, sinking into the not-yet-frozen earth.

Three whynywir landed nearby. They watched calmly with expressionless golden eyes, as if he had always been and would always be in this spot working at this task. The work was strangely soothing. When he finished, Cort was no longer angry, though he felt no friendship for the great birds.

You regret the tiger's death, said one of the whynywir.

It seems so... pointless.

> *Not pointless, no. (Now you*
> *know what is at stake on*
> *Aran.)*
> *This is a valuable lesson.*
> *((well-taught))*
> *His spirit will be reborn.*
> *(perhaps as a human)*
> *((perhaps as a tiger again))*
> *The way of Aran is*
> *perfect. (perhaps even as a*
> *whynywir)*
> *(if only you humans could*
> *remember)*

As Cort folded the skin, he asked, *Do you really believe that?*

> *We know it for a fact.*
> *(We remember.)*
> *As you humans do not.*
> *((mostly))*
> *Would you like to believe*
> *your friend will be reborn?*
> *We are all reborn. ((Even*
> *you.))*
> *(except the trees, who live*
> *forever)*
> *((unless they are*
> *murdered))*
> *Believe it, then,*
> *Corodh-an-Aran.*

And the tiger could be reborn as a human? Or... Cort didn't like the idea...*a whynywir?*

> *Yes. We have been many*
> *things*
> *before we were whynywir.*
> *((We remember.))*
> *(Only a lucky few are born*
> *as whynywir the first time.)*
> *Though we will never again*
> *be else but whynywir*
> *((who would want to be?))*
> *(until we are trees).*

I'd like to think the tiger will be a tiger again, Cort said.

> *Corodh-an-Aran, unless*
> *something very unusual*
> *happens, there will be no*
> *more tigers.*

The whynywir who had spoken stretched and shook its wings. *This would depend on you.* With a few steps, it took again to the sky.

What? Wait! Cort ran after the departing bird. *Why not?*

They will tell you. Listen. The bird sailed over the ridge on the east side of the valley, and was gone from sight.

Cort turned back to the two whynywir who remained. *Why did he say there will be no more tigers? And what do I have to do with it?*

And so we arrive at the purpose of your journey, answered one of the whynywir.

No, I came here because... But Cort didn't want to talk about his dreams with these odd, cold, proud creatures. He felt too vulnerable. *Never mind. Yes, I want to know about the tigers.*

> *On all of Aran, the white*
> *tigers live in only one valley.*
> *The place is far to the south*
> *of the city. ((But not far*
> *enough))*

> *The aliens' machine are*
> *approaching that place.*
> *(Steadily, steadily, they*
> *approach)*
> *In another year, the*
> *machines will kill all the*
> *trees in that valley.*
> *((they that kill everything))*
> *(even the jewel-feathered*
> *onari*
> *((gone))*
> *that used to rise in clouds*
> *bright as sunshine from*
> *their nests in the trees)*
> *((all gone))*

An image of a flock of birds, countless, brilliant, their feathered wings reflecting all the colors of sunlight, floated into Cort's mind, and he felt a wave of sorrow. *Stop*, he begged.

> *(Two years at the most)*
> *And the tigers will die.*
> *((all))*

Cort was silent. What effect could he have on the harvesters? He was just one person. Even with the laser he had taken from the alien Jerrald, even with the soldiers, he could not stand against the technology and power the aliens commanded. If he didn't get killed in the attempt, he'd end up a prisoner, like Dilia had been.

But it is worse than this, added the whynywir.

> *The tigers will surely be*
> *reborn*
> *((as something, though not*
> *as tigers))*

*...but the trees (ah, the poor
trees)*

What can I do? Cort asked. Did the whynywir understand how powerless he was?

*Serve your friend,
Corodh-an-Aran. ((Serve
his family.))
Serve his kind, for they are
in peril. ((Serve Aran.))
Be...
(what your name says you
((what you truly)) are)*

Stay with us, said one of the two whynywir who peered at him. *Stay through the winter.*

*(This much time you have.)
Perhaps you will use that
time
to understand what you
can
((must))
do.*

Cort found this idea decidedly unpleasant. Not seeing Dilia again for a whole year! *I... I'm not sure... Winter must be long up here in the mountains. I don't think I want to be stuck here the whole winter.*

*We know you do not like
us, human. (This matters
nothing to us)
But you are
Corodh-an-Aran. (Aran is*

> *what matters)*
> *Your purpose is what*
> *matters.*
> *((We believe...)) you will*
> *know what you have to do.*

Cort looked at the two birds, watching him as intently as vultures. *How did you know my name?*

Ah, Corodh-an-Aran, we have been expecting you, one said, and the other added,

> *(The trees dreamed*
> *you were coming.)*

Dreams! Cort had to know. He had to face his dreams and overcome them. The whynywir were right, though it cost him to admit it. If he left now, the tiger's death would be for nothing. And he wasn't sure he could live with himself, knowing the danger the other tigers were in and knowing that there was something—however far-fetched—he might have done but didn't. He wrapped his arm around his chest to ease the tension there, and said, *All right, I'll stay.*

The air currents that drifted across the lake on whose shores Cort and the tiger had made their camp were heated and moistened by the lake's warm water. Heavy snow fell on the ridges all around the valley, making them entirely impassable, but the valley itself remained snow-free and green. Cort made a home of sorts in a warm, shallow cave just above the lake.

The moderate climate supported a number of animals too small to attract the interest of the great whynywir but abundant enough to provide a rich diet for the only human in the valley. The red crystal remained silent. Cort developed his skill with the sling and with traps to a degree he had thought was beyond him.

He was so far from his kiri and his friends. So far from Dilia. She must be learning things, just as he was, and like him, her experiences must be changing her. Cort regretted missing even a minute of those changes.

Cort hunted alone, but he wasn't entirely alone. Not if he counted the whynywir as company, though this was a struggle. They rarely talked to him directly. Through the blue crystal, he could sometimes hear their chorused conversations as a kind of harmonious humming. When he stayed completely still and concentrated, he could make out words and sometimes even threads of thought. As nearly as he could tell, they always seemed to talk about the great scheme of things on Aran and their own role in it.

Whynywir, Cort said, *I want you to get a message to Tirei-Sunar. Can you do that?* He wanted to let Tirei know—no, he wanted more than anything to let Dilia know—that he was safe, but that he was spending the winter here.

But the whynywir ignored him. They seemed utterly uninterested in his particular feelings and concerns. Cort didn't like them, but he began to understand that they were neither conceited nor proud. Their shared consciousness was so strong they had no sense of any one individual's particular feeling of importance.

Also—and to Cort, this made a big difference—judging from what he could make of their conversations, the great birds were as completely committed to the well-being of the entire planet as they were indifferent to the fate of any single individual. It was a viewpoint he could respect, though he himself had trouble maintaining that lofty perspective.

One whynywir in particular visited him from time to time. Cort recognized it by its markings, and he surmised by its lightly speckled feathers and relatively small size, that this avian was not long out of the nest. Sometimes the whynywir sat on a rock that jutted from the ground near the opening of Cort's cave and silently watched him as he butchered or cooked or ate or swam in the warm lake.

There didn't seem to be much point in making conversation since the whynywir never answered him. But it wasn't like there was anyone else to talk to. *We aren't any nearer to figuring out what I'm supposed to do,* Cort pointed out one day.

To his surprise, the whynywir answered. *Are you angry about this?*

Cort sighed. *No. I guess not.*

Then perhaps we are a bit nearer.

What's that supposed to mean? Cort flared. But the whynywir was silent. *Why are you always hanging around here, if you're not going to answer any questions?*

I'll go, the whynywir said simply.

No. Wait.

But the great bird spread its wings and flapped into the sky.

Come back tomorrow, then, Cort called after it. He was hit with a pang of loneliness that reminded him how far away he was from Dilia.

It was a week before the whynywir returned, and Cort resolved that he would try much harder to be patient. When the whynywir came back, it acted as if it had never been gone, as if the lapse in time were insignificant. Perhaps driven by loneliness, Cort said one day, *I don't know your name.*

I am whynywir, the bird replied simply.

You don't have an individual name?

What need is there? We all know who we are.

But you have an individual spirit.

Ah, said the whynywir, *so you perceive it, Corodh-an-Aran. But your name, now—that is a different matter.*

It seemed to Cort that the whynywir liked to talk in riddles. But he had also learned that the whynywir revealed answers only when they were ready—or when they judged that he was ready. He was no longer upset by their ways. *What about my name?* he asked.

What do you know about it?

I know I was named after my father. I know that it means 'justice to Aran,' or something like that.

Restitution, corrected the bird. *Or proper selfhood. Yes, the restoring of Aran's proper self. And your father, what do you know about him?*

He came to the city from the forest somewhere...

A village far, far to the south of here, said the great bird. *And?*

I think he came alone. My mother never spoke of anyone else. I... like to think the village is still there, and not destroyed.

It is still there, said the whynywir. *Some of us flew near there only a few days ago. Do you know your father's history?*

No, Cort said.

Then listen. Your father was named Corodh-an-Aran after his father. The name has an ancient tradition in that village, dating back to the earliest times of your people. It is not only a name; it also carries a responsibility. We whynywir, we watch, we feel, we remember. We are witnesses for Aran, but not actors. Humans, though, can change things. That is the way of it. Your father's grandfather was not Corodh-an-Aran, but his great-uncle was. And so it has always been, the name handed down from father to son or uncle to nephew, or villager to villager, one generation after the next. Protectors of Aran's well-being. The spirits who are born to this name are committed, Corodh-an-Aran.

It was too much to take in. *I'm not committed*, Cort said. *I wasn't born to anything like that. I'm just Cort, a city boy.* But the words rang false even as he said them.

As if the great bird knew, it said, *But you will be. When the time comes, you will be.*

Cort had taken to swimming every morning in the warm lake, his long strokes carrying him to the far shore and then back again. He thought of Neder, who had taught him to swim months ago, and of the other people of his village, and wondered how they were doing. He imagined Dilia beside him on those swims, pictured how much she'd enjoy it, and wished he could share these swims with her. Perhaps she'd have some useful insights on his interactions with the whynywir, too.

One day as Cort came up from the water and stretched, he found the whynywir perched on a rock watching him with its piercing golden stare. *You are very much like your father*, offered the bird. *You even move like him.*

All us humans are alike, Cort answered flippantly—then froze. He forgot to breathe. *You knew my father?*

Oh, yes, the great bird replied. *I knew him very well. Not in this lifetime, of course, but the last.*

Cort sat down on the soft grass between the lake and the whynywir's rock. *What was he like?* he asked.

He was a good human being, Corodh-an-Aran. As you are. A person who took his responsibilities seriously.

Why did he go to the city, then? Cort asked. *I've often wondered about that.*

For the same reason that you will go back, answered the whynywir.

I didn't say I was going back there, Cort answered hotly. It was the last thing he wanted to do. The whynywir stretched from its perch and flapped its wings, and Cort hurried to add, *but I didn't say that I wasn't. Why do you think I'll go back?*

Ah, because the forest is in pain, Corodh-an-Aran. Because they are killing the spirits of our ancestors. Why else?

The spirits of our ancestors? Cort asked. *I thought our spirits were immortal. I thought that we could always be born again.*

Indeed, answered the great bird. *And again, and again, and again, until the spirit grows weary and decides to return to the forest. And then it is born into a tree. And the khena are immortal, like the spirits within them, which dream forest dreams in peace. Until the aliens come with their machines and cut them down, and then the spirits truly die. The dreams of the trees have turned to nightmares, Corodh-an-Aran.*

Cort thought about his own nightmares. If he was ever going to take a chance, now was the time. He took a deep breath and said, *I've been having nightmares.* He described the dreams.

Tree dreams, answered the bird. *These are tree dreams.*

All the whynywir feel them, came an echo from another of the great birds, far away.

*None among us sleeps easily
near the great forest.
Nor have we for a
generation
(Maybe longer)
But among the humans
and the other
lower creatures,
perhaps only you feel them,
Corodh-an-Aran.
Aran needs your help.*

Tree dreams? Cort asked.

> *The great trees dream.*
> *(the immortal trees)*
> *It is their language,*
> *Corodh-an-Aran.*
> *(They are not like us.) ((No,*
> *not like us at all))*
> *More deep-seeing, perhaps.*
> *All who would listen may*
> *hear.*
> *((Ah, but who listens?))*
> *We whynywir listen*
> *(but who among the*
> *humans?)*
> *Corodh-an-Aran listens to*
> *the trees, my cousins, and he*
> *dreams tree dreams.*

The whynywir's elegiac emotion washed over Cort in great waves as it echoed from one avian to another to another. It was the same overpowering feeling that had brought him to his knees when he held the staff of living wood. Cort swallowed, trying to ease the tightness in his throat as he thought of his own tree, far away. His tree, his forest, his dreams. This sorrow was the inner truth of the forest's suffering.

The world of Aran was a single entity in a more profound way than anything his Earth-oriented education had prepared him for. The spirits of the trees and living creatures of the planet were as interconnected as the roots of the great trees, whether they were conscious of it or not. The whynwir were the self-awareness of Aran, made incarnate. The planet itself was alive, and it was calling him.

Cort's nightmares took on a different and profound significance for him—as much as the time he had first learned to talk with the kiri through the red crystal. *But they are in such pain!* Then he understood. *Every death hurts all of them like my mother's death hurt me.*

Every death hurts all of us, too, Corodh-an-Aran.

What can I do? Cort asked.

Whatever you can, the whynywir replied.

What happened to my father? Did he die?

We do not know, Corodh-an-Aran. The trees do not dream of him any longer.

The great bird flew from its rock and came to the ground close by Cort's side, as if it were going to whisper in his ear. *When he left for the city, I was already an old man in my lifetime just before this one, and I was ailing. Did I tell you that we were related?*

Cort's heart stopped. Then it shifted into doubletime, and he flushed with the heat of his racing blood. *Related? How?*

It is of no significance. What does matter is that your father believed that the aliens could only be driven out from within the city. He told me that he would do whatever it took, go wherever he had to—or that he would sire the person that could. He made me promise to look after you, should you come along and need help, and that is why I am born a whynywir, young man, and not a human.

So where...? The question had burned in him since he could remember, and now he was almost afraid to ask it. *Where did he...? What could have happened to him?*

I like to believe that he has traveled to the alien's home world. I like to believe that if he died on Aran anywhere, even in the city, the trees would know of it. But I do not know this for a fact. He may have died in the city or in the scrub woods around it, and maybe the khena would not know. We do not interest ourselves in individual humans. I do not know his fate.

Before Cort could think of what to say, the whynywir stretched its wings, leaped into the sky, and left him alone with his pounding heart.

The mountains were piled so high with snow, blinding white in the sunshine, swirling gray in the storms, that Cort began to think he might never escape this valley, never reach home. Never see Dilia again. He hadn't imagined that being separated from her for this long would be so difficult. When he returned home, he wanted never to leave her again.

And he was jealous. All the people he'd brought back to the khenaran had found homes in various villages there and were enjoying their first winter in their new villages. Everyone but him.

He felt so isolated and alone that he began looking forward to the young whynywir's visits. And now, after the conversation about his father, Cort wanted more than ever to speak with the whynywir again. But the avian did not come for many days, and a storm laid new snow on the mountains.

He had built a fire and was preparing to roast a couple of alandhal he'd trapped earlier that day, when the whynywir descended onto a nearby rock.

Smells good, said the creature, for all the world as if it had never gone away.

Please. Cort gestured toward the birds. *You're welcome to have one of them. Would you prefer it cooked or raw?*

Raw, said the whynywir. *With the skin and all, but I see I am already too late for that. Fresh killed is best.*

Cort spitted one of the alandhal and arranged it over the fire. *Sorry. I would have left it alive if I'd known.*

No matter. The whynywir tore a haunch from the other alandhal's small carcass and set about consuming it, crunching the bones. *We generally eat larger animals anyway.*

Cort thought of the tiger. Of how quickly the great birds had devoured it. *Top of the food chain, are you?*

Of course. Why not? We are the highest life form on Aran, the great creature answered simply. *Not counting the trees, of course. Then next, the humans, then the hunting beasts which are the kiri, and then the other animals.*

You prey on the kiri, though you know they are intelligent.

Humans, too, sometimes, Corodh-an-Aran.

Involuntarily, Cort shuddered. *But why?*

We must eat. The spirit is spared; the meat serves the creatures of Aran according to the way of things. Does this bother you?

No, Cort answered, a little too quickly and too casually. *That is, yes. I guess it does. A little.*

How can this bother you, when all around the trees are being cut and suffering and dying an eternal death? There is no wrong in eating; death of the body is not wrong. But death of the spirit is another matter.

We humans only experience the spirit through the body.

Yes, agreed the whynywir. *That is why it falls to the whynywir to witness and to understand. And to teach you.*

In the silence that followed, crickets chirped in the grass. Cort had a feeling that the great bird was communing with the other whynywir in some way that he couldn't quite sense through the crystal. It seemed to be appraising him through its expressionless yellow eyes. He had a strong urge to say something to fill the silence, but he resisted it. He waited.

Corodh-an-Aran, would you like to see the world as the whynywir see it?

The question shocked Cort out of the stillness into which he had fallen. But he didn't have to think long to know the answer. *Yes!*

Lie back. Close your own eyes; you will use ours.

Cort started to say that he was familiar with the process, but he sensed that the whynywir was not interested in conversation. Silently, he did as he had been instructed. At first, he saw nothing but the red color of sunlight passing through his eyelids. Then the world hovered in indigo sky before him.

The hawk never soared so high. Cort traced the long path of a coastline, interrupted here and there by clouds. For the first time, he sensed the entire planet—blue ocean sparkling in sunlight or dark in cloud shadow, green khenaran rolling away toward the horizon. The sky was almost black overhead.

It's beautiful! he whispered.

As he watched, the whynywir whose eyes he shared circled, revealing a snow-capped mountain range. *You are in that valley, Corodh-an-Aran. Do you see it?*

A tiny green valley no bigger than his thumbnail glistened amid the white mountain snows. But it was too far away to make out the lake by which he lay.

Where is Tirei's village? he asked, wishing for a glimpse of Dilia, or at least of the place where she was, the tiniest bit of a connection.

You will not see the villages, it responded. *They are under the khena.*

He felt a flush of disappointment. *Oh, too bad. But then, where is... Whynywir, where is the city?*

His viewpoint shifted. Another whynywir angled toward the city from the south, the terrain passing swiftly below. *Look to the horizon, Corodh-an-Aran.*

The horizon was brown. *What is that?* Cort asked.

Where they are killing the trees, everything dies, answered the great avian. *But plants return after a year or two. In a moment, you will see... Yes, look now.*

Beyond the great brown swatch, an area of green appeared. In a short time, it was close enough that Cort could distinguish between the texture of the true forest, and that of the scrub woods that grew where the khenaran had been demolished. On a distant hill, Cort could see the climbing brown buildings of the city. Near the top, a patchwork of greenery and white and gray buildings showed Hsu-Lin Base. Towering over it all, but still tiny from this distance, a spaceship waited on the leveled hilltop.

Behold how much of the true forest has been lost, Corodh-an-Aran. The great bird cut a wide circle. Though they flew high and kept the city almost on the horizon as they circled, still the swath of destruction extended beyond them on all sides.

How could they have destroyed so much? Cort wondered. In the whynywir's silence, Cort supplied his own answer. *They must work quickly, and constantly. They must be very efficient.*

From one whynywir to another, Cort's vision shifted. Except for the ever-growing wound radiating from the city, the planet was everywhere peaceful. From high above, there were no signs of habitation of any sort. Large areas of the khenaran covered every continent, and the ocean was broader than the land.

When Cort's sight returned to the inside of his eyelids, night had already fallen. The Hunter and Kiri moons were setting across the lake to the west. The whynywir that Cort thought of as his companion had gone. Awed, Cort stood slowly, still deep in the vision of the planet. Then he stretched, and returned to his cave to sleep.

⁂

Why is it, Cort asked the young whynywir a few weeks later, *that the humans on Aran look so like the aliens from Earth, rather than the whynywir and the animals that live right here?*

The answer to that question lies deep in the history of your race, Corodh-an-Aran. Your people, too, came here from the stars, thousands of years ago. But they had a much different attitude than the aliens who are here now. Your people wanted to belong here. They used their technologies, not to destroy Aran, but to learn from it. When they came here to live, they changed. They changed what they were. They brought Aran into themselves, into their nature, so that they would be part of this world, no longer aliens.

Brought Aran into themselves? Cort considered how the eyes of the city people were hazel or gray, dark or light brown or even sometimes blue, the colors of the aliens' eyes, but those of the forest people were golden. Like the whynywirs' eyes. He thought of Dilia's eyes that had turned blue when she lived among the aliens, but were golden now, and of his own eyes, too. *Yes,* he said, *it makes sense. Then the crystals...* He touched the red crystal and the blue one at his hairline.

...are products of your ancestors' technology, the whynywir said. *There are not many crystals in the world, Corodh-an-Aran. The whynywir control them, at the request of your ancient ones.*

And I have two. Why did you give me two, if they are so rare?

For the same reason that Aran gave you the kiri, the whynywir answered. *Because you have need of them.*

⁂

In the spring, the khenaran was ablaze with flowers that carpeted every space where sunlight beamed through the trees' branches. Dilia walked an hour to one of the spots she knew where worrinot grew best, a place where its foliage and blooms received bright sunlight but its roots stayed cool and moist. She and Nel had discovered this spot together, but now Nel had returned to her own village with Lor. Dilia missed her. She missed them both, but not as much as she missed Cort. She sighed. It had been so long since she'd seen Cort.

She harvested a basketful of the pale yellow blossoms to make into a salve, along with mint and chamomile. She smiled, anticipating how she could ease the tension Tirei seemed to be feeling lately Poor Tirei, constantly at odds with his daughter Lela, and looking like he carried the weight of the world on his shoulders.

As she walked toward the house she shared with Nel and with Denra's family, Tirei approached her. "Do you have a moment?" he asked.

"Of course," Dilia said. She'd been bothering Tirei excessively all winter asking for news of Cort, until a week ago he'd responded sharply, "Be sure, I will tell you first thing if I ever hear anything from the whynywir." Now, Dilia glanced at the blue crystal near his forehead, but she wasn't about to ask.

The seer followed her gaze and smiled. "He's on his way back," he said.

Dilia's heart leapt, and in her excitement, she almost dropped her gathering basket. She missed Cort more than she'd thought possible when they had parted nine months ago. The winter had seemed endless. "That's wonderful! When will he be here? Soon?"

Tirei drew in a deep breath and let it out with an audible sigh. "No, Dilia. Not soon. Please don't keep asking me about this, I'm sure the whynywir have more important things to do than to track the progress of a single human traveling in the forest. Even Corodh-an-Aran."

"Oh." Her heart fell back into place. "Do you have an estimate? Two weeks? A month?"

"A month or two if he walks quickly and doesn't stop along the way," Tirei said. "Three months, more likely. People along his way from the whynywir to here will want to see him. It will take time."

Dilia frowned. "Why? Why would they want to see him? Is he... okay?"

Tirei gave her a reassuring pat on the shoulder. "Oh yes, he's fine. Corodh-an-Aran will be going to the city to try and stop the harvesting. That's why the villagers will all want to see him for themselves. And that's why his journey here will take time."

Time. Dilia couldn't keep her disappointment from her face. Three months until she would see him, and then he'd turn around and leave again, going to the city of all places. And how on all of Earth and Aran could one man stop the aliens from harvesting?

Chapter 22

Preparing to Return

Spring came late to the mountains that year. The summer solstice was almost upon them before the snows had receded from the pass sufficiently for a human to travel through it. When Corodh-an-Aran left the valley of the whynywir, he took only his sling and his father's knife, the clothes on his back and a cape made of white tigerskin, a sturdy walking-stick, and a heart filled with grief and determination.

You will go back to the city? asked the circling avians.

Cort nodded. *I will do whatever I have to. Whatever I can. I will not forget.*

The peace of the forest be with you, Corodh-an-Aran.

With all of us. He turned and left the valley, traveling alone down the mountain. After a week of descent, Corodh-an-Aran re-entered the khenaran. A ferret joined him there, whom he greeted like a brother. Other kiri also came, in their turn, during the weeks of his journey through the great forest.

People came, as well. Word of the returning pilgrim who wore the white tigerskin spread by kiri, by drum, and by runner. Perhaps, too, the whynywir spoke with those seers gifted with the blue crystals. Villages close to his path sent emissaries inviting him to spend a night or a day with them. Villages farther away sent good wishes and gifts.

He was always polite, always kind. He detoured through the nearby villages, but he would not stay. Corodh-an-Aran had work to do, and he ached to get started.

In dozens of villages, people lined his path, and most were content simply to touch the white tigerskin as the pilgrim passed. Invariably, a few offered to go with him. Corodh-an-Aran might have raised a small army, but these people could not help him. The only people he needed were those who knew the city. He declined the villagers' offers.

He continued to dream tree-dreams, but they were nightmares no longer. "Soon," he whispered to the trees. "Soon. I will end it." Sometimes he would run his hand across the bark of the trees as he passed by, a gentle caress, like touching his mother's cheek.

Cort traveled at a steady lope through the thick summer khenaran, stopping only briefly to eat and sleep, but still, the journey was long. When he reached the great green river, Cort stroked the tigerskin on his shoulder and said, "I'm sorry, my friend, but we must cross once again. At least this time you won't suffer."

Neder greeted Cort three days from his village, saying, "Word of your arrival preceded you." His expression was studiedly neutral, but the corners of his mouth twitched slightly, and his eyes sparkled with a smile.

"It always does. Good to see you, Neder. Good to be home." Cort embraced his friend with a tight hug.

Neder pulled back and looked Cort up and down. "You look older."

The equinox was almost upon them. Cort had been gone for more than a year. He nodded. "It's been a year. You look about the same, though." He took a breath, then asked the one question that had burned within him during his entire journey home. "How is Dilia?" Realizing how close she was now, finally, he started walking again toward the village.

"She's well, and looking forward to seeing you," Neder said, matching Cort's pace. "She's turning into a fine healer. She has an instinct for it and learns quickly."

"That's good, Neder. It's right that she should be a healer, for I have been sent to destroy, and she may need all the skill she has."

Neder searched his young friend's face, perhaps looking for a sign Cort was joking. He must have seen only Cort's grim determination, for he spoke with an expression as bleak as if someone had died. "You've changed."

Cort could remember how he was before visiting the whynywir, but only in a distant way, like a fading dream. "A long winter among the whynywir would change anyone. As for me, I have simply become what I was born to be, no more—and no less."

Neder never looked away. He nodded slowly. "What you were born to be. Corodh-an-Aran. I should have known when you came back with all those kiri. Tirei's always a bit mysterious in his pronouncements, but I should have known right from the start."

Cort put a hand on his friend's shoulder. "Maybe I should have known, too, but I know it now. My life belongs to Aran. I will do what I must."

When Cort and Neder came to the top of the hill where the staff of living wood grew, Cort paused. Which one was the tree? They all looked similar, and he felt a rush of fondness for all of them. But *his* tree stood at the very crest of the hill. It had grown—already as thick around as his waist and three times his height. But it was still dwarfed by its neighbors, and it seemed somehow welcoming in a way that the magnificent larger trees were not. Friendly, almost. Related.

Cort ran his fingers over its bark. It was warm. He could no longer tell where the runes had once been carved. With the contact came a confused rush of emotion—grief and joy together—that clogged Cort's throat and burned behind his eyes. With a sudden insight that took his breath entirely away for a moment, he realized that his dreams and the dreams of this tree—*his* tree—were the same. "No more," he whispered. "I will end it."

"What's that?" Neder asked, tilting his head.

"Nothing, Neder. I'm just talking to the trees."

"Ah." Neder nodded solemnly, slowly, a gesture that spoke of an enormous effort to humor him. "Talking to the trees I should have known."

People were already gathered in the village's central clearing. Most had been working there preparing meat and plant-stock for cooking, sewing and weaving, carving and making tools—but they put their work aside when the two hunters entered the village. Children ran off to gather relatives and friends.

Perhaps it was a village just like any other in the khenaran, but to Cort it looked like home, and his heart ached with his intense but impossible desire to stay. He looked around at faces that were familiar enough—but where was Dilia? Had something happened to her? Cort stopped and turned to Neder to ask, and then Dilia arrived.

She stepped into the common area from a path between two of the houses, walking with an easy poise that made him think of dancing. She held the hands of two small children, and more walked behind her. The light seemed a little brighter, more intense around her. It added an auburn glow to her dark hair, which hung loose, with vines braided into it. Something in the way the air around her sparkled made her complexion golden and her smile radiant.

Holy Aran, mother of us all. If the whole world of Aran, everything he knew, had been shrunk down and then born as a woman, she would look like Dilia, surrounded by children, wearing grace like a halo. Cort felt his heartbeat quicken. How had he ever managed to stay away from this woman for so long?

But he knew the answer: when he'd left, he was still struggling to find his way into adulthood. They both had been. But now... Now he knew what he wanted. Cort was overwhelmed with a feeling of his own unworthiness—unworthy even to stand in her presence. Certainly unworthy to share a lifetime with her, and yet—he would marry Dilia, or he would marry no one. Tightness gripped his throat, making speaking impossible. He sank to his knees in front of her.

Dilia touched his hair softly, as if she wondered at the miracle of his presence. "Get up, Cort. You are so impossible sometimes." She reached out her hand to him. "Come on. Up."

Her offered hand felt like everything that Cort had missed in his life for the last year. He pressed her fingers against his cheek, and then, very gently, he kissed them. "Dilia, I... want to stay here with you forever."

"But you have to leave again," she said. "I know. Tirei told me. But maybe you could stay for a while. You don't have to go right away, do you?"

"Not right away, but soon. I'm going to go back to the city to stop the harvesting."

"Yes, I know." She stroked his hair, his forehead, his cheek.

There wasn't much to say after that. *Hello, I'm back. Now I'll be leaving, good-bye.* Cort climbed to his feet. A few of the children crowded closer around them, others wandered away.

"Are you going to kill the aliens?" Dilia asked. Her tone of voice was studiedly neutral, like an engineer describing the antigravity mechanism inside a gravlev device.

He groaned. "Oh, I hope not. But—maybe. Maybe I'll have to kill some of them."

"Is it going to be dangerous?"

He looked into her soft eyes. "Yes."

"To you? Might you die?"

"To me, yes. And to everyone in the city."

"Then you'll need my help. I will go with you."

His stomach and jaw tightened. There was no way he was going to let her go back there, but he didn't want to get into an argument. Not now, when he had just come home. He forced a smile, hoping it looked lighthearted. "I'm not planning on dying. I'm planning on coming back here and—" A sudden vivid image of the future he wanted for himself took his breath away. He barely managed to continue. "—and marrying you and living a long, happy life in the khenaran with you."

Dilia laughed with delight. But then her face grew serious. "I still don't know whether I'll ever have..." Her voice broke slightly. "...children."

Now it was Cort who laughed. Not out loud, but a deep inner laughter that bubbled through his spirit and tingled to the tips of his fingers. "Look at you," he said. "Just look at you." He gestured to indicate all the children still crowding around her. "You and I will have all the children of Aran."

"Oh." Dilia said, and then with dawning realization, "Oh!" She looked at the children gathered around her, touched one on the head, another on the shoulder, a third on the cheek. "That's good, then. It works for me. But what about you?"

"Dilia, your children are my children. And all the trees of the khenaran are my children too."

She touched his face as gently as she had touched the children all around her. "In that case, won't you please give me a kiss?"

Cort had dreamed of this invitation, imagined it, hoped for it. His chest radiated warmth, yet his hands trembled as he reached out to her. 'He took her in his arms and touched his lips gently to hers, and he kissed her with all his pent-up longing and his lifetime of love.

The next day, Corodh-an-Aran began making preparations for his return to the city. All winter in the whynywir's valley he had considered his options. He had discarded most of his ideas, but two or three showed promise, and he wanted to move forward with all of them. His next step was to visit the alien xenologist, Lennard.

Lennard had established himself as a member of the community, well liked for his quiet good humor and his willingness to lend a helping hand however he could. People had come to see his extensive note-taking as a personal oddity, like a stutter, that became unnoticeable after they'd known him for a while. He had surprised everyone by proposing marriage to Tirei-sunar's daughter Lela, a woman as tiny as the alien was tall. No one—least of all the young bride and her proud father—had any objections, and the couple had married. Everyone in the village had participated in a house-raising, and the newlywed couple now lived next to Lela's father.

Cort remembered Lela as a girl whose braids he'd pulled from time to time, much to her annoyance. She did not seem like a child anymore. She greeted him warmly, then went to brew some tea over the communal fire while Cort and Lennard sat on warm rugs in their airy home.

Lennard didn't seem to have the genetic malleability of the natives—his eyes were the same clear blue as they had been on the base—but he had adapted in many other ways to village life. He wore the dhelo-skin and alandhal-fur clothing favored by the villagers, and used rawhide to bind feathers and other decorations of personal significance into his now-long blond hair. He still suffered from shortness of breath, but this problem was not nearly as pronounced as when he first left the city. In fact, a relaxed *joie de vivre* had settled onto his features as naturally as the color of his skin. He looked ten years younger, and he spoke fluent, easy Arantu. "Tirei says you'll be returning to the city."

"Yes," Cort answered, then with some reluctance added, "I need your help."

Lennard fidgeted with the khena-wood ring he now wore on the index finger of his right hand. Translucent and golden and shining in the sunlight, with deep swirls of rainbow colors, this was the precious material that the aliens killed for. But this ring had been carefully cut from the living tree so that the tree was not harmed, and painstakingly crafted into a wedding ring. "I'm not thinking of going back," he said. "I'm a married man now. I have responsibilities."

Lela returned with tea, smiling at the two men.

"The life of the forest has its attractions, doesn't it?" Cort said. The two men fell silent a moment, sharing this mutually appreciated treasure. "But, Lennard, all this is at risk because of what your people are doing. I have learned beyond doubting that the spirits of our ancestors are in the great trees. That's why your ring is made of their flesh. When we first traveled here together, you spoke to me of laws. Surely the starmen's laws protect us from this slaughter of our ancestors. We need your help. Your children will need your help." It was a low blow, but the point was important.

Lennard looked away. "What can I do?" He spoke in a flat tone and shrugged.

"Get your Earth government involved! Didn't you say the laws were on our side?"

The alien sighed. "You don't understand. The laws would support you if they were killing people—I mean, humans. If there were objective facts. But people will argue that spirits cannot be in trees, and this is simply a matter of your primitive beliefs."

Cort drew an angry breath.

Lennard cut him off with a placatory hand. "Don't misunderstand me. I didn't say *I* believe that. I'm a member of this community now. I've seen the reverence people have for these trees, and I... I feel the same way. If I could stop the harvesting tomorrow, I would. But I'm telling you what people back on Earth will say. Still, as a case involving a deeply held cultural and religious belief, the law may still offer you some protection. Let's say that it does. Even so, the trip to Earth would take a dozen years or so. Who knows how much time after that to make my case? The government moves slowly. The issue will be controversial. This, too, could take years. I think you'd be lucky to see any change in your lifetime."

Even a lifetime was better than never, but Corodh-an-Aran wanted results sooner than that. He wanted to save the tigers. He wanted to save every tree that was at risk. "Can you think of anything to make it faster?"

"I'm sorry." Lennard looked away. "I think we should just live as well as we can, given the realities of the situation."

"No!" Corodh-an-Aran slammed a hand to the ground, and then forced himself to lower his voice. "That's not enough, Lennard. Every day, trees die. I'm going to find a way to end it. And when I do... You said once that your government no longer allows settlement on worlds inhabited by intelligent peoples."

"Yes, that's true."

"I trust that people on Earth would generally agree that my people are intelligent."

Lennard glanced at Lela, who sat calmly beside him. "Of course. But I also said that this law doesn't apply to this world, since we already have a presence here."

"But if you were to suddenly find you no longer had a presence here..."

Lennard shivered. He studied Cort's face. "You mean, hypothetically?"

"Hypothetically," Cort agreed amiably.

"Hypothetically, if we didn't have a presence here, we would not be allowed to establish one."

"Good." Cort smiled grimly. "Then I'll still need your help. Because once the aliens' presence here is eliminated, I'll be counting on you to ensure that it isn't reestablished."

"Wait a minute! Just what do you mean by that?"

"Lennard." Corodh-an-Aran spoke softly. "Someone has to tell your people what we are like. What our values are, and why they're important. Isn't that a xenologist's job? Someone has to make sure that the commandant and the others leave here while they still can, and that there's no resettlement and no retribution."

"What do you mean, 'leave here while they still can'? What are you going to do?"

Cort looked away. He had a few good ideas, but nothing he was ready to talk about. "I don't know yet, but I'd like to avoid having anyone die. I need your help. I need you to go back to Earth."

Lennard fell silent. He took Lela's hand and began stroking it gently. He studied her fingers intently, as if this was the last time he would ever see them.

Cort's jaw hurt from clenching. He was angry at Lennard for changing his mind and refusing to return to Earth, where he belonged, and marrying into this village instead. Angry at Lela for wanting him, at Tirei for allowing the marriage. He was angry at himself and his terrible purpose that threatened to tear apart these two people who obviously loved each other. He said nothing.

It was Lela who broke the silence. "I will go with you, even to Earth. You are my husband."

Lennard looked sharply at his wife and shook his head. "No. I think the air on Earth may not be very good for you. And our world is so... different. So complicated."

Cort remembered how giddy the air around Hsu-Lin Base had made him feel and how weak Dilia had become, and he understood Lennard's concern. But this was bigger than one person's fears. "Maybe it's possible for her to adjust... over time." He certainly hoped so. He wanted to believe that his father might be alive on the aliens' home planet. "My people can adjust to a lot of things."

"Let me think about it," Lennard said.

When Corodh-an-Aran asked after Aj, he learned that the former soldiers had settled in a number of different villages, exactly as Cort had planned. Two had even returned with Denra, friends after their initial hostile encounter. Aj himself had settled in a village several days' journey to the east.

Now, though, Cort intended to disrupt his old plan and their new lives. Together with his ferret kiri, Cort set out to find the former sergeant.

Aj greeted Cort in the khenaran a day from his village. "I wasn't at home," he apologized, "but I heard you were coming."

For a moment, Cort wondered how Aj had found him. Then he caught the glitter of a red crystal at Aj's hairline. "You're a hunter!"

"Thanks to your example." Aj grinned. "Without you, they wouldn't have thought it was possible for a clanless person to have a kiri. But now they say that anything is possible, so long as the forest has need."

Cort hated pulling Aj out of his new life and obvious pleasure at being a hunter, but he steeled himself. It was necessary. "This brings me to the point of my visit."

"Ah... so it's not just a pleasure call, eh? I expected as much. They say you are going to drive the aliens away and save the trees. You're going back to the city, right?"

"Word does get around. Yes, I am, and I need your help."

"You have it," Aj said without hesitation. "I think some of the others will join us, too. We like it here in the khenaran. If you're working to save the forest, we're with you. Are you going in after the power station?"

Although Cort had thought about the power station and still considered it his most likely option, he hadn't discussed these half-formed plans with anyone, and he felt an odd reluctance to speak them out loud. He swallowed, but they would have to be discussed sooner or later. "Yes. Yes, I think so."

"It's a good plan!" Aj responded enthusiastically. "We were all assigned to the power station before Jerrald took us out to hunt you. I think we were the only off-duty squad around at the time you left, and you know the power-station guards are highly trained, as far as that goes. I know how to access the current security codes. The codes change every day, of course, but the routines for accessing them—never."

"Good!" Cort allowed himself to feel hope. "How many of the soldiers do you think will come back and help?"

"Not all," Aj answered. "Some have married and settled down. One man already has a baby. We'll have to ask them and see, but I'd guess we'll get at least half a dozen."

Lor trudged up from the stream, two heavy buckets of water balanced on a pole across his shoulders. He had no complaints about the burden. In fact, it wasn't much different than bringing water back from the fountain to his house in the city. No, it was better than that. Lor never tired of the khenaran, and one of its miracles was the diversity of plants that grew among the great trees, each in its little niche. How subtly they tended to grow near complementary plants.

Nel had taught him so much in the past year. He smiled, thinking of her. He passed through an area crowded with large-leafed fan-like plants whose fruit, Nel had told him, could be boiled into a syrup that relieved colic in babies. And she'd said they always grew near—yes, there it was—the tiny frond-like vines of throatease, from whose leaves a tea could be brewed—

"Greetings, my goodman."

Lor jumped, nearly unbalancing his load. "Wh—what?"

Someone vaguely familiar looking sat on a rock, as still as if he'd always been there. The person stood. "Lor."

Recognition hit him. "Cort!" He carefully set down his buckets, and then gave his old friend a hug. "What's with the city talk?"

Cort returned the embrace, grinning. "Get into the mindset, my goodman. Going retro to the city, blast the starmen back to Earth."

"Oh... no, Cort." Lor backed away, hands out, and stumbled over one of his buckets. He narrowly missed upending it as he fell.

Cort extended a hand to help Lor to his feet. "Necessary mission." The smile lingered on Cort's face, but his eyes had turned serious and hard. He had changed, that was for sure. He was as lean and ropy as a wolf, with a tiger skin draped over his shoulder and his jaw set with purpose.

Lor had dismissed the rumors about Cort as idle talk by people who didn't know his friend the way he did. But now he wasn't so certain. Maybe the rumors weren't false. Maybe he didn't know Cort at all. "No, not necessary. Not for me. Let's cut the city talk, okay? We're forest people now, right? You coming for a visit?"

Cort studied him in silence, maybe just a heartbeat too long. Then he picked up both buckets as easily as if they weighed nothing, handed one to Lor, and hoisted the other to his shoulder. "Right, Lor," he said. "A visit." He headed down the path toward the village.

Lor hastily grabbed his pole and followed.

It was one of those miracles of life in the khenaran that Lor still hadn't gotten used to, how people always seemed to know something an instant before it happened. *He* certainly didn't. Probably never would. But here people were, already starting to gather as Cort strode into the village. They touched him, a pat on the shoulder or fingers to the tiger skin, as if he conveyed some kind of benediction that might be transmitted to them through their fingertips.

Cort suffered the strange ritual with the quiet dignity of a man being given his due—until he spotted Tonio. "Teacher!" he cried out. Then he turned to Lor. "Tonio taught me everything I know about clans."

"Which isn't much," Tonio said. To Lor he added, "Cort saved my life."

"A fair trade." Cort said.

Okolo made his way through the growing crowd. "Uh-oh. Three of you all in one place. This is trouble for sure."

Cort gave the old seer an enthusiastic hug. "Good to see you again, Okolo."

"Easy!" Okolo exclaimed. "These old bones aren't what they used to be." He pushed Cort's hair back and studied the two crystals at his hairline. "Who would have thought, back then, that those two crystals I sent to Tirei-sunar were both for you?"

Cort nodded, still resting a hand on the seer's shoulder. "Those strange things you said about me kind of make sense now."

"Despite that—what the whynywir told me—I resented you some back then. Taking my grandson from me, and my daughter. But both have returned, and brought me a new son as well." He smiled at Lor, his face creasing all the way into his hairline. He began guiding Lor and Cort back to his house. "And a new grandchild on the way."

Cort turned to Lor, brows raised in surprise. "You're married?"

"Yes. To Nel." Lor turned to look for her among the dispersing crowd, spotted her coming toward him, and beamed. His eyes slipped from her face to the curve of her belly, where the child was growing. "We're going to have a son."

"A daughter," Nel said as she joined them.

"I see." Cort's gaze dropped to Nel's visible pregnancy and then back again. "I guess you're not coming with me at that. Too much danger for a man who's about to become a father."

Nel gave her father a hand as he slowly sat, and then she sat, too. "Is it true," she asked Cort, "that you're going to destroy the city?"

"I'm going to send the starmen home. If I have to destroy the city to do that, then yes, that's what I'll do."

Lor fidgeted and looked away, embarrassed at letting his friend down. "I always thought I'd watch your back, no matter what."

Cort smiled warmly. "Some things do matter more. This is one of them. I'll manage."

"I'd like to name my son after you," Lor said on impulse. "Would that be all right?"

"Lor, mine is not a name to give lightly or for personal reasons." Cort explained the name's meaning, then said, "In my family, it's a blood thing. The name has always been passed down, parent to child. But there could be other people carrying this name, and they may acquire the name in a different way. But this I do know: A person named Corodh-an-Aran will always place the welfare of Aran ahead of his own. Ahead of his wife and even his child. I may fail in the city. Or even if I succeed, I may not be returning. Do you want that for your child?"

Lor swallowed. Was he brave enough to watch his son die? But no, he had to be. If Cort was going to risk his life in the city, and Lor did not have his back the way he should, then by Aran the least he could do was to keep Cort's name and his legacy alive. In his peripheral vision he saw Nel nodding slowly beside him. "It would be a privilege to name my son after you."

"Or daughter," Nel added.

She did have this pesky way of bringing up the daughter issue, but Lor knew it might be true, and knew too that he would love his daughter as much as any son. "What, can a girl be Corodh-an-Aran?"

"I don't see why not," Cort said. "But you really ought to give it some thought before you decide."

Lor wrinkled his nose. "All right. After all, *Cort* is a terrible name for a girl."

Nel laughed. "We'll just have to call her Cora."

Cort returned to his own village, shuffling the bits and pieces of ideas that still resisted falling into a neat plan. He dug out the laser weapon he had taken from the alien, Jerrald. The thing had been a difficult burden, one he could neither carry with him, nor give to anyone. He didn't want to use it, but he had been reluctant to destroy it. It seemed the alien object would be impossible to dispose of. No place on the planet was fitting for it. Cort had finally buried it, carefully wrapped in deerskin, at the foot of one of the great trees. Now he was glad he had kept it.

He studied the alien weapon, turning it over and back in his hands, getting used to the weight of it, studying its controls. *I am like this laser. The little fusion reactor here in the handle will provide power for generations, and so will the purpose in my name. Now I have been powered up and taken off standby and aimed at the throats of Aran's enemies. And I am ready to be fired.*

He tightened his lips in an uncompromising line, hard as his father's knife, straight as a laser beam. *Good.*

He began practicing shooting with the laser. It didn't have the feel and balance of a knife, but when Cort thought of its barely visible, deadly beam as something he threw at his target, the laser began to make sense. He mastered it quickly.

Cort returned to the village just in time to see Tirei-sunar leaving, his spine rigid, fists clenched, and speaking not a word to anyone. The morning after Tirei left, Lennard asked Cort into his small house, where Lela sat, composed and solemn.

"Lela and I are prepared to return to the city with you," he said.

Cort was silent. He hadn't expected Lennard to agree so easily, nor had he expected Lela to come along. He tried to picture an adjustment to his plan that would include one small but spirited woman from the khenaran.

Lennard cleared his throat. "We are prepared to go farther, if necessary."

Farther. To Earth. This would be a major blow to Tirei. "Did Tirei approve?"

"My father will not stand against us," Lela said. She glanced toward the forest at the edge of the village. "He'll be back."

"Are you... Lela, are you sure about this? There won't be any coming back from Earth." Cort thought about his father. Was he still alive? "Perhaps, if… when… Lennard leaves, you might want to return here."

Lela stiffened. She walked closer to Lennard and put an arm around his back. "Lennard is my husband," she said. "I am not leaving him."

When Tirei returned at dinnertime of the second day, Cort was sharing a meal with Neder, who offered Tirei a cup of broth and some meat and moved to make room by his side. "Sit. Eat."

With a sigh, Tirei sat and crossed his legs. In the flickering light of Neder's fire, his tears sparkled but didn't fall. To Cort the seer said, "I could wish that you had never come to this village."

Feeling tears rising to his own eyes, Cort said softly, "I understand, and I'm sorry. I never meant you any harm."

"I know that, Corodh-an-Aran," Tirei said. "You are an elemental force, like a spring storm. You act for the good of Aran. I understand that. But like a storm, you have ripped away the roof of my house and plucked away my child, and were it not for the important work you must do, I would regret your coming here. But it is as it must be."

Cort felt the seer's pain deeply. He swallowed hard. "It's not my fault. The xenologist's job is to return to his people. I *need* him to return, Tirei. He shouldn't have married here."

"And I shouldn't have given my permission." Tirei sighed deeply, as if he had to make room in his chest for his swollen heart. "The whynywir warned me against it, but she loved him so… Against the whynywir's advice, I indulged my child. It's my own fault, if anyone's. I should have known better."

"Still, it may turn out well," Cort said. "Perhaps there is a role that Lela can play in all this. Perhaps the aliens on Earth will listen better to Lennard because Lela is there with him."

"Perhaps," Tirei said, but he sounded tired. He sipped at the broth he had been holding all this time. "I would like to come with you, Corodh-an-Aran."

"What!" Neder exclaimed.

And Cort said, "No."

"If he wouldn't let *me* come—" Neder said.

"I don't want either of you to come," Cort interrupted. He touched the seer's arm. "There's too much risk, Tirei. Maybe I'll make it back, me and whoever goes with me, but maybe some of us won't. Maybe no one will. If I fail, I don't want to bring harm to you, too."

"He's been absolutely adamant," Neder told the seer, giving Cort a glance filled with frustration. "Like a rock. I can't move him."

Cort realized how much he had come to love both of these men.

"The whynywir said that Corodh-an-Aran is to have his way in whatever he wants," Tirei said. "I suppose we'll have to wait here until you come back, Cort. Keep safe. Do what you can for Lela. Don't stay away too long."

"I won't," Cort said. He hoped it was true. "Stay safe, you two. Keep the village safe. No matter what happens out there, you are the beacon I to guide me home."

Both men nodded solemnly.

Cort and Dilia were walking along a narrow stream that flowed swiftly down a rocky course. Moss grew on the rocks nearby, and a cool humidity flavored the air. "I'm going with you," Dilia said. She spoke as matter-of-factly as if the issue had been settled long ago.

Cort lost his balance. He slipped a fraction of a centimeter on a moist rock, feeling for an instant as if the ground had given way. He stopped, making Dilia turn and face him. "No," he said. "You're not."

She bent and rested her fingers in the rushing water, making it flow around them. She looked at him with serious amber eyes. "What about the people in the city, Cort? Have you thought about them?"

"What about them?"

"Isn't there a chance that whatever you do to drive the aliens out may harm the people there? May... kill them?"

He anchored his arms across his chest, set his lips tight. "It won't change my mind. The aliens must go. If a few people die... if city people die, or the people with me die, or if I die, it doesn't matter. We will all be reborn."

"Children, Cort?" She spoke so softly it almost seemed that the words had been formed in the sound of the stream itself. "What about the children?"

He sighed and folded himself onto the ground. There was no answer to this question, no good one. Not when Dilia was the person asking. After a long silence in which the puzzle pieces of his plan rearranged themselves into a new pattern, he said, "What do you propose?"

Chapter 23

Journey to the City

C ort waited in the village's central clearing for the eight soldiers who had agreed to return to the city with him. They were coming from five different villages where they had settled. Dilia waited with Cort. She shivered and wrapped her arms around her chest against the chill of the early morning, and Cort put his arm around her shoulder to offer what warmth he could.

Neder and Tirei arrived a moment later, as did a couple of the soldiers. Children materialized out of the light mist, gathering around Dilia. They seemed to belong near her as naturally as khena trees belonged on Aran. "You are definitely going to have children," Cort said to her.

Dilia stroked the hair of a small girl, who snuggled close against her. "Maybe none of my own, though."

"They are all your own."

She smiled a mixture of pleasure and sorrow but said nothing.

This was one problem Cort could not set right for her. The best he could do was to share it, to give her whatever strength he could. "Yours and mine together," he said, "when we come back."

Her smile brightened, the sorrow in it evaporating like the morning mist. "Yes. When we come back."

It was a promise he had no idea whether he could keep. He looked away from her to see Lennard and Lela arriving—two people who would, if all went well, not be coming back.

"Good morning!" Lennard spoke with a cheerfulness that was just a shade too loud and not quite convincing.

Cort steeled his heart against the guilty feelings lurking there, and he smiled. "Good morning, Lennard, Lela. It's a good day to start a journey, don't you think?"

"And we'd best be going before the day is half over." The new voice belonged to Aj. All eight of the soldiers had arrived. The travelers said goodbye to those who would remain in the village. Dilia hugged each of the children, then joined Cort with tears in her eyes as they set out on their journey.

Despite Cort's warnings of the potential dangers, the soldiers were in high spirits as they walked through the khenaran. They had begun calling him Inei-taru again, sometimes to his face, as if some magic of his would somehow protect them all from harm.

Cort didn't like it. Too much was at stake. It was dangerous for any of them to start thinking they could rely on magical powers.

To make matters worse, Lennard questioned the soldiers every time they mentioned Inei-Taru, and he took extensive notes. Then he approached Cort. "Who is Inei-Taru, exactly?" he asked. "The soldiers all seem to admire him, so why are you unhappy when they call you that?"

Despite his worries, Cort smiled. "Inei-Taru is just a story told to little children, back in the city. You know the meaning of the name in Arantu?"

Leonard considered. "Um... Inei—that would be ancestors, plural, possessive, and Taru, voice. Voice of the ancestors?"

Cort nodded. "Very good, Lennard. Yes, that's exactly it. Inei-taru swoops down on his powerful enemies, usually kingpins, sometimes starmen, too. He steals gold or jewels or other things of value and then uses them to buy food for starving children or to rescue a helpless family from a kingpin's corrupt army. And just as it seems he might be captured, he disappears into the forest, ready to strike again another day."

"Hmm." Lennard made some notes on his tablet. "Robin Hood."

"Who?"

"An old Earth legend, a lot like that. It's based in historical fact, actually."

The idea was not attractive. "Well, I am not an old Earth legend, and I don't want you encouraging them to call me that."

"*You're* encouraging them," Lennard shot back. "I'm just doing my job. You want me to go back to Earth and advocate for your people. Well, if I'm going to do that, I'd better have a first-rate book about Aran, a book everyone will want to read. A book that will make every person on Earth sympathetic to the plight of your people."

There wasn't much Cort could say to that. After a few days, he and Dilia began traveling somewhat apart from the rest of the group. He had been alone for so long that he found the group loud, bumbling, and slow, though not nearly as bad as when they had come out from the city. Dilia was the only one he wanted by his side. He had plenty of time to hunt for food for the group without holding them back. Sometimes Aj joined him on these hunts.

It was late one afternoon, and a storm had soaked them all as they walked. Despite the warm breeze and the golden sunlight that slanted low under the clouds when the rain passed, several of the soldiers complained of their wet clothing and the mud they slogged through. Cort walked away from the group.

Aj followed him. "I'm not sure I believe we will be reborn." he said. They climbed a hill that rose to the left of the path the group followed, emerging in a spot that revealed a far vista to the east. A rainbow arched across the sky's dark clouds.

"Believe it," Cort said.

"But how can we know until we do it?"

"We've done it many times." Cort smiled, looking into the distance and thinking of the whynywir. "But each time we forget."

"Then how can we know at all?"

"Because the whynywir don't forget. Not that I would recommend that anyone be born as a whynywir."

"Sometimes I think I'd like to be born as a fox like my kiri," Aj said.

Cort turned to the soldier-turned-hunter in surprise. "Really?"

Aj looked away. "Maybe a human again," he amended. "It's not so bad being a human, either... these days. How about you, Cort? Have you thought about what you'd like to be born as, the next time?"

Cort looked back at the sky, almost black with storm clouds, yet shining with a full, bright rainbow. Despite the deadliness of this mission, his heart was at peace. "I will be Corodh-an-Aran again. Every time."

Cort discussed his plans with Aj. They went over them time and again, sitting full and satisfied after a long hunt, and before they brought their kill back to the others. Aj had ideas, too, and the two of them worked out as many of the details as they could. How Cort would get onto the base. How Aj and the others would. How to best use Lennard and Lela, and what assignments to give them. What Dilia would be doing. What to do if one thing went wrong, or another. How to join up again afterwards—if there was an afterwards.

Finally, there was no more planning to be done, at least not by Aj and Cort. But the others might have their own perspectives, different ideas of how to act if Cort or Aj were no longer able to lead them. Cort began making the others plan, too. Each person would have something to add.

Sometimes the soldiers would ask, "What are your plans, Inei-taru?"

The question made Cort wince. "Make your own plans," he told them. "You've spent a lot of time on the base. You can probably think of things I don't even know about. Just remember the goal: We have to get the aliens off Aran, hopefully without killing them, although... if necessary..." That was one sentence he never finished, no matter how often they asked. He didn't want to dwell on what might be necessary.

"And another thing," Cort sometimes added, though he didn't feel it would do much good. "You've got this Inei-taru thing all backwards. I'm not Inei-taru. Remember the goal, and take responsibility for it. We are *all* Inei-taru. If any of us fails, the others must continue. I won't be able to do it all myself. You've got to figure out how to succeed, even without me. Work on your own, without me. Plan on it."

After about seven days, when traveling had become routine, Lennard touched Cort's arm and said, "Tell me more about the whynywir."

"There's not much to tell, Lennard." The statement felt false even as Cort said it. He frowned. "Maybe there *is* a lot, but I just don't know how to tell it. They're very different from you and me. I could say that they're the real aliens, but, Lennard, the whynywir are of the forest. They belong here." He didn't add, "Not like your people," but he thought it.

And Lennard must have known. He reddened and looked down. But he persisted. "You know I'm a trained xenologist. I would like—I would *very much* like to meet some true aliens."

"Somehow, Lennard, I don't think you would like to meet the whynywir. Nobody does."

"Oh, but I would!"

Seeing the enthusiasm in the alien's blue eyes, Cort had to look away. "Anyhow, you have a job to do," he said. "I'm counting on you. You have to convince the other starmen to leave. You'll have to go with them, too. And then you have to write that book you keep threatening to write, the one that will convince the people of Earth to stay away from here once all of you leave. I don't want anyone to get hurt."

Lennard folded his arms across his chest and studied Cort from under lowered brows. "How would people get hurt, Cort?"

"They won't get hurt because you're going to help me prevent it."

"But how?"

Cort refused to discuss his plans with the alien. "You'll know when the time comes. Just get everyone onto their starship and away."

"And if there isn't a starship?"

Cort turned to stare at the Lennard. "As long as I have been alive there has always been a starship at the base. Sometimes two. The harvesting never stops."

A silence fell over the group as they approached the river that marked the edge of the khenaran.

Lennard walked glumly, no longer troubled by shortness of breath. He kept close to his wife's side, avoiding conversation both with the soldiers and with Cort. For his part, Cort felt comfortable only with Dilia and in the silent conversations with his kiri.

The soldiers continued to meet, sometimes in twos or threes and sometimes the whole group, discussing their plans neither with the alien and his wife Lela, nor with Dilia and Cort. When they crossed the river, leaving the great khenaran behind, they all pulled their old uniforms from their packs and began to wear them again.

The harvester's heavy tread quivered the tree leaves as it moved into position to strike at a khena. His tree. Cort couldn't let them have it, but there was only one way to protect the tree. He turned, planted his feet, and sank into the earth. The roar of the giant machine drowned his shouted "No!" Even under the ground, sub-bass vibrations shook the bedrock. But his will was stronger than the rock. *You will not. I will not let you.* Cort descended deep, deep into the ground and into Aran's central heat where the rock was liquid. He scooped up a handful of Aran's fire and raced upward, bursting through the surface at the tree's roots. He threw the fire at the harvester, and all Aran held its breath as the fire spread its searing fingers over the huge machine.

Cort opened his eyes to darkness. A residual image of fire burned against the insides of his eyelids. An unusually chilly breeze carried the scent of impending rain. He sat up and slid his finger across his eyelids, erasing the dream, and then rubbed his arms against the gooseflesh that was rising there. An owl whoo-hooted the approaching dawn. They had been traveling for almost three weeks through the woods that surrounded the city, where the khena trees had long ago been cut down.

Hunter. Today is the day. The bobcat sat by his feet. She licked a paw and used it to wash the back of her ear. *It's time to get started.*

He felt the itch the little cat rubbed against and scratched the back of his own ear. Of course it was time, but he wasn't ready. *So soon?*

The bobcat didn't deign to answer.

Cort took in a deep breath. Under the humidity he could already detect the smell of the city—garbage and sweat and dust. He let out his breath. *You'll stay with Dilia, take care of her. When... whatever happens, happens... you'll know it before she does.*

The little cat stood and paced in a tight circle. She returned to her seat and stared at him with unblinking amber eyes. *I will scream danger so loud you will hear it all the way up in the Place of Bad Air.*

He returned the stare. *I will hear you, but Dilia will not.*

Then I will push her out of that foul place with my body against her legs. So I have promised, and so I will do. Hunter, let go of this. It is time.

He could count on the little cat. She would shadow Dilia, would protect her with her last breath. He was procrastinating. He leaned over and touched Dilia's face, stroked her long hair.

She opened eyes still heavy-lidded with sleep. "Mmm?"

"It's time. You should go."

She raised her head and looked around. "It's still dark."

"Not really. It's just cloudy." He nodded toward the east, where the sky had already turned from black to a deep gray. "If you start now, the shops will already be open when you get to the gate." The gang members will be in school or sleeping or at work. The streets will be busy with men and women going to market to buy or sell. The city will be as safe as it ever is.

She sat up and took hold of his hand. "Oh, Cort, don't worry about me."

"Stay away from any soldiers."

"I'll go right to Lor's family's house, like I promised. I won't be alone."

He looked to where the bobcat waited impatiently, but the kiri had already vanished into the woods. Dilia would be less alone than she thought. "One of my kiri will stay near you, a bobcat, but she won't get close to other people, so if you're in a crowd..."

"Cort, stop it. I'll be fine. I'll go to the nurseries and schools, wherever they're caring for the children. I'll warn them to be prepared for... to be ready to leave the city quickly." She smiled mischief at him. "I'll tell them I have seen Inei-Taru, and he sends this message."

Cort gasped. "Don't you dare."

Dilia laughed out loud, stood on tiptoe, and kissed him on the forehead. Then she began folding her bedroll.

He stood, too, and helped her to roll it tight, tie it, and slip it over her shoulder. His fingers touched her hair, caressed her neck. He'd been dreading this moment since they set out.

Dilia took a deep shaky breath, and then wrapped herself in his waiting arms. "I'll miss you."

"It won't be long. A day. Maybe two. Come back this way... afterwards. I'll find you." *By mountain and river and sky, I will find you. By every kiri on the planet.* Afterwards. If there was an afterwards.

"I know."

He pulled back to look into her eyes. "The bobcat will lead you there and stay with you till you return."

Dilia nodded. "Thank you. I'll be all right. But you..."

"I'll be all right, too, don't worry." He kissed her lips, and when she opened hers to him, he had a dizzying moment that threatened to sweep away all his plans.

No. He couldn't. Not now. "Go," he said, his voice hoarse.

Thunder rolled in the distance.

Dilia vanished into the trees.

Chapter 24

Arrival

Now where were those blasted soldiers? Did Cort have to do everything for himself?

The soldiers had camped at a discreet distance both from Cort and Dilia and from Lennard and Lela. But they were easy enough to find. Despite the old saw that soldiers slept quietly, at least two of this bunch snored. And it was getting light enough to see clearly. Cort skirted the sleeping starman and his wife and found the soldiers aligned in two rows to either side of the cold embers of a campfire.

Aj slept at one end of the nearer group, his kiri long left behind in the khenaran.

Cort leaned close to him and said in a normal, conversational tone, "Wake up."

Every one of the soldiers jumped up. About half of them had their stunners in hand and aimed in Cort's general direction.

Cort smiled, but without humor. "You've got to do better than that. If I'd been an enemy, four of you would already be dead. Where's your sentry?"

"Inei-Taru," Aj said, "forgive us."

If he hadn't broken them of this "Inei-Taru" thing, it was too late now. "All right. Fine. But we're only half a day from the city. You need to start thinking like soldiers again. How long until you're ready to go?"

Aj straightened into military posture. "Ten minutes," he said.

Cort nodded and walked a short distance into the woods to be alone, perhaps for the last time. He found a tree of substantial size—though still far shorter than the distant khena—and sat under it. He watched through the owl's eyes as it returned to its roost. The western sky was darkening with an impending storm that growled occasional thunder. But in the east, the sky was turning the rosy pink of clouds reflecting the impending sunrise. Dilia, traveling under the canopy of the trees, was nowhere to be seen.

"You're under arrest, Cort."

The sharp words brought Cort out of his reverie with a breath-catching snap. Aj stood above him, feet braced a shoulder's width apart, Cort's own laser held with both hands and aimed at Cort's chest. Cort had left the laser unguarded in his bedroll, and Aj must have checked. Good for him.

Even though he knew what was coming, Cort's heart thumped wildly, and he went hot all over. Aj was supposed to march him into the city looking like he was under arrest, yes, but it was supposed to be all for show. The laser wasn't part of the plan. Cort's city reflexes took any weapon seriously, especially if it was pointed at him. Especially if the weapon was a laser.

He forced himself to draw a long, calming breath. "Easy," he said, holding a hand up, palm out in appeasement.

"You're under arrest," Aj repeated. "Stand up slowly. Don't make any sudden moves. Keep your hands where I can see them."

Cort stood—slowly and carefully as requested, his mind churning. After all, what had he expected? An arrest celebration? Stumbling and laughing their way into the city? The soldiers were right to do exactly as professional soldiers would. If only they hadn't sprung it on him like this, first thing in the morning, not even one of them smiling. If only they weren't aiming the laser right at him. If only the wild hammering of his heart wouldn't keep pounding a warning that this was for real.

There was a rustling of movement in the camp, and three soldiers came up behind Aj. "We've got the others, Sergeant," one of them said. Two more soldiers brought Lennard and Lela, hands tied, into the clearing. Tears ran down Lela's face, but she stood straight, her shoulder touching her husband's arm, her expression impassive.

"Take Cort's knife, then tie his hands. Make it good and tight." Aj moved slightly to the side so that he could keep Cort covered as the soldier carried out his orders. "If any of your kiri harm any one of us, the soldiers have orders to fire at you. Their orders are to shoot to injure you, but before they kill you, they will kill the alien and his wife."

Lela let out a little cry, quickly stifled as Lennard brushed her arm. Cort's hands were quickly tied.

The hawk was now awake. *I can take one of them,* she said.

Yes, but that would defeat their plans. *No,* Cort answered. *Just stay nearby.* Despite Aj's order, the rope binding Cort's hands was loose enough to work free of. Just as it should be. Time to get into character. To Aj he asked, "Why? Why are you doing this?"

"I told you once before," the sergeant answered gruffly, as he fastened Cort's knife onto his own belt. "We want to go back to the city. After Jerrald died, we couldn't. We would have been suspect. But now, bringing you back prisoner, it's different. You don't think Jerrald headed out on his own, do you? He had orders from the commandant. We all did. We'll get a hero's welcome and a good reward for this, and our old jobs back."

"But what about living in the forest, being a hunter? Are you going to give that up?"

Aj shrugged, not meeting Cort's eyes. "We're going to get our old jobs back. That's better." His voice sounded wavery; he was going to have to be more convincing than this when the aliens grilled him.

But when Aj looked up again, his expression was determined, his eyes hard. "Time to get moving. We've got some ground to cover. You lead. Keep a steady pace. Try anything fancy, and the men have orders to burn your legs." Aj was referring to the stunners that the soldiers still aimed steadily at him. If Aj was a poor play-actor, the soldiers were frighteningly good. They looked like they might actually use the stunners they aimed steadily at his legs, and if they did, he would feel as if he'd been burned alive. He would stay conscious, but he'd wish he hadn't. Cort couldn't help wondering whether some of them were not acting at all. He wondered if he'd ever see Dilia again.

The closer they came to the city, the more disciplined the soldiers became. Cort couldn't have escaped even if he'd wanted to.

From the hawk's viewpoint high above, Cort watched the small procession of soldiers with their three prisoners, himself in the lead, cross the fields that surrounded the city and approach the city gate. A year and a half had passed since the last time he was here.

Aj's squad of soldiers was saluted by the guards at the city gate, and one of them asked, "What's this? Prisoners?"

"Two savages and a renegade. Orders of the commandant."

The guard nodded and said, "Pass."

Nothing had changed in the city, but everything had changed in how Cort perceived it. When he was a boy, the city had been home. It was also a world of adventure and opportunity and a future full of exciting possibilities. When he'd come back for Dilia, the city seemed much smaller. It was a world he had mastered and could succeed in—but he didn't want to. Now, he saw the place was vile. The mud-brick, stone, and wooden buildings were run-down and densely packed with families trying to survive among the garbage and the ruins. The narrow streets smelled of rot and urine. Rats darted across the street from one building to another, even in the daylight. The city was ripe for destruction.

People stopped to look at the prisoners, and as Cort met one pair of eyes after another, all he could read in them was hunger and despair. He hated that Dilia had had to return here.

In the city, their native environment, Aj's soldiers relaxed their guard a bit. Cort could see it in an easing of the stiffness of their backs, in a slight slowing of the pace. In an occasional wavering of their weapons. This was a mistake.

Just ahead, the street opened out into a broad square. From a narrow street to their right, still out of sight at street level, Cort's hawk's vision showed a squad of soldiers in Sleb's uniform approaching. The rivalry between the soldiers employed by the starmen and those working in the city was well known. Sleb's men would not like a squad of base soldiers elbowing in on their territory. Aj's group would have to look like they were just passing through, not a threat but too strong to be bullied—or worse.

"Aj." Cort spoke softly to the sergeant, who now walked just ahead of him. "Soldiers coming in from the right. Not yours."

Aj looked to his right, audibly sucked in his breath, and muttered a swear word Cort hadn't heard since he'd lived in the city. Then Aj gave a quick command, one word, "Alert." Though not aiming directly at the others, Aj's men shifted their weapons so that they were ready to fire quickly if necessary.

Cort clenched his teeth till his jaw hurt. Hands tied, no weapon, not even a knife. And tension bristled like electricity.

As Sleb's men entered the square, they too readied their weapons.

"Easy," Aj ordered. "Just keep walking."

One of Sleb's soldiers gripped his stunner in both hands and aimed toward Cort's group.

Time seemed frozen.

The soldier's face was set in a snarl of bad teeth. His eyes met Cort's. His fingers tightened on the trigger.

Nearby, one of Aj's men fired, a deafening crack.

Sleb's man screamed and fell, clutching at his arm. His stunner catapulted end over end and clattered to the ground.

Another shot, and one of Aj's men fell, clutching at his head. More stunner blasts from Sleb's men made his body twitch, then he lay still, unconscious—or worse.

Two of Aj's soldiers hustled Lennard and Lela toward the base, running while aiming back over their shoulders. Another soldier pushed Cort down, shielding him while returning fire from Sleb's troops.

Civilians ran.

Cort pushed his guard back hard. His only hope was to get out of the crossfire. As Aj's men raced for cover in one direction, Cort ran in the other—back toward the street they had just come from.

It was a gamble. In the open with no cover, Cort sprinted for the shadow of the street with its protective doorways. Only ten steps now... Nine...

A searing pain shot up his spine.

Eight...

His spine burned like fire, stabbed like a thousand knives.

Seven...

A scream shrieked past his lips, came out sounding like something horribly alien. He stumbled.

Six...

He could see the doorway through a haze of red. Only five more steps. Despite the pain, he crawled toward it.

A second stunner-blast hit the back of Cort's head. For a blinding instant, his head felt as if it had exploded. Then blackness.

Dilia had removed everything from her hair—the faded vines and bright feathers, the glistening pieces of khena bark carved into jewel-like beads—then combed it out and tied it back neatly with a thong. She drew a deep, cleansing breath and slowly let it out. She pictured how the wind rippled a meadow full of starflowers. Then she knocked firmly on the door of Lor's house.

It was Nala who answered, Lor's sister. Nala was two years younger than Dilia. She was pretty, with eyes the shade of hazel that was almost green in her perfect oval face, and long blond hair that she wore neatly tied in a long braid down her back. She looked at Dilia with no recognition, her mouth a defensive line. "Yes?"

"Nala, you know me."

Nala's assessing eyes took in her tanned complexion, her animal-skin clothing, her forest-toughened bare feet. "No, I'm sorry, I…" She frowned. "Dilia?"

Dilia relaxed into a smile, letting go her remaining tension.

"Oh, Dilia, you've changed!" Nala threw open the door and stepped aside to let Dilia in.

Dilia laughed. "Well, so have you! When I left here, you were still a girl, but look at you—you're a woman already!"

"You disappeared. People said you were abducted. Maybe sold to the aliens. But you've gone all forest instead?"

"That was true. I was abducted." She needed not to talk about this, the constriction in her throat cutting off all breathing.

Nala's eyes widened. "Abducted? You escaped? No one escapes."

"No, I didn't. Cort rescued me." It was better to talk about Cort. "Remember him?"

"Of course. The boy you lived with. Lor's friend." She frowned, a finger to her cheek, thinking. "He's the one Lor went off with."

Dilia smiled. "We had to get away, so we went to the forest. Best thing that ever happened to me. Besides Cort, of course."

Nala pursed her heart-shaped lips. "You're lucky. But why are you back, if life is so good out there?"

They had come now to the center of it, and everything depended on her answer. "Nala, I need your help. There's going to be... something. An event. Something really big. A lot of people may die. I want to work out a way to get everyone out safely. Or at least the children. To get the children out safely."

Nala frowned, as if she couldn't quite figure out how to take the first step down this path. "Something? An *event*?"

Dilia took Nala's hand in her own. She tried to squeeze her urgency into her friend's hand. "Something. I don't know exactly what, but I believe people are at risk. Possibly the whole city. The children. Help me."

But Nala looked at her with what could only be sorrow. With her free hand, she patted Dilia's. "You have to relax. Why should anything happen?"

It was a question that Dilia could answer, but not in a way that her friend would understand. She took a deep breath. "Look, let's just say that I have true information. Maybe sketchy, but true. We need a plan for getting people to safety." She looked around at the children playing in Nala's house. Six children, none old enough to be in school. The place was crowded. Three girls played with two dolls home-made of rags. Two boys had made a tent of bedrolls and were whispering together intently. A fourth girl rested on a bedroll, her back turned to the others. One or two might be Nala's younger siblings, but the rest were probably children she helped care for. "Especially the children."

"Let's just say," Nala echoed Dilia's words in the flat tones of disbelief.

"Look." Dilia heard the desperation in her own voice. She tried to make it calm. "It never hurts to have a contingency plan, does it? Humor me in this. Suppose—hypothetically—let's say, the ground started shaking."

Nala drew back, removed her hand from Dilia's.

"Hypothetically," Dilia insisted, and she took her friend's hand back. "Just on the chance that something like that were to happen, what would we do to keep the children safe?"

Nala frowned, making a small thinking hum. "The house might fall down. But would it be any safer in the street?"

"Well, at least the roof wouldn't fall in on you, and that's good. But you're right. The narrow streets wouldn't be good. And then, if everyone were running around, there would bound to be a few people who would be up to mischief. Stealing and so on."

"Not from children!"

"Okay, so we try to keep together. Keep the children together. And I think we should try to get outside the walls if the gates are open, where we can get away in whatever direction might be safest."

"But we are talking hypothetically, right?" Nala was starting to look worried, and Dilia figured this was a good thing.

"For now we are. But there are signs—and seers—in the forest who believe this will really happen—and soon."

Nala drew a breath to speak, but Dilia held up a hand to stop her. "I know what you're thinking. They're primitive people, savages. They might be superstitious, maybe even crazy. But Nala, what if they aren't? Out there, the signs are everywhere. It can't hurt to plan, can it?"

Nala looked away, not speaking, as if the answer to a complicated puzzle might be written somewhere on the walls or floor. She frowned. "Last night... there was something strange. I almost forgot about it until now. The ground trembled—not much, kind of like when a heavy cart goes by on the street. It woke me because... the thing is... there was no cart. It was the middle of the night. The street... the whole city... was completely silent. And yet the ground shook."

The two women looked at each other for a silent moment.

"It is coming, isn't it?" Nala's voice was unsteady. "How soon?"

"Very soon." Dilia thought of Cort, wondering where he was. Had he made it safely up to the base yet? "That's why I'm here. I was thinking you might talk with the parents when they come for their children this evening. Get them thinking about going outside the walls in case of... anything. It won't hurt, right? And if something does happen, you'll be glad you did."

"All right," Nala said. "I'll mention it to them."

Dilia grinned with relief. "Thank you. Now, I want to reach as many caregivers as I can. Who else should I talk to?"

⚶

There was a hollow ringing in Cort's ears, and his eyelids hurt when he tried to open them. He didn't have the energy to fight his eyelids. The mother of all headaches pounded through his head. Cort groaned and let his head roll to the side. He focused on his other senses. The smell was musty and acrid and familiar in a way Cort couldn't quite place. His own body—he was sitting, slumped, on a hard, cool floor, and his arms...

Without thinking, Cort opened his eyes. The eyelids weren't such a great obstacle after all. His eyes confirmed what his senses had told him: His arms were tied at the wrists to two large iron rings set into the stone wall. That stone wall, the hard-packed dirt floor, the door with iron bars through which light from alien fixtures filtered dimly—Cort knew the place. He was back in Sleb's prison.

He was going to be sick.

What had happened in the battle between the starmen's soldiers and Sleb's? Did his presence in the prison mean that Aj and the others had lost? Or simply that they had lost their prisoner? It was impossible to know.

He rolled and leaned to his side retching, but the only thing in his stomach was acid.

Cort had to assume that Sleb knew who he was, knew he had already managed to escape once. Why else would he be manacled like this? He had to assume that the kingpin would kill him. His death sentence had been passed when he first broke into the compound looking for Dilia. The fact that he was alive now meant that Sleb wanted him conscious for his own death.

This spoke volumes. The death Sleb had planned for him would not be pleasant.

Cort's only hope lay in escape. He had to loosen the manacles that bound him. He stretched one hand toward the other, but there was not enough leeway in the bindings to reach. He tried to make his hands narrow enough to pass through the loops, but again he failed. In half an hour of effort, gritting his teeth until his head felt like it might burst, Cort succeeded only in rubbing raw spots onto his wrists. But he refused to give up.

He took a deep breath, then bit and pulled at the bindings with his teeth. But all his effort had no effect. The bindings were made of some alien material that was too strong and too tight to loosen. He'd seen this material before. Stas's gang had stolen a box of alien lights, fresh from the starship and not yet opened. They'd been worth good money, those lights, but the box was bound with strips like these. They'd struggled for an hour or more before managing to get a knife sharp enough to cut it. Not even a kiri with its sharp teeth and claws could help with this.

A kiri. The bobcat with Dilia. Was she, at least, all right? *Bobcat? Hunter! You are awake? What do you need me to do?*

I'm... tied up. It was an embarrassing admission. *You can't help me here. How is Dilia?*

She is safe.

Don't leave her. Stay with her. Protect her in case... He couldn't say it. *In case I can't.*

And you, Hunter? What about you?

The little cat seemed genuinely concerned. Cort smiled wistfully. What about him, indeed? *It will help me to know that Dilia is well guarded. That is what I need from you the most. Don't worry about me. I'll figure out something.*

But what?

In the unsavory darkness of the kingpin's dungeon, Cort's whole effort seemed laughable, doomed to failure. He blamed himself for relying too much on Aj and the other soldiers. For not having planned for this particular contingency.

Ironically, here he was back in the very place where this whole adventure had started: Sleb's dungeon. He had come full circle, except that there was no one like Neder here to help him now.

Bound by his wrists in the dungeon of one of the city's biggest bullies, suspended between rage and despair, Cort wept tears of frustration and loss. In all his life, he had never, until now, taken on a purpose and failed to achieve it.

He set his teeth grimly. Nor, by all the stars in the galaxy, would he fail in this one. Perhaps he might still find a means of escape once Sleb's men released him from his bonds. Or perhaps in their secret meetings Aj's men had planned for this contingency, might even now be on their way to free him. And if not... he would take a longer perspective.

He could no longer conceive of a time when the forest's need was not his own purpose. Despite his failure now, Cort was still Corodh-an-Aran, restorer of the forest and bonded to her. In a hundred lifetimes, he had protected her, and if this mission failed in this lifetime, he knew beyond doubting that he would try again in the next. And—sooner or later—he would win. He would win because his purpose was just and because he wouldn't give up, no matter how many lifetimes it took.

In this clarity, Cort reached the calm center of his emotional storm. This death didn't matter to him. His purpose carried him across lifetimes.

Chapter 25

A Public Death

Much later, the soldiers came, frowning, stunners at the ready. "Good morning," Cort said. He was feeling calm, even cheerful. "I assume it is morning."

The lead soldier drew back, eyebrows raised in surprise. "You've recovered rather nicely from that stunner, eh?" he said.

Cort shrugged. "Well enough. I'd appreciate if you would loosen these bonds a bit, though."

The soldier laughed. "He wants the manacles loosened," he said to his comrade in a mocking tone, as if the other soldier weren't right there and hadn't heard for himself. Turning to Cort, he said, "We're going to oblige you, all right. You've got a public appearance to make, and we're barely going to be there on time."

Two other soldiers came into the room, their stunners aimed at Cort's head. The first soldier pulled an implement of alien metal out of his pocket. It might have been either a cutter or a key. He frowned at Cort. "Hold still. You won't be trying anything funny, will you, now?"

Looking at the weapons leveled at him on his left and on his right, Cort was ready to agree. He'd experienced enough of the stunner's effects for this lifetime. "No. If I'm going to make a public appearance, I'd just as soon be conscious for it." *And not in pain.*

The soldier freed Cort's left hand and began working on his right. "Am I going to be executed?" Cort asked. His tone was so matter-of-fact that the guard looked up at him in surprise, seeming unprepared for Cort's serenity.

"Yes, you are." The soldier finished unlocking the manacle at Cort's right hand.

Cort had witnessed public executions three times in his life. There were no standard procedures. Kingpins could execute whomever they wanted because they were powerful enough to do it, and there were no laws. Mostly, they killed in private and without fanfare. But sometimes, the offense was so heinous that the kingpins wanted to teach a lesson. Then they held a public execution. Cort remembered few details. There had been speeches, and then blood, and then free food. The square had been crowded. The pickings were rich for a child who knew how to look for them. The actual execution had seemed consistent with the risks of normal life, and Cort hadn't given it much thought. The whole thing had seemed a kind of holiday.

Now, from the perspective of the one about to be killed, he didn't see it that way at all. His stomach was tight with worry. He hoped he could show dignity and strength during the execution. And, of course, that he could keep his eyes open and his head clear on the unlikely chance he might actually still escape.

"I thought so," he said. He made no effort to resist as the guard tied his hands together tightly in front of his bare chest. Aj had his knife and his laser—as good a recipient of these weapons as any. He thought of Dilia and the life they'd never have together, and he took a shaking breath to calm himself. At least they'd had a chance to say proper goodbyes. They'd both known this could happen.

Corodh-an-Aran's serenity enveloped him like a halo. Though the soldiers didn't lessen their watchfulness, they distanced themselves from him as if he radiated an energy too powerful to resist. He walked, alone but surrounded by soldiers, out into the sunlight.

Two squads of soldiers assembled in the yard in front of the prison. There would be no escaping here, not with this many soldiers. If there was any chance at all, it would be, somehow, in the confusion of the public gathering later. When the men were ready, their leader nodded to Cort, who stood erect and calm.

"Follow these men," the leader said, indicating two rows of soldiers, four abreast, that were in the front of the assembly. "The rest will come after. They are armed with stunners and prepared to use them if you do not follow on your own."

The words had to be said, but the squad leader ducked his head slightly, as if he felt silly saying them and was fighting an urge to apologize.

Cort held his head high, though his stomach was tied in knots. He kept his muscles tight so that he wouldn't tremble and reminded himself that if he had to abandon this life for the next, he would make another, hopefully more successful, attempt on the city. He feared the prospect of his death, quite likely his painful death, but he refused to show any fear to Sleb's soldiers. He walked, erect and purposefully, to the position the soldier had indicated.

He strode straight and tall amid the soldiers, through Sleb's compound and out its front gate. They wound down the hill and into the open square where—was it only yesterday?—he had been captured.

A crowd had already gathered. Some taunted the barbarian prisoner with insults. Others simply gaped at his exotic looks. Still others watched with helpless sympathy.

As Cort surveyed the crowd, he tried to take in every detail. Right in front stood a woman with three children, the oldest already as tall as her shoulder, the youngest no more than six or seven. They would get a prime view of his execution. Would it mean anything to them, or would they remember only the feast that would follow? He thought of Dilia and looked for her, but he didn't see her. Nearby, teenage members of two gangs quarreled, paying no attention to Cort and his escort. Others gathered around the tables where food would be brought. Cort said goodbye to it all.

A platform had been erected in the square, a couple of steps higher than the ground. Easily large enough to support Cort together with his two escorting squads, the platform contained only a low bench at one end and a dais at the other that was raised another three steps from the platform. The soldiers in front of Cort marched up the steps and onto the platform, and Cort followed.

"Halt right there," ordered the squad leader as Cort walked behind the bench.

Cort obeyed.

Two rows of soldiers in front of him arranged themselves in position in front of the dais. Four soldiers moved around behind Cort, stunners ready and aimed at him. The rest of the soldiers did not ascend the platform, but moved in front of it, though whether to protect the crowd from the criminal or him from them was hard to ascertain.

I am here, Hunter, said the bobcat.

Cort scanned the square but couldn't see the small creature. Which was as it should be.

With four stunners guarding him and soldiers all around the platform, if Cort tried to escape, he wouldn't get far. He didn't see how the bobcat could help. Kill a few soldiers, maybe, before a stunner took it down? It wouldn't be enough. There was no way out, not in this lifetime. But he would try again to save the khenaran in his next lifetime, he was sure of it—that was the important thing. He was eager for his death, eager to get out of this hopeless mess. He was eager for a clean slate and a chance to try again.

The square filled with onlookers jostling each other for room as more people arrived. Death was too common to attract so many people. Sleb must have offered a substantial celebration feast.

Cort scrutinized the crowd in the square and the new people as they flooded in from the narrow streets and alleyways. He didn't want Dilia to witness this, but he couldn't help looking for her. And there were certainly plenty of young people among the old, women among the men. But no one wore skins or flowered vines in her hair or seemed to glow in her special way. No, she wasn't there. Good.

A wave of soldiers flowed into the square from its far end. Eight, decked in ceremonial plumes, carried a palanquin, four in the front and four in the rear, bearing its long poles on their shoulders. Cort knew the vehicle. There weren't more than six such in the city, and this one was elaborately painted in Sleb's dark green and gold colors. The kingpin himself had come to watch Cort's demise.

Drumrolls announced the kingpin's arrival, quieting all conversations and shouting. The soldiers parted the crowd easily; no one wanted to be on the receiving end of a stunner. Sleb's escort advanced toward the platform and mounted the stairs. The soldiers bearing the gaudy vehicle struggled to keep it level, and sweat stained their uniforms. They passed behind Cort and his four guards. At the foot of the dais, they carefully put down the palanquin. One of them opened its door and reached in to assist the kingpin. Leaning heavily on the man's arm, Sleb eased himself out of the vehicle amid the heightened excitement of the drums.

Sweat ran down Sleb's face. His thin, fair hair was plastered to his head, making him look almost bald. But he wore thread-of-gold alien silks whose cost would be beyond the dreams of anyone in the square, and rings with Earthish gems sparkled on his short fingers. And one priceless ring of khena wood.

The crowd cheered wildly. No doubt the feast was going to be a good one.

As Sleb ascended the steps to the dais, his breathing heavy with the effort, Cort scanned the crowd once more, looking again for Dilia. But the square was so crowded he could hardly make out any individual faces.

The troops that had escorted Sleb arranged themselves around the dais. The kingpin clearly thought that he needed a considerable amount of protection. Cort wondered from whom—the crowd that cheered him so loudly? Or from himself, bound and held by four soldiers with ready stunners? No matter. Neither was any risk to Sleb this day.

Finally, a single, strongly muscled soldier with a heavy sword ascended the platform and stood directly behind Cort. Cort's breath caught in his throat. Imported from Earth, swords were not weapons of utility; they served only a ceremonial purpose. In this case, the purpose would be Cort's execution.

Sleb raised his arms, and the cheers of the crowd, at least of those nearby, subsided. The drums stopped abruptly, throwing the square into breathless silence. "Let this execution teach a lesson to all who watch!" shouted the kingpin. "This man is a thief! I would have had him executed with his own bone knife, except that he stole it from me." Sleb chuckled at his own joke. Then his voice turned hard. "No one steals from me and gets away with it!"

Sleb didn't mention that Cort and Lor had also kidnapped him and left him in the streets to live or die as fate would have it. Maybe Sleb didn't want to give anyone else the idea.

But Cort smiled at Sleb's mention of his father's knife. "How could I possibly have stolen the knife from you," he called to the kingpin, "when you just admitted that it was mine? Who was really the thief in that case?" Several people in the front of the crowd laughed.

Sleb's features hardened in anger. "Everything you think of as yours is mine, boy, if I want it. I owned your house, and I owned you. You should not have forgotten that." He leaned over to whisper something to one of the guards behind him. The soldier jumped down from the platform and reached into the palanquin, pulling out a package wrapped in dark green silk. As he ascended the dais, the soldier unwrapped the package. He unfolded Cort's white tigerskin and laid it carefully over the kingpin's shoulders.

Cort drew in a sharp breath, meeting Sleb's eyes. The serenity that had enveloped him blew away like the morning mist in a rising wind. He trembled in need and anger and despair. The tiger! How could he have forgotten? Another lifetime was not going to be adequate to his purpose; this one must serve, or all of the tigers would die. He clenched his fists and strained against the rope that bound his wrists.

Seeing his prisoner's pain, Sleb smiled contentedly, a man who was enjoying himself. He drew it out, raising his arms and shuffling in a little dance. "How do I look, boy?" he asked. "Wickedly savage?" He chuckled at his own wittiness, and nearby observers dutifully laughed.

But Cort wasn't listening to the kingpin. For a tiny voice hissed through the red crystal. *Hunter! I am within reach of him. Shall I strike?*

Cort did not hesitate in his answer. *Yes. Take him.*

From among the folds of the tiger skin uncoiled a green snake no longer than Cort's little finger and less than half its diameter. The tiny serpent was barely visible even to Cort, who stood nearby and watched closely. The soldiers, intent on the prisoner and the crowd, saw nothing. The serpent struck the kingpin just below his ear and then disappeared again into the folds of the tigerskin.

A frown creased Sleb's gloating smile as he reached up to scratch the spot just below his ear. Then his eyes widened in alarm and he opened his mouth—but he crumpled to the ground before a sound could emerge, eyes still wide in the horror of his last living moment.

"No," Cort said to his dead captor. "Some things are truly mine."

"I can't *see*!" Dilia and Nala were standing close to the far end of the square. Dilia moved to the right, closer to Nala, then farther away, but the group of tall men in front of them blocked her vision. She wished she weren't so short. "Did you hear what they were saying?"

"No, I couldn't make it out." Nala put a restraining hand on Dilia's arm. "Would you please stop fidgeting? They'll execute the prisoner any moment now. We don't need to watch. It'll be gross. Remember—we're just here for the feast. A lot of people we need to talk to will be here."

"It sounded like Cort, don't you think?" Dilia pulled away from Nala and tried to push between two of the men. But the crowd was too dense, and there was no room even for a person as slim as she was.

"Nonsense," Nala said.

Dilia sighed. "You're probably right. No doubt he's up on the base by now. I wonder who this poor fellow is, though."

"It doesn't matter—" Nala's reply was cut short by a scream from up near the dais, and then by the angry shouts of soldiers and more screams.

"Get out!" someone shouted as the crowd in front began pushing back. Screams and shouts were so loud that Dilia's ears felt like they would explode.

"Hurry!" Nala cried. "We'll get crushed!"

She and Dilia turned and began pushing in their turn. For a tense moment, with the crowd pushing at them on one side and resisting on the other, Dilia was sure she and Nala would be trampled and die.

A piercing cry next to Dilia came from a young girl who had lost hold of her mother's hand. The mother, just ahead, clutching a baby, shouted back, but the pandemonium in the crowd tore her voice from the O of terror on her face and pushed mother and child farther apart.

Dilia snatched up the girl. She held her close and tried—fruitlessly—to close the gap with the mother.

Slowly the crowd behind them began to give way, and they jostled toward a narrow street that led to the produce market. Here, things opened out again. People began running, knocking into produce carts and shoving aside anyone in their way.

But there was room. Room to breathe. Room to figure out what to do next. Room to find the small girl's mother. Even as Nala pulled at her arm, Dilia slowed and looked all around.

There she was! The poor woman, her baby clutched tightly to her breast, had stopped and was looking around frantically. There were circles under her pale eyes, and her cheeks were gaunt.

Dilia waved and began working her way toward her, pulling Nala in her wake.

Seeing her mother, the little girl squirmed out of Dilia's arms and ran to her.

"Thank you," said the mother, tears in her eyes.

Dilia felt awkward. "Anyone would have helped. I just happened to be the one who was there."

"No. Anyone would have trampled my child." The mother hugged the little girl close. "But you picked her up and saved her."

There was heat in Dilia's cheeks. "Well, in that case, you're welcome." And then she told the young mother about the danger that was coming. About being ready to flee. About the need to tell her friends.

"How can there be any danger?" the woman asked.

"The ground shook last night," Nala said. She touched the baby under the chin, and the child smiled at her.

The mother glanced toward the base, where a ship towered over the city. "If there's any danger, the starmen will save us."

Dilia followed her gaze to the starship. "There is danger," she said, "and the starmen won't save us. The starmen will save themselves." Her voice was as bitter as raw *skorb* nuts, her message as hard to digest. Dilia watched the woman shrink inward, clutching the baby more tightly. Dilia had seen that reaction before. Like so many other people, the woman seemed to sense that Dilia had hold of some truth but didn't want to believe her.

What else could she say to convince the woman? To convince all the people she talked with? Dilia could think of nothing. She had done what she could. She turned to Nala. "I want to find out what happened to that poor prisoner. If he isn't already dead, he may need some help."

"You're crazy. Let's just get out of here while we can."

The crowd had thinned, but a pair of Sleb's soldiers ran down the narrow street, stunners at the ready, scowling as if everyone present were guilty of a great crime. The soldiers scanned the market, then turned and marched back into the square. Once they departed, a few brave souls, mostly men, turned and headed back toward the square.

"Scavengers," Nala muttered.

Something about the prisoner, the familiar tones of the distant voice, still bothered Dilia. But Nala was right. Cort would be up on the base by now, so she needed to stay on task and find women with families. The prisoner was not her concern. She looked around the market, where business was returning to normal. "Let's talk with people here."

* * *

The soldiers on the platform, both those near to the dais and those that had been guarding Cort, ran to protect their master. Some of the soldiers from below also ran toward Sleb, but others fired stunners into the crowd. The panic was immediate. People started running from the square, and some of the soldiers chased them.

For the moment, Cort was unguarded. He seized his opportunity.

He slipped down from the platform and joined a group of people that were hurrying to leave the square. Cort moved neither more quickly nor more slowly than the people that surrounded him, though he kept somewhat hunched over, so that his forest hairstyle and his bound wrists wouldn't be too visible to any soldiers on the platform that might look his way.

"Wear this," someone to his right said. Cort looked in that direction. A man about his own age settled a cape of common gray broadcloth over Cort's shoulders and raised the hood over his head.

The generosity was unusual in the city, where people learned early to fend for themselves. "Thanks," Cort said. "I needed that."

"Come with me," said the man. "As soon as we're out of sight of all this, I'll cut your ropes." Moving with the crowd, Cort followed the stranger. About halfway down the main street at the foot of the square, they turned into a narrow alley, apparently a dead-end, for the crowd continued to flow down the street. They huddled into a doorway that fronted on the alley.

The stranger took a knife from his belt, and Cort held up his hands. The rope was strong, but with a few passes, the man sliced through it. Cort studied the man's face. It was unlined and smooth, about Cort's own age, but his expression seemed careworn for one so young, his brown eyes gentle but sad. He looked familiar, but Cort couldn't place him. "Do I know you?"

The young man shook his head. He drew a breath and looked away. "That man murdered my father when my father was as new from the forest as you obviously are," he said. "I didn't help my father then, though I have lain awake long nights regretting it. Maybe doing this for you is my way of making amends."

Then Cort understood why the stranger's features looked familiar, and he knew who had helped him. "Culan," he said.

Culan frowned and drew back. "You... know me?"

"No. I know Neder, your father, and I heard this story from his own lips. He lives, Culan, back in the village where you were born."

"I don't know you," Culan said defensively, a question behind the statement.

"No. I am Corodh-an-Aran. I came to your village after you had already left. I am a hunter and a seer, and I have returned here to destroy this city. You would be wise to leave."

Cort paused, suddenly humbled by a vision of the destruction he intended. "See if you can get others to leave too. I don't want people to die here. You're lucky; you have a home you can go back to. Take as many people with you as you can."

Culan looked at him distrustfully. Cort realized that his hair hid the two jewels at his temple. He pushed the hair back.

His eyes wide, Culan looked at the blue jewel that glittered at Cort's temple even in the shadow of the alley. "You're serious."

Cort nodded.

Culan fell silent, then asked, "You think my father would forgive me?"

"I know he would, if you ask him."

"I'll think about it. You need a place to stay?"

"No. Thanks for the offer, but I'll be busy tonight."

"You need help?" Culan asked softly.

Cort studied Culan's face for a moment—his large, sensitive, sad eyes, the determined set of his mouth. "I think I know now why your father was so proud of you," he said. "Do what you can so that the gate will be open tonight. People will need to leave in a hurry."

Culan nodded. "I'll do it. Good luck, Corodh-an-Aran." He left the doorway, trotted silently up the alley, and was gone. Cort watched for a few minutes. Then he realized that there was one thing he had to do before he was ready to find his way into Hsu-Lin Base.

He wanted his tiger skin back.

Cort walked up the alley, watching the street from the shadow of the alley's narrow opening. The flood of fleeing people had died down. A pair of Sleb's soldiers, stunners on ready, walked by from the direction of the square. Cort shrank back into the alley as they passed, his heart pounding. The soldiers continued on, disappearing around a corner. Cort steeled himself, then stepped out into the street. Keeping to the shadows, with the hood of his cape pulled up, Cort headed back toward the square.

At the place where the street widened out into the square, Cort stopped to look around. A few people remained, wandering back and forth, looking for anything valuable that might have been dropped when the crowd fled. The platform, with its bench and dais, was deserted; Sleb's body and his ornately painted palanquin had been removed. At the far end of the square, eight of Sleb's soldiers were just leaving. Two other pairs of soldiers walked the perimeter of the square, watching. Cort drew a deep breath and walked into the unprotected, wide open space of the square where he had almost been executed.

He moved slowly, scanning the ground like one of the scavengers. He allowed himself only a quick glance at the soldiers from time to time. The group of eight soldiers had gone. One of the pairs of guards was moving toward the street that Cort had just come out of. Cort's heart pounded an alarm, but he studied the ground and refused to run.

The soldiers walked by.

Cort made his movements seem random, scouring the ground here and there. As he did, he worked his way closer to the dais He could see now, in covert glances, the glow of sunlight on something white that was left, abandoned, at the edge of the dais. The tiger skin.

On the street next to the dais, a man casually leaned against the dais, one arm thrown back over the skin as if he was just relaxing. The man wore a cloak, gray like Cort's. Cort couldn't make out his features inside the hood. He hoped he wouldn't have to fight the man for the skin; he had no weapons, unless the tiny serpent was alive and ready to strike again.

Serpent? Cort asked as he worked his way closer to his objective.

Hunter, the serpent acknowledged. *You are whole?*

Yes. And you?

Whole, and ready to strike again.

Cort allowed himself a smile. Despite everything that had gone wrong, at least something was working for him. *Good,* he answered. *Just stay ready, but do nothing until I say.*

As you wish, Hunter.

The problem with using a serpent as a weapon was that he couldn't threaten with it. A knife could be held to a victim's throat with good results; it was most likely not necessary actually to slit the throat. But a serpent... *Give me my tiger skin, or I'll have my tiny serpent sting you* lacked the necessary credibility. Cort reached the dais and stood next to the man, allowing his arm also to lounge carelessly across the rumpled tiger skin. "Nice day," he said.

"I thought you might return," the stranger replied. "After what happened, it seemed reasonable to assume you would want the tiger skin back."

The voice sounded familiar, but Cort couldn't place it. "Do I thank you for looking after it for me?"

The man turned to face him. "It is my pleasure, Corodh-an-Aran."

With a shock, Cort recognized the old man that had advised him the evening Dilia first disappeared. From the shadow of his hood, the man's green-gold hazel eyes smiled. And a blue crystal glistened in a ray of sunshine.

"Who are you?" Cort asked.

"A friend," the old man said. "Let's just say I might have known your father. Let's just say the whynywir might have sent us both to the city together, and after tonight, after all these years, let's just say I am a man who might be going home again."

Cort's eyes lifted for a moment to the blue crystal the man wore. "That would be a long time to be in exile in this place."

For the barest moment, the old man's features twisted into something that might have been sorrow, or regret, or even grief.

The expression was gone before Cort could read it. "It has had its recompenses."

"I'd like to know more."

The man nodded gravely. "I'm sure you would. But time is short at the moment, and I have miles to travel, and you have work to do. I assume you'll be wanting to enter the base."

"Yes, I—"

"Good," said the man. "I thought so. Probably you are thinking to climb the rock wall by the chasm and breach the fence from that direction."

Cort swallowed, wondering if the man was a mind-reader. "I thought about it."

"Unfortunately, it appears that a year or so ago someone actually breached the fence from that direction—or at least the aliens got the idea that someone might have done so. They've installed a repeater at the top of the wall, right in the middle. I would guess that no one will be getting in that way any longer."

"I got in that way once," Cort said.

"Ah. I should have guessed." From the way the old man smiled, Cort was certain that he *had* guessed.

"What would you suggest then?"

The old man nodded toward a street at the far end of the square, where a squad of soldiers from the aliens' base was just entering the square at a brisk march. Sunlight glinted off the Earthish metal that decorated their uniforms. "I believe that your friends over there will take you right where you want to go," he said. "Now, if you will excuse me, I have no desire to go with you." The man started to walk away.

"Wait!" Cort felt suddenly cold. Having only minutes ago escaped captivity and death at the hands of one group of soldiers, Cort couldn't face allowing himself to be captured by another. "Are you suggesting that I turn myself in to them?"

The old man turned. "It depends on your objective," he said. "If you want to get into the base, I know of no other way." He raised an eyebrow. "Perhaps you do, though?"

Cort would have given much for an answer, but he had none.

The old man gave him a slow, deliberate nod and a pat on the shoulder. Then he turned away and walked out of the square.

The leader of the squad was none other than Aj. Cort's heart leapt with a glimmer of hope. He also recognized one of the other soldiers. But the remaining six were strangers. Too many. Aj wouldn't dare help him while surrounded by so many soldiers not of their group.

"I don't have the courage," Cort whispered, though no one was near. "I can't." He gripped the tiger skin so tightly his knuckles turned white, as if it alone might save him from sinking in the deep well of his fear.

He stared at the soldiers, knowing for a certainty that they brought a worse captivity and probably a worse death than the one he had just avoided. But like the old man, he knew of no other way. Cort sighed and allowed the gray cape to fall to the ground. Then he wrapped the white tiger skin over his shoulders and walked out to meet the aliens' soldiers.

Chapter 26

In the Alien Prison

"You're under arrest," Aj said. He drew his stunner and aimed it at Cort. "You're wanted for murder."

Cort's heart did an arrhythmic jump. *Everyone wants me for something—but... murder?* His throat was tight with fear, and he didn't trust himself to speak. Resisting the urge to run, he held out his hands to show that he was unarmed.

Hunter? said the tiny serpent still hiding under the folds of the tiger skin. *Do you need me?*

Not yet, but maybe later. Don't harm these people. Stay hidden.

One of the soldiers searched him methodically, then announced, "Nothing. Not even a knife."

Aj had cut his hair short in the style of the starmen, which the city folk favored. The red crystal, no longer hidden by a fall of hair, glittered just above Aj's right ear. Already, his formerly gold eyes were turning brown, the color no doubt influenced by spending time on the base. He looked straight at Cort, and his expression was as hard as khena wood and as cold as concrete, a man who would do whatever his alien bosses ordered. He spoke gruffly. "Get moving. If you try to escape, we'll shoot."

Cort's heartbeat pounded loud in his ears. He took a deep breath, summoning his courage. Surrounded by soldiers, he walked tall and straight through the gates of the base and into the aliens' enclave, like a prince among his courtiers. He submitted to the routines of an alien arrest in as much dignity as he could muster, though his stomach was tied in a knot. While the prints of his hands and his retinas were scanned into the computer, he answered questions about his name and age and place of birth, and was then assigned a number guaranteed to be unique in the nine colonized worlds. Had he escaped death at Sleb's hands only to suffer something much worse among the aliens?

An alien jailer, along with two alien soldiers armed with lasers, led Cort into the building that served as, among other things, a prison. They passed through a room with a desk, a chair, several cabinets, and an array of four holographic monitors. Stacks of papers and computer equipment suggested a certain amount of organizational carelessness on the part of its occupants. From that room, an empty hallway led to two doorless cells.

The alien gestured for Cort to enter one of the cells. Cort did, and gaped in amazement. The room was as large as the house Cort had grown up in. On the back wall and the wall to Cort's right hung two sets of bunk beds, four beds in all, each with blankets. Sparkling white fixtures in the far left corner suggested sanitary conveniences Cort had only heard of in school. Several changes of clothes and all his material possessions could have easily fit underneath one of the beds, with room to spare.

Cort turned back toward his jailer, but the man and his soldiers were gone. The open doorway was unguarded. Cautiously, Cort walked toward it and reached out with his hand. In the place where a door might have been, he felt a sharp pain, burning as if from a stunner. Quickly, Cort drew his hand back. It looked unharmed. He touched the hand in disbelief.

Cort drew a breath to strengthen his resolve, determined to find a way out even if he suffered some pain to do it. He began a systematic exploration of the doorway, first touching it at both bottom corners, but the effect was the same. Then he stood and was about to try his luck as high as he could reach when the jailer walked back into the hallway. "Stop that," the alien said. "You're setting off the alarm. You speak Standard?"

"Yes. Is this a force field of some kind?"

"Yes. You know about force fields?"

"Like the one around the base?"

"Similar, yes. Touch it, and it'll burn you. Throw yourself at it, and it'll probably knock you back as far as the back wall of the cell, and I wouldn't want to be responsible for whatever injuries that'll cause."

"And if I walk through it slowly?" Cort asked.

"You won't make it through. Ever been hit by a stunner?"

Studying the man's cold, pale eyes, Cort nodded.

"It hurts like that," said the jailer. "Besides, I'll be watching on the monitors. See those?" He pointed to two black boxes anchored to the ceiling of the hallway. "Cameras. I keep an eye on everything you do."

"Lucky you," Cort muttered, and to his surprise the man smiled. Despite having come to know Lennard, Cort never thought of the aliens as capable of smiling. Perhaps it was because they tended to be thinner and more angular than the Arantu, with sharper features, or perhaps because the aliens most likely to be in the city were soldiers. But of course the aliens came in all dispositions, complexions, and sizes, just like his own people. "So what's going to happen to me, then?" he asked.

"The commandant will want to see you. Him and the chief of security. Tomorrow, I guess; they're both busy today."

"So today I just wait?" Cort's jaw was tight with frustration.

"That's right," said the jailer. "Might as well relax."

Relax? Not a chance of that. "What's the penalty for murder among your people?"

The jailer frowned as he studied Cort's face. "Who'd you murder?"

Cort's anger flared. "I didn't! The soldiers said I was wanted for murder." He had a sudden hope that this might all be a misunderstanding. "Didn't they say anything to you?"

The jailer let out a scoffing breath. "They never do. But then, it's pretty rare they bring anyone in at all." He shrugged. "But the answer to your question is, it depends. They won't kill you. We're not like those savages in the city, we stopped executing murderers centuries ago. You'll be deported to one of the labor camps out in the asteroid belt, I suppose, and they'll put you to work. Maybe just a few years, up to lifetime, if it's a serious charge."

"Earth's asteroid belt?"

"Yes, the one in Earth's solar system."

So now that Cort had no desire whatever to go to Earth, they were talking about sending him there! Sending him away from Aran.

Sending him to a place where his spirit might never be reborn, a death worse than death.

He took in a deep breath, as deep as he could make it, then let it out slowly. "I didn't kill anyone." But no, wait. There was Jerrald. But surely they'd understand that was self defense. Lennard was a witness. Surely Lennard would vouch for him. "I have to talk with Lennard, the xenologist."

The jailer looked confused. "Who?"

"The xenologist who just came back from the khenaran with an Arantu wife."

"Ah. Heard about that. I'll try to get a message to him." He studied Cort's face, and his own features relaxed into something that was almost pity. "Meanwhile, how about some food? You hungry?"

The jailer seemed surprisingly kind, and now that he'd asked, Cort realized that he *was* hungry. He hadn't eaten in over a day, and he might need the energy later, if somehow he could get out of here. "Yes, please."

"I'll order you up something." The jailer left. Cort stared bleakly at the cameras and at the unadorned white walls of his cell. Then he slipped a small bone ring out of one of the rawhide thongs binding his hair and threw the ring at the doorway. As the jailer had said, it was thrown back from the force field, bounced off the rear wall of the cell, and clattered to the floor. Cort sighed, picked up the ring, and threaded it back into his hair.

In a little while, an alien soldier entered the corridor. He didn't mention the ring incident. He leveled a laser at Cort. "Stay in the back of the cell." His voice reflected the tired weariness in his face, a person who didn't much care whether he killed the prisoner or not. Cort obliged. A moment later, the jailer entered the hallway with a tray of food.

The smell of roasted meat and other things Cort couldn't identify filled the air. Cort's stomach growled.

The jailer stepped into the cell and put the tray onto the floor. Then he stepped back out of the doorway. A few moments later, the soldier told Cort, "Force field's back in place." He engaged the safety on the laser, holstered the weapon, and left.

Cort stared at the food on the tray in amazement. There was roasted meat with a sauce of some kind, potatoes, an assortment of vegetables, bread… enough food for an entire family in the city below, and this was just the prison fare on the base. He sighed. Then, realizing that he wasn't the only hungry one, he sat carefully with his back to the cameras, and he let the serpent eat whatever it wanted before he took a bite.

"Cort."

Cort lay on one of the lower bunks facing the wall. His mind was too much in turmoil to sleep, and he'd lost track of the passage of time. He rolled over when he heard his name called. Lennard stood outside the doorway of the prison cell. Cort's heart lifted. Maybe Lennard had come to get him out of here. He walked to the cell's opening and reached out a hand to clasp Lennard on the shoulder.

A pain shot into his fingertips, and he jerked his hand away. His nerves screamed that it was burning, but the hand looked perfectly normal. He shook it, as if the fire were something he could cast off, and wiggled his fingers.

"Ouch!" Lennard said in sympathy. "A nuisance, that. It's not actually harmed, is it?" He spoke in Arantu, for which Cort was grateful; it afforded them some privacy, even though every word and movement was captured by the jailer's cameras.

Cort shook his head, continuing to stare at his hand, where the burning sensation was beginning to fade. "Apparently not." At least he hadn't screamed.

"How are they treating you? Is everything all right?"

"They're treating me fine, but it's not all right. Lennard, I have to get out of here." He spoke with barely contained intensity, glancing up at the cameras. The serpent stirred restlessly under the tiger skin.

Lennard gestured with his head down the hallway toward the guard's room. "I can't." He was almost whispering and looked so guilty that Cort was glad the cameras were aimed toward the cell rather than the entryway. Lennard switched to Standard. "The commandant wants to talk with you tomorrow morning. He has that right. I'll be present to make sure he doesn't do anything… illegal. After he questions you, maybe then he'll let you go. I think I might be able to talk him into it, but—"

"Lennard," Cort interrupted with an impatient gesture. He continued in Arantu, "They say I'm arrested for murder. They're going to send me to Earth. I can't do that. I need to get out of here *now*."

Lennard looked crestfallen, a person whose last chance of an easy way out had just vanished. "Oh." He looked around again. "I rather suspected you would say that. I'm afraid that's just not possible."

"It has to be!" Cort wanted to shake Lennard, anything to convey his urgency. He barely stopped the movement in time to avoid another shock from the force field. "Get the jailer to turn this thing off."

"Cort, be reasonable. What am I going to tell him? That I'm just taking you out for a short walk, and we'll be right back?" Lennard nervously twisted the ends of his blond hair, still long in the style of the forest, with rawhide thongs and feathers and beads braided into it, along with, surprisingly, the broken larger half of a wishbone. "No one's going to believe that."

Cort paced the length of the cell and back again. His nervous energy seemed to crackle in his bones like electricity. "This isn't the time to worry about what people are going to think! The life of Aran is at stake!"

"But if the jailer doesn't believe me, he's not going to let down the force field, now is he? But there is one other thing we could try." Lennard pulled a feather from his hair, stared at it a moment as if he had no idea where it had come from. Then he wound it back into his hair and spoke, once again in Standard, glancing down the hallway toward the guard station. "In return for your release, would you be willing to promise you won't do anything harmful to my people and their settlement here?"

Cort paused in his pacing. The offer was tempting. It would be so easy to agree, to avoid the destruction of his immortal spirit and continue to be reborn here on Aran. But the planet needed him to drive the starmen off this world, to shut down their harvesting operations, and the tigers needed him to do it now. Lennard knew that quite well. Lennard had agreed to this goal. Had he changed his mind? There was something about how Lennard fidgeted with his hair. Cort chose his words carefully. "You know I mean no harm to your people, Lennard."

"That wasn't what I asked," Lennard said. His eyes were pleading. What was he not saying?

The commandant! The commandant must have sent Lennard. That was the only explanation for Lennard's change of languages—to allow the jailer to report back. But did Lennard have to go along with it? Was he really so weak? Cort's pulse quickened, and his jaw was tight. "You can tell the commandant I refuse to accept his offer."

Cort's anger must have been evident in his eyes, for Lennard looked away. "All right, he authorized me to offer you that." He shuffled his feet and reached toward Cort, deflecting his hand at the last minute to avoid the force field in the doorway. "I swear I did my best. This was the best deal I could work out for you. Let's face it; your prospects aren't very good right now." He switched back to Arantu. "I thought... if I could get you free... we could go away for a while, maybe visit the whynywir or something. Then later, if you still wanted, you could come back and we could try again."

Cort shook his head. The anger had settled into something cold and hard in his chest. Something deadly calm and as focused as a laser. He answered in Arantu. "No. We have to act now, not later. I have to get out of here. You're not going to visit the whynywir. You and the rest of your people are going back to Earth." If only he could figure out how!

Lennard stared at him for a long, silent moment. In Standard, he said, "It was my obligation to convey the offer." Somehow, his fidgeting had stopped, and he stood tall under Cort's hostile gaze. "It would have been easy enough if it had worked out, but..." He shrugged sadly.

Cort sighed and shook his head again, this time in resignation. There was nothing left to say. He returned to his bunk and lay down facing the wall.

A few minutes later, he heard Lennard's footsteps retreating down the hallway, and then there was silence.

⚜

Dilia looked up at the base. Her view of the buildings was blocked by the wall, but the starship stood, silent and silver, on the hill above. The base was quiet. Where was Cort? What was he doing now? Was he even still alive?

Her thoughts returned to the execution, or, as rumor had it, the *near* execution yesterday. How easily something like that might happen to Cort up on the base, and she would never know. She nibbled at her lower lip. No, she refused to believe that Cort was dead. He was on the base by now and doing... whatever it was he intended to do. And she should get busy doing what she had to do, too. Time to start talking to more people.

She turned her gaze from the base to the market. Farmers had spread out their harvests on mats, and harried-looking people, mostly women, often with small children in tow, walked up and down the aisles, stopping here and there to make a purchase. She fell into step with the nearest person, a woman with two small boys clinging to her skirt. "Handsome boys," she said.

The woman turned her gaze from the fruits and vegetables to Dilia. She had a worry-lined face and squinted a bit at Dilia, her lips in a thin line.

Dilia smiled, and with a slight shake of her head said, "I meant no offense. I would have liked... I mean, I would like to have such fine children someday."

The woman nodded, her expression more open now. "No reason why you shouldn't."

No reason, indeed. Dilia tried to keep her expression pleasant, her voice conversational. "I suppose that's true, if we survive the disaster everyone says is coming."

"Everyone? I heard it was only some fringe troublemakers."

Dilia forced a laugh. "Oh, maybe so, maybe so. But from what I heard, no one is making any money off this. What would it hurt to make sure you're prepared, just in case?"

The woman grunted. "Just in case, eh?"

Dilia nodded toward the boys. "So they'll be safe if... It wouldn't take much, would it? Prepare a small pack for each of you, memorize the quickest way out the gate if... Let's say, if the ground starts shaking or there's an explosion or something."

The woman scoffed. "And if nothing happens?"

"If nothing happens, you'll unpack those packs and at least you'll know the quickest way to the gate if there ever is another emergency." *If nothing happens, it will probably mean that Cort is dead.* "What's the harm?"

Surprisingly, the woman smiled at her. "Maybe you're one of those crazies, or maybe you know something, or maybe this ain't nothing, but I suppose I could take the boys for a walk to the gate this afternoon. It'd be something a little different."

"Good," Dilia said. "I'm glad we talked."

The woman turned to the farmer and began negotiating a purchase. Dilia moved down the street to find someone else to talk to, but the thought stayed stuck in her head. If nothing happens, it probably meant that Cort was dead.

<hr>

Time passed. The uniform lighting gave no clue to the hour of the day or night. Cort suffered his captivity poorly. The stakes were high, and time was short. He paced the cell, which seemed to shrink as his anxiety increased. He forced himself to lie down but then tossed restlessly on the narrow bed.

He had been abandoned by the allies he'd been counting on, Aj and his men, integrated again among the soldiers on the base; Lennard, reduced to an errand boy for the commandant. Only Dilia remained true to his mission. Where was she now? Was she able to convince people to leave, at least some of them? *Bobcat?*

But there was no answer. Perhaps the little kiri was too far away. Or perhaps there was something about the walls of this place. He felt cut off from everything and everyone that meant anything to him, and now it seemed likely the aliens would ship him off to this asteroid belt to die a final death.

I am here, Hunter. It was the tiny serpent, tucked invisibly into the folds of the tiger skin. At least one of his kiri was with him. *I feel your stress. How can I help you?*

Could the serpent help somehow? Cort considered sending it down the hall to sting the jailer. He didn't want to; the man had been kind. But if that meant his freedom... But no, the alien's death would not be enough. The force field would have to be disabled. There was a control somewhere to turn it off, but Cort didn't know where it was or how it worked. And the serpent certainly had no idea. The force field! The serpent couldn't even get out of his cell while the thing was turned on. He shook his head. *Thank you, but you cannot.*

When they came to take him to the commandant, perhaps he would find a way to escape, but clearly there was nothing he could do right now. Somehow, Cort slipped from wakefulness into a fitful sleep.

He woke with a start and didn't know why.

There was noise from the outer room, a sound of scuffling, a thick-sounding thud, a grunt, a clatter of something falling.

Cort jumped to his feet. He stood as close as he dared to the doorway of his cell and peered down the hallway. But he could see nothing in the next room. His pounding heartbeat almost drowned out the continuing noises.

Purposeful footsteps stomped down the hall toward Cort's cell.

Aj came into view. He looked down the hall toward the control room and shook his head. "Wait," he said to Cort, his voice strained.

Cort frowned. Wait for what?

Aj nodded and motioned to Cort to come toward him.

Remembering the force field, Cort stood still until Aj motioned again, more urgently. "Come on. You think we have all night?"

Cort grimaced. He wasn't ready to trust Aj, but when it came down to it, what choice did he have? His heart beat so loud it seemed to echo down the hallway. He prepared himself for pain and reached out to touch the force field.

There was nothing. The force field had been disabled.

Cort stepped out of the cell. His hand went to his belt, ready to grab the knife he no longer had. But he did have a weapon. *Be ready*, he said to the serpent. To Aj, he said, "Did you do that?"

"Of course we did, who'd you think? Inei-Taru?" Aj said. "Go on, into the control room. You'll see."

In the control room, the jailer lay on the floor, perfectly still, either unconscious or dead. Lennard stood at the controls, his back to Cort, scratching his head.

This was beginning to take on the quality of a dream. Next, the white tiger would appear. And then, who knows? Maybe his mother. Or Sleb. "Lennard? What are you doing here?"

Lennard whirled around to face him, his features drawn with worry. "Turning off the force field." And then he registered who stood before him, and he grinned as proudly as a boy who'd hit his first alandhal with a sling. "I did it! I turned it off! You're free!"

Cort groped for words as he struggled to adjust to this turn of events. He felt hot and momentarily dizzy as adrenaline began coursing through his veins. He nodded his thanks mutely to Lennard, then looked again at the jailer.

Aj followed his gaze. "I had to stun him," he said. "I don't want him sounding any alarms for the next few hours. Are you all right?"

"Yes, fine. I..." Staring at the jailer, he said, "You'll have to get him off planet. You too, and Lela."

"So you say," Lennard said. "But it will take a lot to do that."

"A lot," Cort echoed. "That's my job."

"Mine, too," Aj said. "Oh... before I forget. Here's your laser and your knife back." He pulled the weapons out of a pack that leaned against the wall and handed them to Cort. "Now, tell me what you'd like us to do. My men and I are prepared to take over the power station if you'd like."

"Can you do it?"

Aj walked to the door of the building. He opened it a crack, looked around cautiously, then opened the door wider. Several soldiers stood just outside, the ones who had come with them from the khenaran. "Yes, we can take over the station. Jule was in there today. He knows the codes. But none of us has ever operated the equipment. Only the aliens do that."

Cort looked at Lennard.

"Hey, don't look at me! I'm a xenologist, not an engineer!"

One after the other, Aj and the other soldiers met Cort's eyes, their faces as innocent as newborn babies.

"Never mind," Cort said. "I took a course. I'll figure it out."

"Wait, Cort," Aj said. "You should be aware that there'll be damage. Maybe a lot of damage. Jule says that the core has been unstable. Magma flares. They drew the power rods back a bit today, second time in a week."

Damage. Cort tried to understand what this would mean. The power station operated geothermally, tapping into the molten magma at the core of the planet, agitating the magma by nuclear probes, and then powering all of Hsu-Lin Base's needs by the resulting temperature and pressure differentials. If the core was unstable after all these years, had the aliens finally gone too far? Or was Aran itself rejecting the intrusion?

"It doesn't matter." Cort moved to Aj's side and took a deep breath of the fresh night air. "I'm going to take the power station out."

Aj looked long and hard at him, but Cort's determination was unbreakable. He met Aj's eyes, golden to golden, until Aj looked away.

"As you wish, Corodh-an-Aran," Aj said.

There was one last thing. "Lennard. Tonight is the night. I need you to help get these aliens out of here. Every last one of them, so that their Earth laws will prevent them from returning."

The xenologist nodded. "If you can provide some plausible reason, I'll go door to door if I have to."

Cort came back inside and grasped Lennard's arm. "I will. Count on it. You've been a good friend to Aran and to me. I won't miss all this"—he waved his arm to indicate the security building, the base and every alien on it, the entire city—"but I'll miss you. Safe journey."

"You too, Cort." Lennard put his arms around Cort in an awkward hug. "Now get moving."

Cort nodded. He walked into the night, his soldiers following.

The power station wasn't far from the building where Cort had been held prisoner. It was an unadorned building with a square footprint perhaps fifteen or twenty meters on a side and five or six meters high. Like most of the structures on the base, it was made of concrete—not khena wood as the stories had it. There were no windows, and nothing broke the featureless surface of the outer walls except the doorway, no ornamentation, no attempt to make it attractive. The small group kept to the shadows alongside buildings. They saw no one until the entrance was in sight.

Two soldiers, Arantu in uniforms like Aj's, stood just outside the station, talking quietly. They occasionally scanned the area, but with casual just-doing-our-jobs glances that suggested they didn't really expect to see anything out of the ordinary.

Aj touched his stunner, then Cort's laser, and raised a questioning eyebrow, silently asking whether Cort wanted to knock the soldiers out or kill them.

A cool breeze riffed through Cort's hair, cooling the sweat on his forehead. He didn't want to kill anyone unless he had to. He touched Aj's stunner, pointed to Aj's chest, signaling for Aj to knock them out.

Aj pointed at another of his soldiers—Jule, was it?—then himself. He held up three fingers. Aj and Jule would each take one, on the count of three.

Focused entirely on one of the station soldiers, Aj gave three barely perceptible nods of his head. Three... two... one.

Two stunners fired. Their nearly inaudible growl silenced the chirping of night insects in the quiet of the base.

Two soldiers in the doorway crumpled to the ground.

Cort stripped the jacket from one of them and put it on, then tucked the long fall of his hair into his collar.

The door to the power station stood open, no one in sight.

Inside, the vestibule was dark and empty, leading to a closed door beyond. A device hung on the wall, its luminescent clock marking the minutes and hours. "Not security," Aj whispered. "A timeclock. We punch in on our regular rounds."

Cort made a sound of assent and headed toward the doorway beyond. He kept his voice low. "Only two guards?"

"Four. The other two are probably at the other entrance, other side of the building."

"Send a couple of soldiers to take them out. We can't afford to be interrupted."

Aj nodded and signaled to two of his men.

Cort moved to the door at the far end of the vestibule. He tried the handle, and it moved. The door opened to a brightly lit room. A glass wall on the opposite side of the room looked into a large space filled with pipes and machinery that extended visibly quite a bit below ground. A quiet but steady thrumming filled the room. The smell was of nothing natural: alien air, highly filtered, mechanical. Control consoles and informational displays filled the adjacent wall. A man in a white coat of alien fabric and design stood at one of the consoles, his back to Cort, stroking his chin. He had dark hair, cut short, and he was tall and thin-chested—an alien. Beyond him, where he seemed to be looking, a rolling display showed a jagged line trending upward.

"What's that mean?" Cort asked, speaking Standard.

The man startled, his thought train interrupted. "The heat is still increasing," he said, his eyes never leaving the display. "If we allow this to continue, there could be a magma flare. Or worse, a full-blown volcanic eruption. We eased the rods back a bit earlier today, but I'm thinking we need to pull them back a little more." He turned to face his visitor. His eyes widened, alarm growing. He reached toward his pocket.

Cort gestured with his hand—*take it easy*—and gave his most disarming smile. "Sorry if I scared you. Just our routine rounds."

The man frowned, but his hand relaxed. "I don't think I've seen you before. Have I?"

Cort laughed. "Night shift. Name's Cort. The commandant asked my team"—he gestured toward Aj and his men, standing in the doorway—"to check in on you and see if you needed any help."

The alien shook his head. "I don't see how you could help. We don't need soldiers, we need a good physicist."

Cort laughed, hoping it didn't sound forced. "Physics was my best subject in school. I really enjoyed it, but I'm sure I don't know as much as you do. Why is the heat increasing?"

The man straightened his posture and smoothed the lapel of his jacket, seeming to enjoy having an interested student. "The truth is, we're not sure. Our best guess is that the power rods have disturbed something in the core, so we're drawing them back to see if we can ease it back down. You can see how far we've drawn the rods back so far"—he pointed to a gauge marked "Meters x 100" whose indicator was slowly moving upward—"but the temperature hasn't stabilized yet."

Cort looked at the jagged output that marched across its screen, still heading upwards. "It might be leveling off a little," he said. "These things take time. Inertia, and all that. How's the pressure?"

"Decreasing, as you'd expect, with the square of the distance as we pull up the rods." He pointed to another indicator.

"Ah. Square of the distance. We studied that."

The man turned toward him, frowning. "What did you say your name was?" He was reaching again toward his pocket—probably a comm rather than a weapon, but it wouldn't do to have the place suddenly overrun with alien soldiers.

"Sergeant Aj," Cort said. He spoke in a conversational tone, as if there wasn't a worry in the world. "I think a stunner would be better than a laser, don't you?"

Aj fired once.

The dark-haired alien cried out and then fell to the floor, unconscious.

Cort checked the man's pockets, found the comm, and removed it. "Helpful man, don't you think?" he said to Aj. "I'm glad we didn't have to kill him. Could you maybe have a couple of your men drop him off by the door of the infirmary? Don't make a fuss about it, but I want him where he can be found. So they won't come *here* looking for him."

Cort turned to the controls as Aj gave his orders. Temperature still rising, but the rods still coming up. That would be the first thing to change. He found the control just below the "Meters x 100" gauge, conveniently labeled, "Rods." It was set to 1500, and the gauge read 1800. Cort tried to change the setting, but nothing happened. "You have that code?"

"Jule?" Aj said.

"Yes, sir. You enter it here." Jule indicated a small keypad recessed into the panel.

"Do it."

Jule did, and then Cort was able to adjust the depth control. He reset the depth of the rods to 2500, the deepest setting.

He looked up at the temperature indicator. Still rising. Pressure also rising. Good. When the temperature or pressure went critical, there would be a mechanism to safely shut the plant down, but Cort was betting that Aran would shut it down forever before it got to that point.

And if not... he'd wreak what additional destruction he could.

"Lock it in again," he told Jule, and the soldier did. "Can you change the code now?"

"No, sir. Only the aliens can do that."

Cort let out a deep, disappointed breath. "Figures. Well, in that case, that's about all I can do here for now," Cort said to Aj. "Can you and your men hold the power station, in case anyone else shows up? I don't want them messing with my settings."

"We can hold it. But what are you going to be doing?"

"I want to pay the commandant a little visit."

"You going to kill him?"

"Not if I can help it." *Much as I'd like to.* "He has an important job to do." Cort gripped Aj's shoulder, then slipped into the night.

Standing in a flower bed outside the commandant's house, Cort looked into the living room, where what seemed like a lifetime ago he had interrupted the commandant and the xenologist in conversation. Dilia had been so weak that night, she might have died had he not rescued her. He forced himself to unclench his fists. Tonight was not the time to take revenge on the commandant. Besides, tonight the room was dark and deserted.

Cort circled the house. It was almost entirely unlit. The hour must be late. Only a single light gleamed in one room on the other side. From behind a bush, Cort peered into the window.

It was some kind of office or study. A large desk dominated the room, and at the desk sat the commandant, his face in profile, reading from his comm. The desk was piled with papers, and shelves that lined the far wall were piled with papers, books, folders, rolls of paper, and small pieces of equipment.

Cort let his eyes adjust to the dark, then continued his careful circuit of the house until he arrived at its front door. Two alien soldiers stood guard. Cort studied them as he crouched behind a bush, its flowers pale in the moonlight, and odorless. The sentries chatted quietly together, their posture relaxed, and their lasers holstered.

Cort had the element of surprise on his side, and he had a weapon that could easily kill the two soldiers before they even suspected any danger. He didn't want to do that, though, not unless he had no other choice. But the aliens had designed the lasers for crowd control as well as for battle. He examined the controls of his laser and found the 'stun' setting. Hoping it worked as he intuitively thought it might, Cort fired.

One of the sentries went down wordlessly—dead or stunned, Cort didn't know. The other sentry reached for his laser, eyes wide. He drew the weapon.

Cort fired, and the second sentry went down.

He waited a few tense moments to see if any other soldiers were coming, but the night remained silent. He took a deep breath, let it all the way out, and breathed in again. He stepped from the cover of the bush and approached the front door. Both of the alien soldiers lay on the threshold. Their chests rose and fell with visible breathing, but they didn't move.

Cort tried the handle of the door.

It was unlocked.

What was with these aliens, anyway, so sure of themselves?

He went in.

He slipped into the commandant's study, keeping his back to the wall and making sure the doorway he'd just come through was still in his peripheral vision to his left. Aiming his laser carefully at the man, he spoke in Standard, "I understand you wanted to talk with me. I want to talk with you, too."

The alien turned and looked up, half stood, then sat again and reached for his comm.

"No," Cort said. "Don't touch it. Not yet. Face me and keep your hands where I can see them."

The alien commandant did as ordered, his face a frozen mask.

Cort felt a moment of hatred so intense his finger almost squeezed the trigger. How he wanted to kill this man! This alien with his pale, cold eyes, who had hurt Dilia so deeply. This alien who directed the raping of Aran.

But he mustn't—for Aran's sake. His hatred was banded around his chest so tightly he could barely breathe. He brought himself under control with a sound like strangling.

"That's a laser," the commandant said. "Your people are not allowed—"

"It was Jerrald's. Why did you send him after me?"

"You killed him."

He might have dissembled. *No. There was a serpent. I just happened to be present.* But he was tired of lies. "He left me no choice. Don't make me kill you, too." Hatred erupted in him, hot as acid in his mouth. He forced it down, forced himself to lie. "I'd rather not."

"What do you want?"

"I want you to leave."

The commandant snorted, a single syllable of laughter that bordered on ridicule. "Just like that," he mocked, his pale blue eyes glittering in scorn and amusement.

"If you don't leave, you'll be destroyed. All of you. I am giving you warning."

"Ah... warning. Lennard mentioned that you had some grandiose idea about getting us all out. Something about *the spirits of your ancestors*... Do I have that right?" His mocking tone allowed no serious response.

But the over-oxygenated air in the house was beginning to affect Cort, who was no longer feeling particularly serious. He wished he'd shut down the oxygen-generation plant as well as the power station.

"You have that right," he managed to answer, "except that you don't believe it, and we do." Cort remembered that a power shutdown would automatically close the air plant. He giggled, then brought himself under control. He wanted to take a deep breath to calm himself, but he didn't dare. He hadn't expected this job to be so difficult. "Are all your people in the enclave?" he asked.

"No," the commandant replied. He watched Cort closely. He didn't seem as afraid as he should have been. Brave, maybe. Or he was waiting for the poisoned air to have its effect, looking for his opportunity—which, the way things were going, would surely come. "Two are with the harvesters."

"How quickly can they get here?"

"The harvester that just left this morning could probably be back"—the commandant paused and looked up, his eyes moving back and forth as if calculating its likely distance and maximum speed—"just after dawn, if it started right away. The other one is already on its way back, full. It's a little farther out and will travel more slowly. Maybe late afternoon, at best."

Cort wanted to open a window, but as giddy as he was feeling, he couldn't afford to turn his attention from the commandant. He forced himself to concentrate. "And if it jettisoned its load, would it come back sooner?"

The commandant raised an eyebrow. "But why would we do that?"

"Just answer." The only way he could keep going was to pretend that he was acting the part of a tough gangster—the bully Karl, dead all these years. That sounded like fun, playing Karl.

"You could probably cut a couple of hours off the time."

"Order them back, then. Tell the returning harvester to jettison its load. Tell them to make the best speed they possibly can."

"I'm not going to do that," the commandant said.

"Do it," Cort said, "or I'll burn a hole through you and each of your successors in turn until I find a man who will." That sounded fairly Karl-like. He barely managed to turn a satisfied smile into a sneer.

The commandant shrugged. "It doesn't matter," he said. "They can pick up the load later." The implication was, after they had gotten rid of Cort. "I'll have to use my comm to send the message."

"Fine."

The commandant turned to his device. He typed the message, then sat back for Cort to review it. When Cort nodded his approval, the commandant pressed a button to send the message.

"Now you'll have to make preparations to get everyone off the planet," Cort said.

The commandant sat back in his chair, more at ease than anyone with a laser aimed at him ought to be. He smiled. "But why? We've been here for generations. We have no intention of leaving."

What to say? Because you have violated the forest? Because she rejects your presence here? He settled into his Karl-act. "To save your sorry necks," he answered. "This is not a threat. It's a fact. By this time tomorrow, any of you who remain will be dead."

At that instant, two alien soldiers burst into the room. They held their lasers aimed downward, possibly to avoid accidentally injuring their commandant.

Only Cort's unswerving laser, aimed at the commandant's chest, saved him. "Hold it right there!"

The first soldier stopped so suddenly that the rear one bumped into him. They looked from the intruder to the commandant, uncertain.

Cort said, "Drop your weapons. If you try to shoot, I will kill him before I die."

The soldiers hesitated, as if a command from their leader might save them from having to make the decision on their own.

"Now! Or this man is history!" Cort was almost shouting, his good sense lost in the rush of hatred-fueled adrenaline tugging at his trigger finger, ready to fire. And die.

The commandant looked from the soldiers to Cort, and back again. He sighed. "Do it." Relieved of the responsibility, the soldiers let their lasers drop to the floor.

"Kick them over here," Cort said, and the soldiers obliged.

It could be that the commandant had sent an emergency signal when he sent the message to the harvesters, or there could be some kind of surveillance setup inside the house that had flagged his intrusion. Either way, the soldiers' arrival had at least one good outcome. "Now open that window," he ordered the nearest of the soldiers. The man complied silently, and a welcome breeze blew in the window. Cort gratefully gulped deep breaths of it. He picked up the two alien lasers and wedged them into his belt.

"I would have opened it for you, young man, if you had asked," the commandant said wryly. "Now tell me why you think any of us will be dead by this time tomorrow. Are you planning to kill us?"

Cort shook his head slowly. "No," he answered. "You may think I'm here to harm you, but—"

"It's a logical assumption." The commandant nodded toward the laser that Cort still held aimed at him.

"Right. But actually I'm trying to give you time to save yourselves. Aran itself will kill you if you stay."

"Ah." The commandant exchanged knowing glances with one of the soldiers.

Cort realized that the aliens didn't believe a word he had said. And why should they? The starmen had successfully maintained a presence on this planet for centuries. It was easier to think that one savage had gone crazy.

The lights in the room flickered.

The aliens looked around nervously.

The lights went out.

A moment later, the hiss of the poisoned alien air from the air vents fell silent. Bright moonlight flooded the room from the Hunter moon. The Kiri moon looked like a small red bloodstain on the larger moon's face. The only sound was the chirping of insects in the bushes outside the window.

A slight tremor shook the house, and the insects fell silent.

"The power plant!" one of the soldiers said, looking pleadingly at Cort, whose unwavering weapon still pointed at the commandant's chest. "It's been unstable. It could blow."

"I know," Cort said. "It *will* blow. And it will take the entire base with it." He met the commandant's angry, worried eyes. "It will destroy the ship. Get your people out of here while you can. I hope, I just hope you have the time to wait for those people with the harvesters."

"None of my people are out with the harvesters," the commandant said. "It was just an excuse to signal these officers, not that that seems to have mattered. And now, young man, I will make my own decisions concerning how to handle this situation you have made for us." He spoke with authority, as if Cort's laser were not still pointed at him—or as if he believed that Cort wouldn't use it.

Cort sighed. He wouldn't use the laser, and he had no more time to deal with these people. There was nothing more he could say to persuade them in any case. "I'm going to leave. I want you all to wait here in this room for five minutes. If I find any of you following me, I will shoot. Do you understand?"

He waited until each of the starmen spoke affirmatively. Then he edged past the soldiers and shut the door of the commandant's study as he left. Apparently, two was the total number of sentries inside the commandant's house, for the hallway was deserted. He had the front door open when he heard a sound from behind. He dove outside and to the side of the door frame as a finger-thin beam of coherent light shot out the door.

I said five minutes! Cort waited silently. A moment later, one of the soldiers ran out of the house, his laser ready.

Cort shot him from behind. The alien fell.

A tremor shook the ground, and Cort was thrown against the side of the house. The shifting, settling planet roared, and dust rose into the sky. Another tremor immediately followed the first. The sky behind the house boiled red, and the breeze smelled of smoke and sulfur. Somewhere on the base, buildings were burning

Chapter 27

Saving Aran

D ilia woke with a start, her heart pounding. The ground shook again, a long, deep rumbling. The beginning of the end. And where was Cort? Would he be safe?

There was nothing she could do about Cort, but she *could* save some children. Dilia shook away the thought of Cort and sat up. "Nala."

Nala sat up. "I'm awake. Did you feel—?"

"Yes. We have to get as many people out of here as we can. There's no time to spare."

There was a moment of silence, then Nala swallowed audibly. Then she said, "I'll wake the children."

All Dilia's thinking and worrying coalesced into a plan. "Wake everyone up and down the street, especially the parents of the children you care for. I'm going to go wake the others we've talked with, as many as I can. Everyone has to get as far from the city as they can. Now."

As if to emphasize her point, the ground shook again, a more prolonged rumbling.

"But the gate!" Nala's voice broke. "There won't be anyone there to unlock it."

Dilia didn't know what to do about the gate if it was locked. Her planning hadn't gotten that far. She pictured hundreds of people pushing at the gate, trapped. Her stomach clenched into a knot. "I, uh..."

Eyes wide, breathing fast, Nala looked on the verge of panic. "We can't get out the gate!"

Maybe Cort had thought of something. Maybe someone would wake one of the guards. All Dilia knew was that they had to get moving. They'd deal with the gate, if they had to, when they got there. She put a hand on Nala's shoulder, drew a breath, and uttered a falsehood with all the conviction she could muster. "Yes, we can. Don't worry. Cort is taking care of it." She kept her grip firm and looked Nala in the eye until Nala calmed down, nodding shakily.

Dilia parted ways with her, each with an agreed area to alert people to leave. Dilia knocked on all the doors where she knew there were children, and on their neighbors' doors as well. She encouraged everyone to leave the city, to get out and go as far as they could. Every time she said those words, her throat was tight with the fear that the gate would be closed, but after a while, the words got easier to say. Surely, someone would find a way to open the gate.

The ground's shaking grew steadier and more pronounced. Whether or not the gate was opened, Dilia began to wonder whether the walls would stand. Whether any of the city's buildings would stand.

No one answered many of the doors where Dilia knocked. Perhaps these people had already fled—or perhaps they were too afraid to answer their doors. There was no way to know, and no time to investigate. Dilia kept moving. Of those who answered her knock, many had heard her earlier predictions. Urged on by her warning and by the tremors that now shook the ground, they fled. But others backed away from her, pushing back their children, and shut their doors.

Dilia felt her heart would break. She wanted to reach out one more time, to find the right words. But all the words had been said. She quietly wept, and moved on.

The sky was still black when she finally made it to the gate. Ash was starting to rain down on the city, the ground shook almost continually, and the air smelled of sulfur. Dilia breathed a sigh of relief when she saw the gate was open, and then choked on the ash-thick air. People were streaming out of the city, struggling to stay upright on the shaking ground. They and the few belongings they carried were coated in ash. Dilia didn't see Nala, but she doubted she would recognize anyone in the gloom. They would reunite, somehow, outside.

And Cort, would she ever find him again?

No, surely he would find her. He'd be somewhere, out there, and he would find her.

Dilia stepped through the open gate.

The ground shook once again, throwing Cort against the wall of the commandant's house. He thought of Dilia, and his stomach clenched. *Bobcat, where is Dilia?*

The small cat's voice was distant, but audible. *I am with her, Hunter. We are leaving the city now, along with entirely too many humans.* The small creature's distaste for the number of humans was evident. *They are safe.*

If I don't return, you must help them reach the khenaran.

This is a big job, Hunter, and I am not keen on it. I will do what I can, but it will be better if you return.

I will do what I can, too. Cort loped to the side of the house and looked around.

Aliens and soldiers ran in various directions. He wouldn't stand out in the dark. He raced for the power plant.

The ground thundered and heaved beneath his feet. He stumbled.

From a breach in the ground near the power station, molten lava flowed onto the pavement, painting the buildings around it an eerie reddish color and radiating heat. A cloud of smoke or gas, ruddy in the reflected lava-light, hung over the enclave, and the air carried a stench of sulfur.

People moved back and forth among the buildings. Their movements were puzzling; they didn't have the purposefulness of the orderly evacuation he hoped to see.

An instant later, he understood. With the power station down and the fence no longer operating, looters had come up from the city below. Ignoring the unfolding natural disaster, they were taking advantage of an opportunity to gain the wealth of a lifetime. The looters would make the alien evacuation harder, but perhaps they would make it more necessary.

Cort shook his head, smiling. He couldn't blame the looters. Had he still lived in the city, he and his gang would probably have been among them. He only hoped the looters would make it away from the base, away from the city in time.

The ground continued to rumble and shake. When the lava reached one of the alien gardens a flare lit the sky; the grass and bushes were burning.

Cort detoured around the fire, keeping to the shadows behind buildings, bushes, and trees. He sought the owl's vision, and found the nocturnal bird over the woods some distance from the city. The owl was understandably afraid and would come no closer. From this distance the owl's vision was not useful. Cort let it go. He worked his way around darkened buildings toward the power plant.

As Cort slipped behind bushes near one of the houses, he saw the house door open. Two alien soldiers came out, large packs on their backs, their lasers out and ready to fire. Behind the soldiers, an alien man and woman and a child of about ten years followed. The man guided a gravlev wagon that was piled with boxes and bundles and floated a few centimeters above the ground. Behind the family, another two soldiers emerged from the house, and the last shut the door behind himself. All the soldiers carried lasers and warily scanned the landscape, ready to fire. The group headed up the hill toward the starship.

Cort nodded to himself and continued on his way.

The air was hot and thick with a suffocating, sulfurous smell. Fine particles of dark ash floated toward the ground. The shaking of the ground seemed less severe than before, but it was almost continuous, filling the night with a steady roar.

A small fire flared in the pathway ahead of Cort, and acrid smoke burned his eyes. He detoured, rounding the corner of a building, and the power station came into view across an open, paved area. The structure had deep cracks and looked like any moment it might collapse into a pile of rubble. He paused behind the corner of the nearby building to study the situation.

Crouched in the doorway of the building next to Cort were two soldiers firing at the power station, and a third lay on the ground beside them. Another three attackers crouched behind bushes and trees closer to the power station. With the ash that covered everything, Cort couldn't make out who they were. But they were not aliens, for they fired stunners, not lasers, toward the power station. From his hiding place, Cort couldn't see who they were attacking. His heart pounded. He feared it was Aj and his men under attack.

He worked his way along the wall of the building at his back until he reached the next corner. Carefully, he crept around it. Now he could see Aj's men, too, pinned near the entrance to the station. Like their attackers, they were covered with dark ash.

Cort had come around behind the attackers, using the trees and bushes of the aliens' gardens as cover. They were too intent on the attack, too disciplined, and too well armed to be a gang—and too poorly armed to be aliens. Most likely they were Arantu troops loyal to the aliens.

Even as the aliens retreated to their ship, they must have ordered their native troops to recapture the power station. It made no sense tactically; what was happening now was irreversible. The power station was probably the first building damaged, a worthless target. The only motive Cort could imagine was to punish him and the soldiers who had helped him. He thought the alien commandant was capable of it.

As Cort studied the scene, he saw a second squad in the distance moving toward the power station. He hated the idea of killing or wounding these men, whose main fault was that they were ignorant or stupid enough to let themselves be used by the aliens for no good purpose. But he had no intention of letting them kill his friends. Carefully, he aimed his laser at the stunner that one of the soldiers was using, and he fired.

The laser missed. In the murky air, its beam was clearly visible as a thin coherent light with a slightly reddish cast. Cort frowned. It would be too easy for these soldiers to trace his beams back to his hiding place. He wouldn't have much time. He adjusted his aim and quickly fired again, this time hitting the soldier's arm. The man yelled and dropped his stunner, gripping his wounded arm with his other hand. Cort fired again.

He injured five of the enemy and killed two before they figured out that they were being attacked from behind. Two of the soldiers stood and turned, stunners ready. Cort shot one of them. One of the power station defenders got the other one.

Cort aimed again, but instead of attacking, the surviving soldiers ran. As they passed the second squad, they stopped and pointed in his direction. Then all the soldiers ran off.

Cort laughed with sudden insight and with relief. Seeing the laser beams, they must have believed that they were under attack by one or more of the aliens. They must have assumed that their orders had been changed.

Cort wiped his forehead with his hand, and his hand came away black. His white tigerskin was covered with black ash, which made him as unidentifiable as any of the others. Aj and his men would not be able to recognize him until he was quite close. The area in front of the power station was open, offering no cover. Three soldiers defended the station, and three more lay on the ground nearby.

Cort wanted to meet back up with Aj's men and to lead them out. But would they recognize him? If the defenders thought he was an attacker, they would shoot before they could see who he was. On the other hand, he might need his weapon; an attack could come from anywhere. It was a calculated risk. Cort tucked the laser into his belt, and spreading his hands wide in front of him, he headed toward the power station.

A soldier aimed his stunner at Cort, but he didn't shoot. As Cort got closer, he recognized Jule. "That you, Cort?" Jule shouted, barely audible over the rumble of the shaking ground.

"Yes," he answered, then asked, "Where's Aj?"

Jule nodded toward the body at his side, covered with the fine black ash. "Stunned," he answered.

Cort had come close enough that he no longer had to shout. "We have to get out of here. How many men are with you?"

"Three of us standing," Jule answered, with a gesture of his head. The other two men hovered in the darkness just beyond the doorway.

"Aj and two more stunned, and one dead. One ran and may be dead. Out there." He nodded over Cort's shoulder.

Aj and his men had risked everything to follow Cort. Leaving the stunned soldiers behind now was a death sentence. Cort drew a deep breath and straightened his spine. "Pick up the stunned ones and carry them. Follow me."

The ground shook roughly, throwing Jule into the doorway and Cort to his knees.

As Cort stood again, Jule protested, "We'll go too slowly if we have to carry them. And we'll be more vulnerable to attack." His eyes were panicky. He wasn't thinking clearly. In a few seconds the man would simply bolt and run, like a stag with wolves at its heels. The other two men looked to be in the same condition.

"No!" Despite the fear that tightened his chest, Cort spoke slowly, enunciating each word with authority. "We will carry them because we are human beings, and they are our friends. You will do it because I am Inei-Taru to you. I'll take Aj. Two of you carry the other men. My kiri will help me see the way, and I'll lead you out of here." Without waiting for agreement from the others, Cort knelt beside Aj's unconscious body and lifted it over his shoulders like a deer that he was bringing back to the village. He staggered as he adjusted Aj's weight.

Motionless, Jule stared as Cort stood. The soldier's eyes were empty of everything but fear.

"Pick him up," Cort repeated, nodding toward the other body. "Pick him up and follow me." Then he lied with all the conviction he could muster. "We're going to be all right. I am Inei-Taru. Just do as I say."

Jule nodded and picked up the stunned soldier nearest him, and one of his companions did the same with the other stunned soldier.

Cort breathed a sigh of relief. He turned away from the power station. The others silently followed.

In the night of falling ash, one set of faces and clothing was indistinguishable from another, and they were not the only group of people carrying bundles on their backs. The roar of the trembling ground was the only sound as people moved silently wherever they were going. Cort's small group did not stand out, and no one approached or threatened them.

Twice, the ground shook so violently that Cort and the others fell. Each time, he silently hoisted Aj back to his shoulders and waited while Jule and his companion did the same with the other two stunned men. Then he set out again. They slogged through ash up to their knees, barely managing to take one step after another.

From a rise in the ground, Cort turned to look back at the city. The lava flow had run from just below the power plant and reached almost to where the wall of the base used to be. Fires burned in several places. Ash hung in the air like a damp mist, shrouding the distant view, affording only a vague suggestion of blackened buildings and people running in the streets. He wondered where Dilia was, and the children. But the bobcat would have let him know if they had not gotten out safely. Later, he would find her—if he made it out himself.

The power station and most of its surrounding buildings had crumpled into piles of rubble. People still walked and ran among the ruins of the base, and the starship still perched on its hilltop. Cort's view of the path to the ship was blocked by the buildings; he had no way to know if the aliens were preparing to leave. If the aliens stayed, he would have to come back here, but he couldn't bear to think of that now.

His load was growing as heavy as his heart, and there was a long way to go before he would feel safe. Cort started down the other side of the hill. It took an hour to reach the scrub woods, pushing through ash that in some places was thigh-high. They fell so many times, Cort lost count. Each time they picked up their unconscious companions, the bodies seemed to weigh more. He was exhausted. He scarcely had the energy to nod his thanks when one of the soldiers stopped him and took Aj from his shoulders.

Deeper in the woods, much of the ash stayed on the leaves and limbs of the trees and did not reach the floor of the woods. Walking became easier. But here and there around them, a limb that had grown too heavy with its added weight tore and crashed to the ground. Sometimes the path was blocked, and they had to go around through thick vines and scrub brush.

The sky remained dark long after it should have been morning, but slowly the tremors grew fainter, and the rain of ash seemed to lessen.

Hours later, Cort carried Aj again, with the tired soldiers stumbling and shuffling behind him. He walked until the burning soreness in his leg muscles turned to numbness.

They came to a clear, rocky area not far from a river. Ash coated the rocks, but it was barely above their ankles. Cort knelt carefully and put Aj down, propping the soldier's back and head against a tree trunk.

The soldiers flopped down to rest.

Cort was exhausted, but he knew that if he sat down he might not get up easily. He remained standing. Before he could rest, he had to find Dilia. *Bobcat, are you there?*

I am here, Hunter. This stuff is awful.

Cort could picture the bobcat lifting her delicate tufted paws as she slogged through the thickening ash. *Yes, it is*, he said, *but it will end soon. Are you with Dilia?*

I am near her and many other people. I am watching her right now. How is she?

Tired and dirty like everyone, said the bobcat. *But she is fine. And you?*

Tired and dirty, Cort said, *like everyone.*

Cort leaned against a tree and let his eyelids close while he summoned the energy to move again. A blinding flare seared the inside of his eyes. He opened his eyes to see the starship slowly rising against the dark sky. The light of its struggling jets filled the sky.

Cort didn't know if all the aliens were gone, or if some had remained to try to keep Aran for their people. If any remained... Before he left for the khenaran, he'd return to the base one more time to make sure no aliens were still alive there. It was not a task he looked forward to, but it had to be done.

Even if all the aliens had gone, Cort didn't know if Lennard would be successful in keeping them away. Cort didn't even know if Lennard and Lela were still alive. But he had to assume that the two of them had gotten off-planet with the others. And he *would* know about Lela, at least, and therefore probably Lennard. For the khenaran would tell the whynywir, and the whynywir would tell him, if Lela lived or died on this planet.

If the starmen returned, Cort knew beyond doubting that he would do whatever he had to, whatever he could, to keep Aran whole and safe from them, for he was, to the depths of his being, Corcdh-an-Aran.

Along with the soldiers, Cort watched the alien ship struggle upward through the dense atmosphere until it was gone and the sky was dark again. Then he forced himself to stand straight. He was going to find Dilia.

Dilia had been walking for hours. She was exhausted. It must have been daytime by now, but it was dark, and black ash hung in the air like mist, slowing sinking to the ground. Her lungs hurt, and it was hard to breathe.

She held a baby on one hip and had the other arm wrapped around the pregnant mother's waist, helping her along too. A group of adults and children followed behind her. There must have been eighty or a hundred of them at least, more than she'd managed to count. Ahead, a small bobcat, Cort's kiri, indicated a path through the dark woods. Whenever Dilia faltered or fell behind, the animal waited for her. From this, she took encouragement and strength. She hoped the creature was leading her to Cort.

Surely, some people at the end of the group that followed her must have fallen behind, but Dilia didn't have the strength to go back and check on them. She hoped the path that had been trampled by so many adults and children would remain clear enough for them to follow, even in this ash and gloom.

The bobcat led Dilia until the sky began to grow a bit lighter and the distant rumbling had faded. She stumbled into a clearing and looked up to see a man standing there.

Face, hair, clothing—every part of him was covered in ash. He could be anyone.

But the bobcat raced to him and rubbed against his legs. It was Cort, half slumping from exhaustion and yet radiant as he lifted his head and saw her. "Dilia," he said. He stepped forward, arms extended, welcoming.

She gave the baby she'd been carrying back to its mother and stepped into Cort's open arms.

For long moments, she melted into the embracing warmth of him. Then she looked around at the people who were still straggling into the clearing. There were too many to count, but still, so few compared to how many lived in the city. She had saved so few. Her throat constricted into a knot.

"You're crying," Cort said. He wiped the tears from her cheeks.

"I tried, but—" She couldn't speak. She forced herself to swallow. "I tried to save them all, but people wouldn't listen to me. So many people must have died."

He let out a sigh. "Yes, many must have, but listen to me, Dilia. They may have gotten out but just not followed you, right?" He waited, looking at her. "Right?"

"I suppose."

"And they may have left by some other way, not the gate."

"No, how?"

"The wall around the base came down. Probably the city wall did, too, with all that shaking, at least parts of it."

"Okay, but—"

"So, they may have left the city after you, or before you, and you wouldn't have seen them go."

Dilia wiped away a tear. Her fingertips came away black with ash. Maybe she was overreacting, but she felt sure some people would have died. Many people. "They might have stayed in their houses."

"They might be able to dig out later," he said.

Sometimes, he could be so frustrating! "Are you trying to tell me that there was this great volcanic event right near the city, and no one died? That I'm being foolish to worry about it?"

He hugged her tighter. "Oh, my love, no. Most likely some people did die. Maybe a lot of people. Probably we'll never know how many."

"Children too," she said.

He sighed and held her more tightly. "Children too. But the starmen have left, and the harvesting has stopped. The murder of our spirits has stopped, and remember: any Arantu that died will be reborn. Death is not the end, not for us. It's the gateway to a new beginning."

A new beginning! Dilia turned to look back in the direction she'd come. There was no more alien base. No more city. Perhaps the location would, in time, be overgrown with trees. Perhaps even khena trees with the spirits of people who had lived here. Perhaps, in time, all the world would be khenaran again.

Dilia relaxed in Cort's strong arms. A feeling of warmth and peace radiated through her: the entire world spread before them. For the first time, she felt real hope for the future. She turned back to Cort. The ash coating his face and head was streaked with sweat and, was it... yes, tracks of tears. He'd been crying with her or for her, it didn't matter which. She wiped the tears from his face, smearing the ash there. The two crystals glittered at his hairline. There was nobody in all the world like him. She felt grateful and blessed, and with the feeling came a lightness of heart. "It's a long journey ahead," she said, "and a lot of people to care for. But we'll be together. We can do it. Do you want to get started now?"

He drew back enough to look at her face, then gave her a wan smile. "You must have more energy than I do. Let's get these people settled in, and let everyone rest. As you said, it's a long way back to the khenaran. But Tirei and Neder and Okolo and the others will be waiting for us, and they'll welcome these people, too. We're going home, Dilia, and nothing will stand in our way. We have time. Tomorrow, we'll get started." He was smiling, but Dilia could see the lines of fatigue etched on his face. She wanted to hear his whole story, but it could wait.

She kissed him slowly and gently, a kiss that had all the time in the world, and she said, "Yes, tomorrow."

<<<>>>

Dear Reader,

Thank you for reading *Saving Aran*. I know that your time is limited, and I'm honored that you chose to spend it with Cort and Dilia in their struggle to stay together and to free their planet from the aliens.

To be notified of upcoming releases and to receive special content that's for newsletter subscribers only, you can sign up for my more-or-less monthly newsletter at . Here too, you can follow my travels, still only on planet Earth.

If you enjoyed *Saving Aran*, then don't miss the books in the *Ascent of Eden* series—*A Warrior of Eden, Freeing Eden,* and *The Last Lord of Eden*. Follow the lives of the people who would do anything to save their beloved home Eden from exploitation by an interplanetary drug cartel.

If you'd like to see more of the seminal events of Aran's history, both before and after Cort and Dilia rid the planet of the alien presence, I hope you will like *Alien Son*, which will be coming out in the summer of 2022. You'll see Cort again, meet his half-brother from Earth and share his struggles to keep Aran free from Earth's clutching fingers.

I greatly appreciate your help in spreading the word about *Saving Aran*, including telling your friends and fellow readers. And remember, reviews also help readers find books they will enjoy. Please consider posting a review on Amazon, Goodreads, Bookbub, or your blog or website.

To follow me on Facebook:
https://www.facebook.com/gskenneyauthor
To follow me on Instagram:
https://www.instagram.com/gskenneyauthor

Now, here's an excerpt from *Freeing Eden…*

Freeing Eden

by G. S. Kenney

Set back a few feet from the street by a tiny but well maintained garden, the entry to the autobrothel looked inviting. The sun had nearly reached the tops of the buildings on the street's west side, and the garden lay in shadow, its cool, green humidity freshening the air around. The quiet street, with its well maintained and tastefully ornamented buildings, was a pleasant respite from the market, where merchants hungry for a sale accosted passers-by in the streets to hawk their wares, and where by late afternoon the air was heavy with the odors of sweat, leather, cooking oil, pastries, perfumes, and garbage.

No sign announced the name, although the traditional cast-from-brass emblem, a stylized pair of wings, hung beside the heavy wooden doorway. A matching brass knocker was set in the center of the door. Zara reached for the knocker. Its metal was cool under her fingers.

Then she hesitated.

Did she really want to do this?

After a long, hot day dealing with dishonest merchants in the market, she had decided to quit early and unwind. She could still head back to the ship. A quiet drink alone in the ready room, maybe a little music, and—

No, that didn't sound appealing at all. Zara spent half her life alone aboard the Winged Princess. She didn't mind the solitude, but when she was planetside, she wanted someone to talk to. She wished she knew someone besides old Elleren here on Lesurat. The old man was one of the near-homeless who hung around the spaceport hoping for a few coins in return for a kind word. He'd taken one look at Zara, fresh from a month alone in space, and recommended this autobrothel. She'd smiled and thanked him and given him all the coins in her pocket, almost a tiyu, never imagining she'd actually end up here.

The knocker had grown warm under Zara's touch.

She wanted to talk, and given the choices, a baseclone in this place might serve nicely. She'd transported an entire shipment of baseclones a couple of standard years ago, from Bigollo, where they were made, to the mining complex on New Mars. That hadn't been a bad run, not bad at all. She'd reconfigured the cargo area for habitation by the dozen or so baseclone units and given the supervisor a berth in the passenger quarters. Once the ship rotated into the tiny dimensions, bypassing normal lightspeed limitations, the trip to New Mars out on the edge of the inhabited part of the galaxy had taken six weeks. Zara had had time on her hands and helped the supervisor care for the baseclones.

They had no intellect, those failed clones. No language; no human curiosity or initiative. With their remote-control units shut down, the devices attached to the back of their necks at the base of the skull, they were as warm and receptive as sleeping puppies. They would sleep endlessly if they were not awakened and exercised. She'd fallen into mothering even the big, bearded ones twice her size. They'd been easy to talk to, totally uncomprehending of course, not even awake, but in their way gentle and sweet.

Yes, perhaps this autobrothel would be just the thing. She'd find some poor baseclone and talk to him for an hour or two. Of course he'd listen and never once interrupt or argue or try to persuade her to buy something. She'd give him all the motherly affection she could. It would be a pleasure for her, and—who knows—perhaps in some deep recess of his being, the baseclone would be glad of it, too. Zara smiled in anticipation and knocked on the door.

A moment later, the door opened. A middle-aged man with dark, curly hair and nondescript features, shorter than she was, assessed her. "Yes?"

"I… uh, I wanted to… rent a unit." Knowing what the man must be thinking, Zara felt the heat of a blush on her face and was grateful that her dark skin hid it.

"Spacer, eh?" When the man smiled, he looked younger, and kind. "Well, don't just stand there. Come on in." He opened the door wider, stepping back to allow Zara to pass. The room beyond was wood-paneled and carpeted with richly designed rugs of an Ancient-Earthish pattern, geometric designs in warm reds, pinks, blues, and tan. Vases of sweet-scented flowers and bowls of real fruit graced tables that stood near softly inviting couches and chairs that picked up the colors of the rugs.

Zara nodded her appreciation and stepped inside.

"Please. Have a seat." The man motioned toward one of the couches, and sat nearby as Zara sank into the soft cushions. "There's no need to be shy, you know. Lots of people come here. Spacers especially. All the time." He paused and smiled at her. "What kind of unit would you be interested in? We have all kinds, all price ranges, from robounits to baseclones."

"Oh. I didn't realize… I'm looking for a baseclone. Something human."

The manager coughed discreetly into his hand. "I must advise you that neither robounits nor baseclones are considered human, legally speaking. But I do understand. Many people prefer the more human feel of the clones. But the establishment does not allow certain activities with the clones that may be done with the robounits. Baseclones are expensive, and we don't want to see any harm come to them."

Zara's face grew hot again. What kind of pervert did he think she was? She drew herself more upright. "I'm not interested in *activities*," she said stiffly. "I just want someone to talk to for a while."

For a moment, the manager fumbled for words. Then he said, "We welcome your business, of course, and perhaps it isn't in my best interest to say this. But surely you could find a less, ah, expensive alternative for talking. A shop, perhaps, or a bar. Any merchant…"

This was the last thing Zara wanted to hear. "I have been talking with merchants all afternoon. I'm tired of people trying to sell me cheap goods at high prices. That's exactly what I'm trying to get away from."

"Forgive me." He looked as repentant as a sinner at the altar. "I ask these questions so that I can match you with the best possible unit."

"Oh." Zara brushed back a loose strand of her thick, curly hair, and tucked it into her hair band. "Well, go on, then."

"Do you prefer a male or a female?"

"I don't know that it matters." She thought of the baseclones she had transported to New Mars. They had all been male, all gentle. "Male, I guess."

"Ah, good, good. And, to confirm, you're certain that it's only talking you want... or listening, to be precise? The unit will neither talk nor understand you. You do know that?" He held up both hands, palms out, a gesture of pacification. "I just want to be sure."

"I've been around baseclones before. I know. I can do enough talking for any two people all by myself."

He smiled. "I happen to have a unit available now that is, if I say so myself, one of the very finest on all Lesurat. A real treasure." He shook his head appreciatively and clicked his tongue. "But I wasn't planning to put him into service for another week or two. We just acquired him. He's new out of the tanks and not yet conditioned for physical intimacy. The restriction will be in your contract." He gave her a meaningful look.

"Yes. That's fine."

"I think you'll be very pleased with this unit. If, of course, it's in your price range."

Zara hesitated. "How much?"

"I can rent him to you for five hundred tiyus, half of what we would charge in a busier time."

The amount was a month's salary for a skilled worker on Lesurat. Zara scowled. "It had better be a good unit."

"In all my years in this line of work," the manager said, "and of all the baseclones I've dealt with, this one is the very best." He looked at her slant-eyed, then quickly added, "For talking, I mean. Obviously, we don't know yet about his other... uses."

The baseclone sat calmly on the couch in the private room, looking straight ahead. But as the manager opened the door to let Zara in, the unit turned his head toward the sound, tilting it slightly in a gesture that resembled curiosity. He watched her with an utterly naïve openness, and waited.

Zara smiled, and perhaps he might have smiled too. Or she might have imagined it.

"Hello," she said nervously af er she closed the door and locked it. Zara had enjoyed talking to the baseclones she had transported, and though they were completely passive, she had been able to imagine that they enjoyed it too. Like small babies, they brought out a maternal side in her. And besides, after all the time she spent alone, she needed to unwind. She hoped this clone would act the same way as the others—just patiently appear to listen. "It's okay," she explained to him, laughing a little, "I talk to myself, too."

Zara broke eye contact with the unit and looked around the room. It contained no bed, perhaps to discourage "activities" such as those forbidden in Zara's contract. The color scheme ran from cream to gold to the rich russet of the soft carpeting, suggesting refinement and wealth. Next to the couch where the baseclone sat was a table flanked by two chairs. The table was made of a smooth, blond wood, solid wood, not a laminate. She knew how much she could get for it, and the price took her breath away. This autobrothel must cater to a very discriminating clientele indeed.

On the table stood a bowl of fruit, a crystal carafe of water glistening with condensation, two goblets, a bottle of red wine, and two wineglasses. It seemed unlikely that the unit would be able to drink from a glass by himself. Perhaps the second glass was simply for show. Zara couldn't help but wonder in what state a few hours of "activities"—to use the manager's word—would leave such a room, and marvel at a quick calculation of the establishment's maintenance budget. But the tranquility of the room appealed to her, and she nodded slightly in approval.

The baseclone watched her but didn't move. Zara walked over to the couch. "I'm Zara."

He looked at her with what might have passed for interest, moving slightly to make room for her as she sat beside him. The manager had been right; this was a particularly fine unit, far more alert and responsive than the mining units. Unlike them, he seemed almost human. Almost a trueclone. He was also—Zara nibbled at her lip as she studied him—there was no denying it—beautiful. His dark blond hair framed a face that could have been aristocratic, with long, elegant eyebrows and eyes that were to die for. They were a bright, noontime-sky blue, ringed in midnight blue. Zara tried to imagine this clone's creator. She had no way of knowing, of course, but she pictured a handsome man of late middle age, graying at the temples. Perhaps he was the head of a great business empire, or of one of the clandestine crime families, or perhaps a prince. He would be, Zara decided, a man of depth and contradictions, not some squirrelly little back-room accountant, but a man people would follow. It was a good fantasy—but the baseclone hadn't been long out of the tank. His cheeks were still covered in an almost translucent down, the beard not yet starting to grow in.

"You are an unexpected pleasure." Zara found herself reaching toward his cheek. "Uh-oh. Maybe that's outside of my contract." She pulled the contract up on her comm as he watched. "No… it says intimate physical activity. I'd call this friendly, not intimate, wouldn't you?" She reached out again. "Is this all right?"

She lowered the tone of her voice slightly, answered for him, "Yes, of course. Your wish is my desire." She stroked his arm lightly, enjoying the blond hairs on it and the dry warmth of his skin. "You are quite lovely, do you know that?"

With his other hand, the baseclone reached out and stroked Zara's cheek. She drew in a breath of surprise. None of the mining clones had ever initiated action, not unless their remote control units were turned on, and even then, of course, only if someone signaled through the control unit. She felt at the base of his skull and found the dataport. No remote control unit had been inserted. *One of the very finest units on Lesurat*, the manager had said. *A real treasure.* Zara had to agree. She'd had no idea baseclones could be so responsive on their own.

She closed her eyes and relaxed. A few more moments like this and the manager would be breaking open the door, angrily flourishing the contract. Zara sighed. She took the baseclone's hand and held it so that it wouldn't wander toward places that suddenly and unexpectedly ached for his touch. "Tell you what. We'll take turns. I'll tell you something about me, and then you tell me something about you. Or I'll do it on your behalf. Your records seem to be appended to this contract." Not that his records contained anything of interest: baseclone registration number; date of disposal on Bigollo; date of arrival on Lesurat; duty tax paid.

At seventeen thirty local time, a low, melodious chime sounded in the room.

Zara sighed. "Thirty minute warning."

The clone had his arm over her shoulder, and she rested her cheek contentedly on his chest. She could feel his heart beating, and his light breathing stirred her hair.

"I hope you've gotten used to all my talking by now." She twisted beneath his arm so that she could face him. "Wouldn't it be wonderful if you could talk, too?" Zara stroked the clone's cheek, and a slight smile came and went across his lips. "I almost believe you could." She looked longingly at him. "And then I would say, *Hello, my name Zara. Za-ra.*" She pronounced the word carefully. "And you would say, *My name is*—Now, what would your name be?"

"Kell," said the baseclone.

Zara pulled back, her pulse pounding. "What? What did you say?"

The baseclone looked at her with his habitual open gaze, head slightly tilted, as if waiting for something that didn't really matter. He said nothing.

Zara felt a lump in her throat, coupled with an almost desperate urgency. "Please. Please say it again. What is your name?" He watched her silently, and then hesitantly touched her cheek—for all the world as if he were trying to comfort her.

Zara took his hand away from her cheek, kissed his palm softly, and then wrapped the hand firmly in her own. She met his gaze and held it. "Tell me your name. Please. I really want to know."

A tear rolled down the baseclone's cheek, and then another, and Zara felt that her heart would break. "Why are you crying?" she whispered. "Have I hurt you? I didn't mean to." Softly, her fingers traced the track of the tear down his cheek.

Watching her as if mesmerized, the baseclone spoke, slowly. "My... name..." There was a pause long enough to make Zara believe that he would not speak again. Then he added, "...is... Kell."

Zara let out the breath she hadn't realized she was holding, and she allowed herself to fall back against Kell's chest. He wrapped his arms around her.

"Kell," she repeated.

The chime sounded two long tones.

Zara sighed. "Twenty minute warning. I can't leave you here. In this place. This life. By all of space, Kell, you are not a baseclone. There's no control unit in your dataport, but you've been watching and responding to me. I could begin to believe there might be some kind of advanced baseclone I don't know about who can maybe do some of that, but you—! You have feelings—you were crying. And you understand me and can answer; that means you have some intelligence, and you have language. You're not a baseclone, and you don't belong here."

She stood up and walked to the mirror that was mounted on the wall opposite the couch. Straightening her hair's disarray, Zara watched him in the mirror, watching her.

"The papers attached to my contract show you were discharged as a baseclone, but I can't believe it." She took out her comm. "I've transported baseclones, so I have access to the discharge database on Bigollo." She spoke the access code and her password and authenticated her identity with a thumbscan. "I'll use your ID number from the contract." As data appeared on the small screen, she frowned, shook her head, and rekeyed the number.

She shook her head again, more stubbornly. "Something's wrong here. The database on Bigollo says that you died in the tank, and the body was disposed of a month and a half ago." She rubbed the goosebumps on her arms. "But clearly you're not dead, because a couple of weeks ago you turned up here on Lesurat, a baseclone with no name and no owner. But that's false, too. You're a trueclone, not a baseclone. So what's going on?"

He watched her openly, patiently.

"I can't get into the database of creators. There was no need, since I was dealing only with baseclones. There's no clue in the data I have as to who or where your creator might be."

The chime sounded several times, insistently.

"Ten minutes. Not enough time to figure this out. So let's just focus on the urgent question, which is, what are we going to do about it?"

She began pacing up and down the small room. "If the administrators on Bigollo knew you were a trueclone, you wouldn't have been sold here. So most likely, they don't know. That means all I have to do is tell the manager, and he will do the right thing, whatever that is. Return you to the lab, I guess, so that your creator can be found and notified."

She sighed again and turned back to Kell. "On the other hand, this is Lesurat we're talking about. That man is as greedy as the rest of them. Even if he's honest, he'll want very much to doubt me. His purchase papers are in order, and so are the baseclone discharge papers from Bigollo. He'll rely on them. He'll ask himself, *What would a spacer know?* and he'll answer, *Nothing. She's mistaken.*"

Zara pulled at Kell's arm. "Sit up straight, Kell. I'm talking to you. We have to figure this out, and we don't have much time."

Kell obeyed.

"If he's not so ethical, the situation will be the same, or worse. He'll pretend very graciously to accept my comments and thank me profusely and just continue doing what he's doing with you." A shiver ran down her back. "I can't bear to think about that."

As if sensing her distress, Kell touched her arm gently.

"Thanks, Kell." Zara managed a smile that she hoped would pass for reassuring. "You are so much more than a normal baseclone. But touching is not what I need right now. What I need is an idea. I don't suppose you would have that?" She looked at him quizzically, not entirely sure that he wouldn't, but Kell said nothing. He watched her impassively, waiting.

Zara sighed. "No, I suppose not. If you'd had an idea, you would have been out of here days ago, right? I guess I have to figure this out by myself. So, let's see... we aren't going to get any help from the manager here. That means it's up to me. Kell, listen. If I can get you out of here, would you want to come with me?"

Zara studied the clone, but his open expression didn't change, gave no clue to what he might be thinking. *If anything*, she reminded herself. But he looked so vulnerable that her heart ached. "Now, come on. Answer me. If I'm going to put myself on the line for you, I need to know how you feel about it. Would you want to come with me?"

Those beautiful blue-in-blue eyes studied her, seemed to be giving the question some thought. But he didn't answer.

What had she expected?

"Yes."

Zara jumped. "What?"

"Yes," he said. "With you."

Read more of *Freeing Eden* at
https://www.amazon.com/gp/product/B07RCYSBCV.

Acknowledgments

John Donne famously said that no man is an island. This is certainly true of writers. I would like to acknowledge the other people who contributed to this book. My parents instilled in me a love of learning and taught me the values of respect for our planet and for one another that I hope infuse this book. My husband Daniel Kenney, above all others in my life, has supported my writing career even when, sometimes, it meant sacrificing his own time with me. Sweetie, I hope this book, and my others, make it feel worthwhile.

My children, now grown, were my first beta readers way back when. They encouraged me to publish my stories long before I felt ready. Adam and Margot, I see a lot of Cort's and Dilia's commitment to the wellbeing of their planet in the adults you have become. I so clearly remember working through a draft of this very book with you, back when you were maybe twelve and seven years old. At the time, I thought it was the final draft. (I had a lot to learn.)

James Frenkel, my agent and meticulous editor, has also become a good friend, constantly encouraging me. I greatly appreciate how he's always gone "above and beyond."

Thanks, too, to Kim and Milo of Deranged Doctor Design, who created this wonderful cover, and to Laurie Cooper of Pub-Craft, my marketing guru and mentor, and now also a friend.

One of the best things that ever happened to my writing career was becoming a finalist in the 2018 Golden Heart contest of the Romance Writers of America. A lot has happened to the Golden Heart and to RWA in the interim, but my cohort of Golden Heart finalists, the Persisters, are some of the most generous and supportive people

I've ever known anywhere—as well as an incredibly talented group of writers.

Other writers are crucial to any writer for support and feedback. I'm fortunate to belong to two critique groups. Not only have these conscientious readers helped make my books better, but they've also kept me writing to a schedule when sometimes it was the hardest thing in the world to do. And Jeanne Estridge, a fellow Persister, writing partner, and friend, helps me remember to show up at the computer, even when I can do no more than staring at the screen

And you, gentle reader, thank you for opening your heart and mind to these books. I hope to see you again in this journey.

With warmth and gratitude,

G. S. Kenney

www.ingramcontent.com/pod-product-compliance
Lightning Source LLC
Chambersburg PA
CBHW061055210726
48294CB00001B/155